AN ENORMOUSLY ENGLISH MONSOON WEDDING

Christina Jones

WINDSOR
PARAGON

First published 2013
by Piatkus
This Large Print edition published 2013
by AudioGO Ltd
by arrangement with
Little, Brown Book Group

Hardcover   ISBN: 978 1 4713 0408 8
Softcover   ISBN: 978 1 4713 0409 5

British Library Cataloguing in Publication Data available

Printed and bound in Great Britain by
TJ International Limited

To Moonpie—I love you.

With special thanks to Broo Doherty, Emma Beswetherick and Lucy Icke—you were all great when I needed you most.

CHAPTER ONE

'So, how are your wedding plans coming along, dear?' Dora Wilberforce's elderly voice echoed from her shimmering Nook Green garden. 'I bet you and Jay still have masses of things left to do before the big day, haven't you?'

'Actually,' Erin Boswell, teetering precariously on the top of a rickety stepladder in the nether regions of Mrs Wilberforce's extremely stuffy, dark and cluttered shed, called back, 'there isn't that much left to sort out. Most of the arrangements are made—and so far everything's gone really smoothly.'

'Has it? Then you're a very lucky girl.' Dora sounded slightly disappointed at this lack of prenuptial problems. 'In my experience, most weddings seem to cause all sorts of complications in the planning—right up to the eleventh hour.'

Erin shook more grimy particles from her blonde ponytail, wiped dust from the front of her pink vest and beamed into the shed's murk, ridiculously happy in the knowledge that she and Jay were clearly the only couple in the entire world to be having a stress-free wedding.

Then, mindful of the shed's possible immediate horrors, she stopped beaming and concentrated on squinting into the cobwebby gloom. Because this was always the tricky bit of the job.

OK . . . She closed her eyes.

Please, she prayed silently, please, p-l-e-a-s-e, don't let there be any spiders.

Slowly opening one eye, then both, Erin exhaled.

1

OK again. So far, so good—no spiders.

Carry on.

'Oh, I know all about the nightmare wedding stories.' Erin raised her voice a little higher. 'That's all everyone keeps telling us. That there'll be all sorts of hitches and glitches. But honestly, our wedding hasn't caused any problems at all. We've kept everything dead simple. Jay and I knew exactly what we wanted and, of course, it's been easy for us because we've been able to do it without any interference, er, I mean help, from either family.'

'Actually, there's no need to shout, dear,' Dora Wilberforce said. 'I'm not deaf.'

'Sorry. I thought you were still in the garden.'

'No, dear. I'm here in the shed doorway now—ready to give you directions on finding the box. You'll have to fight your way through a few more cobwebs first though. The shed hasn't been touched for years. I'm afraid it looks rather like Miss Havisham's house in there, doesn't it?'

And then some, Erin thought with a shudder. 'Mmm, it does a bit. And it's quite dark. I should have remembered to bring a torch.'s

'Shall I fetch you one from the house, dear?'

'No, I'll manage, thanks.' There was no way Erin was going to admit that she really didn't want to be left alone for even a nanosecond with the threat of spiders. Dora Wilberforce might be old, but at least she'd be *there*. 'My eyes are getting used to it now.'

'Good,' Dora Wilberforce said happily. 'Because actually I've no idea where my torch is and I'd have to search for it and that would have taken even longer and we've wasted quite enough time as it is.'

Erin giggled.

'So,' Dora continued, 'you've made all your

wedding arrangements yourself, have you? You and Jay haven't had one of these newfangled wedding planners?'

'Well, yes we have actually, oooh . . . excuse me . . .' Erin sneezed as a whole veil of dusty cobwebs floated round her. She held her breath. No spiders. Again. Phew.

'Jay and I knew what sort of wedding we wanted, so once we'd written everything down, we met Abbie, the wedding planner at the Swan, and gave her all the details. And now she's working with us to make sure it all happens exactly to plan.'

'Fancy.' Dora chuckled. 'It's all a far cry from my day when the bride's parents provided whatever they could afford, and if you got a bit of a sit-down spread in the village hall afterwards, you were grateful. And most couples had to move in with their in-laws after the wedding 'til they could get a place of their own. Honeymoons were a rare treat, too. If you were lucky you got a weekend in a seaside boarding house, but for most, the wedding night used to be a family occasion, so to speak.'

'Oooh, that sounds terrible,' Erin laughed. 'Thank goodness times have changed. Jay and I have saved up and paid for everything ourselves, so we didn't need to ask anyone else to help out financially. Or to be involved. It's going to be our day, exactly the way we want it.'

'I wish my wedding had been more what I wanted. Mine was a very cheap do.' Dora Wilberforce sounded quite nostalgic. 'Mind you, weddings are big business now, aren't they? Such a lot of money. I s'pose it all makes sense to you young 'uns.'

'Oh, we're not going mad with ours—we're not

3

having a castle and a Red Arrows fly-past and zillions of white doves and Cinderella coaches and eight million bridesmaids, or anything like that—but we do want a lovely day that everyone will enjoy.'

'And your mum and dad, or Jay's, haven't had any say in it at all?'

'None, no.'

Dora pondered this. 'Wish mine hadn't . . . Ah, well. Water under the bridge . . . And I s'pose your mum and dad *couldn't* be involved under the circumstances, could they?'

'Not really, no.'

'But even if they've been left out of the planning stages, they will still be popping over for it, won't they? They'll be here in time for the big day? They're not going to miss it?'

Standing on tiptoe, Erin wobbled again and smiled to herself in the warm darkness. Mrs Wilberforce made it sound as if her parents lived just round the corner in Nook Green, or in the neighbouring village of Bluebell Common or something, rather than an entire world away in Sydney. She still missed them and wished they were closer. Especially now.

But, she had to admit, it had been much easier to plan the wedding without her mum—or Jay's who lived in the Midlands—raising any objections or making unsuitable suggestions or demanding that some ancient and unpleasant rellie simply *had* to be invited.

'Yes, of course they're coming over. They'll be here ten days before. They do know what's happening, though. We've kept them up-to-date with everything on email and Skype.'

4

'Have you?' Mrs Wilberforce, clearly never having heard of Skype and possibly not even email, sounded doubtful. 'That's nice. And it'll be lovely to see them again. Mind, I could never understand why they went all the way to Australia in the first place. Rose and Pete were Nook Green people, born and bred. A trip to London or a holiday in Majorca was a big adventure for them.'

'Mmm, yes, it was a bit of a shock to everyone.'

'I know it was for your dad's job but surely he could have found something nearer?'

'Not at the time. Anyway, they're really settled over there now and I've been happy living with Uncle Doug, and it means Jay and I have been left well alone to plan the wedding ourselves. It's all gone really smoothly. There's absolutely nothing that can go wrong now.'

Dora Wilberforce gave a little snort. 'Now you be careful, young Erin. Don't you be too cocky. Remember, there's many a slip twixt cup and lip.'

Erin giggled. 'My nanna used to say that too.'

'Ah, a wise woman, your nanna. And such a jolly lady. We've all missed her so much at the Yee-Hawers Over Sixties Line Dancing Nights, not to mention the monthly Cheese and Wine parties.' Dora sighed wistfully. 'How she loved her glass or two of Blue Nun with a nice chunk of Caerphilly on a cream cracker. Ah, the life and soul, Muriel used to be. Always laughing, always the first up on the floor, always the last to leave. Still, nothing stays the same for ever, dear, does it?'

Guessing the question was rhetorical, Erin simply shook her head and continued her rummage among Mrs Wilberforce's stored clutter.

'You must miss her too,' Dora Wilberforce

said sadly. 'What with your mum and dad being in Australia and everything.'

'I do, yes.'

'And she'd have loved to see you wed,' Dora sighed again. 'Such a shame she got taken away.'

'Taken away?' Erin chuckled. 'That sounds a bit dramatic. She was hardly abducted by aliens, was she?'

It had caused more than a bit of a hoo-ha in the village when Muriel, her sprightly widowed nanna, had put a lonely hearts ad in a national oldies magazine, had been contacted by, met, and fallen whirlwindly in love with the suave, also widowed and slightly younger Colin, and gone to live—in sin, according to the more strait-laced Nook Greeners—with him in his homeland of Malta.

'Anyway,' Erin finished robustly, 'she was very happy to be *taken away*, actually. And she and Colin will be coming to the wedding.'

'R-e-a-l-l-y?' Dora Wilberforce exhaled noisily. 'Muriel's going to bring her fancy man back to Nook Green, is she? Well, I never . . .'

Erin laughed to herself. That would give the Yee-Hawers Over Sixties Line Dancers something to gossip about at their next hoedown—and then some.

Holding her breath for a moment, she carefully wiped a stray cobweb from her face. Fortunately, again, luck was on her side and there wasn't a spider attached.

She exhaled.

'So, yes, my entire scattered family, all five of them, or six if you count whoever Uncle Doug brings as his plus one—and none of us are sure who that will be—will be on my side of the wedding room to see me married.'

'Surely, Doug will be partnered by young Gina, won't he, dear? They've been walking out together for some time now.'

'Who knows? I hope so because Gina is so lovely and really good for him—far too good for him, really—but you know what he's like.'

'Hmmm. Once a Lothario always a Lothario. He's a naughty boy, your Uncle Doug. Such a bad reputation with the ladies.'

'And still mightily proud of it, sadly.'

Although he was hardly a boy, Erin thought as she leaned even further into the shed's upper recesses. Doug was in his mid-fifties, but as he'd clung on to the ethos of his 1970s laid-back love 'em and leave 'em hippiedom, his romance track record was pretty rocky.

Erin sighed. 'I'm sorry, but I still can't see the box you wanted in here.'

'Can't you? Oh dear. The shed's a bit cluttered I'm afraid, dear. And the light bulb went months ago. The box is walnut with mother-of-pearl inlay. Top shelf to the right. You really can't miss it.'

Erin thought she probably already had. Several times. Mrs Wilberforce's garden shed was crammed from floor to ceiling with boxes and bags and broken things that no one would have made any use of for generations.

Still, it was her job as junior partner, negotiator, valuer and most importantly, accounts person, in her Uncle Doug's Old Curiosity Shop—"collectibles and curios for all"—to spend her working life rooting around among other people's unwanted detritus, and, apart from the daily spider hazard, she absolutely loved it.

Taking another deep breath, Erin felt gingerly along the top shelf with one hand while clinging tightly to the top of the ladder with the other. Choking quietly on the clouds of dust, she reached even deeper into the sweltering gloom and tried not to fall.

'Any luck?' Mrs Wilberforce's voice was nearer now. 'Oh, do take care, dear. You were such a cack-handed kiddie. Always had your knees plastered up or your arm in a sling. Mind, you were a fearless little thing. A proper tomboy. You haven't changed all that much in the twenty-seven years I've known you, dear.'

Erin pulled a face in the sultry darkness. Thanks so much, Mrs W. Nothing like bolstering a girl's ego.

'And,' Mrs Wilberforce continued, 'I don't want you to break any bones on my account. Not so soon before the big day.'

'I'm not keen on hobbling down the aisle on crutches either, so I promise I'll be careful. And I haven't fallen off my bike or grazed my knees in the playground for some time now. Ah, I think I'll just have to reach forward a bit more and move some of this stuff—I can see a box just over here . . .'

'Good girl,' Mrs Wilberforce's voice sounded delighted. 'Not long to go now to the wedding though, is it?'

'Seventh of September. Six weeks and three days and ooh—about four hours.'

'Not that you're counting?' Mrs Wilberforce chuckled. 'Bet you can't wait, can you? Young Jay's a smashing bloke, and everyone speaks so highly of him. He's the best vet we've ever had in Nook Green.'

8

Erin nodded in proud agreement on Jay's behalf. He was, without doubt, the best vet *anywhere* in the whole wide world.

As she'd found out two years ago . . .

CHAPTER TWO

Two years ago, very early on a similar scorching July morning, and still wearing her pyjamas, Erin had hurtled bare-footed out of Uncle Doug's front door and raced across the green that gave the village its name, slithering on the dew-soaked grass, and crashed into the Nook Green Veterinary Surgery, carrying her beloved cat, Florence, inert in her arms.

'I need to see Mr Howes,' she'd sobbed incoherently over the desk to her receptionist-best-friend Sophie. 'Now, Sophie! I've just found Florence lying on the kitchen floor and she's been so sick everywhere, and I know she's dying!'

'Oh, sweetheart.' Sophie had leaned across the desk, touching Florence's immobile grey head and handing Erin a tissue. 'How awful—but Mr Howes has left. Retired. Remember? I told you. He sold the practice. We have a new vet now—Mr Keskar—and he's fully booked and we're not even open yet and—'

'I don't care!' Erin had sobbed even louder. 'Is he here?'

'Yes, but—'

'Then ask him to see Florence. Now. Please, please, please. You're my best friend. Pull strings! Please, please, please Sophie, just ask him.'

'OK. Look, go and sit down—the first appointment hasn't arrived yet. I'll just go and have a word with Jay.'

'Jay?'

Sophie had hurried out from behind her desk. 'Mr Keskar. Jay Keskar. He's lovely, Erin, and brilliant. Try not to worry.'

Being far beyond worrying and unable to sit down in the tiny waiting room, Erin, cuddling Florence's motionless body against her with tears dripping into the smoky, silky fur, had paced frantically up and down.

'Erin . . .' Bella, Erin's other best-friend-from-childhood, and the practice's veterinary nurse, clattered into the waiting room and hugged her. 'Sophie's just told me. Oh, poor you—poor Florence. Jay's said of course he'll see you now. Come through.'

Dry-mouthed, tears falling unbidden, and her heart thundering, Erin had followed Bella into the surgery.

'Hello, Miss Boswell,' Jay Keskar had smiled kindly at her. 'Sophie and Bella have told me all about you and Florence. I've called up her notes on the computer, and she's young and been a very healthy girl so far. Please just put her down on the table and I'll have a look at her.'

Vaguely aware of Jay Keskar being tall and lean and dark, with silky blue-black hair and amazingly gentle deep brown eyes to match the kind smile, Erin laid the almost-unconscious Florence carefully on the table.

'Thank you for seeing us,' she'd sobbed. 'Thank you so much.'

'No problem. Now, let's have a look . . .'

Jay had asked several questions while carrying out his examination, and Erin, stroking Florence, sniffling and frozen with fear, had tried her best to answer them coherently.

'OK.' Jay had smiled reassuringly. 'Her temperature's through the roof—so we need to get that down straight away—that's what's causing the floppiness. I'm going to take some blood tests to rule out anything nasty lurking underneath, and I don't think she's been poisoned. My guess is that she's been foraging and eaten something unpleasant and she's suffering a severe reaction ... if I'm right, then a couple of injections and a course of antibiotics followed by a special bland diet should have her back on her paws pretty quickly. I'll just get Bella to help me. If you'd like to wait outside for about ten minutes, I'll be as quick as I can.'

'Is she going to die?' Erin had sniffled behind the soggy tissue. 'She isn't going to die, is she?'

'Not if I can help it.' Jay had smiled again, his voice calming and reassuring. 'I'll run the tests and call you back in. Try not to worry, Miss Boswell.'

The waiting room had been no longer empty, and the two women with overenthusiastic dogs and the man with a very vocal cat in a travelling basket, chattered gaily with the relaxed air of people whose animals were in for routine treatment and who knew no heartbreak lurked behind the surgery door.

They'd all stopped talking and stared at the distraught Erin, in her pyjamas, with a mixture of amusement and shared pet-owner sympathy.

Pacing up and down again, she'd ignored them and scrubbed at her eyes with the now shredded

11

tissue.

Jay Keskar, she'd thought, had been so much better and kinder and gentler than the brusque Mr Howes. But if anything happened to Florence . . . Oh God, if anything happened to Florence . . .

And ten minutes was going to seem like ten hours.

'Feeling better? Told you he was good, didn't I?' Sophie had leaned across the desk in the reception cubicle. 'And smoking hot.'

'*What*?'

'Jay's soooo fit. He's to die for,' Sophie had whispered.

'Do not use the "d" word!' Erin had hissed back.

'Ooops, no, sorry—but you must remember me and Bella telling you we had some right dweebs come to look round when Mr Howes wanted to sell up, and then we said how gorgeous Jay Keskar was and we couldn't believe it when he bought the surgery? And amazingly he's *single*. We both fancy him like mad. So does every other female pet-owner in the village, sadly.'

Erin had shaken her head. She had some vague memory of Sophie and Bella enthusing wildly over their new young Indian boss, but hadn't listened much at the time as she'd been recovering from being two-timed by Mike-the-plumber-from-Newbury and had been sworn off men for ever.

'I didn't really notice.' Erin had blown her nose. 'But he seems very kind and efficient—and as long as he makes Florence better he can look like Quasimodo for all I care.'

'Didn't *notice*?' Sophie had looked scandalised. 'He's *scorching*.'

'I don't care,' Erin had sniffed. 'I only care about

12

Florence.'

'Erin.' Bella had opened the door. 'If you'd like to come back in now.'

Her stomach in knots, Erin walked back into the surgery.

Florence, looking sleepy but very alive, had been sitting up on the examination table and Erin had burst into tears again.

Jay Keskar had laughed and handed her a printout. 'The blood tests were all negative. Look, kidneys and liver function—all perfectly normal. No trace of FIV or FIL—I know she's had her boosters but you can't be too careful. I think she's probably scavenged something like a dead mouse or a gone-off frog. She's responded extremely well to the injections as you can see.'

'Thank you,' Erin had whispered, picking Florence up and hugging her, and being rewarded by a faint but distinct purr. 'Oh, thank you so much.'

'My pleasure. You can pick up Florence's pills and the food from Sophie at reception. Make sure she has plenty of water to drink to counteract the dehydration from the vomiting, and if you'd make an appointment for a couple of day's time, I'll repeat the injections. But I'm confident that when I see Florence again she'll be as right as rain.'

And muttering her thanks over and over again, Erin had hugged Florence even more tightly, and practically skipped from the surgery.

And, by the time she and the fully restored Florence had made their second appointment, she'd realised that Jay Keskar was not only the greatest vet in the whole wide world, but also the sexiest, most drop-dead gorgeous man she'd ever seen.

After that appointment, much to Sophie and Bella's amazement, and despite having seen her at her absolute worse—incoherent, pyjama-clad, wild-haired, red-eyed and runny-nosed—Jay had phoned her and asked her out, and the rest, as they say, was history.

In just over six weeks' time, they'd be married and she'd become Mrs Keskar, and she and the equally besotted Florence, would be moving into Jay's picture-pretty cottage next door to the surgery.

She simply couldn't wait.

CHAPTER THREE

Jolted back to the present, Erin realised Dora Wilberforce was still chattering.

'. . . and I've always said you make such a lovely couple. With him being all tall, dark and handsome and you looking like a little blonde fairy-doll—even if you are a bit of a ragamuffin at times.'

Another ego boost there. Ta, Mrs W. Erin grinned to herself again.

'It was so kind of you to send me an invitation, dear. I'm really looking forward to it.'

'Good. We wanted all our friends in the village to share our day, and as I've got such a small family, my side was going to look pretty bare without friends.'

'Whereas Jay has lots of family to ask, does he?'

'Millions.' Erin sneezed more dust. 'It'll be all family on his side and our friends on mine. It's

14

worked out really well.'

'And you're just having Sophie and Bella as bridesmaids, are you?'

'Yes—oooh—atishoo! Excuse me.' Erin sneezed again as she dislodged several decades' worth of grime from the shed's ceiling. 'Sophie and Bella and I made this pact when we were at primary school. We always said we'd be one another's bridesmaids.'

'Lovely. The three of you have always been best friends, haven't you? But doesn't Jay have any female relatives who want to be bridesmaids too?'

'No, well, not exactly. He's an only child as well, and he's got so many zillions of cousins that we couldn't just ask one or two of them without offending the others.'

Mrs Wilberforce laughed. 'No, I can see that would have been tricky.'

Tricky? Erin chuckled. It would have been a total nightmare. Jay's extended Indian family—and friends of friends who'd all become honorary aunts, uncles and cousins—stretched to every corner of the globe. There would have been an international incident if they'd even *tried* to choose a bridesmaid from the dozens of candidates.

'And are their bridesmaids' frocks pretty?' Dora queried. 'I do like a pretty frilly frock at a wedding. Pink or blue is always lovely, I think.'

Erin smiled. Sophie and Bella definitely weren't wearing anything frilly, and certainly not in pink or blue. 'You'll have to wait and see . . .'

'Oh,' Dora sighed impatiently. 'So I suppose that means you won't tell me about your frock either? You *are* wearing a frock, aren't you?'

'I am. And it's absolutely gorgeous—and it's a

huge secret.'

Dora sighed again. 'Well, just so long as you're intending to walk down the aisle looking like a princess rather than an urchin in those tatty jeans you usually live in.'

'Jay's mum says much the same,' Erin laughed. 'She says—whoops . . .'

The ladder suddenly rocked backwards. Erin clung on with both hands and giggled. 'Ohmigod.'

Mrs Wilberforce sounded disapproving. 'I bet she doesn't say that. From what little I've seen of Deena Keskar, I'd think a profanity was the last thing she'd utter. A proper lady, she is.'

Oh, yes, Erin thought. Jay's mum, Deena Keskar, her future mother-in-law, was certainly a proper lady: always elegant, always perfectly groomed and perfectly poised.

It was going to be an awful lot to live up to.

'Anyway.' Dora Wilberforce clapped her hands. 'We've wasted enough time on wedding chatter, dear. Try and find the box, there's a good girl.'

Erin shook her head, giggling again.

Ah—was that it? Over there? Tucked behind all those old newspapers? Erin stretched upwards again. The ladder shuddered.

'Erin . . . You've gone very quiet now . . . Are you sure you're managing, dear?'

'Yep, sorry. I'm still looking, and the ladder just had a bit of a wobble.'

Teetering on the top platform of the stepladder, Erin stretched out for the box. Clouds of dust puffed into Mrs Wilberforce's shed's airless gloom.

'Gotcha!' Erin muttered triumphantly. Then, 'Whoops-a-daisy . . .' followed by 'Oooh, no—don't let me fall . . .'

16

Giggling, she swayed wildly as the weight of the box threatened to send her tumbling inelegantly down the dozen grubby rungs to the equally grimy floor. She grabbed the side of the ladder with one hand, balancing the box with the other, and slowly made her way downwards.

Halfway down and she hadn't slipped or dropped anything. Result!

Then she screamed.

Instantly rigid with terror, Erin clutched the box and stared at the enormous spider.

The spider, having appeared nonchalantly over the top of the box, stared back. Feeling the sweat tingle across her scalp, inch down her neck, then snake icily along her spine, Erin whimpered.

The massive spider rocked backwards and forwards on the lid of the box on long, hideously hinged legs. Her eyes still fixed on the spider and exhaling slowly, Erin swallowed.

'Did you shout? Are you still OK in there, dear?' Mrs Wilberforce called cheerily from the shed's doorway.

'I've-found-the-box,' Erin muttered through clenched teeth, not taking her eyes from the spider, and wishing upon wish that she'd insisted on Dora Wilberforce—even if she was nearly ninety or whatever—doing her own dirty work.

'Oh, good—about time too. Well, bring it out then, dear,' Mrs Wilberforce continued gaily, 'so's we can take a peep inside and see what's what, out here in the sunshine.'

Rooted to the spot, paralysed with fear, Erin swallowed again. 'I can't.'

'Why not, dear? I know it's a bit heavy, but surely . . . ?'

The spider made a sort of jerky false move forwards across the lid of the box. Then it stopped and bounced up and down menacingly.

Instinctively, Erin wanted to drop the box, slide down the remaining steps of the ladder and run as far away from it and the spider and Mrs Wilberforce's dark stuffy shed as possible.

But she couldn't. Because if she dropped the box, as all arachnophobes know only too well, the spider could go absolutely *anywhere* . . . and a spider you can't see is far, far worse than one that you can . . .

The spider, clearly enjoying the confrontation, made another stuttering forward move across the mother-of-pearl inlay.

Erin gave in and screamed again.

'Dearie me.' Mrs Wilberforce, elderly and emaciated, with skin like tanned leather and silver candyfloss hair, and with a grubby tea towel knotted round the waist of her ox-blood-and-mustard-splodged 1950s summer dress, finally appeared at the bottom of the ladder. 'What on earth is happening in here? Are you sure you're OK, dear?'

'Spider . . .' Erin muttered, still not taking her eyes off the threatening spread of eight thick brown hairy legs. 'It's enormous.'

'Oh, the shed's full of 'em,' Mrs Wilberforce chuckled. 'At least, at this time of year. Come the autumn they'll all be heading indoors for a little bit of how's yer father.'

Erin winced. She knew all about the indoor influx of autumn spiders. She spent the weeks of mists and mellow fruitfulness in a state of abject terror, scouring every corner of Uncle Doug's cottage armed with chestnut oil sprays, two-handed, like a one-woman SWAT team.

'You're shaking from head to foot.' Mrs Wilberforce frowned as she puffed on to the stepladder behind Erin making everything sway wildly. 'Don't tell me you're afraid of spiders?'

'No, no . . .' Erin exhaled again, staring transfixed at the monster, because she knew the minute she looked away it'd make a dash for her fingers and if it touched her then she'd simply die on the spot. 'I'm not afraid of them at all. Oh no—I'm far, far more than that.'

'Goodness me.' Mrs Wilberforce shook her head, leaned round Erin and scooped the spider gently into her hands. 'Bless it. It's only a little tiddler.'

'Tiddler?' Erin whimpered. 'It's a flaming tarantula.'

Mrs Wilberforce laughed wheezily as she made it to the floor. 'Hardly, dear. Look, he almost fits into the palm of my hand.'

'Nooo!' Erin turned her head away. 'Take it away. Please.'

'All right, no need to have hysterics, dear. But honestly, what's to be scared of? Clever little buggers, spiders. And they can't hurt you, you know.'

Hurt, no. Maybe not. Scare to death—oh, yes, yes, yes.

Erin tumbled inelegantly down the stepladder and watched in fascinated horror as Mrs Wilberforce cooed lovingly at the spider and headed out of the shed for the raspberry canes with it cupped in her hands. Its legs overflowed between her gnarled knuckles, waving gaily as it was liberated amongst a riotous bed of golden nasturtiums and purple nettles.

'There. All gone.' Mrs Wilberforce beamed at

19

Erin and spoke kindly as if to someone of limited mental faculties. 'Now come out here and bring the box and let's get down to business, there's a good girl. I haven't got all day.'

Erin, still shivering and feeling very sick, but not waiting to see if the spider's entire family were hovering in the musty shed waiting to pick up where their eight-legged chum had failed, scuttled out into the searing July sunshine.

Mrs Wilberforce's country cottage garden was the pride of Nook Green. And that was saying something. The tiny Berkshire village took its gardens very seriously indeed. Dora Wilberforce had won "Best in Village" for as long as anyone could remember.

Hollyhocks and lupins, cosmos daisies and cornflowers, sweet peas and poppies all spread themselves in fragrant rainbow beds between pathways of springy grass and beneath stunted fruit trees, before tumbling on and forming several multicoloured oases around perfectly tended vegetable patches.

Like the rest of Nook Green, it was chocolate-box perfect and always sent the townie tourists into paroxysms of ecstasy.

Keeping as far away as possible from the raspberry canes just in case the spider decided to have a second shot, Erin placed the walnut box on a sun-bleached picnic table and wiped her sweating palms down her cut-off jeans.

'Better now?' Mrs Wilberforce asked kindly. 'Would you like a cold drink? I've got some ginger beer on the go.'

Erin, her legs still shaking but her heart rate at least starting to return to somewhere near normal, shook her head quickly. Everyone over a certain age in Nook Green always had ginger beer on the go. The Women's Institute sold ginger beer plants every Christmas at their bazaar, and they self-perpetuated at an alarming rate. Every pensioner's larder was awash with cloudy Kilner jars and small explosions.

'No thanks. Honestly, I'll be OK in a minute.'

Mrs Wilberforce blew dust from the top of the box. Most of it landed on her upper lip. She looked like John Cleese.

'Bit of a funny business you're in for someone who's scared of spiders, if you ask me. You must spend half your life rooting through people's sheds and attics and what-have-you looking at their junk. Spiders everywhere, I'd have thought.'

Erin, still trembling, nodded again. Since she'd been working for Uncle Doug, spiders had become a terrifying occupational hazard. She'd passed up on several lucrative deals because the family heirloom in question had more eight-legged protectors than the Vatican City had guards.

She really must get round to some phobia hypnotherapy. She'd put it on her to-do list.

Just as soon as the wedding was over.

'I only remembered these Staffs a couple of days ago,' Mrs Wilberforce said, wrestling with the box's dusty clasp. 'Seemed a shame to leave them mouldering in the shed when they might bring me in a few bob. And—' she surveyed Erin with a wry grin '—I wanted to deal with you rather than your Uncle Doug. You're more likely to give me a fair price. Your Uncle Doug's such a rogue—I know he'd just say—"Staffordshire pottery figurines? There ain't much of a market for them. Tell you

21

what, I'll give you a fiver to take 'em off your hands." Now wouldn't he?'

Erin giggled and nodded. He probably would.

As the owner of the Old Curiosity Shop, Doug Boswell had his shelves crammed with other people's cast-offs—all purchased for a fraction of their worth if he could get away with it.

And much as she adored him, she had to admit that Uncle Doug was well known in and around Nook Green for his ability to charm and wheedle and obtain the lowest price possible.

'Uncle Doug never cheats anyone, though,' Erin said stoutly. 'But he is in business to make a profit. And there's an awful lot of Staffordshire about. The market's flooded with certain figures. Not even the Americans want them any more.'

'Ah,' Mrs Wilberforce concurred, finally snapping the box open and stepping smartly back from a further cloud of dust, 'that's as maybe. But they might want these, mightn't they?'

Shielding her eyes from the sun, Erin peered cautiously into the box—just in case some other massive arachnid had taken up residence.

Dora Wilberforce clucked her tongue in frustration and shoved the straw packaging to one side. 'There you are—not a spider in sight.'

Erin smiled her thanks and looked into the box. Nestled amongst the grubby straw, two sneering highwaymen, with very red lips, a lot of eyeliner, and resplendent in vibrantly hued frock coats, frilly shirts, thigh boots and long curly wigs and brandishing cocked pistols, sat astride two prancing horses—one bay, the other jet black.

They looked like a pair of nineteenth-century Grayson Perrys.

Erin picked each one up carefully, shook off the straw, and turned them round, checking the marks. 'Flatbacks. About 1840. Dick Turpin and Tom King. Oh, they're lovely. In perfect condition. Not a mark on them.'

As always, when finding something unexpectedly ancient and lovely, Erin felt a rush of pleasure and thought she had the best job in the world. And, spiders apart, she really enjoyed working for Uncle Doug, and he'd admitted she was pretty good at the valuations.

She looked at Dora. 'Are you sure you want to get rid of them? They'd look just right on your mantelpiece.'

'Can't abide 'em,' Dora Wilberforce snorted. 'Belonged to my damn ma-in-law. She had 'em on a shelf in her kitchen. I hated her and I hated them. No, you tell me what they're worth, young Erin, and I'll be glad to see 'em go.'

Erin laid the figures carefully back in the box and pushed damp strands of her hair back into the dusty ponytail. She knew Uncle Doug would offer Dora £25 for the pair at most, and Dora would probably be delighted.

'Well, if you sent them to auction you'd possibly get a really good price. I know some American collectors are paying a lot for these.'

Mrs Wilberforce's pale-blue eyes twinkled with delight. 'Really?'

Erin nodded. 'Definitely. Shall I give you the details of the local auction houses and—?'

'No, dear, thank you. It's far too much faffing around.' Mrs Wilberforce shook her head. 'That's why I gave you a ring. I'd rather have a few quid in me pocket right now. You give me what you think they're worth to you and we'll shake hands on it.'

Not sure that she wanted to shake Dora Wilberforce's hand—not when it had been in very recent contact with that spider—Erin frowned. 'OK, if you're sure. Um, I'll give you a hundred pounds.'

'Oh, that's a fortune to me, dear!' Dora Wilberforce beamed as they shook on the deal. 'Thank you so much. No doubt your Uncle Doug'll send 'em to auction and double his money, but I'm more than happy, dear. Cash?'

'Cash,' Erin confirmed, flicking her briefcase open and pulling out her laptop and her business wallet. Then she counted out the twenty-pound notes on to the table and filled in the details on the computer.

Dora Wilberforce quickly tucked the money into the pocket of her ox-blood splodged frock. 'Thank you, dear. Oh, and is that your mobile telephone ringing?'

Erin winced as the *Steptoe and Son* theme tune—Uncle Doug's idea of a jokey ringtone, which she'd really have to do something about—again, as soon as the wedding was over—echoed from her bag.

Tucking the laptop under one arm and the walnut box under the other, Erin scrabbled for her phone and checked the caller.

Jay. Her heart gave a little skippety-skip of delight.

She looked at Mrs Wilberforce. 'It's Jay. Do you mind . . .?'

'Not at all, dear. You go ahead. I'm not one to stand in the way of young love.'

'Hi.' Erin answered the call, beaming. 'No—I've just finished at Mrs Wilberforce's. Yes, it did take a bit longer than I'd planned, but there was a spider—no, don't laugh! Not funny! I've got to take the stuff back to the shop and catalogue it, then—*what*? When? Oh, Lordy . . . Yes, of course—um—it'll be lovely . . . But can we get a table? Oh, have you—that's lucky . . . How? Right, are you? OK, I'll drive myself over. I'll see you there, then. Love you, too. Bye.'

'Problems?' Dora Wilberforce asked cheerfully.

Erin shrugged, pushing her phone back into her bag. 'No—well, not really. Jay's parents have been in Reading on business and have finished early and want to meet us for lunch on their way back to Birmingham.'

'That sounds lovely, dear.'

'Mmmm.' Erin nodded. 'It is. But they want to meet us at the Swan. And as Jay's finished surgery and is already in Maizey St Michael on a house call, he's managed to get a table and—'

Dora beamed. 'Ah, the Swan's where you're getting married, dear, isn't it? Have Jay's mum and dad been there before?'

'No. And we really didn't want them to see it before the wedding. We wanted it to come as a lovely surprise.'

'I expect they'll want to see it, though, dear. They'll be so excited . . . and they're bound to love it, aren't they?'

'Oh, yes,' Erin said happily. 'They'll absolutely adore it. There's no doubt about that.'

CHAPTER FOUR

'Wow!' Jay pulled Erin into his arms and kissed her. 'You look amazing.'

'Thanks.' She kissed him back, wondering dizzily if she'd ever get tired of kissing him and knowing that she wouldn't. Never. Ever. 'I had to make some sort of an effort for your parents.'

In a remarkably short time, she'd managed to rush home, shower off the grime from Dora's shed, wash her hair, change into a floaty blue and lilac summer dress, and even remembered mascara, blusher, a slick of lip gloss and a carefully measured squirt of her beloved Prada Candy.

Lunch at the Swan meant being suitably dressed; lunch at the Swan in the achingly elegant company of ma-in-law-to-be, Deena Keskar, meant pulling out as many sartorial stops as possible.

Erin peered round the Swan's car park for the Keskars' Mercedes. The sun glimmered and shimmered from a mass of expensively gleaming paintwork, but not, as far as she could see, Tavish Keskar's pride and joy.

'I can't see the car, aren't they here yet?'

Jay shook his head. 'No—and you mean all this gorgeous girly stuff and make-up isn't for my benefit?'

'Nah, course not.' She giggled. 'Why would I make any effort for you? We're getting married in six weeks—I've captured you—it's all downhill from here. You won't see me in anything except trackie bottoms and dirty T-shirts once that ring's on my finger.'

Jay shook his head. 'I could always call it off.'

'Yeah, right.'

He kissed her again, and she kissed him back and they smiled dreamily at one another.

'We're very lucky to have booked this for the wedding, aren't we?' Erin sighed, staring across the sparkling-jewelled sweep of gravelled drive to the Swan: centuries old, mellow and swathed in a tumbling mantle of blue wisteria

Surrounded by the curve of the River Maizey, the Swan gave the impression of having been built on an island, with gently swaying willows, enticing pathways snaking between immaculate lawns, tumbling trellises and hidden arbours. The vast grounds sloped gently away to a glistening lake, encompassing a plethora of fragrant pastel-coloured flower beds, with weather-worn rustic bridges criss-crossing the irregular paths of the Maizey's many tiny tributaries.

It was, Erin thought, the most beautiful place on earth.

'Mmm. I just wish we could have kept it a secret from Mum and Dad for a bit longer.'

'Me too,' Erin agreed. 'It would have been lovely to hang on to the wow factor until the wedding day. Still, they're going to love it, aren't they?'

'Course they are.' Jay took her hand. 'They'll be knocked out. Anyway, rather than fry out here in the car park, shall we go and have a drink down by the river until they arrive?'

'Oh, yes—something long and cold.' Erin nodded. 'A spritzer would be great. In fact, anything but ginger beer. Dora Wilberforce offered me ginger beer—as an antidote to the spider—the Nook Green cure-all.'

27

Jay chuckled as they walked hand in hand towards the Swan's imposing entrance. 'Ah, yes— the spider . . . want to tell me about it?'

'Not really.' Erin shuddered. 'Same as usual. I'll get some help soon, I promise, but right now I'd rather talk about something else. Why are you in Maizey St Michael anyway?'

'I'd finished morning surgery early and I had a house call,' Jay said, as they ducked under the Swan's low arches in to the dim coolness of the shady bar. 'Or rather, a farm call. I did what I could, and I think it'll be OK, but—' he smiled at the barman '—oh, hi, two white wine spritzers, please—oh, yes with soda, not lemonade—thanks.'

As the barman bustled with glasses and bottles, Erin gazed round with renewed delight at the glorious glowing panelling, the curving deep stone staircases, the sculpted archways, the gleaming leaded-light windows, as she always did when they came to the Swan.

In a tiddly bit over six weeks' time, the whole fabulous place would be filled with everyone she and Jay loved, celebrating their marriage.

Oh, she was so lucky . . .

Fighting the urge to do a little happy dance on the spot, she contented herself with just sighing blissfully.

'Are you booked in for lunch, sir?' The barman clinked ice.

'We are, yes.' Jay said. 'But we're waiting for my parents to join us. We're going to have our drinks down by the river—could you point them in the right direction when they arrive, please?'

'Of course.' The barman smiled, placing the tall glasses, tantalisingly beaded with ice-cold droplets, on a tray. 'A good choice, the river, on a day like this.'

Jay nodded agreement, and paid for the drinks, then skilfully whisked the tray away from Erin's outstretched hands. 'It's OK. I'll carry it. I'm all for equality but I'm also desperate for a cold drink—you're wearing heels and you might drop the lot before we get out of the door.'

'True,' Erin giggled. 'Today I'm practising walking in sandals that aren't just flip-flops.'

'Because you're wearing heels with your wedding dress?'

'Don't pry about my wedding outfit. It's not allowed. And I'm practising because I'm wearing heels on my hen night. Actually—' she wrinkled her nose at him '—I'm going barefoot on our wedding day.'

'Oh, good.'

They laughed together. It was so lovely, Erin thought, to be madly, insanely in love, and blissfully happy, and be best friends and understand one another so well. And then to be married as well . . .

Oooh . . .

She really, really, really couldn't wait for the wedding day.

Six weeks and counting.

'Ouf!' Erin exhaled as they stepped from the cool darkness of the Swan and into the full glare of the sun. 'Anyway, sorry—I think we got a bit side-tracked by shoes, or lack of them. You said you were in Maizey St Michael because you had a farm visit, which I know isn't the best sort of call-out for you, and . . .?'

'A pony with a damaged hoof.' Jay carried the drinks across the lawn. 'Luckily it was something

I could deal with, but again, I'm a small animal specialist and this is such a rural area I really need someone in the practice who can handle the needs of the farm livestock. I'm having to turn a lot of work away at the moment.'

'I know.' Erin nodded as they made their way across several tiny weather-worn bridges. 'And you'd like to keep it all in-house rather than passing it on to other practices? That makes sense. So, are you going to advertise?'

Jay shook his head. The ice cubes danced in the spritzers. 'No, actually I was thinking of offering Kam a partnership.'

'*Kam*?' Erin erupted with laughter, luxuriating in the cooling breeze from the river, as they eased themselves onto rustic benches beneath the willows. 'Your cousin Kam? Are you mad?'

'Kam's a great equine and bovine specialist, you've agreed I need a partner—I thought you liked Kam?'

'I love Kam,' Erin chuckled. 'You know I do. I adore Kam. Kam's amazing—and he'll be a fabulous best man—but a partner in the practice? You know what he's like. You won't get a minute of work out of Sophie and Bella. And every woman in Berkshire will be queuing round Nook Green, drooling, much like they were over you until I took you off the market.'

'That's a very sexist remark.' Jay raised his eyebrows in mock-horror. 'And, OK, I'll admit we Keskars do have something of an animal magnetism.'

'Which is why you're vets?' Erin giggled. 'And don't be so big-headed. But, seriously, as long as you can keep the slavering hordes at bay, I think it's a great idea. But would Kam give up his current job to join you?'

'I think so. He's a locum for the Cumbrian practices at the moment—a partnership would be a great career move for him. And I could certainly do with him. Still—' Jay reached for her hand across the table '—like your spider phobia treatment, it's something that can wait until after the wedding.'

'Mine can, yours can't.' Erin stroked his fingers. 'I know how pushed you are. Honestly, I think you should ask Kam sooner rather than later. Ring him tonight and see what he says.'

'Mmm, I might just do that.' Jay smiled gently at her. 'So, what about your morning? What happened at Dora Wilberforce's—apart from the spider?'

Erin sipped her spritzer, told him about her morning and laughed with him as they talked, watching the eponymous swans gliding past on the unruffled river, the water reflecting the cornflower-blue sky.

The honey-sweet air was filled with butterflies and birdsong. The sun danced in dapples across their entwined hands on the tabletop. And there wasn't another soul in sight. Just the two of them, madly in love, with their whole future stretching blissfully ahead of them.

Perfection.

'Jay! Darling!'

Erin jerked her head up, rudely dragged from the romantic rural idyll.

Deena and Tavish Keskar were carefully picking their way across one of the rustic bridges towards them.

As always, no matter how carefully she'd prepared, Erin felt instantly scruffy and slightly grubby as soon as she saw Deena. Stifling a groan, she watched the elegant vision, arctic cool in sleeveless pale-green linen and nude heels, sweep as gracefully as the swans on the Maizey, towards them.

Jay was already on his feet, and they all indulged in the ritual mutual mwah-mwah cheek-kissing and hugging.

'Erin!' Deena embraced her in a cloud of sweet-scented something so obviously expensive that it had probably involved passion flowers and unicorns and angels and hummingbirds. 'How lovely you look.'

'Thank you,' Erin said, still slightly dazed by the perfumed embrace and catching a glimpse of tiny emerald studs glinting in Deena's ears beneath the glossy black bobbed hair. Emeralds to go with the pale-green linen, of course. Emeralds echoed in the many golden bangles that slid sinuously up and down Deena's slender brown forearms. 'And so do you. As always. I know I've got an awful lot to live up to.'

'Nonsense.' Deena smiled. 'It's the other way round, darling. You're a very beautiful girl—so young and fresh. I always feel like some ancient crone when we're together. You're going to be such a spectacularly gorgeous bride I might have to hide myself away in a corner.'

'That's hardly likely, is it?' Erin said, right on cue, knowing exactly what was expected of her. 'After September I shan't be known as Jay's wife in Nook Green, but simply as "that girl with the stunning mother-in-law".'

Everyone laughed.

Jay and Erin exchanged grins as a mollified

Deena preened and headed for the table.

Tavish Keskar beamed at Erin. 'What a beautiful spot.' He helped his wife onto the bench seat after brushing it free of any minute traces of rustic debris. 'Just right on a day like today. Let's hope the weather holds for the wedding, eh?'

'I've got everything crossed.' Erin smiled at Tavish.

Despite being slightly intimidated by her, Erin was very fond of Deena, but she absolutely loved her future father-in-law. He was an older version of Jay, easy-going and laid-back; and although his black hair was threaded with silver and the laughter lines round his dark-brown eyes were deeply etched he was still a very attractive man.

Deena flicked at imaginary grime on the table then reached across and held up Erin's glass, inspecting it carefully. 'I always find you can judge the standards of an establishment by the cleanliness of their glasses, don't you, darlings? I always check for leftover lipstick or finger smudges.'

Erin fought down the urge to say that there would be *nothing* like that on the Swan's glassware and simply nodded.

Having satisfied herself that everything was hygienic, Deena smiled. 'So, how have you both been? Working hard, no doubt. We've heard so little from you recently.'

'Yes, sorry. We've both been busy,' Jay nodded. 'With work, and the wedding.'

Tavish nodded. 'Ah, yes—not long to go now. Everyone back home is getting very excited. Your mother has bought at least nine new outfits.'

Deena laughed and flapped her glass-free, perfectly manicured hand, but didn't deny it. 'I only hope I won't clash with your mother, Erin. Do you know what colours she's chosen?'

'The last time I spoke to her, she was wanting to wear peach.'

'Oh.' Deena looked disappointed. 'Peach? Such a bland colour I always think. Always makes pale skin look washed out. Why peach?'

'I've no idea.' Erin shrugged, knowing that her mum had probably found something vaguely mother-of-the-bride suitable in peach in a Sydney second-hand shop and didn't give a tuppenny fig whether it would make her look washed out or not. 'I do know she wants to wear a hat though. A very big hat. Dad was worrying about getting a massive hatbox into the hand luggage.' Erin giggled. 'My mum is so not a hat person. I've told her it doesn't matter. She doesn't have to wear one. It's not that sort of wedding.'

'Well, no—' Deena frowned '—a hat, if she's not used to wearing one, might be a little uncomfortable. Maybe she could opt for a fascinator?'

Erin shook her head. 'You haven't met my mum. My mum in a fascinator would look like an electrocuted emu.'

'Erin, darling!' Deena raised both perfectly threaded black eyebrows in horror. 'That's not very nice.'

'No, seriously. My mum is the loveliest person in the world, but she's the first to admit that she can sabotage the smartest of outfits. She's much happier in—um—more casual clothes.'

And that, Erin thought to herself, was putting it kindly. Her mother had no interest whatsoever in fashion, in clothes, in shopping. Rose Boswell had no idea what suited her, neither did she care. She wore what was comfortable; most of her clothes were charity shop buys or old favourites, worn until they fell to pieces.

Rose Boswell and Deena Keskar were light years apart.

Jay drained his glass and glanced at his watch. 'I think it's probably time for lunch. We can't wait to show you the dining room. It's got sensational views.'

'Mmmm.' Deena smiled. 'We did have a little peek just now, actually.'

'Did you?' Erin frowned, slightly annoyed. 'Oh . . . but you wait until you see the rest. We'd hoped to keep it as a lovely surprise for you, but—'

Deena giggled. 'Oh, it will be, and we have a stunning little surprise of our own for you too, darlings.'

Oh, God, Erin thought.

Tavish cleared his throat. 'I thought we'd agreed not to say anything until . . .'

'Oh, I know, but it's *so* exciting.' Deena flapped her hands. Jewels sparkled in the sunshine. 'Sorry. No, no, Erin, darling, you carry on. Our little surprise will keep until we have lunch.'

Erin and Jay exchanged amused glances. Deena's surprises were usually notoriously expensive, expansive, huge and totally impractical gifts. The loft in Jay's cottage was full of them.

'And we're both very much looking forward to seeing the rest of the Swan,' Tavish said firmly. 'Aren't we, Deena?'

Deena nodded. 'Yes, we're delighted to get an early glimpse at where you're having your reception. The restaurant is certainly gorgeous and

35

the whole place—what little we've seen of it—looks very nice indeed. But . . .'

'But?' Jay raised his eyebrows. 'There's a but?'

'Well, yes, darling.' Deena beamed. 'It all seems a little confusing. You still haven't told us where you're having the ceremonies. The invitations merely said the Swan—which we knew was for the reception—and we all assumed you'd be sending separate invitations for the rest.'

'What rest?' Erin frowned. 'Rest of what? We're having everything here. That's what it says on the invitations. Our ceremony is taking place in the marriage room, the wedding breakfast is in the dining room, we've got the ballroom for the dancing, and the grounds for the entire day. We're having a buffet during the evening's entertainment, and we've booked rooms for everyone who wants to stay overnight, with breakfast the next morning and—'

Deena laughed. 'Really? That all sounds wonderful, and I know that's what it says on the invitations, but surely, you can't actually be *getting married* here? I know it's a beautiful old manor house, and it's in a stunning location, and it still looks like a minor stately home, but it's *an hotel.*'

'With a designated wedding room,' Erin said. 'It's licensed for marriages.'

Deena nodded. 'Yes, yes, I understand that. Most Indian wedding ceremonies—and I'm talking here about the actual marriage only—take place in venues that have been blessed for the occasion these days. Not everyone wants to wait for the temple to become available. But even so, there are still a few things I simply don't understand and need to clarify.'

36

Just as Erin was going to speak again, Jay did a silent wide-eyed, head-shaking warning. 'Maybe we could talk about the arrangements over lunch?'

'Good idea.' Tavish stood up and winked at Jay. 'Your mother thinks she's been kept out of the wedding loop for far too long. She's got all sorts of questions that need answering.'

Erin groaned inwardly. Trust Deena to arrive now and put a bloody spanner in the works. Just when they'd got everything running so smoothly. What on earth was she talking about anyway? Why would she imagine that their wedding was going to take place somewhere else? Oh, why did people have to *interfere*?

Crossly, Erin swung her legs over the rustic bench and caught the heels of her unfamiliarly high sandals on the edge of the table. One sandal flew off across the rustic benches and disappeared into the riverside undergrowth.

Erin groaned. Loudly.

The swans stopped and stared at her with haughty disdain.

Oh Lordy, Erin thought, mortified as she bunched up her frock and hobbled lopsidedly to her feet. In front of Jay's perfect parents, too. And just when she'd wanted to be all elegant and sophisticated.

'Oh, dear.' Deena stared at Erin, clearly trying not to laugh and holding out her hand. 'Are you OK, darling?'

'Fine, thanks. I'll just have to look for the sandal,' Erin sighed, clasping Deena's perfect pearly-nailed proffered hand to steady herself.

Deena smiled again. 'Jay's searching for it now. Shall Tavish and I start making our way to lunch?

37

We don't want to be late, do we? And I can't wait to show you both our surprise.'

Erin forced a smile. 'I'm sure we'll love it.'

Jay had quickly retrieved the errant sandal from the long grass and held it out while Erin slid her foot into it.

'There you go, Cinders.' He grinned at her. 'You shall go to the ball.'

'Ta, but lunch'll do nicely right now.'

'Mmm, me too. I'm starving. Although, much as I love Mum and Dad—' Jay glanced towards the rear view of his parents, making sure they were out of earshot '—a picnic for two, by the river, sounds a pretty good alternative at the moment.'

'I wish,' Erin muttered. 'What the heck is your mum on about?'

'I've no idea, but I suspect we're about to find out that it's all about tradition, ritual and culture.'

'Oh, goody. And the surprise?'

'Probably yet another bejewelled elephant ornament to join the rest of the herd in the loft.'

'That's what I thought,' Erin giggled. 'Oh, well, we'll just have to look suitably thrilled, won't we?'

'We've had enough practice, haven't we? And— er—right,' Jay said loudly as they caught up with the elder Keskars, 'we're all sorted now and I'm starving.'

'Me too, and I can't wait to have a good chat about these arrangements. And to share our wonderful surprise, which you're both going to love.' Deena slid her arm through Erin's and they set off towards the first rustic bridge with Jay and Tavish behind them. 'Oh, and if you're going to be wearing heels on your wedding day, darling, maybe you should have a few deportment lessons before the wedding. I know a very good—'

'Mum!' Jay frowned. 'Erin doesn't need lessons in anything at all—least of all deportment.'

Erin shot him a grateful glance. 'And actually, I've just told Jay I'm going to be barefoot at the wedding.'

'*What?*' Deena looked at her in horror. 'Why? We're Hindus, darling, not Jains. There's absolutely no cultural or religious need for you to go barefoot.'

'Joke, mum,' Jay chuckled. 'And Erin will be perfectly OK with heels on the big day.'

'Well, of course. But—' Deena pouted playfully '—I was only trying to help.'

'We know you were,' Tavish interrupted smoothly. 'But I'm sure, as Jay says, Erin will be perfectly poised on her wedding day and won't need any help from anyone else.'

Erin shot him a grateful look too.

'Maybe not,' Deena said. 'But this is the most important day in our lives, Tavish. I don't want anything to spoil it.'

'It's pretty important to us, too,' Jay said quickly.

Deena paused on the crest of the rustic bridge and looked over her elegant shoulder. 'Of course it is, darling. But you, obviously more than Erin, should be aware of just how important family honour and tradition is. The entire family is open to scrutiny at a wedding. We're all on show. Which is why I think it's high time I found out exactly what you've got planned, before we lose all credibility.'

CHAPTER FIVE

'Jay's booked the table over there by the window,' Erin said excitedly, as they walked into the Swan's beautiful dining room. 'The one with the view across the—Oh! There's someone sitting there!'

Erin glared at the stunning woman with the smooth, dark-honey skin, large perfectly made-up dark eyes and layered chocolate-brown hair shot through with auburn highlights feathered round a traffic-stoppingly beautiful, high-cheekboned face who was browsing the menu.

'The cheek of her! We'll have to ask her to move and—'

The rest of Erin's sentence was lost in a shout of amazement from Jay, and laughter from Deena and Tavish, as the woman abandoned the menu, uncurled herself and flew elegantly across the dining room on killer heels.

'Jay!'

'Nalisha!'

Erin frowned in complete disbelief as the tall, slender woman, who looked as if she'd just sashayed from the pages of some exclusive glossy fashion magazine, squealed with delight and entwined her arms round Jay's neck and kissed him.

A lot.

'What the . . .?' Erin shook her head.

'Our lovely surprise, darling,' Deena gurgled happily. 'Nalisha's one of Jay's oldest friends.'

Erin blinked. Was she? Really? It was news to her. She'd never heard of a Nalisha, had she?

Erin suddenly felt a cold lump of fear grip her

heart. So *this* was the big surprise, was it? This was what Deena and Tavish had brought them? The stunningly gorgeous Nalisha.

Oh, great.

Instantly knowing she'd really, really have preferred to be surprised by another bejewelled elephant or twenty, Erin tried to smile.

Her lips didn't quite make it.

Which wasn't surprising, was it? After all, what woman really wants to see some scorching female curled like a second skin round their fiancé?

Not her, that was for sure.

And she knew she'd never heard of Nalisha. Ever.

'Erin,' Jay laughed, his arms still clasped round Nalisha's slender waist, 'this is Nalisha. Nalisha— my fiancée, Erin.'

'It's wonderful to meet you at last.' The long-legged vision in the short, fitted coffee-coloured lace dress with her arms still entwined round Jay's neck, beamed. 'I've heard so much about you.'

And I've heard sod all about you, Erin thought, still managing to smile. 'Er—thank you, and it's lovely to meet you, too.'

Liar!

It *might* just have been lovely to meet Nalisha if she'd known she existed and if Nalisha had been some even averagely pretty woman. But *this*? This was definitely *not* lovely on any level.

And why, again, did she feel so scruffy and grubby? Because, Erin told herself darkly, in comparison to this elegant, glorious vision of perfectly groomed Indian womanhood in a designer outfit that must have cost a fortune, she looked

41

like a chain-store-dressed *child* in her now slightly crumpled summer dress and high street sandals.

Euueewch . . .

Jay managed to extricate himself from the hug, and beamed at his parents. 'How on earth did you manage this? Last time I heard from Nalisha, she was still working in California and—'

'Sir? Madam?' The maître d' hovered beside them. 'Your table is ready and . . .'

'Yes, sorry.' Jay grinned. 'We can all catch up when we've ordered.'

Nalisha, Deena and Tavish, still laughing and chatting, headed for the table.

Jay, beaming, grabbed Erin's hand. 'How fabulous is this? I can't believe Nalisha's here. Oh, you'll love her, Erin. You'll be such great friends.'

Erin swallowed. Now was not the time to turn into some shrewish fishwife and screech 'Never in a million bloody years,' however much she might want to. 'Um—yes, I'm sure we will be. But who is she? Have I heard of her?'

'I'm sure you have, and you did write her name on the wedding invitation.'

Erin sighed. Yes, she probably had—along with dozens of Jay's other female friends and relations with very pretty Hindu names.

Jay hugged her. 'Nalisha and I grew up together. Our parents were friends and neighbours, and Nalisha and I were both only children, much the same age, so we just knew each other from being kids.'

OK. Keep rational. Sound calm.

'Oh, right. How nice. Sort of like a reality version of Friends Reunited?'

Jay beamed. 'Yeah, I suppose it is. Nalisha was

42

exactly like a sister to me while we were growing up, and it's so great to see her again.'

'And you're still in touch with her?'

'We've kept in touch, yes.' Jay smiled. 'Not so much recently because I've been so busy with work and the wedding plans. But we email occasionally, and we do try to catch up on Facebook as often as possible. I knew she'd be over here in time for the wedding, of course, but she didn't tell me she was coming home early.'

Erin frowned.

Jay laughed. 'Don't look at me like that. Do you tell me all about your Facebook friends, and people from your past that you text or email, with chat and old photos and "do you remembers?"?'

'No, of course not. They're not important to *us*.' Erin felt quite proud. She was handling it well now the initial shock had worn off. And it wasn't as if Nalisha was a *threat* or anything, was it? Especially as she lived in America. Which was a huge bonus. 'So Nalisha will be able to tell me all your embarrassing teenage secrets over lunch, will she?'

Jay chuckled and pulled her even closer. 'I sincerely hope not.'

Erin stared across the Swan's dining room. Nalisha was now giggling with Deena. The maître d' was still twitching.

Jay squeezed Erin's hand. 'We'd better sit down before he explodes.'

'What? Oh, yes, right.' Erin nodded as they moved towards the table. 'And honestly, I'm really happy for you if you haven't seen each other for so long . . . oh, thanks.'

Jay pulled out Erin's chair. Deena, Erin noticed had rearranged the seating so that Nalisha was

43

between Erin and Jay.

Oh, great. And, Lordy, Erin thought, as she was engulfed by a fragrant wave of Nalisha's expensively heady, exotic scent, she even wears the same perfume as Deena.

'Honestly, it's simply wonderful to meet you.' Nalisha leaned towards Erin. 'I can't wait to get to know you better—I know we're going to be such good friends. And nothing Jay's told me about you does you justice. I'm so pleased that you and he are so happy and are getting married.'

OK, Erin thought, Nalisha's clearly a very nice person.

'Um . . . Thank you. And, er, I'm so glad you'll be at the wedding.'

'So am I,' Nalisha laughed happily. 'I would have come over from the States for your wedding anyway, of course, but because of my new post in London, I have some unexpected free time—and here I am.'

Bugger, Erin thought. Not living in America any more, then. Sod it. And, yes, here you are. As a special treat for my fiancé. *My* fiancé.

'You're moving back to the UK?' Jay said happily to Nalisha. 'Permanently? Wow. I never thought that'd happen. I thought you loved the California job?'

'I did. But, you know, life changes . . .'

Deena peered over the top of her menu. 'I know Nalisha's far too modest to say this, but she's been headhunted over here. An offer she couldn't refuse, as they say. She's taking a sabbatical before moving down to London in September, so she was back home visiting the family, and we thought this—bringing her with us today—was too good an

44

opportunity to pass up.'

I bet you did, Erin thought darkly.

'So—' Erin looked at Nalisha, trying very hard not to let any of her rapidly mounting insecurities show '—your family live close to Jay's in Birmingham, do they?'

'Solihull, actually.' Nalisha nodded and leaned even closer to Erin. 'Not Birmingham. Yes. And as Jay and I grew up together—our parents are best friends, did he tell you?—Deena's always been like a second mother to me. She's absolutely wonderful, isn't she?'

'Oh, yes, wonderful.'

'You're so lucky to be having her as your mother-in-law.'

'I am, yes.'

Well, she was. As opposed to a future mother-in-law who was an axe-murderer or a serial poisoner or something.

'I think we should order,' Jay said as the hovering waiter tried not to appear too obvious. 'Otherwise we'll all be here at supper time.'

Everyone laughed and diligently studied their menus. Erin wondered sadly what had happened to her appetite.

'And then,' Deena said, 'we really must get down to discussing this wedding.'

Erin and Jay exchanged glances.

Nalisha chuckled. 'And as weddings are definitely not my area of expertise, I'll keep well out of that.'

Hallelujah, Erin thought. She smiled sweetly at Nalisha. 'So, you're not married?'

Tavish spoke before Nalisha could answer. 'No, not our Nalisha. She's an independent career woman. A highly qualified corporate lawyer. And a very much sought after one. And I doubt if there's a man in the world who's good enough for Nalisha.'

Erin squinted sideways at Nalisha. This, surely, was the point where she giggled a bit and denied it.

Nalisha didn't. She merely smiled and slowly crossed her supermodel legs. All the men in the restaurant stopped eating and watched.

Jay grinned. 'And even if there was such a man, he'd have to be very brave to take Nalisha on. She certainly has a mind of her own. I can't see her settling for domesticity.'

Nalisha, now studying her menu, still said nothing, but her sleepy pussycat smile spoke volumes.

Huh, Erin thought. No need to spell it out. There's Amazingly Clever and Stunningly Beautiful Independent Nalisha—and then there's little non-corporate, not-been-to-uni me, who simply can't wait to be married, and work for a year or so, and then have babies with the man I love more than life.

Nalisha was clearly a glorious Indian role model for the sisterhood and Erin now decided she and Nalisha would have absolutely nothing in common and couldn't wait for her to be taken back to Birmingham—ooh, no, sorry, Solihull—by Tavish and Deena.

Then she wouldn't have to see her again until Nalisha was just one more very beautiful Indian woman at their wedding. Another immaculately manicured hand to shake in the greeting line-up. Another bejewelled and sensuously sari'd guest.

It couldn't be a minute too soon.

Oh, Erin thought miserably as she stared at the

46

menu, why the hell had Deena invited her today?

Having eventually ordered, and by now exhausted the discussions about Tavish's business meeting in Reading, interviewing a new supplier for his small pharmacy, and Deena's sourcing new products for her salon, along with Nalisha and Jay exchanging general chit-chat about people Erin had never met, it was as if no one actually wanted to make that first opening gambit regarding the wedding, just in case.

Lunch-time conversation hummed from the other tables, but not from theirs. Erin stared out of the wall-long ranks of floor-to-ceiling arched windows, open to the drowsy midday heat, across the glorious view down to the river. In six weeks' time, this centuries-old room would be transformed for their wedding breakfast.

It would be so amazing, and incredible to think that when they next sat in this fabulous dining room, she would be Mrs Jay Keskar and the happiest woman in the world.

She simply couldn't wait.

But . . .

Erin pleated the white linen tablecloth between her fingers. She and Jay had spent ages with Abbie, the Swan's wedding planner, and the chefs and the restaurant manager, explaining what they wanted, and it had all been so exciting. Now, she felt a little knot of anxiety in the pit of her stomach, and it wasn't *all* to do with the beautiful woman now sitting between her and Jay.

Surely Deena Keskar couldn't start playing the cultural heritage card and *interfere*, could she? And even if she tried, it was far too late to change anything, wasn't it?

The wine waiter arrived, dispensing the bottles of mineral water they'd ordered, as they were all either driving, or returning to work, or both—or in Nalisha's case, because she was apparently *dieting*.

Tavish poured drinks all round.

Deena raised her glass and smiled. 'Well, I must say this place is absolutely gorgeous. Very clever of you two to have found it. I love it.'

Phew. Erin exhaled, let go of the tablecloth and smiled across Nalisha at Jay. It was going to be OK.

'Yes—' Deena nodded as their first courses arrived '—it'll be perfect for either the *sagai* or the *sanji*.' She looked across the table at Jay. 'Which of them are you holding here?'

'Neither,' Jay said shortly, his forkful of goat's cheese tart suspended. 'We've explained all that. We're having our wedding here—our entire wedding day: our marriage and the reception and—'

'What or who is a *sagai* and a *sanji*?' Erin frowned over her untouched mushrooms. As Jay and his parents were vegetarians, she'd already decided to forgo the bliss of the Swan's fabulous pâté today. Now she didn't even want the mushrooms. 'They sound like an Indian double act. Like an Eastern Ant and Dec.'

Both Tavish and Deena looked at her doubtfully. Jay stifled a chuckle.

'Oh dear,' Nalisha said softly, slicing a tomato into skin-thin slivers.

'Surely Jay's told you? The *sagai*—' Deena leaned forwards '—is the Indian engagement party. The ring ceremony. A celebration of your betrothal. It's held a week before the wedding ceremony.'

'Oh, we don't need to worry about that, then. We

48

got engaged on my birthday—as you know—and we didn't bother with an engagement party,' Erin said, watching the sun dance in prisms from her diamond solitaire. 'We just had a few drinks with our friends at the Merry Cobbler in Nook Green and then we went all out for dinner and—'

'But you must be having a *sagai*.' Deena looked shocked. 'It's traditional.'

'Um,' Erin said, 'maybe for Hindu weddings, but ours isn't one of those, is it? Although, because it's a *fusion* wedding, we've incorporated loads of Indian stuff into our day. It's very important to us to have a celebration of both cultures, but we're not telling anyone the details because we want it to all come as a lovely surprise.'

'Everything's coming as a surprise to me at the moment,' Deena sighed. 'I really can't believe that you haven't organised a *sagai*. Still, never mind— leave it with me. Your parents will be here a week before the wedding won't they, darling?'

'Yes,' Erin said with a nod, 'but—'

Deena smiled. 'Then that's settled. We can have the *sagai* when they arrive. No, no, I don't want to hear any arguments on that front—humour me, Erin. Please.'

'Best just nod and say nothing,' Nalisha whispered. 'When Deena is in full Indian Mamma mode it's the only way. Trust me.'

Erin stared at Nalisha in surprise. Maybe Nalisha *was* going to be a friend after all. However, nodding and saying nothing simply wasn't Erin's way.

She looked across the table at Deena. 'But, honestly, we haven't got time for a saggy, er, *sagai* and nowhere to hold it, and no one is going to want to come to another party just a week before the

49

wedding anyway, and we've got our hen and stag nights too.'

Nalisha shook her head sadly.

'Why on earth wouldn't everyone want several parties? Everyone loves a party.' Deena beamed. 'Anyway, let's not worry about that now. You can leave the *sagai* to me. Right now, we seem to have far more important things to talk about. I'm very disappointed that you haven't incorporated a *sanji* in your plans.'

'Told you to say nothing.' Nalisha played with her salad leaves and laughed quietly. 'You'll regret it . . .'

Jay shook his head. 'Please don't interfere, Mum. I know you're doing all this with the best of motives, but—'

Erin, delighted that Jay *was* on her side, gave him a 'no, it's OK, leave this to me, please' look across Nalisha. She really, really didn't want a stand-up Keskar family row in the Swan's hushed and illustrious dining room. Diplomacy had never been one of her skills, but she felt she had to at least try.

'This, er, *sanji*? Is that right? What is it?'

'It's a Hindu wedding reception,' Jay said quietly. 'A light-hearted evening of dancing and music and lots of food. It's supposed to be a chance for the families to get to know one another better.'

Erin nodded happily. She could cope with this. Diplomacy was much easier than she thought. 'That's OK then. We're having one of those. A bit of fun for everyone after the formality of the ceremony and the meal and the speeches.'

'Oh, thank goodness for that.' Deena looked mollified.

'But ours is an evening reception, here, straight after the wedding,' Jay said. 'As in all normal British marriage ceremonies.'

Erin wrinkled her nose. 'Well, yes, of course it is. Why wouldn't it be?'

'Because,' Nalisha said quietly, 'Indian weddings have the reception the day *after* the wedding.'

'Wow.' Erin chewed and eventually swallowed a mushroom. 'That must be exhausting. Well, we couldn't do that anyway, because the day after our wedding we'll be at Heathrow to go on honeymoon and—'

Deena frowned slightly. 'Oh, really, it's such a shame you and Jay weren't a couple when any of our family have been married, darling. Then you'd have been to their weddings and know exactly what we expect a wedding to be. Nalisha would have known *exactly* what to expect, wouldn't you, darling?'

Nalisha held up an elegant hand. 'Please don't involve me in this. You can't expect Erin to know about all our cultural celebrations, can you? Yes, of course I'd have known, but then I'm a Hindu, and Jay and I have been to so many Indian weddings together . . .'

'Have you?' Erin said sharply.

'Masses.' Nalisha smiled. 'We were always one another's plus-ones.'

Bugger, Erin thought, this just gets better and better.

Deena pushed her plate away. 'But surely Erin, you must at least know that our cultural heritage is one of strictly observed traditional rituals? And none more so than at a marriage?'

Tavish put down his fork with a clatter. 'I think

51

there are a lot of things we need to talk about here, Deena. And possibly privately. It seems to me that Jay and Erin have organised their wedding day to include something of both cultures—which is wonderful—and maybe we should leave it at that today.'

Deena shook back her glossy black hair. The emerald earrings danced with green prisms. 'And risk being a laughing stock? And risk everyone saying afterwards that the poor couple didn't have any *poojas* or a Mandap Mahurat, not to mention the *pithi*? And risk being accused of allowing our only son to have a cheapskate wedding?'

CHAPTER SIX

'Excuse me.' Erin's brief sortie into diplomacy was instantly forgotten. She pushed her mushrooms away. 'Clearly unlike Nalisha, I have no idea what any of those things are, but whatever they are, we're not having any of them. And Jay and I have saved like mad for this wedding. We haven't asked you, or my parents, for any financial input at all, because it's our day. It's going to be the wedding we want, the way we've planned it. I can assure you there'll be absolutely nothing cheapskate about it.'

'Sorry, darling.' Deena smiled. 'Of course there isn't. Not for a British wedding—it all sounds rather lovely. But Jaimal is Indian and—'

Nalisha laughed.

'Mum!' Jay clattered down his knife and fork. 'You haven't called me Jaimal since I was eleven years old! And . . .'

52

'But Jay's British,' Erin said, with an awful sinking feeling that things were once again spiralling way out of control. 'He was born here. In Britain. In Birmingham.'

'Solihull, darling,' Deena corrected quickly. 'Not Birmingham.'

Nalisha laughed again.

'And you're British, too.' Jay looked at his parents. 'Both my Naanis and Daadas were already living in Britain when you were born. You've told me the stories often enough. How they scrimped and saved and made enough money to leave Gujarat.'

Erin took a gulp of her ice-cold mineral water. Despite the Swan's tables being well spaced, she was aware that their conversation was causing a certain amount of interest amongst the other diners. She really couldn't blame them for eavesdropping. If she weren't so painfully involved, she'd be riveted herself.

'Exactly,' Deena said in a placating voice. 'That's exactly why you have to acknowledge your roots. My parents, and your father's, sacrificed everything for us, as we did for you. The marriage ceremony, especially the marriage of our only child, is a time for repaying those sacrifices.'

'Look,' Erin put in, 'and I know how grateful Jay is for everything you've done for him. But really, without being rude, for us, the wedding is a confirmation and celebration of our love and our commitment to one another, and the opportunity to be able to show that love and commitment publicly in front of our friends and family.'

'Dangerous ground,' Nalisha whispered. 'I'd back off now if I were you.'

Erin shook her head.

Jay nodded. 'Erin's absolutely right, Mum. Oh, I'll never forget what you've sacrificed for me, which is why we want everyone we know and love to be here to share our day. But when Erin and I get married, it's just that. Our wedding day. Our day. No one else's.'

Nalisha sighed.

Erin wanted to cheer and stamp her feet and hurl her arms round Jay and kiss him. With Nalisha in the way it'd be tricky but she was sure she'd manage it somehow.

Deena pursed her lips but mercifully remained silent as the waiter removed the empty starter plates, which were immediately seamlessly replaced by their main courses.

'Oh, this looks and smells delicious.' Tavish wafted the steam from his vegetable linguini towards him.

'It is,' Erin said quickly. 'The food here is out of this world. As you'll discover at the wedding breakfast. We've chosen a menu to suit everyone, again a fusion of East and West, and plenty of veggie dishes, and—'

Nalisha, who had hardly touched her first course, leaned towards Erin. 'I'd give up if I were you. You're flogging a dead horse, as they say. Deena has her own agenda. Honestly, just agree with everything and then go your own sweet way.'

'But . . .'

'Seriously,' Nalisha said softly, 'leave Deena to me. We have a lovely long car journey home to Solihull. I'll talk to her then.'

Erin smiled. She suddenly decided she liked Nalisha. A lot.

'Thanks.'

'No problem.'

Jay beamed at them both, clearly delighted that they were getting on so well.

'Anyway,' Deena said with a smile, 'let's get back to the matter in hand while we still have time, darlings.'

Jay and Erin exchanged raised eyebrow looks of *Oh, Lordy, do we really have to?*

Deena smiled. 'You see, Erin, from our point of view, this fusion wedding will just be a watered-down version of yours and Jaimal's backgrounds, won't it? Neither one thing nor the other? Erin, darling, I love you. I'm delighted that you're going to be my daughter-in-law—I couldn't be more happy with Jay's choice of a future bride, but—'

'But?' Erin frowned. 'But? Go on, please. Don't stop there. I can't wait to hear the rest.'

Nalisha sighed heavily, looked at Jay, and shook her head. Despite her brave words, Erin saw the look between Nalisha and Jay and felt a pang of fear.

Nalisha and Jay: the perfect, beautiful Indian couple.

In the two years she and Jay had been together, their differences had never been mentioned by anyone, least of all themselves. There *were* no differences for heaven's sake. Never had been; never would be.

Or would there? Was Jay, now reunited with Nalisha who knew everything and everyone that mattered in the Keskar culture, secretly feeling the same way as Deena?

Jay sighed and looked at his mother. 'Whatever

55

Erin says, Mum, we really don't want to hear any more objections. This is the twenty-first century. We're not having an arranged marriage. Erin isn't coming to me with a dowry. We don't care that we have different backgrounds. We haven't even considered it. For God's sake—we're marrying each other because we're in love and want to spend the rest of our lives together. This is getting ridiculous.'

Erin, giving Nalisha a triumphant glance, swallowed in relief. He *was* completely on her side. Yay!

Tavish shook his head. 'Jay, you shouldn't speak to your mother like that.'

'No, Tavish, it's all right. I'm sorry,' Deena said quickly. 'Erin, darling, please don't ever think that we would prefer anyone else for our daughter-in-law.'

Not even the exotically and expensively fragranced Nalisha? Really?

Erin knew that she had to be grown up here, and that one wrong word could ruin things for ever.

'Thank you. And I'm sorry, too. I shouldn't have said anything. It's just, well, I'm feeling a bit bombarded by all this Indian ritual stuff when our wedding is already arranged. That's all.'

'That makes two of us,' Jay said. 'And I really can't see the point of carrying on with the conversation. Can we change the subject, please?'

'What a good idea,' Nalisha said softly.

Deena played for time by moving a slightly less than perfect piece of cucumber to one side of her plate. 'All right, yes, of course. But because I don't want to upset either of you, can I just reiterate that even if Jay's the first person in our family not to be marrying within our culture, we absolutely adore you, Erin. Don't we, Tavish?'

Erin felt it was all being a bit overdone now.

'We do,' Tavish said, smiling kindly at Erin and saving a glower for his wife. 'We couldn't be happier.'

Oh, good, Erin thought, hoping that the conversation would now change to something far less inflammatory. Politics would be good.

'Exactly.' Deena nodded. 'And we're not completely archaic, you know. It's simply very important to us that our wedding traditions and rituals are observed.'

Some hope, Erin thought, irritably. Deena wasn't going to let it go, was she? Bugger.

'Why?' Jay shook his head. 'Come on, Mum. When did you and Dad last go to the temple, if it wasn't for someone else's wedding? You're no more committed than we are.'

'That's not the point.'

'It's exactly the point,' Jay insisted. 'Neither Erin nor I pay more than lip service to the religions we were born into. That's why we're having a civil ceremony.'

'Goodness me!' Tavish dropped a snaking loop of linguini from his fork. 'A *gay* wedding?'

Nalisha chuckled.

'Nooo.' Erin, much cheered now by Jay's support, blessed Tavish for his great comic timing. 'That's a civil partnership.'

'Tavish knows that.' Deena sighed at her husband. 'We went to one when Kishan married Daman. It was very nice.'

'You've actually been to an Indian gay wedding?' Despite still being cross with Deena, Erin was fascinated. 'Blimey.'

57

'Fortunately both families are very forward thinking. There was no problem.' Deena inspected a cherry tomato. 'But even they had a *sagai* and a *sanji*. A lot of the boys wore saris.'

Nalisha smiled. Erin giggled. So did Jay.

'There you are.' Jay looked far more relaxed now. 'And the temple roof didn't collapse, did it? And Kishan and Daman's families haven't been condemned to hell fire, have they? Times are changing, Mum. Honestly, no one in the family is going to worry that we haven't stuck exactly to the old ideas. They'll just be happy to have been invited to our wedding—whether it's totally traditional or not.'

'They are.' Tavish mopped up the last of his sauce and gave his wife a warning look across the table. 'As we are. Honestly.'

'Good,' Jay said. 'And we know you'll all have a wonderful time. And so will Erin's family. So please don't go on about cousin Alisha's fabulous marriage in the Wembley temple, or cousin Mittul's wedding that lasted for three weeks, or any of the other family stuff, because this is *not* going to be an Indian wedding.'

'That—' Deena captured a last piece of Lollo Rosso '—is becoming abundantly clear. Oh, dear . . . All right. I can see that I'm not going to win on all counts here. But there are some things that I'd still like to discuss.'

Please, nooo, Erin thought, pushing her plate away. Just when it all seemed to be getting sorted. And as if there wasn't enough to worry about. Now it wasn't just if she tumbled off her wedding shoes, or found a spider in her bouquet, or any of the million things she'd previously imagined could go

58

wrong.

Now, just when she'd got Nalisha into perspective—well, almost—Deena was going to *insist* on things, and those things were going to cause a massive, massive problem, she just knew it.

'No, no pudding, thank you.' Deena waved away the dessert menu. 'Like Nalisha, I have to think about my figure.'

Like Nalisha, a teeny-weeny size 10 at most, and toned and honed to perfection, Erin thought, sighing.

'Well, I'm going to have the honeycomb mousse,' Tavish said happily. 'With the Jersey cream, please.'

'And me, thank you.' Jay smiled. 'Erin, have you decided?'

'Nothing for me, thanks.' Erin, having hardly eaten anything, shook her head. 'I've got another dress fitting really soon and I can't afford to have put on an ounce.'

'Ah.' Nalisha's eyes sparkled. 'The wedding dress? Fabulous. I want to hear all about what you're going to be wearing.'

'Not a chance.' Erin refilled her water glass. 'My mum's been begging me to tell her about it, too. My lips are sealed.'

'Oh.' Deena fluttered her eyelashes. 'Come on, darling. Mind you, I can guess at the colour, and probably the style.'

'Can you?' Erin frowned. 'Really? Because no one, apart from Sophie and Bella who've been with me at the fittings because they're having their bridesmaids' dresses from the same shop, have seen it or know anything about it at all. Unless—' she shot a look at Jay '—they've said something to you at work? And you've told your mum and—'

'Whoa!' Jay held up his hands. 'More than my life's worth to cross-question Sophie and Bella I can tell you. They're so loyal to you that they wouldn't tell me anything—not that I've asked. I want to be stunned along with everyone else.'

Deena and Tavish laughed.

The two puddings arrived and Jay and Tavish fell on them with murmurs of appreciation.

Deena leaned eagerly towards Erin. 'Yes, I completely understand that you'd want to keep the details secret, darling, but obviously it will be red and gold with possibly a touch of white or cream and heavily embroidered and gorgeously bejewelled. A ceremonial sari is always—'

'What ceremonial sari?' Erin giggled. 'I'm not wearing a sari!'

Deena looked as if someone had just slapped her. 'Not-wearing-a-sari?'

'Sheesh,' Nalisha murmured. 'Another wrong move . . .'

'No.' Erin shook her head. 'Why would I wear a sari? For the umpteenth time, it's a fusion wedding, which is why Jay is going to wear a Nehru suit and I'm wearing . . . well, a traditional Western wedding dress—and that's all I'm going to say about it.'

'But you have to wear a sari,' Deena insisted. 'Jaimal's bride *must* wear a sari.'

Here we go again, Erin thought.

'Don't call me Jaimal,' Jay mumbled round a mouthful of honeycomb. 'And whatever wedding dress Erin's chosen I know it won't be a sari. Why on earth would it be a sari?'

'Because—' Deena's eyes flashed '—we will all be wearing saris or *lehengas*. Nalisha will be wearing a sari, won't you, darling?'

'Yes, probably. But that's because I'm Indian. Erin isn't. She's bound to be wearing a Western wedding dress. It is a fusion wedding.'

Erin wanted to kiss Nalisha.

Deena sighed heavily. 'But every woman on our side of the family will be wearing saris or *lehengas* and they'll all expect Erin to do the same.'

Erin exhaled. 'Then maybe you should tell them that I won't be. That way they won't be shocked on the day, will they?'

'Cool,' Nalisha whispered. 'Well done.'

Deena merely frowned.

Jay laughed. 'Look, Mum, Erin and I are delighted that all my aunts and cousins will be wearing saris or *lehengas*. Just as all the ladies on Erin's side of the family, and our friends, will be wearing their best outfits. And, as Erin says, I'm wearing a Nehru suit, so you have no complaints there—oh, and before you ask, no there will be no ceremonial turban with it and—'

'No *turban*?' Deena's voice travelled up several octaves. 'Why on earth not?'

'Because we're not Sikhs, because turbans are not part of our heritage or religious dress code, because I am not wearing a Hindu wedding turban for anyone, because I've never worn a turban in my life, and because I'd look and feel a complete prat.'

Nalisha and Erin looked at one another and snorted with laughter.

'Jaimal!'

Tavish put down his spoon. 'Deena, you and your sisters and mine, and the other girls in the family will be splendid in your saris and what have you. But I think the children here have made it perfectly clear that their wedding outfits are already chosen,

61

and they both sound ideal for this fusion wedding, so maybe we should leave it well alone.'

'And you'll look gorgeous in a sari,' Erin put in quickly as it looked as if the elder Keskars were about to have a very public row. 'I've never seen you in one. You've always worn Western clothes. You're like a walking advert for Per Una and Phase Eight.'

'Yes—' Deena's eyes were flinty '—but *not* on ceremonial occasions. As mother of the bridegroom, I shall definitely be adhering to the correct dress code, even if no one else is.'

Ouch, Erin thought, trying to clamp her lips together so that nothing unforgivable could escape. She did a quick eye-meet with Jay and was relieved to see that he was actually trying not to laugh.

Oh Lordy, I love him so much, Erin thought. She'd cope with Deena and the *sagai* and the saris and Nalisha and all the other stuff later. With Jay, she knew she'd cope with anything.

'OK, so we know, very clearly, that Mum and Nalisha and the aunts and cousins will be wearing saris and *lehengas* and Erin won't. What about you, Dad?' Jay looked at his father. 'Are you going to be wearing a Sherwani tunic and churidars to our wedding?'

Tavish glanced down at his trademark neat chinos and white sports shirt, and chuckled. 'No, I'm not. Like you, I'll be wearing a Nehru suit. And that's as far as I'm going too.'

Thank goodness for that, Erin thought, wishing that her future parents-in-law would shut up about the bloody wedding. Surely there was nothing left to say?

The gods—of whatever religion—were smiling

on her.

Deena glanced at her watch. 'Tavish, it's getting late—we're not even going to have time for coffee. We really ought to be going. I have a client at three-thirty.'

Oh, goody, Erin thought.

Deena ran a beauty parlour and therapy centre. She was absolutely ace at head massages and eyebrow threading and fitting elaborately decorated acrylic nails.

'And I'm in surgery, and Erin has to be back at work, too,' Jay said. 'No, put your wallet away, Dad. It's all taken care of. This is our treat.'

Some treat, Erin thought darkly, managing to stretch her lips into a charming daughter-in-law-to-be beam at the same time.

Tavish scraped up the last drops of his Jersey cream. 'Thank you both, then. It's been lovely. And it's hopefully answered all your mother's questions and put her mind at rest.'

Judging by the way Deena snorted and snatched at her Radley bag as she stood up, Erin reckoned Tavish was going to get both barrels of thwarted fury all the way back home. She hoped Nalisha had her iPod to plug in and drown out the worst of the barrage.

'Not entirely,' Deena said. 'But it has at least given me some idea of what's needed before September. So much to do, so little time. Now, darlings, we'll have to fly. Thank you for a lovely lunch and we'll be in touch very soon.'

Can't wait, Erin thought darkly, as they thanked the Swan's staff, and trailed out of the dining room.

Nalisha, her arm now linked snakily through Jay's, turned every male head in the restaurant.

Outside in the car park, the early afternoon sun broiled relentlessly in the cloudless sky and the Swan's shady dining room and tastefully hidden air con was very quickly a thing of the past.

Nalisha hugged Erin, then moved away and kissed Jay. Erin tried not to look, or listen as they laughed together.

Be grown up, she told herself. Nalisha will be whizzing up the motorway in a few moments and you won't have to see her again for weeks.

'Bye then.' Nalisha beamed at Erin. 'It's been lovely to meet you.'

'And you.' Erin smiled fixedly as Jay helped Deena ease herself into the Mercedes and held the door open for Nalisha.

Nalisha paused and smiled secretively at Erin. 'I'm so pleased we're going to be friends. And don't forget what I said. Leave Deena to me.'

'I will—thank you.' Erin wondered just why she'd worried about Nalisha who was clearly a very nice woman indeed and simply an old friend of Jay's and no threat whatsoever.

'Oh!' Nalisha smiled suddenly. 'Your sandals, Erin! I hadn't noticed them before. How sweet.'

Erin looked down at her pale-blue, slender-strapped sandals and laughed. 'Thank you. I've been practising—rather unsuccessfully—walking in heels before the wedding.'

'Oh, I love them.' Nalisha continued to smile. 'It's amazing how well the cheap shoe shops can copy the designers these days, isn't it? I had an original pair of those a couple of seasons ago when they were fashionable.'

Erin's mouth was still open as Nalisha slid herself into the Mercedes.

'Well,' Jay said, waving as Tavish started to drive away. 'That wasn't too bad, was it?'

Was he *mad*? Hadn't he *heard*?

'And it was fabulous to see Nalisha again.' Jay, clearly unaware of Erin holding herself tightly in check, slid his hand down her arm and stroked her fingers. 'I'm sorry it went a bit astray. But no one can spoil our wedding day, Erin. No one. Not even my mother.'

'What?' Erin was still smarting. 'Possibly not, but she's having a damn good try.'

'She means well. Honestly.'

'Mmmm. Maybe. And what about Nalisha?'

Nalisha the two-faced bitch woman from hell.

'Who's Nalisha?'

Jay kissed her, and despite everything, she melted. It was OK. Nalisha was on her way back to Birmingham—oooh, no, Solihull, darling—wasn't she? And now it was just her and Jay. Together. As it always would be.

'Oh,' Erin sighed happily. 'I do love you.'

'I love you, too. Such a shame I have to be in surgery this afternoon, because I really, really want to—'

The Mercedes came to a sudden halt on the gravel and reversed slowly.

Deena leaned from the window. 'Oh, darlings, Nalisha and I have just had such a wonderful idea. As she's going to be at a bit of a loose end until she takes up her new job, why doesn't she come down here and stay in Nook Green for a couple of days? She can help you with all the little odds and ends that are bound to crop up before the wedding.'

Nooo! Erin screamed silently.

'And she'll be able help Erin out with any of

those awkward little cultural queries that are bound to occur,' Deena continued, still smiling.

Over my dead body, Erin thought.

'Oh, I don't need any help at all,' Erin said through gritted teeth. 'I'm perfectly well organised, thank you. It's a lovely offer, of course, but . . .'

Jay shrugged. 'Well, if Nalisha wants to be bored to tears in a very tiny Berkshire village, then I'm sure we'd love to have her for a few days, wouldn't we?'

No, we bloody wouldn't, Erin, thought crossly, trying not to look at Nalisha, smiling smugly in the back of the car. Nalisha is clearly a grade-A cow.

'Fabulous!' Deena beamed some more. 'I'll leave the arrangements to you then, darlings. Byeeeee!'

CHAPTER SEVEN

'So, when does she arrive?' Doug Boswell clambered over several packing cases in the back room of the Old Curiosity Shop, easing his long ripped-jeaned legs carefully to the floor. 'Nalisha— this stunning Indian woman that you seem to dislike? She'll be here soon, won't she?'

'Don't remind me. The day after tomorrow. Fortunately it means we'll get tomorrow's dress fitting out of the way before she gets here,' Erin said, straightening up and inelegantly wiping dust from under her nose with the back of her hand. 'Jay's booked her into the Bates Motel for three days.'

'The Bates Motel?' Doug chuckled. 'Seriously?'

Erin nodded. 'It's what she deserves.'

Esme Bates ran a small hotel—the White House—all very genteel and very twee, on the outskirts of Nook Green. Esme was about ninety but she had an IQ of about six million and had very, very high standards.

Doug laughed. 'Wouldn't she prefer to stay at the Merry Cobbler?'

'She'd probably prefer to stay at the Ritz but it isn't going to happen,' Erin snorted. 'And I'd prefer it if she stayed in Solihull for ever and ever and ever.'

'You really don't want her here, do you?'

Erin frowned at her uncle across the shop. 'Oh, well spotted.'

It was a week after the Keskars visit to the Swan. Early August had followed late July and settled steamily into what the red tops still called a Proppa Scorcha. And, with only five weeks to go, it seemed to Erin that all her carefully organised wedding plans were rapidly unravelling. And now Nalisha was coming to stay for a few days. And Nalisha, who had *promised* to have a word with Deena about interfering, was clearly a two-faced bitch.

Jay had thought it was a great idea, and Erin had found it impossible to tell him that she really, really didn't, without sounding jealous and insecure and needy. And Nalisha's parting shot about her cheap sandals might have not been as cruel as it sounded, might it? Maybe . . .

'But there's never been anything between Jay and Nalisha, has there?' Doug sliced through a wodge of gaffer tape and delved into the packing case. 'Romantically, I mean?'

'No, I don't think so. He says not, but honestly I'm not sure. I'm not sure about anything any

67

more.'

'Erin, you have to trust him. Believe him. You can't start doubting him now. Although why on earth he'd risk upsetting you by having this woman to visit, I have no idea.'

Erin sighed. 'Oh, you know Jay. He's got this deep-rooted honour-your-parents respect thing, which is good—usually—so, he doesn't want to say anything to upset Deena. And, believe me, this was Deena's idea.'

'Well, yes, she can be very persuasive.' Doug grinned. 'But even so, I still think Jay should have the balls to tell his mother to mind her own business.'

'If only it was that easy. You know what Jay's like when it comes to family. He'd never dream of saying anything like that.'

'Pity.' Doug stretched and flexed his shoulders. 'Hell, it's hot.'

'Mmmm—far too hot. Anyway, I've decided that I can cope with Nalisha for a couple of days. Even if she does think she's going to try to persuade me that Deena's right, and I should go all-out Indian for the wedding.'

'Some hope,' Doug mumbled from the depths of the massive box. 'I don't envy Jay, though. He's the one caught up in the middle. You don't think he'll be *swayed* by all this sudden parental pressure, do you?'

'God, no.' Erin frowned. 'At least I hope not . . . No, surely not? Not after all we've been through to get the wedding organised the way we want it. He wouldn't—would he?'

'Don't ask me.' Doug shook his head. 'I just think that if Deena keeps on and on at him about what's right in her eyes for her only son's wedding, he might feel that he has to give in on at least some of the points—what with the family honour code and everything.'

Erin exhaled. The idea was too ridiculous for words. 'No way. I know Jay too well. I know that would never happen.'

'Good, that's OK then. Now, what have we got here—ooh, nice—lots of blue and white china. You can do a window display, Erin, love. That'll bring the punters in—the tourists all love a bit of blue-and-white.'

Erin laughed. 'OK—but you were lucky. Buying those big boxes at auction without having a clue what was in them. It could have been a real load of rubbish.'

'Rubbish,' Doug said sternly, pushing his floppy sun-streaked hair away from his eyes, 'is our stock in trade. One person's rubbish is our bread and butter.'

'Nice mixed metaphor.' Erin grinned, blowing sawdust from a massive blue and white serving dish.

'And—' Doug grinned back across the storeroom '—actually, these all came as a freebie.'

'Really?' Erin cradled the serving dish carefully in case the brittle aging meant that any pressure would smash it to smithereens. She examined it more closely. It was grimy but perfect. 'How come?'

'I sold Dora Wilberforce's Staff highwaymen at a stonking profit, then I bid for the cases unseen with some of what I made. See? Blue and white freebies.'

'God help me—I'm related to Mr Micawber.' Erin shook her head, carefully putting the serving dish out of harm's way. 'It's a good job you leave

69

the accounting to me.'

'Why else would I employ you? You're spider-phobic and feel so sorry for everyone who wants to sell their family heirlooms that you pay them way over the odds. I only keep you on because you're a whizz with the books and the paperwork and keeping the accountant happy.' Doug winked. 'So, what do you reckon to changing the window display this afternoon?'

'Fine by me. But the way things are going, we might as well forget the blue and white and have a window display of Indian artefacts instead. Nalisha's on her way to stay, Jay's invited Kam to be a partner at the surgery and he's coming down to have a look round, Deena thinks I'm getting married in a ceremonial sari, *and* she wants Jay to wear a bloody turban!'

Doug laughed. 'No, sorry—but that's not a bad idea, actually. Oh no, not the turban, that's terrible—I mean the Eastern display. You could start this afternoon—a nice window filled with red and gold, draped in sari silks, and some bejewelled elephants and a few little gods and goddesses scattered everywhere and—'

Erin shook her head and lifted a fat blue and white teapot aloft. 'And I'll throw this at you if you even *think* about it.'

'Check that teapot for spiders first, then,' Doug chuckled. 'You wouldn't want an incy-wincy falling out on you, would you?'

'Eeeuwww.' Erin shuddered, quickly putting the teapot down. 'No, but seriously, I think it would be lovely to have an Indian display for the week before the wedding. I'm sure we can find some stuff in here or scour the salerooms. But not yet.

70

Not now. If Deena gets wind of it she'll think she's already won us both over to all things Indian, and she hasn't.'

'I don't understand the woman.' Doug sliced through the tape on the second packing case. 'You and Jay have always made it clear that your wedding was going to be a happy mix of both cultures, so I can't see for the life of me why she wants to hijack it.'

'Oh, it's all to do with heritage and traditional rituals or something.' Erin frowned at a pile of dusty mismatched blue and white saucers. 'Have we got the cups to go with these? Oh, yes . . . in that box over there . . . Um, yes—Deena seems to think the wrath of the gods will be heaped upon the heads of the Keskar dynasty if we don't have a *sagai* and a, um, *sanji* and all the other stuff. And now there's bloody Nalisha to cope with as well.'

'Who might not be as bad as you think once you get to know her properly.'

'She'll be *worse*! She's breathtakingly beautiful, she's amazingly intelligent, she knows everything about Jay, she's single and Hindu and totally sodding perfect for him.'

'Whoa,' Doug said reasonably. 'Jay clearly doesn't think so. Otherwise he wouldn't be marrying you, would he?'

'No, I s'pose not.' Erin sighed. 'Oh, this is all so annoying. I just wish Deena had kept her nose out.'

Doug chuckled. 'But, seriously, if Deena wants you to add a few parties, I can't really see the harm if it suits both factions.'

Erin paused in matching up cups and saucers. 'There aren't any damn factions. Or at least, there weren't. And Deena won't be happy with any half

71

measures, believe me. Whatever she says, it has to be full-on Indian or nothing at all.'

'But that's as daft as your mum insisting everyone at the wedding wears twinsets and pearls and drinks tea out of bone china and eats cucumber sandwiches.'

Erin giggled. 'And don't suggest that option to Mum, either. You know what she's like for everything Ye Olde English since she's been in Australia. I couldn't cope with an all-out cultural war. Oh, was that the shop bell? A customer?'

'You go and have a look, love.' Doug buried his head into the packing case. 'It might be Gina.'

'Why don't you want to see Gina?' Erin frowned across the storeroom. 'Have you had a row? Or have you just lost interest? You have, haven't you?'

Doug shrugged.

'Oh, you're useless. She's so lovely. Most men would give their eye teeth for someone like Gina. Gorgeous, single, no baggage, drop-dead sexy, easy-going, *and* she owns a pub . . . Gina is perfect for you.'

'She certainly thinks so.'

Erin put her hands on her hips and surveyed her uncle with mock severity. 'Honestly, you're hopeless. You sound like some truculent teenager rather than a fifty-something grown-up. It's way past time for you to settle down.'

'Easy for you to say.' Doug grinned lazily. 'You and Jay are rock solid—and your mum and dad met at school and haven't glanced at anyone else since. This whole family is so boring when it comes to romance.'

'Nanna wasn't. Otherwise she'd still be line dancing in the village hall and making ginger beer, instead of living it up in Malta with Colin.'

'True.' Doug looked slightly chastened. 'That must be where I get the genes from. Still, now Ma's left the village it was clearly left to me to uphold some sort of family mystique in the affairs of the heart.'

'Mystique? Crap. It's just your excuse to keep playing the field. Well, if you let Gina slip away, someone else will snap her up and you'll regret it for the rest of your life. If you carry on like this, before very long you'll be all old and wrinkly and unlovable, not to mention unloved.'

'Ta,' Doug chuckled. 'I clearly have so much to look forward to. And please be an angel and go and see who's in the shop. If it isn't Gina, it might be a customer clutching cash, and we don't want to let anyone escape, do we?'

Giving her uncle a last pretend frown of disapproval, Erin brushed the dust from her shorts, vest and ponytail, manoeuvred her way round the boxes, crates and piles of stock and out into the shop.

Like every other building in the charmingly rustic centre of Nook Green, the Old Curiosity Shop was low ceilinged, uneven floored, wonky walled and totally impractical for the twenty-first century. Unlike every other building in the centre of Nook Green, the Old Curiosity Shop wasn't, and never had been, a cute picture-perfect cottage.

The Old Curiosity Shop was an ancient slatted wooden shed. Or rather a series of ancient slatted wooden sheds all knocked into one. True, it had new large display windows looking out over the green, and the crumbling wood was now covered with a mixture of the delightful patina of age and a cascade of ivy, and sprouted emerald velvet cushions of moss and lichen from every crevice, but it was still a shed.

The dim interior was illuminated by dozens of second-hand lamps, and crammed full with collectibles, curios, old furniture, even older paintings and just plain junk. Shelves and tables wobbled under pyramids of books and ornaments. It looked chaotic, but Erin and Doug knew exactly where everything was.

'Hello, Erin.' Gina, stunningly pretty in her late thirties, with a mass of brown curls, and dressed in white shorts to show off her endless tanned legs and a vividly coloured low-cut top, which made the most of her cleavage, gave a tentative smile. 'Is Doug around?'

Sod it, Erin thought. She hated having to lie. 'Er, um, well, he had this huge consignment in from the sale rooms this morning and—'

'OK. Don't bother.' Gina sighed. 'It's all right. I just wondered, that's all. Just tell him, when you see him, that I'm still short-staffed so I'll be working in the pub this lunchtime as per usual. If he fancies a pint he'll know where to find me.'

'OK.' Erin smiled gently. 'I'll tell him. But, Gina—'

The bell pinged again.

A hot and harassed-looking couple with two bored teenagers in tow, both attached to mobile phones, looked startled in the open doorway.

'Hello.' Erin smiled. 'Sorry if the bell made you jump. It's in the doormat. We have to keep the door open on hot days otherwise we'd suffocate in here, and if we're in the stockroom we wouldn't know if anyone was in the shop and then—'

74

'Erin,' Gina, always the businesswoman, hissed. 'They're *customers*. They don't need to know that stuff. Just serve them.'

Erin grinned and sailed straight into saleswoman mode. 'Please come in and look around. If there's anything particular you're looking for, please ask.'

'Better,' Gina said approvingly, easing her long legs round a triangular table piled high with faded cloth-bound books. 'Anyway, I'll be off now. Just pass the message on to Doug—if you see him.'

Erin nodded, watching her make her way across the green towards the Merry Cobbler. Damn Doug! Stupid man!

As Gina disappeared, Erin carefully negotiated the crowded shop and beamed cheerfully at the newcomers. 'Lovely day, isn't it?'

The teenagers looked up from their texting and scowled at her.

'Too bloody hot for traipsing round places like this,' the man said. 'Brenda here said she'd seen this shop advertised on the internet and thought it would be a good place to pick up some more crap. Bit of a magpie is Brenda. Picks up crap at car boots, jumble sales, junk shops like this—you name it, Brenda can find crap in it. Our house is bloody full of crap.'

Brenda smiled happily and said nothing.

The teenagers looked up, still texting, still scowling, and nodded their agreement.

'OK.' Erin took a deep breath and looked hopefully at Brenda. 'So, do you collect anything in particular?'

Quickly, clearly before her family could chorus 'crap', Brenda nodded. 'At the moment I'm collecting Wade Whimsies miniatures. I had them as a child and they got thrown out when my mum had a blitz. I loved them so much. I can't see any here, though.'

'Oh, yes, Wade Whimsies—lovely. And we do have some, over here.' Erin led the way through a maze of various small cupboards and three wing-backed chairs, round a glass case of moth-eaten stuffed owls that she never liked looking at because they looked so mournful, and pointed to a glass-fronted cabinet. 'We've got quite a few of the original 1950s Disney editions in here. We've got nearly all the *Lady and the Tramp* characters and some from *Bambi* and—'

Brenda clasped her hands together and gave an ecstatic sigh. Her family groaned.

The doormat pinged again and Sophie, her short black hair standing up in excited spikes, jigged up and down on the doormat. It sounded like a really bad rendition of 'Jingle Bells'. 'Erin! Quick! Can you get away for lunch? Now?'

Erin paused in unlocking the cabinet and shook her head. 'Sorry, Sophie. I've got a customer and please-get-off-the-doormat.'

'Oooh nooo! You must be able to escape,' Sophie squeaked, still on the mat, still jigging, still accompanied by a series of discordant and intermittent chimes. 'Erin, please. It's a matter of life and death!'

'Get-off-the-mat and . . . what?' Erin suddenly felt sick. 'It's not Florence is it? She hasn't been run over?'

Sophie stepped off the mat. The cacophony stopped. Brenda and her family looked relieved.

'God, no. Sorry if I scared you, sweetheart. Florence was happily sunning herself on Doug's windowsill when I came in. No, it's nothing like that.'

Erin exhaled. 'Then why? No, honestly, I can't.'

'Step away from the Wade miniatures.' Doug appeared from the storeroom and removed the cabinet key from Erin's hands. 'Do not touch the Wade miniatures.' He grinned at the still-cooing Brenda. 'So, do we have anything here to add to your collection?'

'Oooh, yes,' Brenda breathed.

Her family groaned again.

'I,' Erin said, lowering her voice and glaring at Doug, 'am perfectly capable of serving this lady.'

'I know,' Doug said gently, unlocking the cabinet and handing Brenda a tiny Lady and Tramp. She squealed in delight. 'But I owe you one. With Gina—yes, I was listening, and you were very tactful—and now Sophie seems about to burst if she doesn't tell you something. So, you go to lunch and I'll man the fort.'

'And manage to avoid Gina in the pub without feeling too guilty?' Erin shook her head. 'You're such a coward, not to mention totally insane, but I'm not going to have to be told twice. I'm off.'

She beamed at the still-cooing Brenda and the rest of Brenda's glowering family, and picked her way across the shop to Sophie.

'OK. I'm all yours. Now what's so desperate?'

'Nalisha's here! Already! She's in the surgery!'

CHAPTER EIGHT

'She can't be.' Erin's heart sank. 'She's not due for two days.'

'Well, she is, and ohmigod,' Sophie breathed, 'she's so funny, and so friendly, and soooo beautiful. You never said she was that stunning.'

Erin groaned.

'And her car!' Sophie's eyes were wide with excitement. 'Wow. It's a BMW sports convertible. It's like something out of a Dior advert. And . . .'

'Yes, OK, but why the heck is she here today? Oh God, that means I'll have to see if Esme Bates has any rooms available and—'

'Whatever.' Sophie grabbed Erin's arm. 'We can sort it all out while we have a drink. That surgery is like an oven and I'm gagging. Come on.'

And with her arm linked through Erin's, Sophie hurtled across the green towards the Merry Cobbler.

*   *   *

'. . . and she said she'd come down two days early because she was at a loose end and couldn't wait to get involved in things here,' Sophie said as she and Erin sipped iced cider under a big striped umbrella at a table outside the Merry Cobbler. 'She said she didn't tell Jay because she wanted it to come as a surprise.'

'Oh, it has.' Erin swirled rapidly melting ice cubes. 'All of it. Believe me. And what has Jay said to her?'

78

'He hasn't seen her. He doesn't know she's here yet. Neither does Bella. They're doing an emergency Caesarean on Mrs Blundell's Yorkshire terrier.'

'Oh, poor little Tulisa! How many puppies is she having?'

'Probably far too many for a Yorkshire terrier, but she'll be fine. Jay'll make sure she's fine. We really don't need to worry about Tulisa, do we? I want to know all about Nalisha. Is she really Jay's ex?'

'No! She's just his best friend from childhood.'

'Yeah, right. That's like you saying your best school friends were Johnny, Brad and George.'

'Shut up!' Erin giggled. 'They grew up together. She's like his sister. That's all. And where is she now anyway? She's not involved in the Caesarean too, is she?'

Sophie chuckled and blew bubbles into her cider. 'Nah. She wanted something to do while she waited for Jay, so I've left her sitting behind the reception desk. We're closed for lunch but she's going to man the phone. She knows where I am if we get an urgent call.'

Erin frowned at Sophie. 'You sound as if you actually like her?'

'I do, well, what little I've seen of her. She's nothing like you said. Not stand-offish at all. She's really friendly and she let me skip off to lunch early, and she says she'll do my correspondence filing and my online updates, too.'

'Is that allowed? Patient confidentiality and all that?'

'She's practically family. And I'll let anyone do my filing.'

Erin shook her head. 'Didn't she want to see me? Did you tell her you were meeting me and we were going to the pub?'

'Yes, but she said she'd prefer to wait for Jay.'

I bet she would, Erin thought darkly.

'Well, as soon as I've finished this cider, I'm going to start as I mean to go on,' Erin said. 'Nalisha and I need to have a little chat.'

'About the wedding?' Sophie leaned her elbows on the tabletop. 'She said she had some advice for you.'

'Bloody hell. Is there any part of my life you haven't covered?'

Sophie giggled. 'You're soooo jealous of her!'

'No I'm not! I'm just annoyed that she's here early, with no warning, when we really don't want her, and that she thinks she can advise me on my own wedding, that's all.'

'Well,' Sophie said, grinning, 'if it meant I could end up looking as gorgeous as she does, I'd let Nalisha advise me on *anything*.'

'Listen to yourself—you've gone all girl-fan. So sad.' Erin drank the last of her cider and stood up carefully, making sure she didn't rock the table and send the glasses flying. 'I'm going to see Nalisha and be pleasant and welcoming, and then ring Esme Bates and see if she can bring her booking forward.'

'Or she could stay here.' Sophie nodded towards the pub. 'Gina does B&B, doesn't she?'

'Did I hear my name being taken in vain?'

Erin groaned as Gina undulated sexily out of the Merry Cobbler's rose-covered doorway to collect glasses. 'Hi, Gina. No—Sophie was just wondering if you had a spare room.'

'Been chucked out of your flat, have you, Soph?'
Gina blew strands of hair away from her face. 'Too
many all-night parties? And yes, I've got a couple of
rooms free.'

'It's not for me. It's for Nalisha,' Sophie said.
'You know, Jay's *friend*.'

'Ah yes—' Gina gave Erin a sympathetic glance
'—I've heard all about her. And I thought she
wasn't coming for a few days and when she did she
was staying at the Bates Motel.'

Erin flapped her hands. 'She's here now, but
don't worry, I'll go and see Esme Bates and sort it
out. I wouldn't want to inflict her on you.'

Sophie giggled. 'Erin's jealous.'

'Oh, God! Grow up! I'm not jealous—just
annoyed.'

'Understandably.' Gina smiled kindly, then
flapped her curls away from her face. 'Jeeze, it's
hot out here. Mind you, it's even hotter inside and
there's only me and Part-time Pearl and old Sam
to serve. Part-time Pearl is already complaining
about her "poor ol' feet giving her gyp", and Sam's
gone selectively deaf today and is slower than a
snail, love him. If you hear of anyone even slightly
able-bodied looking for bar work I'll snap 'em up.
Er, by the way, Erin, did you see Doug? Did you
mention . . .?'

'Yes and yes. He's, er, busy with a customer at
the moment, though. He'll . . . um . . . probably be
across as soon as he's free.'

Gina smiled happily.

'Right.' Erin stood up. 'I'm off to sort out
Nalisha's accommodation. I may be some time.'

Now cursing herself for having given the still
smiling Gina false hopes, Erin took a deep breath

81

of scorching air and set off across the green towards the vet's surgery.

Nook Green sweltered. A heat haze hung motionless over the village. Everywhere was silent, somnolent, drowsy. A few villagers gossiped idly in whatever shade they could find. A radio played muted nostalgia from an open window and the air smelled of scorched, baked earth.

Scrunching her way diagonally over the tinder-dry grass, kicking up little puffballs of dust, Erin was so immersed in her thoughts that she hardly felt the sun prickling the top of her head and the sweat trickling down the back of her vest.

And for the first time in months, her forthcoming marriage to Jay wasn't the thing that was uppermost in her mind. Well, not directly at least. There was Doug and Gina to worry about now, and the two-faced Nalisha and possibly a further clash with Deena.

Erin gulped the warm, stifling air and sighed heavily. Usually, the pretty familiarity of the village acted as a balm whatever her problems. But not today. Today, the symmetry of Nook Green—with St Lawrence's church at one end of the green, the Merry Cobbler at the other; the Old Curiosity Shop to one side and Jay's veterinary surgery opposite; and all of them linked together by an uneven circle of skew-whiff cottages and mellow redbrick houses, not to mention the Nook Green Stores and Post Office—failed to comfort her.

She was almost unaware of the canopy of delicious shade offered by the lacy tracery of the towering sycamores and horse chestnuts, of the glorious fallen-rainbow cottage gardens, or the distant shouts of children playing on the Nook

Green recreation ground on one of the myriad lanes that radiated in high-hedged ripples from the centre of the village.

Even the hotly exotic scents of flowers and the incessant babble-over-pebbles trickle of the Nook—yet another tributary of the River Maizey—as it wandered aimlessly through the green's tussocky grass, both of which usually delighted her, went unnoticed.

Oh, sod Doug and his cavalier approach to his love life. And sod Deena Keskar and her interfering, however well intentioned. And even more sod Nalisha for—well, just being Nalisha.

Erin quietly opened the door of the vet's surgery and almost recoiled. It was like an oven. A fan whirled pathetically on the reception desk, spitting puffs of warm air back into the stuffy room, and pools of sunlight shimmered hotly across the waiting-room floor.

Nalisha didn't look up. Her head bent over a sheaf of papers, she sat behind Sophie's desk, seemingly unaware of the heat. Wearing a gossamer-thin blue and green sari, Nalisha looked mermaid cool, unruffled and elegant.

And stunning.

Erin flicked the trailing strands of her ponytail away from her face, once again feeling irritably sweaty and grubby in her shorts and vest, and wondered what it was about Indian women that made them appear so immaculately untouched and untouchable.

'Nalisha . . .'

Nalisha looked up quickly from the pile of letters, blinked, then smiled. 'Erin! Oh, it's so nice to see you again. And you look so, er,

83

workmanlike.'

'That's because I've been working.'

'Ah, yes, in the junk shop.'

'Antiques actually. And this is a lovely surprise. We weren't expecting you until . . .'

'I know.' Nalisha shook back her glossy hair to display cobalt-blue chandelier earrings shimmering against the perfect melted-chocolate skin. 'I do hope it won't be inconvenient. I needed to escape.' She smiled conspiratorially at Erin. 'Much as I adore my parents, they still fail to realise that I'm grown up when I go home. I was in danger of being smothered.'

Oh, if only . . .

Erin smiled, thinking that if she'd needed to escape that much, Nalisha must have been able to find masses of more exciting locations than sleepy Nook Green. She really didn't trust her motives an inch.

'Mmm, I think all parents are the same.'

'Indian ones, definitely.' Nalisha jangled an armful of glittering blue and green bangles and indicated the desktop computer. 'Oh, and I'll have to have a word with Jay about his systems here. It's all so archaic.'

'Sophie still organises the correspondence the way she did it for Mr Howes,' Erin said quickly, angry at *any* criticism of Jay. 'He owned the surgery before Jay and liked letters to be personal. Jay agrees. And everything clinical is on the computer. It all works perfectly.'

'Really? How quaint. Still, I suppose it's probably quite up to date for you out here in the sticks.'

'God, yes. We've only just stopped using quills.'

Nalisha narrowed her pussycat eyes. Then she

84

laughed. 'I don't think Jay needs you to fight his battles for him.'

'I know he doesn't.' Erin smiled back, hoping the smile reached her eyes. 'So, while he's still in surgery, would you like me to check if the Bates Mo— er, the White House has any vacancies for the next couple of days? It's a lovely place and—'

'Actually—' Nalisha flicked her silky dupatta over her shoulder '—I've cancelled my room there. Deena said it wasn't necessary. And I'm not just staying for a few days. I'm staying for the rest of the summer. Oh, and Deena said as I'm practically family, that I could stay here. In the cottage. In Jay's spare room.'

CHAPTER NINE

For the rest of the summer? In Jay's cottage?

'*What?*' Erin shook her head. 'But you can't! I mean, does Jay know?'

If this was Jay's idea she'd kill him—and then call off the wedding.

'Not yet,' Nalisha said softly. 'I can't wait to tell him. You see, Deena said, as you and Jay aren't going to be living together until after the wedding, there'd be plenty of room . . .'

Erin groaned. Bloody Deena! And Nalisha couldn't—*couldn't*—share Jay's cottage. Not for weeks, not even for a few days. She just couldn't!

'Actually, I find it very sweet that you and Jay are so circumspect.' Nalisha's voice held a hint of laughing malice. 'I'd have thought, given his very obvious, er, charms, you'd have moved in here with him ages ago.'

Erin clenched her fists. She really, really wasn't going to rise to this. The reason she and Jay didn't live together was *because* of Deena—Tavish, too, but mainly Deena—who had made it abundantly clear that living together before you were married was a slur on good Indian families. Even in the twenty-first century. She and Jay had gone along with it to keep the peace, and also because Erin had thought it would be rather romantic not to move into the cottage until after the wedding, and, of course, with her living just across the green, they still managed to have plenty of secret sexy sleepovers.

And none of it was Nalisha's business. None of it!

But could she rest for one second, knowing that Nalisha was going to be spending nights and nights under the same roof as Jay? Of course she trusted Jay, but she didn't trust Nalisha one little bit . . .

Oh God, this just got worse and worse by the minute.

'Oh, this is going to be so much fun.' Nalisha pushed the files and folders away and stood up in a waterfall whisper of silk. 'I thought once I'd visited all the relatives and exhausted the retail therapy, the gap between my jobs would be boring, but not now. I can't wait to get busy and organise everything here. Not just this ridiculous computer set-up, but all your wedding poojas as well.'

'We're not having any poojas,' Erin said sharply. 'And weren't you going to speak to Deena about that?'

'Was I?' Nalisha frowned. 'I really can't remember. No, I'm going to have a lot of fun sorting out a mehendi night for you. Oh, and then there's the tilak . . .'

Erin sighed heavily. 'Forget it. I'm not that ignorant of Indian ceremonies, you know. OK, the *sagai* and *sanji* may have bypassed me, but I know all about mehendi—that's a sort of Indian hen night with lots of sweets and rituals and henna tattoos, isn't it?'

'Well done.' Nalisha's eyes glittered. 'It traditionally prepares the bride-to-be for her passage from innocent virgin to red-hot lover, but clearly, in your case, it'd be far too late.'

Erin laughed. 'Years. And my perfectly normal and absolutely traditional British hen night is already organised, thank you. And as for the tikka—'

'Tilak. That's for Jay actually.'

'What's for me? Something nice, I hope?' Jay, having shed his gown and mask but still in his operating scrubs and drying his hands, appeared from the surgery and stared at them in astonishment. 'Nalisha?'

'Surprise!' Nalisha shimmied from behind the desk and hurled herself into his arms.

'Yes, isn't it?' Jay looked at Erin over Nalisha's head, his eyes asking a million questions.

Erin, as always on seeing him, felt her heart do a little bumpety-bump of divine-pleasure-mixed-with-lust. Seeing him with Nalisha in his arms hurt more than she could ever say.

She returned the eye-meet and raised her eyebrows. 'Nalisha's arrived early. Isn't that wonderful?'

'Er, yes . . . I mean—' Jay grinned '—two beautiful women waiting for me—what more could a man ask for after a tricky operation.'

'Erin's assured me that me being here a bit early won't be a problem, which is very sweet of her. And we've just been talking—' Nalisha smiled, not moving away from him '—about the wedding celebrations and—'

'How's Tulisa?' Erin broke in, not caring if she was being rude or not. 'Is she doing OK?'

'Mother and babies doing fine.' Jay grinned, gently removing Nalisha's arms from his neck. 'All nine of them.'

'Nine? Blimey.'

'Yorkshire terriers don't usually have more than four pups per litter, so yes, Tulisa needed a bit of help, but she's a tough little girl. Bella's just tidying them up and we'll keep them all in overnight and monitor them for a few days to make sure she's feeding them OK, but they should all be fine to go home as soon as the stitches come out.'

Nalisha yawned. 'Too boring. I've honestly never understood, Jay, why you've wasted your incredible brain and amazing surgical talents on being a vet. You could have become a proper doctor and specialised in real life-saving, life-changing surgery and done, well, anything.'

'Jay is a proper doctor. A very talented surgeon. And a bloody good one,' Erin said hotly. 'For animals.'

Nalisha shook her head. 'I still fail to see why.'

'Because I love animals.' Jay said quietly. 'Because animals need care and good medical treatment and life-saving surgery and procedures, just as much as humans do.'

'Rubbish.' Nalisha shook her head. 'I simply can't understand why anyone could become

88

emotionally *attached* to an animal.'

Erin sucked in her breath. Even if she'd liked Nalisha before, that would have been the death blow.

'Good job we're not all the same, then, isn't it?' Erin said quickly. 'And thanks to Jay's brilliance, Mrs Blundell will be delighted that her beloved Tulisa and the puppies are all going to be OK.'

Nalisha gave a derisory sniff. Erin ignored her.

'Anyway,' Jay said quickly, 'Bella will be on call overnight if they need her—which I'm sure they won't.'

Bella lived in the flat above the surgery so it was easy for her to nurse the relatively few in-patients.

Erin grinned. 'If I know Bella, Tulisa and the puppies will all be upstairs with her as soon as your back's turned. Her flat usually looks like a menagerie. I'm just glad they're all OK.' She took a deep breath. She was going to be grown up about this. 'Right, sorry for interrupting you, Nalisha. Obviously you and Jay will have loads to talk about, and I've got a window display to sort out for Uncle Doug so I'll make myself scarce and—'

'You can't just leave me like that,' Jay said in mock horror. 'I'm a man in need of a stiff drink. It's not every day I bring nine new lives into the world.'

'Save the celebrations for tonight,' Erin said. 'It might be a bit cooler then. And you've got afternoon surgery to get through, not to mention hefting all Nalisha's luggage into the cottage.'

'Uh?' Jay frowned. 'Why would I do that? Why aren't we going straight to the Bates Mo— er, the White House?'

'Ah.' Erin gave a mock groan. 'Silly me! Another change of plan. Nalisha's staying in your cottage.

89

Didn't you know?'

'No, I didn't.' Jay looked shell-shocked. 'Nalisha?'

'Your mother said it would be fine.' Nalisha pouted prettily. 'I'd assumed she'd mentioned it to you. Oh, it won't be awkward, will it?'

Come on, Jay, Erin willed. This is where you tell her that it'll be very bloody awkward indeed.

'No.' Jay grinned. 'It'll be great.'

Erin groaned.

'We'll have time to catch up properly, and the spare room is always made up for anyone who can't stagger home.' Jay looked delighted. 'It's a great idea, isn't it, Erin?'

Erin looked at him. Men! Didn't Jay have a *clue*?

'Oh yes. Great,' Erin said coldly, 'I'm so glad that's all sorted. And once you've moved Nalisha's luggage in, she can tell you all about the tikka.'

'Tilak,' Nalisha corrected. 'As you well know. That's what we were discussing, Jay, when you came in.'

'Oh, I'm not having a tilak,' Jay said cheerfully.

'Your mother said I must try to persuade you.'

'Did she?' Jay frowned. 'Well, she's going to be disappointed then. Honestly, I don't want a tilak ceremony, which—' he looked at Erin '—traditionally excludes women and involves all the men of the family gathering together and saying prayers while the nearest male relative applies the tilak mark to my forehead to mark my passage from—'

'Virgin to red-hot lover?' Erin raised her eyebrows.

'*What*?'

'Well, I'm just guessing here, but as Nalisha's

90

kindly explained the meaning behind my mehendi, I'm assuming that this tilak-thingy is much the same for you.'

Jay laughed. 'And as I'm sure you've explained to Nalisha, you'll be having a normal hen night and I'm having a stag night with my friends. As per good old British traditions.'

'I have, yes.'

Nalisha shrugged. 'To be honest, I couldn't care less one way or the other. But I promised Deena I'd try. Which I have. Now, can I move my stuff into the cottage and have a shower?'

'Of course.' Jay looked slightly confused. 'Um—where's your luggage?'

'In the car.'

Erin stared at Nalisha. Was she going to make no move to help with her own bags? Nope, clearly not.

Outside, in the dazzling sunlight, Jay and Erin blinked at the super-expensive, dark-blue sports car. There were designer bags piled into every spare corner.

'Hell, is all that luggage hers?' Jay frowned. 'It's an awful lot for a short stay.'

Erin raised her eyebrows. 'Oh yes—another little point Nalisha failed to mention. She's not here for a few days, she's here for the rest of the summer. She's staying until the wedding.'

Jay sighed. 'Erin, look, I do realise this must seem a bit . . . well . . . odd to you. But you are OK with it, aren't you?'

Erin sighed. 'I suppose so. Although obviously I'd prefer it if Nalisha was only here for a couple of days and staying at the Bates Motel as arranged and . . .' She stopped. 'No, OK. Seriously, Jay—think about it. How would you feel if I casually mentioned one of my exes was moving into Uncle Doug's with me for a few weeks?'

'I'd find it a bit strange, I suppose, and wonder why. But I trust you absolutely, and anyway, this situation is completely different. Nalisha is *not* one of my exes, is she?'

'Maybe not. But she's a very beautiful woman who's a lifelong good friend, and who clearly knows far more about your past than I do. It just seems a little bit . . . well, odd.'

Jay hugged her. 'I know it must seem like that to you. But honestly, Erin, Nalisha and I are like brother and sister, and it's just great to see her again after all this time. Also, this will give you plenty of time together and I just know you'll be great friends.'

Erin sighed. She had to face it: Nalisha was here for the duration, Jay was happy, and, unless she wanted to risk having an almighty row, she'd just have to accept the situation.

But it didn't mean she had to like it. Or Nalisha.

CHAPTER TEN

'. . . and she's been amazing.' Bella grinned happily from the passenger seat, across the scorching interior of Erin's hatchback, the following day. 'She's so sweet and so friendly, which is unusual in someone as gorgeous as she is. She's not up herself at all. And she's showed me how to use shaders on my face to hide the freckles and—'

'She doesn't like animals,' Erin interrupted as they left the leafy high-banked Berkshire villages behind

92

and headed on to the mad dash rush of the A34's dual carriageway. 'So I have no idea why you think she's so wonderful.'

'Crap.' Bella's bright red curls bounced in the gush of hot air through the open windows. 'Don't know where you got that from. She *loves* animals. She spent ages with me last night, making sure Tulisa and the puppies were OK. I'm so glad she's staying for the rest of the summer. Oh, and she's promised to show me how she does her eye make-up too.'

Clever old Nalisha . . . Erin sighed again and flicked a glanced through the rear-view mirror. Ever since they'd left Nook Green Bella had been singing Nalisha's praises. Sophie, on the back seat, was apparently singing along to Jethro Tull, and fortunately so far hadn't joined in the Nalisha fan-fest.

'And—' Bella frowned '—what the heck are you playing?'

'Jethro Tull,' Erin said, turning up the volume.

'Jesus,' Bella groaned. 'Never heard of him.'

Sophie leaned forwards between the seats. 'He invented the seed drill, I think. Don't you remember Miss Forbes saying so in history?'

Erin and Bella shook their heads.

Bella frowned. 'He should have stuck to inventing and not bothered with the singing then. He doesn't sound very happy.'

'He's a they, and it's one of Uncle Doug's CDs. He must have left it in here.' Squinting into the relentless afternoon sun, Erin overtook a dawdling smart car and pulled back into the left-hand lane. 'I quite like it.'

Bella shook her head.

Erin concentrated on driving and tried not to think about Nalisha. The previous evening she, Jay and Nalisha had gone to the Merry Cobbler for an alfresco pub meal in the sunset, and the entire evening had been filled with Nalisha's elaborate stories of family weddings and parties, and each story, it seemed to Erin, had been carefully chosen to show just how much Erin was letting the Keskar side down by being an outsider.

As soon as Jay had disappeared into the pub for refills, Nalisha, dressed in skinny white jeans and a gorgeous coral-pink top, had leaned across to Erin.

'So, are you getting nervous about the wedding?'

'No. Not at all.'

'I'd be terrified by now,' Nalisha had laughed, looking as if she'd never been terrified of anything in her life. 'But of course, as it's a fusion wedding, at least you won't have to endure the hours and hours of full-on Indian ceremonies. Although it clearly isn't what Deena wants.'

Erin had sipped her cider and tried to stay calm. 'No, it isn't.'

Understatement.

Nalisha had delicately nibbled an olive, then laughed. 'And of course, as you're not even wearing a ceremonial sari . . .'

'No, I'm not,' Erin had said quickly. 'And please don't think you can persuade me because—'

'God, I wouldn't dream of it.' Nalisha had wriggled the top a little lower. All the men in the beer garden watched. 'A girl's wedding dress has to be her choice and hers alone. After all, it's the most wonderful outfit you'll ever wear, isn't it?'

Erin had nodded, still not trusting Nalisha an inch.

Nalisha had laughed. 'Poor Deena will be so disappointed. She loves everyone to be dressed in full ceremonial splendour. I remember at Jay's twenty-first . . .'

Erin had sat back, taking sips of now lukewarm cider, listening to story after story of Jay's parties, celebrations and family festivities—all of which had included Nalisha—feeling her confidence draining away with each one.

'. . . and then, when he graduated, well, that was simply spectacular.' Nalisha had stirred the remains of her G&T. 'Deena and Tavish were so proud. Well, we all were of course. So they hired the function room at the football ground—Premiership, of course—and we had a party for thousands. Oh, but you must have seen the photographs . . .'

Erin had nodded. She had. She just hadn't realised that Nalisha had been there, or just how massive the celebration had been. How massive any of the celebrations had been.

Jay's parties had clearly always been hugely flamboyant affairs.

So, she'd wondered miserably, did Jay secretly want a massive Indian wedding? Was he only going along with the fusion idea to please her? If he'd been marrying Nalisha, the full-on poojas and parties would have happened as a matter of course, wouldn't they?

And everyone—including Deena and Tavish—would have been delighted.

In fact, if Jay had been marrying the sumptuous, fragrant, corporate lawyer Nalisha, then Deena and Tavish would be far happier than they were right now, wouldn't they?

How desperately disappointed must Deena and

Tavish really have been when Jay had announced his engagement to a comprehensive-school-educated village girl who worked in a junk shop?

Erin had groaned inwardly. She'd never had any doubts before, but now . . .

'Sorry to have been so long.' Jay had emerged from the pub at that moment. 'I got caught up in a conversation with Gina—are you two getting to know one another?'

And Erin had nodded miserably and taken another mouthful of cider.

*   *   *

'And I noticed you didn't come back to Jay's last night,' Bella said now, raising her voice above Jethro Tull.

'Uh?' Erin jerked herself back to the present. 'Sorry?'

'You didn't spend the night at Jay's.'

'How do you know that?' Erin was shocked. 'Were you checking up on us?'

'Nah, not really. I was last-minute checking on Tulisa and the puppies and Mr Duncan's Smurfy who's in for fasting blood tests—you know what Mr Duncan's like for sharing his fry-ups which is why Smurfy is possibly diabetic—and I heard Jay and Nalisha come home—alone.'

And disappearing into separate bedrooms, please God, Erin thought—as she'd thought nearly all of her sleepless night.

'Checking up on us, as I said.'

'Well—' Bella grinned '—maybe just a little bit.'

'Actually,' Erin said haughtily, 'Jay and I'd decided earlier—even before we knew that she, er, Nalisha was coming to stay—that we'd give the overnights a miss until after the wedding. It seemed sort of romantic, you know, because we'll be spending our wedding night at the Swan, then going straight off on honeymoon, and then, when we're back, I'll be living at the cottage and it'll be like a fresh start for both of us.'

'As born-again virgins? Yeah right,' Bella chuckled. 'You and Jay can't keep your hands off each other. You won't last five minutes. Not that you'll have much choice now she's in the cottage. Those bedrooms are way too close together for any sort of privacy. Shame—Nalisha's not only sodded up your love life good and proper, but also Nook Green's early morning entertainment.'

'Sorry?' Erin frowned, concentrating on the unbroken line of shimmering vehicles ahead of her.

'Oh, you know, you scampering home across the green in the pearly dawn in nothing but your knickers.'

'I never did!'

'Gotcha!' Bella laughed. 'But you did—once.'

Erin blushed, remembering. 'That was in the early days and it was a mistake.'

'Mr Lumley at the Post Office Stores still talks about it when he brings his guinea pigs in for their toenail clipping. Says it gave him a whole new lease of life.'

Despite her misgivings, Erin giggled. Fortunately, a white van man tailgating the hatchback took up the next few minutes of her concentration and her early-in-love misdemeanours were instantly forgotten.

'Why doesn't he back off? There's nowhere to go—we're all nose to tail in both lanes. He's

97

flashing his lights now—oh, and waving . . . God, is there something wrong with the car?'

'Nope.' Sophie leaned forwards. 'I just waved at him. He's quite cute. And now he's realised it's a car full of women and he's giving us the full benefit of his testosterone.'

Erin snapped Jethro Tull into silence mid flute solo and glared at Sophie in the mirror. 'Don't encourage him—or anyone else—please. It's tricky enough driving in this traffic. I'm practically suffocating in this heat, and the sun's blinding me. I really don't need you behaving like a teenager on a school trip.'

'Oooh, who's a grumpy guts, then?' Sophie smirked. 'Who's just a teensy-weensy bit tense and jealous?'

'Grow up!'

Sophie and Bella giggled.

The white van man leered and gesticulated. Erin, thoroughly hot and bothered and wishing for the umpteenth time she had a car with air con, gesticulated back.

Tense? Jealous? Her? Of course she wasn't— was she?

Oh, only another five miles to go . . . Only another five miles . . .

CHAPTER ELEVEN

'OK.' Linda, the co-owner of Elle-Cee Bridalwear, nodded happily at Erin. 'Have you got your wedding shoes with you?'

'No. Sorry. I never thought about them.'

'Not a problem. Just stand on the box then, it should bring you up to the right level, while Carol fetches the frock. I think you'll find that those last-minute tweaks to the lacing at the back and the slight rearranging of the net have worked brilliantly to make it fit like a glove.'

Erin, having discarded her cut-off jeans and vest and luxuriating in Elle-Cee Bridalwear's ice-cold air conditioning, stepped obediently and bare-footed on to the red plush covered box in front of the bank of wall-to-wall mirrors, and felt a wave of dizzy euphoria.

Not even Nalisha could spoil this moment.

The vast fitting room at the back of the shop was glitzy and glamorous, with the mirrors reflecting a zillion lights like a conglomeration of constellations, and had several velvet sofas and little glass-fronted cabinets displaying glittering tiaras and chokers and earrings. While the dresses all frilled, frothed and flounced in gauzy perfection in the front showroom, the fitting room was a sanctum of serenity.

'You don't look as though you've put on any weight, or lost any,' Linda said cheerfully, casting a professional eye over Erin in her bra and knickers. 'Always a good sign. Although we can make alterations up to the eleventh hour. And are these the undies you'll be wearing on the day?'

Functional lilac cotton covered in small grinning Garfields? Hardly.

Erin shook her head. 'No—why, does it matter?'

'Of course it matters—well, not the pants so much because your frock isn't slim-fitting, but the bra certainly. And your dress is strapless so you'll need some good support.'

'I've bought a basque.'

'Lovely—bring it with you when we do the final fitting then. You'd be amazed at the ladies I've seen who don't even think about the undies until the last minute.' Linda threw a tape measure round her neck like a stole, and reached for a pincushion, which she slid on to her wrist. 'I'm not anticipating we'll need to make any other changes today, but you never know. Do you want your bridesmaids in to watch?'

'Not at the moment,' Erin said, suddenly aware of the lights showing up cellulite on her thighs where she was sure there hadn't been any before. Damn it. 'When I'm in the dress and laced up, then yes. Are they OK out there in the shop?'

Linda nodded. 'We've got theirs ready to try on once you're done. Ah, now no tears—here's Carol with your dress.'

Carol, as tall and slim and dark as Linda was tiny and rotund and blonde, hauled a huge cotton-swathed armful into the fitting room.

'Afternoon, Erin. All ready for this?'

Erin gave a little jiggle of excitement. The dress—an Ian Stuart design—was the most astonishingly beautiful thing she'd ever seen. It would blow any ceremonial sari out of the water and she just knew Jay would be speechless when he saw her floating down the aisle on their wedding day; and she, for once, would feel delicate and feminine and exactly like the fairy-tale princess she'd always dreamed of being.

'Are you wearing you hair up or down on the day?' Linda asked, as Carol manhandled the acres of glorious ivory taffeta and lace frothed with silvery pearl tulle, dancing with a million

100

tiny shimmering diamanté stars and floating on a never-ending mass of net underskirts, from its cover.

'Down,' Erin whispered, as always completely overcome when she saw the dress. 'And we're not wearing tiaras or anything. We're just having tiny flowers in our hair.'

'Lovely.' Linda nodded briskly. 'Then I think perhaps a choker—possibly really thin strands of silver and grey pearls on invisible wire. Delicate and beautiful, and not too much, but just filling in the gap between your hair and your cleavage. Same for the bridesmaids. We can sort out all those last-minute things when you come for your last appointment. OK, stand still and we'll pop this over your head. Close your eyes. We'll tell you when to look.'

After a few minutes of being smothered in the most fabulous dress in creation, Erin's head emerged from the layers and Linda and Carol fussed round, pulling it down, easing it up, frou-frouing it out, lacing laces and securing hooks.

'There, all done,' Carol said. 'You can look now.'

Erin opened her eyes. 'Oh . . . oh . . .'

'Succinct,' Linda chuckled. 'Is that "oh" in a good way?'

'That,' Erin whispered, gazing at herself in the multiple mirrors, 'is "oh" in a stunned, incredible and "oh my God is that really me?" way. It's totally, totally fabulous—it fits perfectly—and even without proper make-up or my hair done it's simply amazing. Oh, now I'm really going to cry—you've transformed me from a scruff into a princess.'

'Ian Stuart always manages to do that,' Linda said, kneeling down and rearranging a few more layers of glimmering net. 'And this one could have been created for you.'

'You cry away, Erin,' Carol said cheerfully. 'You look absolutely stunning. And I honestly don't think we'll need any further alterations, do you?'

Erin, gently stroking the froth of billowing layers, almost afraid to touch the exquisite fabrics, gazed at herself again, teary-eyed and still unable to quite take in what she was seeing. 'No. It's just so amazing. You don't need to change a thing.'

'You do look gorgeous, love.' Linda stood up again and surveyed Erin with motherly pride. 'Breath-taking. The dress is a dream. And we see masses of brides, obviously, and not all of them make me feel like this.' She reached for a tissue. 'Oh, sorry.'

Carol sniffed. 'Shall we all have a good cry and get it out of the way? And if you're happy with it, shall I call the girls in to have a look and try their dresses on now?'

'Yes, please.' Erin sighed blissfully, and had a little careful twirl on the box. 'Whoo—it's gloriously heavy. Oooh—whoops . . . Nearly went then. Mind you, I've got a feeling this dress would act as a cushion long before I hit the floor.'

'Don't even think about falling over,' Carol said sternly, heading for the door. 'Not now, and especially not on the Big Day. It'd take an entire army of bridesmaids to dig you out of those skirts. OK—here come the girls.'

As soon as Carol opened the door, Bella and Sophie tumbled in.

'Wow!' Sophie gasped. 'Wow and wow! Every time I see this dress it just gets more and more amazing. You look sensational.'

'Bloody hell!' Bella shook her head. 'That's exactly how I want to look on my wedding day if I ever get lucky enough to have one. Oh bugger, I think I'm going to cry.'

'Everyone else has,' Linda said, 'so feel free. And when you've finished, get undressed and I'll fetch your dresses. I've only had to make minor alterations so they should both be good to go. You're OK with stripping off out here, aren't you? You don't need the changing room?'

'God, no.' Bella tugged off her T-shirt, her eyes still riveted on Erin. 'We've been dressing and undressing in front of each other since infant school.'

Sophie unzipped her jeans. 'Jay will be knocked out when he sees you in that, Erin, not to mention completely overcome with lust—and oooh, I'm just filled with deep, deep envy.'

Erin giggled.

'Here we are then, ladies.' Carol bustled back with the bridesmaids' dresses, swathed in white linen on padded hangers. 'Now, who's the size ten?'

'Me,' Sophie said.

'And I'm the fat bridesmaid.' Bella grinned. 'There always has to be one.'

'Shut up.' Erin grinned back. 'You're curvy and voluptuous and sexy. And what size is your dress? A standard size fourteen at most?'

'Yeah.' Bella nodded. 'As I say, the fat bridesmaid. You're a dinky size twelve, Sophie's a stick insect and that leaves me.'

'Size fourteen is perfectly normal and healthy,' Linda said briskly, 'so let's have no more of that nonsense. We recently had an entire bridal party—bride and six bridesmaids—and not one of

103

them was under a size twenty-four, and blooming gorgeous they looked too. Mind, they'd all chosen full skirts and hooped petticoats so they had a heck of a job getting up the aisle. I heard they all went up sideways.'

Everyone laughed.

Carol unzipped the covers from the bridesmaids' dresses and handed them to Sophie and Bella. As they slid into them, Erin, still totally overcome by the fabulousness of her own wedding gown, sighed with delight.

Short, strapless, slim-fitting matching creations in folds of ivory silk, taffeta and tulle, with layered pearly net skirts the colour of morning mist and covered in tiny sparkling rhinestones, the bridesmaids dresses were utterly gorgeous.

'Should've shaved my legs,' Sophie groaned, posing and pouting in front of the mirrors and fluffing at her short spiky hair. 'And remembered to bring the right shoes . . . but I think we look pretty damn hot.'

'Yeah,' Bella admitted, smoothing the net skirt over her hips, 'this is definitely the most incredible dress I've ever worn. It even manages to make me look quite slim. I love it to bits.'

'You both look fantastically beautiful,' Erin sighed. 'Sod it. I knew I should've picked ugly bridesmaids.'

Sophie and Bella poked their tongues out. Erin laughed.

'So what's the overall colour scheme for the wedding?' Linda asked, pulling and pushing and tucking at Bella's dress as Carol did much the same to Sophie's. 'Flowers? Table decs?'

Erin gave another little flouncy swirl in the

mirrors. 'Well, as Jay's Indian, we knew straight away that the main colour scheme would be cream and red with touches of gold—traditional Hindu marriage colours—which is fine, because this fabulous dress is mostly cream and I know he's going to be wearing a cream Nehru suit.'

'And then,' Bella put in, 'because of the lovely pearly grey bits in the dresses, the bouquets, buttonholes, corsages and table flowers are all going to be a mix of scarlet lilies and pale grey feathers.'

'Will that work?' Carol looked a bit doubtful.

'Absolutely,' Erin said. 'Abbie, the wedding organiser at the Swan, has done swatches and everything. It all looks amazing. The grey is more silvery, so it'll be like silver and gold amongst the main Indian theme of red and cream. And don't ask me any more details because it's all secret.'

There was a knock on the fitting room door.

Linda paused in straightening Bella's hem and frowned at Carol. 'Not a customer in the shop, surely? I thought the outside door was locked and we put the "closed for private appointment" notice on the front door?'

'I think I did.' Carol frowned. 'I always do. Maybe I forgot.'

The door opened.

Oh, God . . . Erin groaned.

Nalisha . . .

CHAPTER TWELVE

'Is it OK to come in?' Nalisha, wearing a flimsy rose-sprigged dress and vertiginous heels, smiled at everyone. Then she stopped. 'Oh, wow! Erin! That dress is awesome!'

Awesome? Erin groaned. OK, Nalisha had just come back from living in the States, but . . . *awesome* . . . really?

'I'm so sorry, but you can't come in here.' Carol looked flustered. 'The front door should have been locked. Didn't you see the notice? This is a private fitting and—'

'Oh, that's fine.' Nalisha beamed happily. 'I'm practically family, aren't I Erin?'

Bloody nerve! Erin swallowed her anger and glared at Nalisha. 'Please go away. I don't want anyone to see my dress.'

Bella and Sophie stopped smiling at Nalisha and blinked at Erin. Linda and Carol just stared.

'Oh, of course. I'm so very sorry if I've intruded.' Nalisha looked contrite. 'I didn't realise that it was private. I was just desperate the see this sensational dress. Sorry, Erin, I should have thought.'

'She's seen the dresses now,' Sophie said quickly. 'She might as well stay. And where's the harm?'

Erin shook her head. Where to start? Why was everything to do with her previously perfectly planned forthcoming wedding now going rapidly pear-shaped?

She sighed. 'OK. But—' she frowned at Nalisha '—how on earth did you know where we were? I mean, no one knew, except . . .'

106

'Er—' Bella looked a little embarrassed '—I might just have mentioned it. Last night. In passing.'

Dear God.

Linda and Carol continued to look anxiously at Erin.

Erin, who wanted to hit someone—preferably Nalisha—glared at Bella.

'Is it OK, Erin?' Linda asked.

Erin simply shrugged. 'I suppose so.'

Sophie and Bella beamed again.

'Thanks, and, seriously, you do look absolutely amazing,' Nalisha said. 'All of you. Especially Erin. That dress is totally out of this world. It's an Ian Stuart, isn't it?'

Erin nodded. 'Yes, and please, please, don't breathe a word of what it's like to Jay or anyone. I wanted to keep this a secret from *everyone*.'

'I wouldn't dream of it. My lips are sealed.' Nalisha smiled. 'You know you can trust me.'

Oh yes, of course.

Nalisha continued to smile sweetly. 'Seriously, Erin, I won't say a word. I thought Deena may have been right when she said I should try to persuade you to wear a ceremonial sari for the wedding, but she wasn't. She was totally, totally wrong.'

Erin allowed herself a little mental jig of triumph. One–nil!

Everyone else nodded happily. Bella and Sophie looked smug.

'And—' Nalisha's eyes sparkled as she gazed at Bella and Sophie '—the bridesmaids' dresses are just too cute. You both scrub up really well, sweeties.'

Sophie and Bella preened.

Cute? Sweeties? Why had Nalisha suddenly gone all gushing West Coast? Couldn't Bella and Sophie see how false she was? Erin wanted to laugh. The woman was a complete phoney.

Nalisha stroked the skirt of Erin's dress. 'Fabulous. Truly. This is soooo you. Seriously, if you'd gone down the traditional sari route, and had to wear all that heavy drapery, not to mention being bedecked out in Jay's Naanis' heirloom gold jewellery, you'd have looked just like some old dowager.'

Ever-so-slightly backhanded compliment there?

'Thanks—I think,' Erin muttered. 'So, does this mean, now you know I'm definitely not going to be wearing a sari, and you've realised at last this is going to be a British-style fusion wedding, you're going to tell Deena exactly that?'

Nalisha fluttered her impossibly long eyelashes. 'Erin! I'd never intended to *interfere* in your wedding plans. Yes, I may have given Deena the impression that I'd try some gentle persuasion simply to keep the peace, but honestly, the minutiae of your wedding to Jay actually doesn't concern me at all. I'm in Nook Green to help you, not hinder.'

Bella and Sophie almost clapped their hands.

'OK.' Carol looked relieved that harmony had been restored. 'I think we're all finished here for today, ladies. So, let's get you out of the dress before anything gets damaged. Stay there a moment, Erin, and we'll be with you shortly.'

As she and Linda started unzipping Bella and Sophie, Nalisha smiled. 'Oh, please let me help. I know I shouldn't be here and it was so kind of Erin to let me stay. I'd like to do something.'

'OK.' Linda nodded. 'You can start unhooking

108

Erin. But very, very carefully. And make sure when you undo all the criss-cross lacing that you keep the ribbons flat—they're a bugger to iron.'

Nalisha nodded obediently.

Once more overcome by a waft of Nalisha's exotic scent, Erin watched in the full-length mirror as the slender and perfectly manicured fingers carefully unhooked the dozens of tiny fasteners at the back of the bodice, and undid the lacing, and tried not to feel slightly uncomfortable.

Linda and Carol dressing and undressing her caused her no problems at all, so why did this feel so embarrassing? So wrong?

'There,' Nalisha said softly. 'All undone.'

'Thanks.'

Erin hoped Nalisha would go away now before she had to display the functional bra and pants, not to mention the cellulite.

'You know—' Nalisha met Erin's eyes through the mirror '—your choice of dress has honestly come as a massive surprise to me.'

'Has it? Thank you.'

Nalisha smiled, her voice still a whisper. 'Mmmm. As I said earlier, it's so perfectly you. You see, several of my girlfriends had this design last summer when it was fashionable. I certainly didn't expect to see it again this year.'

CHAPTER THIRTEEN

'It's quiet in here this afternoon,' Gina said, stepping carefully over the Old Curiosity Shop's doormat so as not to activate the bell. 'Where is everyone?'

Doug, who was sitting on an ornately carved carrier's trunk, and clearly in the middle of pricing up some Bristol Blue glassware at the back of shop, looked up in surprise. 'Er, oh, hello, Gina. Um, Erin's gone for another wedding dress fitting with Sophie and Bella, and I guess all the would-be customers have died from heat exhaustion on the way here.'

Gina wriggled in her short denim skirt and sat gingerly on the edge of a rocking chair that also contained an ancient teddy bear, which might or might not be a Steiff but probably wasn't, a kaleidoscope and a box of beautifully veined marbles.

She glanced across the shop at Doug, loving as always the sight of him in his faded Levi's and much-washed festival T-shirt. He looked, she always thought, like some legendary hippie rock god.

Then, in case he noticed the longing, she stared down quickly at her sparkly flip-flops, not wanting to see the disinterest in Doug's eyes. It had taken a lot of courage to walk into the Old Curiosity Shop. Her suntanned feet were dusty from the grass and her vermillion nail varnish was slightly chipped. She sighed. How disappointing of her feet to look so scuzzy and let her down.

'I've got the opposite problem.' Her voice sounded falsely cheerful, even to her. 'Too many people. The pub was heaving this lunchtime. We were run ragged. Every man and his dog in the village seem to want a cold drink today. I've left Sam and Part-time Pearl in charge at the moment, but you know Sam's knocking on and Pearl's a raging hypochondriac and liable to down tools at the drop of a hat. She's even worse since she did that Silver Surfer's course at Daisy Bank, because now she can just tap her imaginary symptoms into her laptop and come up with some obscure disease that's going to kill her within minutes.'

Doug nodded but didn't answer. Or laugh. Once, he would have laughed with her.

Gina ploughed on. 'Even together they can't cope with it all, so unless I can get extra staff I'm going to have to go back to closing in the afternoons.'

She stopped and took a breath. Oh, hell, she thought to herself, listen to me. Babbling on. Straining to make small talk with a man who has seen me naked. Get a grip, woman.

Doug held a carafe towards the light, inspecting it for flaws. 'Funny—I'd have thought there'd be any number of ladies in the village just looking for a few hours' work in the pub.'

'Not in the school holidays. Any of the mums who might be able to cover some shifts in term time are all otherwise occupied. And anyone unemployed doesn't want just part-time work because it eats into their benefit payments.'

'Mmm, I suppose it would. You can't blame them for that.'

Gina sighed again. Doug was just as bad. Why on earth were they discussing the weather and the ups and downs of their respective trades when they'd rolled and tumbled and made love for months? Was the relationship really over? She felt the cold grip of fear in her stomach.

She tried again. 'Nice glass. I've always loved Bristol Blue.'

111

Doug nodded but still didn't look at her. 'Bought it for a song at the auction in Newbury yesterday. I thought I'd better get it priced up while Erin's out of the way. She'd probably smash most of it at the moment.'

Gina smiled. It felt wrong to smile so she stopped. 'Because she's got wedding nerves and her hands are all shaky?'

'Mmm, you could say that.' Doug put the glassware down and finally looked across the shop at her. There was no twinkle in his eyes. 'All this wedding malarkey seems to be getting to everyone at the moment. Erin's still having a bit of a problem with Jay's family. They want her to agree to incorporate more of the Indian celebrations and customs. Which at first I thought was a bit of an imposition, but now, honestly, thinking about it, it seems quite reasonable.'

Gina, noticing the lack of warmth, cringed inwardly. 'I hope you haven't told her that.'

'Not in so many words, no. I know she needs me on her side, but I honestly don't see why she's getting so upset about what Jay's family must see as sensible suggestions for their only son's wedding.'

Gina frowned at him. 'Well, yes, if Jay and Erin were at the planning stages and asking for suggestions from both sides and that's what they wanted, but they're not, and it isn't. As I understand it, from what Jay and Erin have told me in the pub, all the arrangements are made, have been made by them and they're giving a nod to both cultures, but basically having the totally non-religious wedding they both want. Why on earth would Jay's family want to interfere now?'

'I'm guessing that Deena and Tavish fondly

112

imagined that, as their only child, Jay was organising a traditional Hindu wedding. I think it's come as a bit of shock to them to discover he wasn't. And I also gather that's why Nalisha's here—to use her feminine charms and wiles and do the iron fist/velvet glove thing on Jay.'

Gina looked away and studied her feet again. She was very much looking forward to the wedding. To being Doug's plus one and sitting on Erin's side of the Swan's marriage room. She'd even bought her outfit. She had an awful feeling that she may not be needing it now.

'And you think they should cancel all their plans and embrace the painted elephants and white horses and millions of sari-clad ladies throwing rose petals, do you?'

'Hardly.' Doug shook his head. 'But I don't think it would hurt if Erin accepted that Jay's parents have certain expectations and would like more of their culture expressed in the ceremony they've chosen. Hindu weddings—the few I've been to—are so colourful and fun-filled and exciting. We could do with a bit of that life and vibrancy round here.'

'But it's Erin's day,' Gina insisted. 'And Jay's, of course, and no one should be allowed to interfere in what they've chosen.'

Doug shrugged. 'OK, we clearly don't see eye to eye on it, and anyway I'm steering well clear of it all from now on. Weddings are not my area of expertise, really. Been to loads, seen them disintegrate, mopped up after the divorces, and never had one of my own.'

'Nor me,' Gina said shortly. 'But I live in hope.'

Eugh, she thought. Stupid, stupid thing to say.

113

Doug smiled for the first time. 'I hope you'll invite me then.'

Bastard, Gina thought, but she managed to smile. 'Oh, you'll be top of the guest list.'

Doug laughed. 'You're funny. You can always make me laugh. We haven't laughed much lately though, have we? We've hardly seen one another.'

She waited for him to add that he'd missed her, but it didn't come.

'No. Well, we're both busy and—'

'We've always been busy.' Doug pushed his hair away from his eyes. 'It never stopped us spending time together before, did it?'

Gina shook her head. She'd washed her hair specially that morning, so that it would curl to her shoulders and bounce and shine in the sun. Doug had once said he loved her hair because it was all free and wild and messy and reminded him of the summer girls of his youth.

She'd worn the denim skirt and the pin-tucked broderie anglaise top for the same reason.

Sad cow.

She leaned forwards slightly. The marbles rattled in their box and the kaleidoscope dug into her bare thigh. 'So, are you saying—?'

'I'm not saying anything. Just stating a fact. We seem to have drifted a bit, that's all. I certainly didn't expect to see you in here today.'

'Well, you haven't been in the Merry Cobbler for ages, so I thought one of us should make the effort to catch up. Oh, I'm not stalking you,' she said, hoping that the words sounded jokey, fearing that they didn't. 'If you don't want to see me any more just say. I mean, of course, you'll still *see me* because obviously we live and work opposite one another, but if you don't want to go out with me any more, then please tell me.'

Jesus, she thought, now I'm not only babbling but I sound as if I'm about fourteen.

She swallowed. 'What I really mean is, I hate the way you seem to be avoiding me recently.'

'I'm not really avoiding you.' Doug sighed, pushed away the glassware, the price tickets and the marker pen, and looked at her. 'It's not you—'

'Oh, please' Gina glared at him. 'Not the "it's not you, it's me" rubbish. We're both too old for that sort of crap.'

'But it is me. I don't know what I want. Never have. Well, except this place. This place and an easy life.'

'Without me in it?' Gina felt the icy knot of fear and pending heartbreak rise from her stomach to settle painfully somewhere beneath her ribs. 'That's OK. You don't need to say any more. It would have been nice to know sooner, that's all.'

'Gina.' Doug stood up. 'You're a really great girl. We've had some good times. But . . . but . . .'

'But it's over.' Gina stood up too, making the rocking chair squeak backwards and forwards and sending the teddy bear slumping sideways. 'That's all I needed to hear.'

'No, it's not like that at all. I'm just rubbish at relationships. And I think we both want different things. I've never wanted to settle down. I'm scared of settling down. And you want someone who will make a permanent commitment. You want a proper relationship, not an on–off affair, which is all I can offer.'

Absolutely determined not to cry or appear needy or, even worse, to grovel and say she'd be happy to take any sort of relationship as long as it was with Doug, Gina shrugged. 'So, roughly translated, that means you think I'm desperate? That I want to get married? That at thirty-eight, my biological clock is ticking loudly and telling me that it's time for me to have children before it's too late, and that I don't want to spend the rest of my life as a sad and single woman running a pub? Right?'

'No . . . no . . .'

'Yes, yes, actually.' Gina looked at him. 'Well, not the desperate bit, but the rest, yes. And what's so wrong with that, Doug? I've got no family and I don't want to be alone. I'll be forty in two years' time. I'll probably work in the pub trade until I'm in my sixties, and then what? If I don't find someone to love who loves me in return, someone to share my life with, someone I can have adventures with, or be cosily complacent with, I'll tell you what—I'll retire, and be as bored and lonely as hell. And you?'

'Much the same.' Doug's smile was wistful. 'Only I'm about fifteen years further down the line than you are. Erin told me I'd end up as unloved and unlovable, and she was probably right.'

Definitely right, Gina thought, but she didn't say so.

She felt such an utter fool. She'd lived and worked in Nook Green for two years, and in that time had watched Doug drift in and out of relationships with a succession of women. Why the hell had she thought she would be any different?

'We should have had this conversation ages ago,' Gina said. 'It's a shame you're such a coward.'

'Gina . . .'

'No, please don't say anything else. You've made it perfectly clear where we stand, which is all

I wanted to know.' She headed towards the door, childishly tempted to leap up and down on the doormat and send the bell into a jangling tailspin. 'And please don't think this will mean you can't drink in the Merry Cobbler in the future. It's your local. Always has been. We can still be civil to one another. We don't need to be adolescent about this, do we?'

'Gina . . .' Doug moved quickly across the shop, skilfully avoiding the mountains of stock. 'Please don't walk out on me. I want us to be friends. I don't want to lose you.'

'You already have.' Gina stepped over the doormat, feeling quite proud of herself, knowing that she would bawl like an idiot the minute she was alone. 'Goodbye, Doug.'

CHAPTER FOURTEEN

'You know,' Jay said, sleepily stroking back Erin's hair and gently kissing her neck, 'thinking about it, I'd say that was a triumph all round, wouldn't you?'

'You're so big-headed,' Erin giggled, reluctantly rolling away from him and reaching for her clothes. 'Ouf—I really should have a shower now but I'm due at the Weedons' to price up their unwanted furniture in—oh Lord—about ten minutes ago.'

'And I have a fully booked surgery in less than that time, so I won't be showering either, which means we'll probably both get a really bad reputation regarding personal hygiene.' Jay propped himself up on one elbow and watched her dress. 'Not to mention for sneaking off for some

117

illicit passion, because I doubt that went unnoticed either in this village. And actually, I wasn't referring to the afternoon delight performance being a triumph.'

'Really?' Erin stopped in pulling her blue vest over her head and freeing her ponytail and grinned at him. 'That makes a change.'

Zipping up her shorts, knowing she really should be leaving but feeling too delightfully languid to dash off anywhere, she wandered to the window of Jay's bedroom. Their bedroom soon. Very, very soon. In four weeks' time.

Not soon enough.

She leaned her hands on the uneven sill and looked out of the open window.

Nook Green shimmered silently under the relentless sun. Anyone hardy enough to be out in the afternoon heat was seeking refuge beneath the trees on the green, or sitting on the banks of the brook, relishing the icy cold water on their feet. The village was swathed in a motionless haze; the grass was burned away to a bronzed stubble, the leaves hung dusty and immobile, and even the cars crawling, by necessity, on the narrow road round the green seemed to be doing so more slowly and sleepily than usual.

'No,' Jay said, dressing quickly in his scrubs and coming up behind her and sliding his arms round her waist. 'Actually, I was thinking about how well Nalisha's settled in over the last week and how great it is that you've made her so welcome.'

Men, Erin thought again. Jay had no idea at all.

Nalisha . . . Erin sighed, leaning back against Jay's gorgeous body. Oooh, the absolutely last thing she wanted to think about right now was Nalisha.

118

Nalisha the two-faced bitch. Nalisha who slept in this cottage. Nalisha who was miraculously out of the way today having gone to visit some old uni friends which meant she and Jay had some time to be alone. For once.

She said nothing.

Jay kissed her hair. 'When Mum rang yesterday, she said Nalisha told her she was really happy here. And that, according to Nalisha, all the wedding plans are going in the right direction. So that's fantastic, isn't it?'

'What?' Erin frowned, praying that Nalisha hadn't divulged details of her *clearly unfashionable* wedding dress to Deena. 'Are you and Nalisha having secret discussions about our wedding with your mum?'

'No, of course not. But you know what Mum's like. She wants everything to be perfect. And I don't want to hurt her feelings by keeping her out of the loop. I do love my parents.'

'I know. And I adore mine. But I wouldn't allow them to interfere in our wedding.'

'And I'm not allowing mine to interfere either— it's just—' Jay sighed '—after a lifetime of being brought up with this strict family code of obedience and respect, I find it really hard to argue with them.'

'I'm not expecting you to argue with them. I'm just peed off that Nalisha feels it necessary to be telling your mum anything at all about our wedding, and I'm just expecting you to stick to your guns. *Our* guns.'

Jay laughed softly. 'I know. And I am. I will. To be honest, if Nalisha being here means that Mum lays off ringing *me* every day and insisting that we

119

change all our wedding plans into some Gujarati five-week matrimonial festival, then long may it continue.'

Erin relaxed back against him again. She mustn't think about Nalisha now. She mustn't allow Nalisha to spoil what little time she and Jay had together. The blissful illicit sneaked hour of passion had flown by. For the umpteenth time she really regretted the decision to not spend any more nights at Jay's cottage until after the wedding.

Mind you, she thought, as Bella had pointed out, with Nalisha now in residence, and the cottage being literally two-up two-down, with the addition of a tiny bathroom on the upstairs landing, their love life would be severely curtailed.

She pulled away from him. The desire to stay was too great and they both had work to return to. Erin managed to move away from the temptation of Jay and the lovely view from the window.

Jay pulled her back and kissed her. 'I love you. And, honestly, if Nalisha keeps Mum from interfering our wedding I suppose we should count ourselves lucky.'

Whatever . . .

'We really have to go.' Erin moved away and gathered up her bag and her sandals. 'You go and prescribe worming tablets and flea sprays and I'll go and inspect the Weedons' unloved furniture for dry rot.'

'And spiders?'

Erin shuddered. 'I'm hoping the furniture will be in the house and not in some arachnid-infested shed. See you tonight, then? Uncle Doug's going out so we'll have his place to ourselves.'

'Great. Is Doug out with Gina? Have they kissed

and made up?'

'Not a chance. He's blown that good and proper. Stupid man. I've told her we still want her to come to the wedding on her own, or, even better, with some stunning man in tow so that Uncle Doug realises what a total prat he's been. I'm not sure she's going to though.'

Jay shook his head. 'She was certainly very cut up about it. And she's such a lovely woman, too. I'm sure he'll regret it.'

'So am I. And I'm sure he already is. Anyway, before we dash off—about tonight, I'll feed you, OK? Pasta salad? It's far too hot for anything else.'

'Sounds good to me. Just you, me and Florence—Oh, is that my mobile? Any idea where it is?'

Erin giggled. 'Well, as we threw everything everywhere, it could be, well, anywhere. I think it sounds as though it might be under the bed.'

Groaning, Jay knelt down and retrieved the phone. 'Damn. Gone to voicemail. Hope it wasn't urgent.'

'If it was anything to do with the surgery, Bella or Sophie would have let you know.'

Jay listened to the message, then laughed. 'It's Kam. He's resigned from his job in Cumbria, forgone his period of notice and his salary, and he's on his way down.'

'Now? Already? Blimey. He didn't hang about. He must be keen.'

'He is, and the sooner he gets here the better as far as I'm concerned,' Jay said. 'I'm turning away such a lot of large animal work, and I really could do with a second vet in that empty room in the surgery for the domestic animals too.'

121

Erin nodded, then stopped. 'But unless he's bringing his own, he'll need another nurse, won't he? And somewhere to live?'

'We'll advertise for a nurse if he needs one, but use the agency from Newbury for the time being and he can stop at the Merry Cobbler until he finds something more permanent. Why are you laughing?'

'Because, when Kam rolls up, Sophie and Bella will think all their birthdays and Christmases have come at once.'

'Lucky Kam—no, don't glare at me like that. I managed to escape their clutches, didn't I? And Kam's far more used to being lusted after than I ever was. But if he makes good time, it'll put paid to our cosy meal this evening.'

Bugger, Erin sighed. Then she smiled. 'Oooh, I don't know. I think Florence and I could just about cope with having dinner with two devastatingly drop-dead gorgeous men.'

'See?' Jay shrugged. 'You're merely weeks away from being my wife, and even you are smitten by Kam.'

'I'm not, actually.' Erin grinned. 'Kam's far too much of a playboy ladykiller for me—even if I was interested, which I'm not. Why would I be? I've got you. Kam's not a patch on you. You're the most fabulously sexy man in the entire universe.'

'Aw.' Jay grinned. 'You say the sweetest things.'

'All true.' Erin laughed. Then stopped. And groaned. 'Oh—and the cosy dinner for two wouldn't have happened anyway. We'd forgotten about Nalisha. She'll be back tonight, won't she?'

'Don't think so. I think she's staying over. That's why it would have been simply perfect and we could have sneaked away to your bedroom afterwards.' He kissed her, very slowly. 'Sod it—we're free of Nalisha playing chaperone, and now we've got Kam.'

'That's families for you. Always there when you want them, and even more so when you don't.'

Jay laughed. 'Too right. Oh, damn it, I'm really going to have to fly now, and I don't want to go. I'll see you later, and I love you.'

'Love you too. Always.'

Erin sighed happily. It was all going to be OK.

CHAPTER FIFTEEN

'Thanks for a great meal.' Kam Keskar smiled at Erin across the table in the garden of Doug's cottage. 'Exactly what I needed after the journey from hell.'

Dusk was falling, casting lilac shadows across the tiny lawn and the curved flower borders, and the air was still, warm and musky-sweet.

'It was only a pasta salad, hardly Heston Blumenthal,' Erin said, as Jay collected the plates and Florence entwined her grey silky body round the rickety wrought-iron chair legs looking for scraps.

'It was a pasta salad fit for the gods. You'll make someone a fantastic wife one day.'

'Me,' Jay laughed, leaning across the table towards his cousin. 'Remember? In four weeks' time. So don't waste your time flirting with my fiancée.'

'As if.' Kam sighed. 'You don't happen to have

123

any sisters, do you, Erin?'

'No, sorry.' Erin lifted Florence onto her lap. 'And I can't believe you're ever short of female company. Last time we met you were, um, going out with your nurse.'

'He's always, um, going out with his nurse,' Jay chuckled, balancing the empty bowls on top of the plates. 'Didn't you bring the latest one with you? Was that Asha? Or Pakshi? Or—no—what was that fiery one called—Roshni?'

'All old news.' Kam stretched his long legs in faded jeans out in front of him. 'I've wiped the slate clean. I shall start a fresh life here in Nook Green, with a fresh nurse, and—'

'Do all your veterinary nurses have to be Indian?' Erin asked. 'Isn't that a bit, well, insular at best and racist at worst?'

'No way. It's simply a coincidence that all the nurses I've had when you and Jay have been around, have been Indian.' Kam laughed. 'I've had nurses from every corner of the globe.'

'He means that literally.' Jay shook his head. 'We'll have to make sure the one he gets this time is Kam-proof. Maybe older, sort of comfy middle-aged, happily married with a nice little family. Totally immune to his dubious charms.'

'Ah, but does such a woman exist?' Kam smiled. 'I haven't met one yet. And, on the same subject, in my role of best man, I'm guessing I get first pick of the bridesmaids?'

'No way. Hands off. Sophie and Bella are my oldest and bestest friends.' Erin shook her head. 'They don't need their lives messed up by you.'

'You are so boring.' Kam grinned. 'I suppose I'll just have to find other diversions to keep me

124

occupied.'

Erin let Florence slide to the ground, and peered suspiciously at Kam. 'What sort of diversions? Nothing to do with our wedding?'

'No, well, not directly.' Kam leaned back in his chair. 'Although the family has asked me to check on a few things.'

'Oh, not again.' Erin groaned so loudly that Florence stopped trying to catch a moth in the herbaceous border and stared at her. 'Not you as well? Once and for all—our wedding plans are in place, we're having the marriage we both want, and there's absolutely no point in you trying to say anything different.'

Kam laughed. 'I'm not going to try and change anything—well, not much. It's just that when Jay's parents heard I was coming to live and work here, well, I was given some very specific instructions regarding the wedding rituals.'

'Which I *do not* want to hear. OK?'

'You're really very beautiful when you're fierce. You're very beautiful anyway, of course, but when you're angry your eyes really blaze—like turquoise diamonds.'

'Bleugh.' Erin made a throwing-up gesture. 'Wasted on me, Kam, thanks all the same. Save all that crap for your hordes of devoted followers. And please, don't think you can move into Nook Green and, like the rest of the family, try to reorganise our wedding, because you can't.'

Kam laughed lazily, poured more wine for them both and topped up Jay's glass. 'OK, now just hear me out. As best man, I'm traditionally supposed to make sure Jay's wedding has all the proper Hindu ceremonies. I also know none of this is what either of you want. But I've got an idea. No—don't say anything. Just trust me and I'll make sure family honour is satisfied, and you get the wedding day you want.'

'How? Why?'

'By being devious. And because if I was Jay, all this interference would drive me crazy.'

'Really?'

'Totally. I'd run a mile from the organised rituals and tradition and non-stop celebration. If I loved someone enough to want to spend the rest of my life with them, then I'd make sure it was just me and her, and the rest of the world could go to hell.'

'*What*?' Erin frowned. 'But that's exactly how we feel. So why on earth are you trying to force Jay into something you don't even agree with?'

Kam laughed. 'I'm not, believe me. That's why I asked you to trust me while I work out a way to keep everyone happy.'

'And that's Mission Impossible.'

'I can see it probably seems like that to you now. You must think that our family are suddenly determined to turn the happiest day of your life into some three-ring circus.'

'Oh, yeah. Complete with clowns.' Erin drained her glass.

Kam poured her another refill. 'I know it must seem crazy to you, but it's been instilled in us from birth to honour these deep-rooted traditions, along with a massive respect for our heritage. And for our parents, a marriage ceremony is the biggest event in *their* lives. In their eyes, this isn't about Jay and you, this is about Indian family honour.'

'Of course it's about me and Jay! It's our damn wedding! And Jay is *not* Indian—well, yes he is—

but he's also very, very British.'

'We both are.'

'Exactly. You were both born here, educated here, and live totally Western lives. Why the hell do you all think Jay'd want to revert to the traditions of a way of life he's never known?'

'I don't.' Kam shrugged. 'I know he doesn't. Which is why I'm on your side. But I've also got to keep Jay's parents sweet.'

'So you're going to be a sort of double agent?'

'Yeah, something like that.'

'I still can't see you outwitting foxy Deena . . . Oh, sometimes I wish we could just forget the whole damn thing and run away and get married on some deserted beach in the middle of nowhere or something.'

Kam leaned back in his chair. 'Which, in Jay's place, is exactly what I'd do. I've always fancied eloping.'

'Who's eloping?' Jay appeared from Doug's cottage carrying a tray of fruit salad and bowls. 'Anyone I know?'

'Erin and I were just having a bit of a discussion about the wedding, and I said if I were in your shoes I'd run away from all the meddling,' Kam said, reaching for the tray. 'That's all.'

Erin looked at Jay. 'And I've told him it's a topic that's now closed. I think we've covered it enough for a lifetime.'

'So do I.' Jay sat down and took her hands across the table, then grinned at Kam. 'So you can keep your mouth firmly shut regarding our wedding, OK?'

'OK. But if you'd just hear me out, you'd realise that I'm not—'

Jay shook his head. 'No—just butt out, Kam. We've both had more than enough. Now, as soon as we've finished here, we'll go over to the Merry Cobbler and see if Gina can sort you out a nice single room until you can find a place of your own.'

Kam gazed at the cottage in the twilight and then lazily round Doug's pretty country garden. 'Can't I stay here? Don't you have a spare room for a totally knackered vet?'

'No,' Erin said quickly. 'Sorry. Well, actually yes, there is a spare room, but my mum and dad are having it when they come over for the wedding. And they're staying for two months—so sadly, no, there's no room at the inn.'

'Is that a biblical reference?' Kam grinned. 'Or are you telling me that I won't find anywhere to sleep at the pub either?'

Erin pulled a face across the table at Kam. 'I wouldn't dare make a biblical reference—you'd probably report me to Deena and Tavish for insurrection. And I don't know if Gina has any rooms free at the Merry Cobbler. But—' she smiled over her wine glass '—if she hasn't, we could always book you into the Bates Motel.'

Jay laughed. 'You wouldn't wish that on him?'

'Oooh, don't tempt me.'

Kam frowned. '*The Bates Motel*? Seriously?'

'Well, now Nalisha's not staying there, we know there's a vacancy.'

Kam looked at Jay. 'Ah, yes. I'd heard the divine Nalisha was not only back in the UK but here in the village and living in your cottage. Is that for real?'

'Sadly, yes,' Erin said quickly, dispirited by the mention of the 'N' word. 'And it's something else I really don't want to talk about.'

128

Jay and Kam exchanged 'talk about it later' looks across the table.

'Anyway,' Erin continued, 'if you don't lay off our wedding plans, we'll take you to the Bates Motel by force and book you in for the duration.'

'Please don't.' Kam spooned fruit salad into his bowl. 'The pub sounds much nicer. I just wish you'd both trust me.'

Erin, now halfway down her umpteenth glass of wine, sighed. 'No woman should ever trust you. You should come with a health warning. But, just for the record, we're not having any sort of Indian pre-wedding parties—not for you, for Jay's parents, or for the Maharajah himself. Last, final word.'

CHAPTER SIXTEEN

'It's a lovely room,' Kam said, smiling at Gina across the bar in the Merry Cobbler. 'And a great price. Thank you so much.'

'You're more than welcome.' Gina, still looking woebegone but clearly trying very hard not to show it, managed to smile back. 'I'm glad you like it.'

'Why wouldn't he?' Erin whispered to Jay, listening to the exchange from their corner table. 'It's not the Bates Motel. It's above a pub, it looks out across the green, it's a stone's throw from the surgery, he gets breakfast chucked in, and Gina has just said she'll do his washing.'

Jay laughed. 'Absolutely. And she's possibly the most beautiful landlady in the country. What's not to like?'

Erin sipped her wine slowly. She'd had too much

to drink really. This would have to be the last one tonight or she'd be feeling rubbish in the morning.

Jay ran his finger down her cheek. 'Sorry if Kam was one Keskar too far tonight. Don't worry about anything he said. Together, we can ignore all of them and just carry on. Together, we can do anything. Right?'

'Right.' She smiled sleepily at him. He really was the loveliest man in the world. 'Oh, I wish we were already married and all this stupid meddling was over.'

And Nalisha had gone to live in London for ever and ever. But she didn't say it.

'Me too,' Jay sighed. 'Still, it won't be long now, will it?'

Too long, Erin thought. Still too many days left for outside interference.

Oh, to hell with it all.

She relaxed back in her tapestry-cushioned carver chair, too tired to worry about anything else tonight. The Merry Cobbler was still very warm, despite all the leaded-light latticed windows being thrown open, and hummed with convivial conversations.

Tiny table lamps glowed, throwing splashes of gold across the shabby but comfortable room, and behind the bar, Gina and the elderly Sam were still very busy.

At the end of the sweltering evening, most people were drinking round the outside tables, but while Gina had shown Kam to his room, Erin and Jay had just collapsed into the nearest corner of the pub.

'Last orders please!' Gina moved away from Kam and energetically rang the old ship's bell that hung from a twisted rope at the end of the bar. 'Last orders, ladies and gents, please!'

There was a flurry of activity as the Nook Greeners all scraped chairs across the quarry-tiled floor, and eased themselves from behind tables, and shuffled forwards to buy their final drinks.

'Hello, dears,' Dora Wilberforce, dressed rather incongruously in a fringed denim skirt and a loudly checked blouse, and smelling strongly of Yardley Lavender, paused beside them. 'Lovely to see you both in here. What a blistering hot night though, isn't it? My ginger beer just wouldn't suffice tonight after the line dancing. Me and the rest of the Nook Green Yee-Hawers have all been rather naughty and popped in here for a nice cold lager and lime or two.'

'Good idea.' Erin smiled brightly, gazing at the rest of the geriatric bunch crowded round the Merry Cobbler's largest table, all dressed in cowboy boots and Stetsons and looking like an elderly faction of the Village People's appreciation society.

Dora patted Jay's shoulder. 'And it must be nice for you to have some of your own type here in the village, dear. We all love seeing that new stunning Indian girl in the village, especially when she wears all those lovely bright saris. A regular little blaze of colour, she is. And now—' she motioned coquettishly towards Kam '—you've got another handsome young man of your ilk to keep you company. There's some as don't think it's in keeping with the village, but not me. I've never been narrow-minded in that way. Well, I better get on and get the last round in before Gina calls time. I'm so looking forward to the wedding, dears.'

Erin and Jay stared after her.

131

Erin giggled. 'Was that, um, politically correct or not?'

'God knows.' Jay shook his head. 'Probably not, but who cares. Love her.'

Kam, laughing at something Dora had said to him, elbowed his way back through the Yee-Hawers and pulled up a chair.

'This is great. Fabulous pub, really nice room, and a very sexy landlady.'

'Glad you like it, but please leave Gina alone,' Erin said quickly. 'Don't mess about with her. She's lovely and my friend and she's been hurt enough.'

'Erin's Uncle Doug has just finished their relationship,' Jay said. 'It's left her a bit bruised and battered.'

Kam raised his eyebrows. 'Is your Uncle Doug *mad*? She's gorgeous and funny and friendly—and she owns this place.'

'Completely barking.' Erin nodded. 'As I've told him many times. But honestly, Kam, he hurt Gina badly, so please leave her alone.'

'OK.' Kam leaned back in his chair. 'I'll stay well away. Pity, though, because she's stunning. Oh, and talking of stunning women, am I allowed to mention Nalisha now?'

'If you really have to,' Erin said, smiling sleepily at Jay. The wine was starting to kick in rather nicely. 'But I had hoped tonight would be a Nalisha-free zone.'

Jay grinned. 'Go on then. How did you know she was here? Did Mum tell you?'

'No, she texted me as soon as she knew I was thinking of working here.'

'Really?' Jay raised his eyebrows. 'The speed of the family grapevine never ceases to amaze me.

132

Why did she text you, though? Oh—you're not, are you?'

'No way,' Kam laughed. 'For some unknown reason, Nalisha never gave me a second glance. I always thought that maybe you and she would . . . well, you know. You were always together at all the family weddings and parties and . . .'

Erin was suddenly wide awake.

'As best friends,' Jay said quickly. 'As I keep explaining to Erin. So, go on, why did she text you?'

Erin fiddled with the stem of her wine glass.

Kam grinned. 'Just being friendly, she said. Long time no see and all that. And getting in touch again now we're all going to be Nook Green. Although I do think it's a bit weird that she's staying in your cottage and Erin isn't.'

So do I, Erin thought, but didn't bother saying.

'None of your business.' Jay grinned. 'And Erin's fine with it, aren't you?'

'Oh yeah. Fine.'

Kam laughed. 'Oh, well, I'll see her when she's back tomorrow, no doubt. I might have to take her out to dinner—just to catch up, of course.'

'Oh, of course.'

Oooh—ker-ching! Erin suddenly grinned to herself. The perfect solution. Kam and Nalisha . . . Nalisha and Kam . . .

Yay!

Kam stretched lazily. 'Right, I'm getting another drink. What would you like?'

'Nothing for me, thanks.' Erin shook her head.

'Or me,' Jay said. 'And Gina will be calling time soon so you'd better hurry.'

'OK. I'll just go and chat up the gorgeous Gina and—no—Erin, don't look at me like that—I'm joking. I know when to steer clear.'

'Really?' Erin smiled, still mulling over the delightful possibilities of a Kam-and-Nalisha scenario. 'Remember, I'm watching you.'

'So's every other woman in the pub.' Jay grinned as Kam sauntered back to the bar. 'Damn—I'm clearly not number one on their lust list any more.'

'Only because they all know you're strictly off-limits.' Erin grinned.

'Sod it—I knew there was going to be a drawback to getting married.'

Erin laughed, then swirled the remainder of her wine round the glass. 'When did you and Kam last see Nalisha, then? It must be ages ago if she's been working in America.'

'Don't know about Kam, but I last saw her a couple of years ago, just before I came here and she went to California. We were both leaving our present jobs and moving elsewhere, with much better prospects, so we had a weekend away to celebrate.'

'*What?*'

Jay frowned. 'A weekend away. Her family and mine. Not just the two of us—it wasn't like that. It was never like that.'

Erin studied the tabletop. Years of beer stains and cigarette burns had been lovingly polished into a glowing golden sheen.

So, the gloriously stunning, highly qualified, two-faced Nalisha, who knew Jay inside out and upside down, and who was clearly an eagerly accepted part of the whole huge extended family, had spent a weekend with him, had she?

OK, with the rest of the family, and before he'd moved to Nook Green and before she'd even met him. But even so . . .

Nalisha, it seemed, had been automatically considered as Jay's plus one for *years*. And not just when they were children.

Hmmm . . . Erin sighed heavily. But Nalisha wasn't marrying Jay, was she? Jay had chosen her, not Nalisha, hadn't he? And no one could change that, could they? Could they?

'Are you still awake?' Jay said softly.

'What? Oh, yes. Sorry.' Erin smiled at him. 'Miles away. Just thinking.'

He leaned across the table and took her hands in his. 'As long as it's about me, that's cool.'

'Of course it's about you. It's always about you. Ego satisfied now?'

'Totally,' Jay laughed. 'Oh, I just wish we could go back to the cottage tonight. Together.'

Erin stifled a yawn. 'We could, actually, as Nalisha is staying over with her friends. Although I might just be asleep before we made the stairs.'

'Damn.' Jay grinned. 'I bet I could wake you up though.'

Erin was suddenly swamped with lust. Again. 'Mmmm, I think you probably could . . .'

'So, shall we go?' Jay asked softly. 'Kam's still chatting to Gina at the bar and she hasn't called time yet. I'll tell him we're off now.'

'OK.' Erin pushed her glass away and stood up. 'Oh shit.' Her heart plummeted into her flip-flops.

Bella and Sophie had just appeared in the doorway, followed by Nalisha.

Nalisha hadn't seen them, but she'd definitely spotted Kam. Her eyes widening, she gave a little scream of delight, and hurtled through the throng and threw her arms round him.

'Oh, bugger! What the hell is she doing here?' Erin frowned, watching as Kam hugged Nalisha and was clearly ordering her a drink. She secretly hoped he'd get her rolling drunk and drag her upstairs to his room, but was pretty sure, given Sod's Law, that he wouldn't.

'No idea.' Jay shook his head. 'She must have changed her plans. But we could still go. She'll be ages yet.'

Erin looked across at Nalisha, with so much of her superb body displayed in her linen shorts and her sliding-off-the-shoulder T-shirt, and shook her head sadly as all the earlier lovely lustful feelings simply fizzled away.

'Sorry, but it just wouldn't seem right, knowing she was in the cottage. In the next room. It'd be like being a kid again, all furtive and tense and not making a noise, waiting for your parents to suss you.'

Jay sighed. 'I must have had such innocent teenage years compared to yours.'

Erin shrugged. Bloody Nalisha had ruined things—again.

On purpose?

'Wow!' Bella sidled up to them and jerked her head towards the bar. 'The red-hot man with Nalisha. Who's *he*?'

'He's Jay's cousin,' Erin said, still feeling extremely grouchy. 'He's called Kam.'

'Wow! And are they—you know? Together?'

'Not yet.'

'Goody.' Bella grinned. 'Fat and ginger still stands a chance then?'

'If you're quick. And you and Sophie haven't been out with Nalisha tonight, have you?'

136

'What? No. Me and Soph've been to the cinema in Newbury. Crap film. Nalisha pulled up in her car as we got here. But doesn't she look *amazing*? I wish my legs looked half that good in shorts.' Bella continued to stare at Nalisha and Kam. 'She said her night out was pretty boring so she'd come home. Why?'

'Because she was supposed to be staying in Oxford.'

'Well, she didn't, obviously. Oh, look, excuse me—I must go and get a drink before it's too late.'

'There's just a teeny tiny space beside Kam if you hurry.' Jay smiled. 'Although it looks as if Sophie might be getting in there first.'

'Nooo!' Bella shrieked, and thrust her way between several of the Nook Green Yee-Hawers.

'You just failed to mention to Bella that you'd offered Kam a partnership and that he'd be working with you, didn't you?' Erin said. 'Which means of course that he'll also be working with her and Sophie. Was that deliberate?'

'Absolutely. I didn't know he was going to take me up on the offer or arrive so quickly, but now he has I'll leave it to him to make the introductions. And leave them to squabble over him. Maybe then he'll have something else to concentrate on and he'll back off from flirting with Gina, and messing with our wedding arrangements.'

'Good thinking.' Erin, still cursing Nalisha with warty-toad-type curses, picked up her bag and followed Jay towards the bar. 'Oh, look, Bella and Sophie are both trying to buy him a drink now. Let's make a break for it before they revert to the playground and start pinching and doing Chinese burns and pulling each other's hair out.'

137

Kam, his arm round Nalisha's shoulders, and happily squashed between Bella and Sophie, winked at them as they said their goodnights. Bella and Sophie flapped their hands in farewell but didn't take their eyes from Kam.

'Goodnight, Nalisha,' Erin said quietly as they passed. 'So sorry your plans didn't work out.'

'Actually, they've worked out perfectly.' Nalisha smiled. 'I never had any intention of staying away tonight . . .'

CHAPTER SEVENTEEN

Only three weeks to go. Only three weeks until she became Mrs Jay Keskar.

Erin, in her shorts and vest pyjamas and the insanely high—and even more insanely expensive—cream-satin-and-silver-net-delicately-studded-with-tiny-organza-rosebuds wedding shoes, teetered across the kitchen's quarry tiles and crossed off another day on the *Antiques Roadshow* calendar.

She picked up Florence and did a little careful, if slightly unsteady, happy dance round Uncle Doug's kitchen. Florence looked at her in horror, struggled from her arms and wriggled free, marching away out through the open door.

Erin watched her go, smiling fondly, then stalked up and down, doing catwalk turns between the fridge and the oven. Perfect. The shoes were perfect. She'd been breaking them in every morning for the last week. On 7 September, she'd glide—positively glide—down the aisle of the Swan's marriage room with not a wobble in sight. She'd show Deena Keskar and bloody Nalisha that she had poise and elegance. In spades.

Another gloriously hot day beckoned. August was still following on nicely from the rest of the summer. And the long-range forecast promised there were no storm clouds on the horizon. No threat of a breakdown of the heatwave in the foreseeable future. No rain expected for weeks. Which, Erin admitted, was probably bad news for farmers and gardeners, but absolutely great for someone who wanted a blissfully hot and sunny wedding day.

Still wearing the heavenly shoes, Erin put fresh food and water into Florence's bowls and set them down outside in the shade. Florence, now sprawled in the herbaceous border, stopped her intensive grooming, stared at her and the bowls, and then carried on washing.

'Suit yourself, lady. You know where it is when you want it.'

Erin swayed back into the kitchen, made coffee and toast as she sang along to the radio, and stacked the remainder of the previous night's plates into the dishwasher. There was no sign of Uncle Doug. He was an early riser, so she assumed he'd already left for the Old Curiosity Shop.

Or not come home last night.

It was too much to hope, she knew, that he'd be cuddled up with Gina in the Merry Cobbler. That was definitely all over. Stupid man. And poor Gina. Her heartbreak had been obvious to everyone, even though she'd put on a brave face and tried very hard to hide the puffy eyes behind huge sunglasses.

Erin sipped her coffee. Damn Doug.

Still, everything else seemed to be going OK,

she thought. Kam had settled happily into both the Merry Cobbler's guest room and his role in the vet's practice, and had quickly become a firm favourite with every female farmer and pony club mum for miles. Jay was delighted with the rise in income, not to mention the sharing of the workload.

And the agency nurse, Renata, that Jay had employed to work with Kam, was perfect and had agreed to become a permanent fixture. A statuesque and sweet-natured redhead, she lived happily in Maizey St Michael with her partner Julia, and was totally immune to Kam's charms.

'I swear I didn't know she was gay,' Jay had chuckled. 'We never touched on that side of things at the interview, obviously. I know Kam thinks I did it on purpose, but I simply went for the best candidate for the job. And of course, Bella and Sophie are delighted with her. No competition.'

Erin laughed again at the memory, and stretched luxuriously.

Of course there was still one fly in the ointment. One sneaky, slinky, two-faced fly . . .

Nalisha had somehow managed to collect quite a fan club. No one else seemed to realise just what a bitch she was. Uncle Doug was positively slavering; Gina thought she was 'a nice woman'; she'd shown Sophie how to make several shortcuts in her admin, and miraculously had overcome her aversion to animals and been, as Bella kept saying, 'a total star' in helping out behind the scenes in the surgery.

And when she hadn't been whizzing off in the snazzy sports car catching up with friends, she'd admired Dora Wilberforce's garden and praised her ginger beer, given Part-Time Pearl some herbal concoction guaranteed to help 'her poor ole feet', had charmed everyone in the local shop-cum-post office, and had a geriatric fan club hanging on her every word among the Yee-Hawers and had promised to come along to their next dance night.

And, most importantly, she appeared to have kept her word and not breathed a word about Erin's clearly 'outdated' wedding dress. The whispered and delivered with a smile slight still rankled.

Sadly, the Nalisha–Kam thing didn't appear to be happening, although he had taken her out— much to Bella and Sophie's chagrin—on a couple of evenings, but Erin still lived in hope.

But Erin wasn't going to think about Nalisha today. Today was Saturday. Jay only had morning surgery, and she'd be working until two o'clock, so they'd have the rest of the afternoon free. They'd made an appointment at the Swan with Abbie, the hotel's wedding organiser, to make sure all the last-minute touches were in place.

Bliss.

And then, three weeks today . . . Three weeks today . . .

Whoo!

Erin munched her toast as she danced again round the sun-dappled kitchen. Nothing, not even Nalisha-the-cow, could possibly mar her happiness on a day like today.

Their wedding, Erin knew, going to be perfect. She'd been so silly to worry about it.

All she had to do now was lovingly return the fabulous shoes to their cream satin box, shower and dress, and pop to the Old Curiosity Shop and in a very few hours, she and Jay would be with Abbie at the Swan making sure their final arrangements were still all in place.

And three weeks today . . .

*   *   *

Erin was still chanting the mantra when she walked into the shop.

'Dear God!'

She stared in horror. Uncle Doug, looking wild-haired and wild-eyed, was heaving a dusty and moth-eaten chaise longue into one corner. The rest of the shop floor had been miraculously cleared, and all the furniture and books and ornaments were stacked round the edges.

'Have you gone mad? Where's all the stuff gone? Are you planning to have a party in here? Have you been here all night? And what the hell is going on?'

Doug stopped in his heaving, dropped his end of the chaise longue, straightened up and wiped the sweat from his face. 'Way too many questions. And actually I'd hoped to have it finished before you came in.'

'Have what finished exactly?' Erin stared round the shop in amazement. 'Oh, no—you haven't been to a house clearance without telling me? We're not going to have an entire three-bedroomed house's junk in here again, are we? Last time you did that no one bought any of it and it cost us a fortune to hire someone to take it all away again, and—'

'Even more questions. You should be in investigative journalism.'

'Just tell me what's going on.'

'Right. Well, I've had a little internet delivery.' Doug puffed. 'You know I like the odd dabble in and out of the eBay shops—well, this deal was too

142

good to pass up under the circumstances. Got it all for next to nothing.'

Erin winced. She'd heard those words—or similar—many, many times before.

'OK—so what is it and when's it arriving?'

Doug looked slightly shifty. 'It's already here. Out the back in the yard. That's why I haven't been to bed. They wanted to make an overnight delivery. Big lorry, you see. Less disruption for the village. I'm surprised it didn't wake you.'

'I slept like a log, didn't hear a thing—but it must be furniture.' Erin frowned. 'Otherwise you wouldn't have cleared all this space. Do we really need more furniture, though? We make more money from the tourists buying nick-nacks and the out-of-print books and general collectibles. And the locals who come here to buy furniture are few and far between in the summer. So, why . . .?'

'It's not furniture.'

Erin's heart sank. If it wasn't furniture, what on earth could Uncle Doug have bought that needed most of the shop to house it?

She looked sternly at him. Oh God—not a menagerie of stuffed animals? Or a train set? A whole model railway layout that needed all the floor space? She wouldn't put that past him.

'There's something you're not telling me—oh, and you said "under the circumstances" . . . what circumstances?'

Doug smiled. Guiltily. 'Ah, well—do you remember we said that coming up to your wedding it might be a nice idea to have a little Indian-themed window display?'

'Mmm. I remember saying that I'd happily go along with it during my wedding week but not

143

before, and anyway, the blue and white china still looks lovely, and we've sold loads to the browsers, and I really don't want to spend this morning changing the window display again and . . .'

'You won't have to. Not yet anyway. This, um, new consignment is just for the interior of the shop. Not the window.'

'Tell me what you've bought.'

Doug smiled again. Erin still thought he looked very shifty. 'Well, I thought, now Jay has both Kam and Nalisha in the village, it might be nice to show our solidarity.'

'What-have-you-bought? Something Indian, obviously, but what? No, no, don't bother. I'll go and have a look myself.'

'Erin! Wait!'

Too late, she thought, forcing her way through the piled-up cabinets and chairs and rickety tables to get to the storeroom, and through that, out into the yard.

The sun, beating down across the uneven rooftops, dazzled her for a few seconds. She blinked. All she could see in the yard were lots of tall white pillars.

What the heck? Had Doug bought an online Indian temple? A do-it-yourself shrine? She blinked and stared again. No, no, not pillars . . . Not smooth enough. Too lumpy. Lots of individual tall lumpy things, most of them at least as tall as she was and some even taller, all covered in white sheets.

'Erin.' Doug appeared behind her. 'I really didn't want you to see this until I'd got it organised properly. Don't touch the sheets, love. Please.'

Ignoring him, Erin twitched back a corner of the

144

nearest sheet. And yelped.

'It's a life-size Marc Bolan!'

'No, actually, it isn't.'

'It is! Look at the black curls and the eyeliner! Why the hell have you bought a statue of Marc Bolan?'

'Er, actually, I think that might be Krishna. I need to refer to the accompanying catalogue to be sure, but yes, it looks like Krishna.'

'It looks like Marc Bolan.'

'Yeah.' Doug surveyed it with his head on one side. 'Yeah, I can see the likeness now you mention it.'

'Once again, why have you bought a statue of Marc Bolan?'

'It's not Marc Bolan. It's Krishna.'

'And the others?' Erin gritted her teeth and clenched her fingers tightly into her palms, staring at the collection of white shrouds. 'A full line-up of the Sweet? The Glitter Band? Mud?'

'They're *not* nineteen seventies glam rockers, love. They're gods and goddesses. Indian gods and goddesses.'

'Jesus Christ.'

'Not him, no. Just Indian. Erin, don't touch the sheets. Don't . . .'

Erin glared at him and stalked round the yard crossly whipping back the sheets.

'Ohmigod!'

She stared at the collection of larger-than-life-size plaster figures with mounting horror. Gaudily painted in vibrant colours, their flowing multilayered saris and ceremonial robes adorned with lots of golden painted jewellery and much glittery embellishment, they towered above her.

And she even recognised some of them.

Ganesh, Lakshmi, Shiva and Vishnu she knew. Even Krishna, now she realised it wasn't Marc Bolan. All these were displayed in tiny shrines in Jay's cottage, gifts from his parents when they'd visited various temples. Erin loved them: loved their made-up faces, and their beatific smiles and their ornate rainbow clothes. Loved the flowers and animals scattered at their feet. Loved the stories behind them. Loved their links to Jay's gentle cultural and religious heritage.

But the ones in Jay's cottage were small discreet figurines, a couple of inches high, not mostly nearly six feet tall, and not so many of them.

She counted the statues quickly. Eighteen. *Eighteen!*

'We can't keep them. You'll have to send them back.'

'I can't.' Doug rattled various sheets of paper. 'Er, it's a done deal. Um, I was expecting them to be a lot smaller—you know, like little ornaments, and I thought they'd look lovely in the shop window with a lot of sari silks and some golden bowls and—'

'You didn't think to check on the sizes?' Erin knew she was in danger of becoming hysterical and tried very hard not to screech. 'When you ordered them?'

Doug looked abashed. 'I thought the measurements were in centimetres, and I don't do metric, as you well know. I did think it was a bit odd that they said they'd deliver, as most things go in the post, but as it was a free delivery I wasn't going to quibble and . . .'

Erin counted to ten and exhaled slowly. The sun

146

hammered down on the top of her head.

Stay calm. Stay calm.

'So, what exactly do you intend doing with them? Given that you can't return them, no one is going to want to buy them, and you *cannot* put them in the shop.'

'Of course I can put them in the shop.' Doug tried another sheepish smile. 'That's why I've cleared all the space. Why can't I put them in the shop?'

'Because I'll bloody resign and leave you to do your own accounts, that's why! Look at them! They're more than human-sized and some of them—like Ganesh—are also quite . . . well . . . fat. And there're eighteen of them! That's like having eighteen very tall, chunky people standing in the middle of the shop! We can't move when there're three in there! We won't be able to get any customers in and you'll go bankrupt in a week!'

OK. Calm down. Calm down. And breathe.

Doug looked a little shocked at the outburst. 'Hardly, love. That's why I cleared the space, though. So there'd be room for the customers if the statues all stood in the middle.'

'And do what? Stop any customers we might have, the ones who aren't breaking their necks to own a life-size statue of an Indian god that is, seeing what else we have in stock? Actually buying something?'

'Well, no . . .'

'What—' Erin was now on a roll '—was the point of me spending all last winter having the website designed? Getting us linked to all those telly show antique and collectible sites? Getting listings on all the Berkshire tourist trail sites with the coach tour companies? It's worked miracles for the business, but we'll be a laughing stock if all the customers find when they get here is a whole coterie of Indian idols!'

Doug sighed. 'Don't keep shouting at me. OK, I might have made a bit of a mistake . . .'

'*A bit of a mistake*? No, being stupid enough to lose Gina was a bit of a mistake—this is a bloody disaster!'

'Calm down, love. It's not that bad.' Doug looked slightly worried. 'Look, why don't we get them inside and just see how they fit? We might be able to integrate them somehow.'

'Integrate them? Give me strength! And just how do you think we're going to get them inside? They must weigh a ton. How many people delivered them?'

'Um, about half a dozen or so. Quite big blokes they were, too.'

Bloody hell!

'And where exactly do you think you're going to get another half a dozen or so people to help you move them from the yard into the shop?'

'I thought I'd ask round the village. And Callum's here, so he can help.'

Callum Prior, an adenoidal teenager with blank eyes, a baseball cap and his jeans hanging halfway down his backside, was the Old Curiosity Shop's Saturday boy.

Erin sighed. 'Most people in this village are even older than you are. Anyone daft enough to say yes will end up with a hernia or heart failure or both, especially in this heat. And Callum can't manage this lot on his own.'

'I thought we could ask Jay—and some of his

148

friends—and Kam, of course. They're all young and fit and strong.'

Erin sighed. 'Jay and Kam will be at work until lunchtime, and we're going out this afternoon, and anyway, we really, really don't want all these, er, statues in the shop, do we? Oh, for someone usually so astute in business, someone who can turn a profit on almost *anything*, you're just plain daft sometimes.'

'So I've been told.' Doug surveyed the statues sorrowfully. 'Well, if they have to stay out here for the time being, maybe we could make them into some sort of feature. You know, like a sort of visitors' shrine?'

'Why? We need the yard for deliveries and stacking up reclamation stuff. And even if the tourists did suddenly decide they wanted to look at eighteen Indian gods and goddesses—though God only knows why they would—there's bound to be some sort of health and safety issue about letting people wander about in a delivery yard.'

They stared at one another. The yard was unbearably hot. The statues were giving off a rather unpleasant old-paint musty smell.

The doormat bell rang, echoing distantly through the shop and out into the yard.

'Hello!' A female voice called from inside the shop. 'Anyone at home?'

Bugger, Erin sighed. A customer. She raised her voice. 'We're out here in the yard. Just coming . . . no, don't come through here—oh . . . Nalisha.'

Nalisha, wearing a pink and silver sari, blinked batwing eyelashes in the sunshine. 'Ah, here you are—why's the shop so empty? I just thought—Oooh, wow! Awesome!'

149

Erin pulled a face.

Nalisha sashayed between the statues making little chirrups of excited pleasure.

'Lovely, aren't they?' Doug said cheerfully, making puppy-dog eyes at Nalisha, and obviously delighted to have found an ally. 'I was just saying to Erin that—'

'Lord Krishna,' Nalisha breathed, stroking the solid black curls, 'with butter on his fingers. Exactly right. And—' she moved round the towering figures, cooing blissfully 'Lord Vishnu, oh, and Matangi, the Dark One. Oh and there's Lakshmi! Isn't she gorgeous? Oh, they're simply fabulous! I haven't seen anything like this outside the temples. Where on earth did you get them?'

'Ask Uncle Doug,' Erin said shortly. 'Although possibly it's best not to know the exact details.'

'They're not stolen,' Doug said quickly. 'They were left over after a refurb, apparently.'

Erin, deciding it was honestly better not to delve too deeply into the statues' origins, looked at Nalisha. 'Do you recognise all of them, then? I mean, I know some of them because Jay has *tiny* gods in the cottage, doesn't he?'

'Ganga, Annapurna, Balarama, Ganesh . . .' Nalisha ignored her and continued to drift delightedly round the gods and goddesses, reverently touching a crown here, a flowing robe there. 'Oh, so many, and they're perfect in every detail. Perfect. They're wonderful—you're *so* lucky to have them.' She looked at Doug. 'Clever old you.'

Doug preened and looked hopelessly infatuated.

Erin shook her head.

Nalisha smiled at him. 'Are they for sale?'

150

'Too right.' Erin snorted. 'Why? Would you like to buy them?'

'Oh, I'd love them, but they'd take up so much room and, at the moment, I have nowhere to keep them.' Nalisha made it sound as if she was reluctantly turning down a litter of pedigree puppies.

You could always go and buy a mansion in London and move out of my fiancé's cottage, Erin thought, managing to smile sweetly.

Nalisha beamed at Doug. 'But I do have an idea about where they can go.'

'Share it, please,' Erin said. 'Because Uncle Doug wants them to go into the shop, which is ridiculous, and—Oooh, no!' She glared at Nalisha. 'You haven't got some crazy idea about them being involved in the *non-existent* mehendi or tilak, have you?'

Nalisha had somehow managed to shimmy her way very close to Doug. She touched his arm. 'Erin is so funny about this wedding, isn't she?'

'Hilarious.' Doug nodded, still looking besotted. 'Almost as funny as Sarah Millican.'

'Actually,' Nalisha said, narrowing her eyes at Erin, 'it's nothing to do with your wedding, although now you come to mention it, maybe that's not a bad idea.'

'It's a terrible idea.'

Nalisha smiled and wriggled her dupatta over her shoulders. Doug looked on admiringly.

'Just teasing,' Nalisha said with no humour in her voice. 'Actually, I've been thinking about a little project. Something to bring a bit of life into the village. I love it here, of course, but there's so little to do. I need something to get my teeth into while

151

I'm here.'

As long as it's not Jay, Erin thought, you can get your perfectly veneered molars into anything you damn well like.

Nalisha looked at Doug. 'So please, please promise me you won't sell the gods and goddesses until I've thought about it a bit more.'

'You've got first refusal.' Doug beamed.

'Thank you.' Nalisha beamed back at him. Then she looked at Erin. 'Oh, I almost forgot why I came over in the first place. I was taking the early morning phone calls at the surgery before Sophie got in, and Jay's last appointment has cancelled, so he says as long as things go OK, and unless he gets another emergency, he'll be ready earlier than you'd thought and he wondered if you could get away by midday instead of two o'clock.'

'Yes, of course. But why couldn't Jay tell me himself? We do have mobiles.'

'He's in surgery. Operating. He had a call-out really early this morning. He took the pick-up.'

Erin exhaled. She wasn't even annoyed that Nalisha knew all this before she did. She knew only too well that taking the pick-up, the convertible vehicle that Jay used as an animal ambulance, meant that something serious had happened.

Loving animals, she always tried really hard not to be squeamish about aspects of Jay's work, knowing that as a vet's wife she was going to have to distance herself from the occasional heartbreak and trauma. But it was impossible not to feel a heart-rending compassion for the animal, or to put herself in the place of the animal's owner, and share the pain and suffering.

'Oh God, is it—?'

Nalisha, clearly nowhere near as emotionally involved as Erin, shook her head. 'I've no idea. Jay said it was going to be a very tricky operation. Kam's assisting. Renata and Bella are in there, too. I just popped my head round the theatre door.'

'And was it . . .? I mean . . . going OK?'

'Honestly, I don't know. I'm not really involved, am I? It's a dog. A big dog. A road accident.'

Erin groaned. She couldn't bear it. Poor dog, poor owner. But if anyone could work miracles it would be Jay.

The shop's doormat jingle-jangled again in the distance.

'Ah, customers,' Doug said happily, walking quickly across the yard, clearly delighted to escape further censure. 'Callum isn't great on haggling. I'll have to go and explain why we've got so much space in the shop. I might even have to start moving the stuff back if Krishna and co are staying out here.' He grinned at Erin over his shoulder. 'Have to go, love. So much to do. So little time.'

'I'll come with you.' Nalisha smiled slinkily. 'We can have a little chat about the statues.'

Doug beamed and stood back gallantly to allow Nalisha to pass, then he winked at Erin.

Erin watched them disappear through the Old Curiosity Shop's storeroom doorway then looked thoughtfully at the gods and goddesses.

'Right, are you lot listening? If you've got any influence at all, please, please, please, manage to remove bloody Nalisha from my life as soon as possible. Oh, I don't mean violently or tragically or anything—just let her have to dash off to her new job early or something. OK?'

'Who are you talking to, Erin?'

153

Erin jumped, then laughed guilty at Callum. 'God! Don't do that!'

Callum, all Converse trainers and designer pants showing above his jeans, gawped at the statues. 'Christ! They're random! Were you praying to them?'

'No, just thinking aloud.'

'My mum does that too. Old people seem to do it a lot,' he said kindly. 'I only came out here for a fag. Is that OK?'

'Fine. I'm just going.'

Callum lit a cigarette and stared at the statues again. 'Doug does get hold of some crap sometimes, doesn't he?'

Erin nodded. 'Oh, yes.'

'Mind,' Callum said, blowing a plume of smoke into the still air, 'that hot Indian woman is gonna buy them, I reckon. I sorta listened in. She wants 'em for the village hall.'

'*What?*'

'Ah.' Callum grinned. 'She's going to have a dance thing. Like the old line-dancing stuff what my Nan goes to, only Indian. She says she could use the statues for it.'

Erin laughed. 'Oh. My. God. An Indian dance class? Is that what she's planning? Bollywood comes to Nook Green . . . magic.'

Callum looked doubtful. 'You reckon?'

'Oh, yeah.' Erin grinned, delighted that the Old Curiosity Shop would no longer be crowded out by Ganesh and co, and wickedly thrilled that Nalisha was going to make a complete idiot of herself. 'I reckon. Thanks, Callum, you've just made my day.'

CHAPTER EIGHTEEN

'. . . so, we've been through everything, checked and cross-checked. All OK so far?' Abbie, the Swan's wedding planner and organiser, leaned across her very tidy desk, pushed her laptop away and tapped her folders. Her office was painted in creams and pale blues and had icy air conditioning. It was calm, and cool, and gorgeous. Much as she was. 'Good. So, we're all happy, are we?'

Erin nodded and squeezed Jay's hand. Well, she was. With the wedding arrangements at least. 'It all seems to be perfect, thank you so much. We don't want to make any changes at all. We just thought it was a good idea to check, and also to let you know that the flowers have all been ordered now and the table displays will be delivered here on the morning of the wedding.'

Abbie checked a white clipboard. 'Lovely. I know you wanted to use your own florist. And the rest of the decorations? You're still happy to go ahead with what we've arranged? In the marriage room and the dining room? No changes there?'

'None at all,' Jay said, sounding very relieved. 'And everything else we've ordered has arrived, has it?'

'It has.' Abbie nodded. 'And it's all totally gorgeous.'

'And you have the plans we drew up with the restaurant manager? For where everything has to go?'

'Absolutely,' Abbie confirmed. 'No need to worry about any of that. And we can't wait to get going on it, to be honest. It's so exciting to be doing a fusion wedding. So much more interesting than a few pink helium balloons and roses and a swirl of glitter on the table. And only three weeks to go now. You must be so excited?'

'We are.' Erin grinned happily. 'I've regressed to childhood and I'm counting off the sleeps.'

Jay chuckled, leaned across and kissed her cheek. 'Me too.'

'Ah, bless,' Abbie cooed. 'It's going to be an amazing day.'

Jay and Erin, now leaning together, looked at one another and beamed with a sort of contented almost-married smugness. Erin sighed happily. Yessss! No one could interfere now. It was all going to be absolutely perfect.

Almost . . .

'Oooh, yes.' Erin sat up quickly, 'There is one other thing. The seating plan—we need to make some changes.'

Jay frowned. 'Why?'

Erin leaned forwards. 'We've got twenty circular tables for ten guests on each, haven't we?'

Abbie nodded.

'And we've now got a possible one, and definitely another two, guests to fit in somewhere.'

'We have?' Jay frowned at her. 'Do I know them?'

'Kam's plus one. He's bound to bring someone— although I haven't got a clue who at the moment. And then there's Renata and her partner Julia. We can't leave them out, can we?'

'God, no—OK—so is there still room on one of the friends' tables?'

Abbie flipped through the folders, found the

appropriate page on her laptop, and tapped with a perfectly manicured nail. 'You want them seated together?'

'Please.' Erin nodded. 'They won't know anyone really, so at least they'll have each other to talk to until everyone gets nicely squiffy and all the social niceties go out of the window. Er,' she added quickly, ' not, of course, that our wedding is going to degenerate into a brawl or anything.'

Abbie smiled stiffly. Erin realised she'd had Botox. It was reassuring to know that all that poreless porcelain perfection wasn't natural. 'Of course not. But even the most strictly regimented weddings loosen up nicely towards the end, don't they? Right—well, at the moment, we have enough room on the table with your bridesmaids' plus ones—are they still unnamed?'

Erin chuckled. 'Mmm. Bella and Sophie are both going out with someone at the moment—that's a different someone, not the same one—but neither of them are looking to be long term and may well change a couple of times between now and the wedding day, so we've left it open. You can add Kam's nameless plus one there too. And who else is on that table?'

'Let's see, as well as the nameless plus ones, we've got . . .' Abbie scrolled down, 'Mrs Dora Wilberforce, Mr Ted and Mrs Mary Blundell, Mr Sid Duncan . . .'

'Village friends,' Erin said approvingly. 'And they're all quite old and friendly and most of them are patients at the surgery, so that should be a nice mix. Ideal for Renata and Julia.' She looked at Jay. 'OK with you?'

'Fine with me.' Jay smiled. 'So, that's everything,

157

is it? No more last-minute invitees? We're all done and dusted?'

'Well, now we're digging into the murky depths, there's going to be a bit of a hitch on my side of the first family table,' Erin sighed. 'Because obviously Uncle Doug isn't going to be with Gina, and we still really want Gina to come, but not to feel uncomfortable, so we don't want her sitting with Doug.' She looked at Abbie. 'There may be a bit of eleventh-hour rejigging needed there. I'm so sorry to mess up the plans.'

Abbie stretched another smile. 'Believe me, compared to most, your plans are inch-perfect. A few last minute pluses or minuses on the guest list are neither here nor there. We'll be able to sort out the tables right up to the minute you're making your vows. We've had to deal with far, far worse things than that.'

'I can imagine.' Jay pulled a face. 'Anyway, I really do think that's it for now. I can't think of anyone else we've missed, can you, Erin? I think we're all sorted at last.'

'Wonderful.' Abbie whizzed through her laptop. 'Remember, we're very flexible and you're paying us to make your day perfect so your wish is our command, as they say. Let's just have one last look while you're here. Oh yes, you're still agreed with going against the traditional set-up of splitting up the parents, and putting Jay's together on the groom's side and vice versa with yours, Erin?'

Erin nodded. 'We thought they'd all be more comfortable with that. More relaxed. They'll have hardly met before the wedding, and there'll be plenty of time to mingle later. And as my mum and dad live in Australia and I haven't seen them for ages, I really wanted them both beside me.'

'Absolutely understandable.' Abbie flicked a bit more. 'Right, I think that's it. No problems at all.'

'Wonderful, thank you.'

Erin stretched and gazed out of the window. The Swan's glorious grounds were fleetingly visible through Abbie's white vertical blinds. As soon as they left Abbie, she thought it would be lovely to stroll down to the river with Jay and sit on the bank, dabbling her burning feet in the cool ripples of the Maizey. The opportunities to be alone together without interruption were few and far between these days.

On the way to the Swan, they'd talked about the influx of the eighteen Indian gods and goddesses, and Nalisha's plans for them, and Jay had laughed. They'd also talked about Jay's lengthy and complex operation on the dog, which had, fortunately, been a resounding success, and the dog—Milo, a sort of greyhoundish-lurcher with heart-melting eyes, according to Jay—was now being intensively nursed by Bella and Renata, who were acting like proud mother hens with a new chick, and keeping his once distraught but now very relieved owner updated with hourly phone calls.

And now, all their plans were in place, and the rest of the afternoon stretched deliciously ahead in glorious freedom.

They were just shaking hands with a relieved-looking Abbie when there was a gentle knock on the door.

'Come in!' Abbie called cheerily.

'Hiya.' A young man with rainbow dreadlocks, which seemed to be at odds with his very severe Swan uniform, beamed into the office. 'Sorry

159

to interrupt, Abs. Is this the Boswell–Keskar wedding?'

'It is.' Abbie nodded.

'Great. Hoped I'd catch them before they left.'

Abbie blanched. 'Oh, heavens—we've just finished. Please don't tell me there's a hiccup?'

'No . . . well, not really.' Rainbow Dreads beamed some more. 'It's just that we've had a delivery of decorations for the wedding and I wondered if, um, Mr Boswell and Miss Keskar would like to see them before we put them into storage?'

'Other way round, actually.' Jay smiled kindly. 'And are you sure they're ours? I thought Abbie said everything we'd ordered had already arrived some time ago.'

'It has.' Abbie looked at her screen again, then frowned at Rainbow Dreads. 'Are you sure you've got the right wedding?'

Rainbow Dreads nodded. 'Totes, Abs. We haven't got another Indian-themed one booked, have we?'

'Ours isn't just Indian-themed,' Erin said quickly. 'It's fusion.'

'Call it what you like,' Rainbow Dreads said happily. 'This stuff is very Indian. It says so on the labels. They've got little Taj Mahals on them. And elephants. The labels, that is. And it says "Boswell and Keskar Wedding" all over it. Must be yours, huh?'

Jay nodded. 'Maybe it's something that was missing from our original order?'

'There was nothing missing,' Abbie said tersely. 'I've checked everything off personally.'

'D'ya wanna see it or not?' Rainbow Dreads

160

asked kindly. 'Or shall we just label it up to go with your other stuff until the wedding day?'

'No, no, we'll have a look at it,' Jay said. 'I'm really curious now. And if it isn't ours we can arrange to have it sent back.' He looked at Erin. 'OK with you?'

'Absolutely,' Erin said quickly, hoping they'd manage to escape from Abbie and Rainbow Dreads and the wedding decs that clearly weren't theirs so they could have time for some blissfully cool solitude down by the river.

Abbie stood up. Despite the heat and the fact that she was wearing the Swan's corporate navy-blue suit, Erin noticed she looked completely immaculate and unruffled, while Erin in her baggy white linen trousers and pink T-shirt felt like a limp rag. It simply wasn't fair.

'Right.' Abbie nodded at Rainbow Dreads. 'Leave it with me then. I'll show Jay and Erin to their storeroom.'

'Ain't in their storeroom,' Rainbow Dreads said cheerfully. 'Or anyone else's storeroom. Far too big for the storerooms. It arrived in a huge lorry. It's in the back delivery courtyard. We're gonna have to put it somewhere else.'

Erin closed her eyes. Please, please, please, don't let it be another load of life-sized Indian gods and goddesses.

'*Too big?*' Abbie sounded like Lady Bracknell decrying a handbag. '*Too big* for the storerooms?'

'Massive,' Rainbow Dreads confirmed. 'We was reckoning we'll have to use the big shed behind the swimming pool for it. The one where we store the marquees and that sort of stuff.'

Jay grinned. 'Then whatever it is certainly isn't

ours. We've only ordered garlands and small Ganesh statuettes and table lanterns and candles and some silky drapes in the appropriate colours for the wedding and—'

'Maybe we should just go and see what it is?' Erin squeezed his hand, thinking the sooner they got this latest problem out of the way, the sooner they could sit by the river and chill out. 'Then, if it's a mistake—which it obviously is—it can be returned to wherever it should go.'

'Come along then,' Abbie said briskly. 'Let's not waste any more time. Follow me.'

And with Jay and Erin and Rainbow Dreads in pursuit, she click-clacked efficiently out of her office, along several beautiful corridors, beneath various stone archways, and through a massively studded oak door.

Outside, in another of the Swan's lovely mellow-walled delivery courtyards, where even the one used for the most prosaic of purposes was awash with tumbling roses and fragrant borders and a fountain sending shimmering droplets across the golden flagstones, chaos reigned.

Several other corporately clad Swan employees, although none of them quite so eye-catching as Rainbow Dreads, stood round several highly loaded pallets. The towering contents were swathed beneath multiple layers of opaque plastic.

Erin and Jay simply stared. Erin's heart was sinking fast. Please, nooo—not more statues. Anything but more statues.

'What on earth is it?' Abbie practically stamped her stilt heels. 'Has anyone even looked yet?'

Everyone shook their heads.

'Whatever it is, it's definitely not ours,' Jay

162

whispered to Erin.

'Well—' Abbie looked quite fierce now as she scanned the Swan crowd '—who signed the paperwork? Aiden?'

'Yes, me.' Aiden, about the same age as Rainbow-Dreads, with razor-cut hair, an earring and an elaborate neck tattoo, nodded.

'And?' Abbie glared. 'What did it say? What have you signed for?'

'Wedding decorations for Boswell and Keskar,' Aiden ventured. 'And I checked there was no outside damage to the packaging and everything was intact. I ticked off the pallets. They all tallied. I do know my job.'

Erin wanted to give him a round of applause.

'Well, let's look then.' Abbie strode forwards. 'Goodness me, do I have to do everything myself? Anyone got a Stanley knife so's I can just nick the corner of this nearest one and see what it is?'

Several knives were offered. Abbie selected the nearest one, opened it and slid the point along one of the plastic layers, then lifted a corner.

Erin blinked, suddenly dazzled by a billion reflections dancing from a million prisms.

'What the f—. Er . . .' Abbie caught herself just in time, 'I mean, whatever is it?'

She slid the knife through some more of the wrappings. Golden columns, heavily embellished with droplet crystals and entire galaxies of star-burst sequins towered upwards.

'Jesus,' Jay groaned. 'It's a bloody *mandap*.'

'A *mantrap*?' Erin frowned. 'Are you sure? It's far too pretty and twinkly for a mantrap.'

'A *mandap*,' Jay corrected. 'It's an Indian wedding stage—a tent—like a mobile temple

163

within, well, anywhere you want to put it. There'll be umpteen pillars, all covered in jewels, and matching pedestals, and a pleated silk canopy roof dripping with diamanté, and gaudy thrones and swathes of gold-leafed organza for the walls.'

Oh, goody.

'Then there must be some mistake, mustn't there?' Erin looked hopefully at Jay.

Jay didn't look too sure.

Abbie was now slashing at the plastic sheets with all the ferocity of a serial killer on a spree.

Everyone else, including Rainbow Dreads and several of the Swan's visitors who'd wandered out of the public rooms and clustered round to watch, was silent, staring in awe as the madly exotic components of the *mandap* appeared incongruously in the old courtyard, glittering and dazzling in the scorching sun.

'Cool!' Rainbow Dreads breathed ecstatically. 'It's just like something out of *Bride and Prejudice.*'

Several of his colleagues tittered.

Jay frowned at him. 'You've seen that film? Really?'

'I've seen them all.' Rainbow Dreads nodded. '*Hide and Seek, Pyaar Impossible!, Bumboo . . .*'

Aiden nodded earnestly. 'See, me and David dance a lot, so we love all that Indian film stuff. Bollywood isn't gay, you know? Wicked music, cool moves and seriously hot women—what's not to like?'

'Er, nothing,' Jay said, straight-faced.

Erin stifled a giggle, knowing Jay had never seen a Bollywood film in his life.

Aiden grinned. 'We started off with street, because David saw himself as the next Ashley

Banjo, but everyone was trying to be Diversity and it got a bit crowded, so we started copying the Bollywood shapes. David's pretty hot.'

David, a.k.a. Rainbow Dreads, looked suitably proud.

'Really?' Erin smiled. 'Then you might like the new dance class that's starting in Nook Green, then. Strictly Bhangra, apparently.'

'Wow,' David looked animated. 'Really? Cool.'

'I'll let you know if and when it happens,' Erin promised, giggling inwardly. 'They'll definitely be short of men, especially men who can dance.'

'Ta.'

'Erin,' Jay hissed.

'What?'

'Forget canvassing for Nalisha's dance class for a moment. What are we going to do about the *mandap*?'

'God knows. It's, um, absolutely huge, although it's very pretty, but the Swan has a marriage room so we don't need a temple, even if we were having a Hindu wedding, which we aren't, so I suppose it'll have to be sent back to whoever bought it.'

Jay nodded. 'Exactly what I was thinking. It must be a mistake. It can't be ours. It'll have to be returned.'

Erin did a little mental happy dance.

Abbie stopped slashing and triumphantly waved a delivery note. She scanned it quickly then looked at them.

'Oh, it's definitely yours. It says so. What the f— um, devil we're supposed to do with it though, I have no idea. Oh, it looks as if there's a lengthy personal note in here, too.' Abbie shook out the paperwork and squinted at it. 'Oh, crap, over my

165

dead body.'

'What?' Jay frowned, his fingers entwining with Erin's and squeezing them encouragingly. 'What does it say?'

Wordlessly, Abbie handed the letter across to Jay. Erin stood on tiptoe and read it at the same time over his shoulder.

To dearest Jaimal and Erin
A little early wedding present, darlings. To be erected and used in the Swan's dining room following your ceremony. We understand now that the marriage service will, for legal licensing reasons, have to be boringly civil and fairly British, but we feel there's no need for the reception to follow the same trend. And as you've made it clear that you won't be around for an authentic next-day sanji, we thought this would bridge the gap. We know you'll adore it.
With much love, Mummy and Daddy

CHAPTER NINETEEN

'So Jay and Erin are off making the final arrangements at the Swan this afternoon, are they?' Gina said to Kam, as she collected glasses from a very busy, very hot, Merry Cobbler. 'It's all so exciting.'

Kam, leaning on the bar in his faded jeans and T-shirt and nursing an almost-finished glass of lager, laughed. 'They seem to think so. It'd scare me rigid.'

'Oooh—' Gina pulled a mocking face '—what a

surprise. Another commitment-phobe. You men are all the same.'

'And I'm deeply insulted.' Kam grinned and swirled the dregs of his drink. 'You've clearly misunderstood me.'

Gina chuckled. 'Isn't that what they all say? "She didn't understand me."'

Kam sighed and smiled. 'Oh, you're such a cynical woman. And I do hate being unfairly typecast.'

Gina, in skimpy orange shorts and a tight white vest, undulated her way through the crowded pub, clattered empty glasses onto the bar and raised her eyebrows. 'Unfairly? Really? Blame Jay then. He's told us all about your lady-killing activities. And I believe every word.'

She slipped behind the bar and served two customers with cider on ice before grabbing the empties again.

Kam laughed. 'You shouldn't believe everything you hear. And what I actually meant was, if I ever found my Erin, the love of my life, my soulmate, like Jay has, then I wouldn't want the sort of big bash British wedding they've chosen. That's all.'

'Really?' Gina stopped shoving glasses into the washing-up machine. 'And what would you choose? The full-on five-week Indian ceremonial fiesta? The sort of thing that you and the rest of your relatives seem to have been trying to persuade Jay and Erin into?'

'God, no.' Kam finished his drink. 'I've already told Erin I'd run a mile from all that. I'm happy to be Jay's best man—and I'm having a bit of fun winding him up by trying to convince him that he absolutely must have a tilak and a *sagai*, just as

167

Nalisha is teasing Erin about her mehendi—but no, that wouldn't be for me either.'

'Really? So you're on his and Erin's side in all this wedding malarkey, are you?'

'Totally.' Kam grinned wickedly. 'But Jay and Erin haven't really grasped that yet.'

'And wouldn't it be kinder to tell them? I know Erin's getting herself pretty screwed up over all the outside interference from Jay's family, and this close to the wedding it's the last thing she needs.'

Kam nodded. 'I've already told Erin I'm trying to work out a way to keep everyone happy.'

'Call me cynical, but from what I've seen, I reckon that's going to be impossible.'

'Oh, nothing's impossible. You'll all just have to trust me.'

'Trust you? Never in a million years.'

Kam laughed. 'Funny, that's more or less what Erin said, too. But seriously, I'll do my best to make sure they have the wedding they want.'

'Hmmm—and I'll believe that when I see it. Oh, sorry—have to go.' Gina smiled at the new influx of customers. 'Hello, lovely day—what can I get you?'

Sailing into landlady mode, Gina pulled pints and smiled to herself. Kam fascinated her, and not, she told herself severely, simply because he was smoking hot, either.

It'd be nice to have time to chat to him properly. To find out more about him. It was one of the reasons she loved running the pub. Gina was infinitely curious about everyone. But Kam's deepest darkest secrets would have to keep for another day. The Merry Cobbler was heaving and Sam and Pearl were both trying to serve three customers at once.

Gina served a very young couple with a Coke and two straws.

Poor little things, Gina thought, watching them fondly as they curled together in a far corner. They had so much to learn. Give them a few weeks and one, or both, of them would have their hearts ripped to shreds and their dreams trampled into dust, like she had. By Doug.

And the one before him.

Pushing her hair behind her ears and sighing, she reached for another clutch of empty glasses, took an order for three salads and a jacket potato with prawns for the outside tables, and gazed irritably at the empty ice bucket and the equally empty sliced lemon and lime tray.

'Let me do something to help.' Kam slid in behind the bar. 'It's madness in here today. I've never worked in a bar, so I'm probably rubbish at serving people or pouring drinks, but I can collect glasses, take food orders, operate the washing-up machine and get ice and slice lemons and—'

'Are you sure? You've been in surgery all morning. You must be exhausted.'

'I'm fine—and Milo is doing well now. And Bella and Renata will ring me if they need me to check on him before Jay gets back.'

'I thought vets were never off-duty? I know Jay works all hours and is constantly called out. Many's the time he's been in the middle of a meal here with Erin and had to drop everything and dash off.'

Kam nodded. 'It's hardly a nine-to-five profession, true. And yes, I'm on call, but my mobile's switched on, so unless I get a shout, I'm all yours.'

'Then you've got a job,' Gina said quickly. 'Dive

in. Pint pulling is easy once you get the hang of it—there's a slop bucket for your mistakes. Anything you don't understand, don't bother asking.'

Kam laughed, deftly removed the glasses from her hands and slotted them into the washer. 'So if I'm chief bottle washer, who's the cook?'

'Oh, that's me as well.' Gina grinned, pouring three pints of beer from separate taps at the same time. 'Why? Are you a closet Jamie Oliver?'

'God, no. Can't cook, won't cook, that's me. You need more staff. You can't do all this alone.'

'Bless you.' Gina swept the three perfectly poured pints of beer onto the countertop, took the money, played chopsticks on the till's buttons and dispensed the correct change. 'I'm not doing it alone. I've got Sam and Pearl. And I've probably been doing this since before you went to uni. It's second nature.'

'Nonsense. Oh, not the second nature bit, that's all too obvious. But the other.' Kam chopped lemons and limes into chunks. 'Unless you were serving in a pub while you were in infants school, of course.'

'Flattery,' Gina chuckled as she eased past him to head for the kitchen, then stopped again to serve the never-ending flow of customers, 'will get you everywhere. And, as you're a surgeon, could you slice the lemons and limes a bit more delicately, rather than hacking at them like that? They go further sliced.'

'OK. Sorry. But seriously, you need a break.' Kam sliced diligently, piled the fruit into the tray and reached for the ice bucket. 'Do you ever take time off?'

'Course I do. Every night at closing time.'

'You never have an evening off?'

'Very rarely. Not ever when it's busy like this.'

'Take one.'

'Are you mad? Look at this place.'

'OK—but soon? Take an evening off.'

Was he asking her out? As if! Gina didn't answer him. She could make a complete fool of herself here. Again.

'Impossible. Right—' Gina eyed the sea of customers '—who's next?'

Kam shrugged and disappeared to refill the ice bucket.

Phew.

One day though, Gina thought as she served non-stop on autopilot, maybe she'd take Kam's advice and surprise everyone and down tools for the night. Obviously not for a date with Kam, but maybe just to do nothing at all.

She'd taken evenings off for Doug occasionally, although their dates had usually been late-night affairs after closing time. Still, dates with Doug, late or not, were never going to happen again, were they?

Maybe one day perhaps she'd find a nice experienced couple to take over the Merry Cobbler for a fortnight and she'd disappear to the Caribbean . . . Well, OK, maybe not the Caribbean, that might be a little bit too ambitious for someone who'd never travelled outside Europe, but then, why not? What was to stop her? What was to keep her in Nook Green anyway?

Not Doug any more, that was for sure.

Gina pushed her way into the kitchen and set about microwaving a potato, assembling a prawn Marie Rose and tossing several salads.

171

Anyway, she would be taking a whole day off soon, wouldn't she? On the day of Jay and Erin's wedding she was closing the pub and not even bothering to look for a stand-in manager.

Most of the village would be at the Swan, either for the entire day, or at least the evening. There wouldn't be any customers here—and she'd have a whole day off.

Ah, bit of a flaw there . . . She'd been invited as Doug's plus one, hadn't she? And now she was Doug's minus one, and there'd be someone else in her place. And she simply couldn't bear that.

The realisation hit her like a solar-plexus punch.

'Sod it!'

She piled the plates onto a tray, walked backwards through the kitchen door and yelled unnecessarily loudly at Sam.

'Sam! When you've got a minute! Service for table eight outside!'

'And manners don't cost nothing neither.' Sam, wizened and lined, with little tufts of gingery hair appearing in odd patches—more oddly on his face than his head—giving him a sort of malevolent goblin look, grabbed the tray from her and started to shuffle off through the throng. 'Please and thank-you gorn out of fashion, has they?'

'Sorry, Sam,' Gina groaned as he disappeared. 'I'm turning into a bitch. And it's all Doug's bloody fault.'

Kam, squeezing past from the cellar with unopened bottles of Chardonnay in each hand, looked at Gina in surprise. 'Are you OK?'

'Sorry, yes.' Gina clutched a handful of empty glasses. 'Don't take any notice of me. I'm absolutely fine. What about you? Not too crazy for you, is it?'

'No way. I absolutely love it. I think I might have found my true vocation.'

'Good.' Gina smiled. 'Because I was wondering if you'd mind hanging on and helping out, at least until the rush dies down.'

Kam pushed the wine bottles into the chiller cabinet. 'I'll work for as long as you need me.'

'Thanks. You're a lifesaver. Oooh, sorry—yes, you are, aren't you? So that's a bit clichéd.'

'I love a good cliché,' Kam laughed. 'And actually, I'm really enjoying this. I'll be happy to help out anytime I'm free and you're short-staffed.'

'I think I'm just going to do a cartwheel of happiness,' Gina giggled. 'And you'll certainly bring the girls in. I can just see Sophie and Bella and the rest propping up the bar now, simply ogling. You'll increase my profits no end.'

'I'm looking forward to the cartwheel. Let me take those glasses . . . thanks. And I think you're overestimating my appeal.'

'Rubbish—you know Sophie and Bella both fancy you like mad.'

'I couldn't possibly comment.'

Gina looked at Kam, now bending down to restock the glass-washer. She really couldn't blame them. He was definitely the most divine man she'd ever seen.

The afternoon buzzed busily on and Kam, Gina noticed happily, was a very quick learner, the slop bucket wasn't too full, and the customers seemed to like him a lot.

Not just a pretty face then.

'So, where's Nalisha this afternoon?' Gina queried as she and Kam criss-crossed behind the bar. 'I know I'm probably the only one in Nook

173

Green who understands the friendship and doesn't find it odd that she's staying with Jay, but I hope she hasn't gone to the wedding planning with them.'

'No. Even more bizarre than that. She's apparently up at the village hall with whoever holds the key and is in charge, making arrangements to start a Bollywood dance class. Or at least that was what I heard from Callum Prior when he came in just now for a much-needed alcopop.'

'Really?' Gina laughed. 'We're going bhangra, are we? Well, it'll make a nice change from Billy Ray Cyrus. I might even be up for that.'

Kam grinned. 'And I'll come along and watch— but dance? No way? I've had my fill of Indian dancing. It was compulsory at every bloody wedding and party I've ever attended, and I've definitely got two left feet. Anyway, according to Callum, Nalisha has made arrangements with Doug to decorate the hall with some Indian statues and . . .'

Gina listened, while pouring shandies and lager tops, to some amazing cock-and-bull story about an entire army of life-sized Indian gods and goddesses and how Doug was involved.

'. . . oh, and sorry,' Kam looked contrite as he finished, 'Erin told me about you and her uncle. Maybe I shouldn't have said anything about that part of it.'

'No you're fine. Doug's history.' Gina smiled, creating the perfect creamy head complete with shamrock on the perfect pint of Guinness. 'And Doug always did have a way of buying completely useless tat and then somehow emerging quids in. The statues sound amazing.'

'They do, and if you could allow yourself a few seconds away from this place, you could see for yourself.'

Gina shook her head. She'd love to see these wondrous Indian statues, but it'd have to wait until Nalisha had managed to move them to the village hall. She could hardly drift over to the Old Curiosity Shop any more and just smile at Doug and say she was popping into the yard to admire his latest acquisitions.

She'd never be able to just pop over the green to see Doug again.

Goodness me. She gave herself a good mental shake. She'd always been a glass-half-full girl and no one, especially not Doug Boswell, was going to change that.

'According to Callum,' Kam continued 'Nalisha's been busy finding anyone with transport and is intending to move the statues into the hall later. We could go and help.'

Gina nodded slowly, savouring the 'we'.

'We could, couldn't we? Sam and Pearl could cope without me for half an hour or so, I'm sure. Yes, OK, let's do it.'

Was she going mad? She'd never left the Merry Cobbler on a whim before. Ever. She looked again at Kam and decided she was probably going very mad indeed.

'Great—and actually, there's something else I want to talk to you about, and that will be the perfect opportunity. Away from the pub and the customers.'

Gina smiled. 'That sounds—oh, what the hell?'

There was a sudden howl of anguish from the other end of the bar.

Gina stopped smiling. 'Oh, damn, could you go and see what Pearl wants, there's a sweetheart. I'm guessing it's a barrel change, so tell her I'll be there in a minute.'

'OK. But is changing a barrel something I can do?'

'I'm sure you'll be able to do it with your eyes shut—get Pearl to tell you what to do. She knows well enough, she's just not strong enough to manage it herself. Thanks, you're a star.'

Then feeling very hot, wondering what on earth Kam wanted to talk about, and pretty sure she was going to make a huge fool of herself—again— Gina tried not to think of exactly why she would be skiving off and going to the village hall tonight. She knew it had very little to do with the Indian statues . . .

Oh goodness, she thought, pouring two white wine spritzers, get a grip, woman. He's not interested in you. Never will be. Grow up.

Taking the money for the drinks, she pasted on her best landlady smile.

'All done—it was easy once Pearl told me what to do—and we didn't flood the cellar or anything. I've got another string to my bow,' Kam said happily as he came back up the steps with a simpering Pearl. 'And that's scary.'

'What?'

'The grimace. It's scary.'

Gina chuckled. 'Really? I was trying to look cheerful.'

'You always look cheerful. You've got a gorgeous smile. You really don't need to do the grimace thing.'

'It wasn't a grimace thing. It was a welcoming smile.'

'Looked like a grimace to me.'

She laughed. 'And I take back all I said earlier. You're no lady-killer if that's an example of your chat-up lines.'

'One of my best, actually. So, why were you grimacing? Was it because I mentioned Doug earlier? Or because you don't really want to come to the village hall?'

'No! I-was-not-grimacing. I'm smiling. There. Look. Now, what have we got there on the order spike? Four lots of fish and chips—OK—microwave here I come again.'

'Oh, if it's microwaved I can manage that.'

'Sadly, you can't. You need a basic health and hygiene certificate even to set foot in the kitchen. You just carry on being the best-looking cellar man I've ever had.'

'Duh!' Kam laughed. 'I spent over six years training as a vet, only to be labelled a cellar man, did I? But I do like the "best-looking" though.'

'Barmaid's patter,' Gina said quickly. 'Blarney. Stock phrases.'

'Damn. OK, I know my place. I'll just go and collect some more glasses then and remember to tug my forelock.'

Gina laughed as he vanished between the crowded tables and she started, again, to serve the never-ending stream of customers.

'Sam!' Gina hollered down the bar. 'G&T, ice and a slice, four times, for ladies in the beer garden! Sorry, I've got fish and chips to do and everyone else is busy.'

Sam shuffled along the bar and cleared his throat loudly as he reached for suitable glasses. 'Ah, right. No sweat, love. He's a good worker that Kam, but what did I tell you? It's getting more like bleeding

Bollywood every day in here.'

'Do-not-be-racist!' Gina hissed, heading for the kitchen.

'Ain't being racist,' Sam grunted, swiftly managing to assemble a clutch of exquisite G&Ts. 'Merely stating a fact. And now we're having Indian gods and what have you in the village 'all, saints preserve us.'

'Were you listening in on my conversation?'

'Nah. I ain't got time for that. Young Callum Prior told me. See, now that young N'lisha's got her claws into the Yee-Hawers, you mark my words, the whole village'll be like bleeding *Goodness Gracious Me* in no time.'

'Now you *are* being racist.'

'Nah, I ain't. That were Peter Sellers and Sophia Loren. It were lovely. Nothing racist there at all.'

'An entire bloody generation ago!' Gina hissed. 'Things were different then. Oh, let me get these fish and chips done. Sam, serve the ladies outside, and just try to be nice to people.'

'I allus try.' Sam grinned gummily at her. 'I'm a godsend, I am.'

Gina laughed and crashed through the kitchen door, now horribly aware that there was absolutely no one left behind the bar except Kam and Part-time Pearl who had been coyly telling him she thought she had a touch of malaria and was about to pass out.

She hoped Kam could cope on both counts and thought he probably could. Kam, she thought, as she counted out frozen cod fillets and grabbed a massive bag of chips, could clearly cope with anything.

Kam, Gina thought, smiling to herself, as she

took four plates from the dish-rack and spread the portions of fish and chips onto the plates and set the industrial-sized microwave, was pretty damn amazing.

And tonight, they'd be together at the village hall. Talking.

'Oh, dear,' she said to herself as she watched the microwave's timer on countdown. 'Gina—stop it right now. He's stunning and he knows it. You are on a very slippery slope.'

Somehow, she didn't seem to be listening.

CHAPTER TWENTY

Nook Green appeared deceptively tranquil. Twilight; still and warm; dusk sweeping across the chocolate-box scene in gentle shades of lilac and dove grey; a few lamps glowing in cottage windows; the air filled with the scents of stocks and honeysuckle; bats and moths giving spectacular ghostly aerial displays; several shadowy figures walking dogs on the green or sitting beneath the trees beside the Nook; fragments of laughter floating from the drinkers in the pub's beer garden.

A perfect summer's evening in a rural idyll.

Almost.

In the Old Curiosity Shop, Doug, having been very recently relieved of the Indian gods and goddesses by Nalisha, and having spent most of the afternoon and evening hauling everything back into place in the shop, sat exhausted and forlorn.

He slumped in the rocking chair in the darkness, and thought miserably there was nothing worse

179

than being alone on a Saturday night when the whole world was out there partying somewhere, that despite Nalisha paying him, he'd made a complete financial balls-up with the Indian statues, and also that, after his exertions, he was probably going to collapse and no one would find him for hours until it was far, far too late.

In the Merry Cobbler, Sam, left in charge of the late shift with Part-time Pearl who was now convinced she might have a touch of beriberi and might pass out at any minute, thought longingly of his cottage and his comfy chair and a cheese and pickle sandwich and a glass of stout in front of the late-night telly film. He couldn't wait for the clock to tick round to last orders and eyed the lingering customers with deep, deep loathing.

In the vet's surgery, Bella administered an already-much-improved Milo's night-time medication, was rewarded by a slobbery kiss and a madly wagging tail, and wondered sadly when it was going to be the right time to tell her current man— waiting impatiently upstairs for her in her flat—that he, like so many others before him, was no longer her Mr Darcy and therefore he might as well get out of her bed, get dressed and go home.

In the village hall, a very mixed bag, including Nalisha, Gina, Kam, Sophie, Callum, Callum's dad because he owned several vehicles, a few of the Nook Green yoof, and the entirety of the Yee-Hawers—all having been three-line whipped by Dora Wilberforce—puffed and sweated as they manhandled the last of the Indian gods and goddesses from the back of various vans and pick-ups.

Panting, groaning, straightening out aching

limbs, they smirked about the deal Nalisha had done with Doug Boswell, and hoped loudly that the statues would all fit inside the village hall.

Kam and Gina, taking a breather before the next stage of rehoming the gods and goddesses, and inspired by the awesome presence of the Lords Krishna and Vishnu and the rest, were now huddled in a corner also hatching a rather devious little plan of their own.

And in Jay's cottage, Jay and Erin were having a row.

They hadn't discussed the *mandap* since leaving the Swan. They'd decided, over a meal at the new Italian restaurant in nearby Daisy Bank, that discussing the *mandap* could wait until they got home.

Which it had. And now they were.

'No.' Erin paced up and down Jay's snug living room, her ponytail swinging furiously from side to side. 'It's got to go back. Seriously, Jay. We can't use it, we certainly don't need it, and we definitely don't want it.'

Jay, sitting on the edge of the deep-cushioned sofa in the dusk, ran his hands through his hair. 'I know, and I completely agreed with you before I knew it had been sent by my parents. Now, they'll be so hurt if we return it.'

'Then they shouldn't have sent it in the first place. I don't want to hurt them, insult them—whatever—either, but they should have asked us first.'

'They obviously wanted it to be a surprise. Look, I was thinking, maybe we could rearrange the dining room for the reception. It's a huge room. We could erect the *mandap* at one end and then—'

181

'No!' Erin sighed. 'I. Don't. Want. It. And if that sounds petty and childish and self-centred, then so be it. We've planned how the dining room is going to look—we've got everything organised, chosen the decorations, everything—and we need space for the evening reception as well. We need the dance floor and, well, the other things. There simply isn't room for the *mandap*. Please, just tell them thank you, but it doesn't fit in with our plans, and hopefully they can return it and recoup their money.'

'It'll have cost them a fortune.'

Erin stopped pacing. 'I know that, Jay. I'm not stupid. It's huge and beautiful, so that's very obvious. And I don't want to sound rude, but that's not our problem, is it? We couldn't have made it clearer that our wedding was fusion, secular, and already planned. Actually, I'm pretty insulted that your parents just assumed they could ride roughshod over everything we've planned. Both of us. Not just me. Or is it just me?'

'Is what just you?'

'The fusion ceremony? I'm not forcing you into a wedding you don't want, am I?'

Jay sighed and leaned back amongst the pile of sofa cushions. 'Of course not. You know that. But I really don't want to insult, upset or dishonour my parents in any way.'

Erin counted to ten. 'I know all that. I understand all that. But what about me? Is it OK to upset me?'

'Of course not.' Jay rubbed his eyes. 'You know I'd never ever make you unhappy, but please try to understand my position.'

Erin sighed, walked over to the window and

182

leaned her hands on the sill, staring out across the twilight garden. She hated arguing with Jay. He was always so laid-back, so easy-going, that they rarely disagreed about anything major. Yes, of course they'd had rows, like every couple, but they were few and far between, and usually brief and ended in hugs, kisses and laughter.

But this was different. This should be the happiest time of their life. This morning she'd known it was, and now, thanks again to his bloody family, it clearly wasn't.

'I do understand.' Erin continued to stare out at the garden even though she couldn't see it. 'I understand that you're having to choose between your parents and me. No, don't say anything. I don't mean that in some sort of threatening way. I mean, one of us is going to be upset over this damn *mandap*—and the rest of the Indian stuff—and it's easier for you if it's me, isn't it?'

Jay laughed. It didn't sound very funny. 'Strangulated syntax, but I think I get your drift. And yes, OK, I suppose so. Because you're here, and you're far more reasonable, and because we can discuss it.'

'We're not discussing it, though, are we?' Erin didn't turn round. 'There's nothing to discuss. We're just going round and round in damn circles. You know, as well as I do, that whatever intentions your parents had for sending the bloody *mandap*, we are not going to use it.'

'I love my parents. I don't want to hurt them.'

'Oh, God,' Erin sighed. 'I *know*. It's one of the reasons I love you so much. All this honour and respect and decency and cherishing your elders— all stuff that seems to have been lost from our

183

culture—but this isn't about being disrespectful, Jay. This is about being sensible. And about standing up for me. I want you to stand up for me.'

'I'll always stand up for you,' Jay said quickly. 'Although you rarely seem to need it. You're perfectly capable of fighting your own battles. Oh, look, maybe if we went up to Solihull tomorrow and saw Mum and Dad and talked to them face to face, it would be easier.'

'No it wouldn't. They'd just be lovely, and charming, and delicately upset, and I'd feel like a complete cow and you'd turn into the dutiful son, and then we'd both give in. We'd end up compromising and having things that neither of us want. Jay, either you ring them and explain to them about taking back the *mandap*, or I will.'

'I don't think that would be such a great idea, either.' Jay frowned. 'Look can we leave it for tonight, it's getting late and—'

The phone on the small coffee table beside the sofa rang loudly.

Both Jay and Erin, used to hearing only their mobiles, stared at the landline with some astonishment.

Jay leaned across and lifted the receiver. 'Yes? Oh God, is it? Sorry, Bella. Yes, I'm home now. I'll switch it on. No, I haven't been drinking so I'm fine to drive. Will I need the pick-up? Oh, Kam's got it anyway—OK. And is Kam still on call too? Great— get hold of him then please, and tell him to pick me up at the cottage. I'll just go and grab my kit.'

'Emergency?' Erin asked.

Jay nodded, already on his feet, pulling his phone from his pocket. 'Yes. Bella was trying to ring me on my mobile but it's been switched off. I hadn't switched it back on since we were with Abbie.'

Erin smiled. 'Just go and sort out whatever the emergency is.'

'Picton's Farm, apparently according to Bella. Cattle. Needs two of us. I'll just go and get my stuff and Kam's from the surgery and meet him outside.' He kissed Erin briefly. 'Will you let yourself out and lock up? Or you could stay if you like.'

Erin sighed. She'd like very much indeed. But she wasn't going to stay. Not while Nalisha was there. Sod it. 'I'll go home. Hope everything goes OK at Picton's. Take care. I'll see you in the morning.' She stood on tiptoe and kissed him. 'I love you.'

'I love you too. Madly. You know that. And I'm sorry about the *mandap*.'

'Me too. We really shouldn't fall out over Elton John's gazebo, should we?'

Jay laughed and kissed her. A lot.

They stared at one another then reluctantly Jay moved away. 'I'm going to have to go.'

'I know. So am I, before Nalisha arrives from wherever she's been tonight. I'll see you in the morning.' She kissed him again. 'Jay—sorry.'

'Me too. I love you.'

And he was gone.

CHAPTER TWENTY-ONE

In the village hall, Gina stood back and admired their handiwork. The Indian gods and goddesses stood proudly round the room, looking like imperious, gaudy and ever-so-slightly out of place

185

wallflowers waiting to be asked onto the floor at a Saturday night dance.

'I think we can call this a success, don't you?' Gina blew her tousled curls away from her face. 'It looks amazing.'

'It does,' Kam agreed. 'And you're OK with my little, um, idea?'

'I think your little idea is a brainwave.'

'Good.' Kam smiled at her. 'And of course it'll have to be our secret.'

'Oh, of course.'

'And, as we haven't got much time, we'll have to have regular assignations to check and counter-check the development of our plans?'

'Can't wait,' Gina laughed, noticing the rest of the villagers casting dubious looks in their direction. 'We'd better join the others before they start noticing that we're whispering in corners and get paranoid.'

Nalisha, now workmanlike in jeans and a white shirt knotted at the waist and showing an awful lot of toned midriff, smiled happily. 'Thank you to everyone for helping, and for agreeing to come to my first dance class.'

Dora Wilberforce, her hair awry and her second-best summer frock—droopy beige with bottle-green geometric splatters—covered in dust, clapped her hands in delight. 'They look wonderful. Such a clever idea of yours, young Nalisha, to bring a bit of life back to the village hall.' She chuckled. 'And I do like getting one over on Doug Boswell.'

Sid Duncan nodded vigorously. 'It's a great idea, duck. We needs a bit of summat different, and these here gods and goddesses are right perfect as a backdrop for your Bollywood sessions.'

Nalisha smiled some more. 'As long as the other people who might use the village hall don't object to being watched over by the Lords Krishna and Vishnu and the rest.'

Gina shook her head. 'I can't see it being a problem. Quite the opposite in fact. They'll be a talking point. Something no other village hall has got.'

'That's true,' Dora Wilberforce said vigorously. 'It might even help to bring people back here. There's no youth club any more, and the Cubs and Brownies and what have you all meet in the new community hall at Bluebell Common now.'

'Ah, and Weight Watchers has moved to Daisy Bank,' Mary Blundell added. 'And the mums and toddlers group go to Maizey St Michael. It's mostly just been us line dancers that have used the hall here for ages.'

Sid Duncan broke in. 'And we need to get them—and more—back again. And this might just do it. There's no one nosier than villagers—so as soon as they thinks we've got something special here, they'll come back in their droves, you see. And as the village hall key holder, Nalisha, my duck, anyone who has any complaints will have me to answer to.'

'Great.' Nalisha smiled. 'So, I'll get some flyers printed off on my laptop and we'll all meet up here next Tuesday evening, at about half past seven for our first Bollywood dance lesson?'

'Too right, dear,' Dora Wilberforce said cheerfully. 'I for one can't wait. It'll make a nice change from side-stepping and thigh-slapping to "Achy Breaky Heart" for the umpteenth time.'

'And bloody Zumba,' Mary Blundell said with

feeling. 'I signed up for Zumba at Maizey St Michael. Dr Jermaine said it was good exercise. Daft bat, she is. Ten minutes in and I thought I was going to die.'

'That's because it's meant for the youngsters,' her husband Ted said. 'You're way too old for it, duck.'

'Believe me, she isn't.' Sophie laughed. 'I started going to Zumba, too. With Erin and Bella. We all came out of the first class scarlet-faced, panting and unable to walk straight. I think we'll all happily swap it for a bit of Bollywood. And we'll have to ask Renata and Julia to come along as well. You'll have a full house of ex-Zumba-ers on your first Tuesday, I reckon, Nalisha. Natalie, who runs the Zumba classes, will be after your blood.'

Gina laughed. 'Mmm, I fell foul of Zumba too. Although at least mine was nothing to do with Natalie's class—it was in the privacy of my own room with my Wii Fit.'

'Really? I'd have paid good money to see that.' Kam grinned.

Gina smiled cautiously back.

OK, they were friends, and now they had a shared secret, but was he *flirting* with her? No way. She knew this was a very one-sided attraction that could—as always—end in tears. It was doomed from the start. Not, she told herself quickly, that there was going to be any start as such.

Kam must be at least three years her junior, and gorgeous, and able to have any woman he batted his long, long eyelashes at. Why on earth would he be interested in her? Someone who was rattling towards forty and with a rubbish track record when it came to men? Of course he wasn't flirting with her. He was probably just being kind.

Get a grip!

Gina shook herself. 'Well, I'll be here. If Sam and Part-time Pearl cope tonight, they can do their worst for a couple of hours in the Merry Cobbler next Tuesday.'

'And, as I said earlier, you can definitely count me out,' Kam said with a laugh. 'I've had enough bhangra dancing to last me a lifetime. It was the least cool thing any teenage boy could do, in my opinion.'

'Shame on you,' Gina teased. 'I was so looking forward to seeing you in the full regalia, strutting your stuff.'

'Not going to happen.' Kam grinned at her. 'But I'll come along and watch you, as promised. I can give helpful hints from the sidelines.'

They smiled at one another again. Gina, feeling suddenly uncomfortably warm, looked away first.

'Anyway,' Kam said, 'I'd better be getting the pick-up back to the surgery and cleaned out ready for its proper purpose. I must admit I never expected to have Hanuman, Saraswati, Indra and Ram as passengers in the back of my truck.'

'They really are spectacular.' Gina moved away from him, and walked among the towering statues, stroking the fabulously coloured plaster saris and jewels and dupattas. 'Wonder why on earth Doug bought them in the first place?'

She stopped and smiled to herself in surprise. She'd actually managed to say the D word without the little pain jabbing under her ribs and taking her breath away.

'I gather he thought they were going to be smaller and make a window display,' Nalisha said.

'Doug Boswell's loss—our gain.'

Gina gave a mental cheer and was just about to say something else when Kam's phone rang.

He grabbed it and listened.

'OK, Bella. I'm on my way. Yes, I'll pick Jay up. Has he? Good. Thanks.'

Gina paused in admiring the haughty faced and heavily earringed Bhuvaneshwari. 'Call-out?'

'Yes, afraid so. Would you like a lift back to the pub?'

'No thanks.' Gina shook her head. 'It's only a quick walk across the green. Hardly worth the trouble and you've got far more important things to do. But thanks for the offer. Have you got your key if you're going to be late?'

'Yes thanks. Hopefully we won't be very long and I'll be back before you lock up.'

They all watched him go.

'God,' Sophie, said wistfully, 'he's soooo bloody fit.'

Gina nodded to herself. He certainly was.

'Kam's a bad boy,' Nalisha said softly. 'But with a good heart.'

'Mmm, I'm sure he is,' Gina sighed.

She could have sworn Bhuvaneshwari was laughing at her with a knowing look in her heavily kohled eyes.

'And didn't you and Kam ever . . . well . . . you know?' Sophie looked at Nalisha. 'I mean, with you knowing the family so well, you and Kam must have been thrown together all the time. I don't know how you could resist him.'

'Easily.' Nalisha smiled. 'Kam's my friend but definitely not my type. There's no chemistry there at all. Anyway, I was far too much in love with

190

someone else when I was a teenager to give Kam a second thought. And since I've grown up—well, nothing's changed. I know he's simply not for me.'

Gina, realising she'd been holding her breath, shook her head, moved away from the statues and clapped her hands. 'OK, everybody, are we all done in here? Good. So, who's for a last drink on me to say thank you?'

She was almost flattened in the stampede for the door.

CHAPTER TWENTY-TWO

'Why are you sitting in the dark?' Erin, having found Uncle Doug's cottage empty, apart from Florence sprawled out luxuriously on a windowsill in the still-stifling dusk, peered into the Old Curiosity Shop. 'Oh, and you've moved everything back in again. Blimey. On your own?'

'Yes,' Doug said wearily. 'All on my own. Like I've been all day. Like now. Alone again— naturally.'

'Do not quote Gilbert O'Sullivan's saddest-ever song.' Erin avoided the bell-ringing doormat, manoeuvred her way through the once-again crowded shop and perched on the edge of a rickety table. 'And don't go all maudlin on me.'

'Yeah, well.' Doug moved in the rocking chair. They both creaked. 'Maudlin's how I feel. Along with knackered and pissed off.'

'Poor old thing. And where are the gods and goddesses?'

'Nalisha has taken them to the village hall.'

Erin laughed.

Doug frowned. 'It's not a laughing matter.'

'No, sorry. It's just you made it sound like she was taking them for an outing or to play bingo or something. You mean, Nalisha's installed them in the village hall already?'

Nalisha certainly didn't hang around.

'She has. I was just glad to see the back of them.'

Erin smiled. 'Agreed, they possibly weren't the best purchase you've ever made. Never mind, you'll have to make your money back on something else. You've made mistakes before and put them right in your next deal.'

'Yeah, whatever. Nalisha had half of Nook Green with her to help move the statues. I thought I was going to have to pay them to take the damn things away. I felt it was a bonus that I got away with that. And anyway, why are you here? Where's Jay? How did the Swan go?'

'Best not to ask,' Erin sighed. 'Long story. Which I might just tell you over a pint. I desperately need a drink and you look like you could do with one or several.'

'I could do with a dozen. But I haven't been over to the pub since . . . well, for ages. I'm not the most popular person in the Merry Cobbler at the moment, am I?'

'Your own fault. And I think Gina is far more grown up than that. Although you were a complete prat to finish with her. She's so gorgeous. Blimey, Uncle Doug, she turns heads whereever she goes and the pub's always full of men with their tongues hanging out. She's absolutely sex on legs. Some other bloke will snap her up within days and then you'll be sorry.'

Doug groaned. 'And that's supposed to make me feel better, is it? Don't you think I've been over and over it? I know how damn sexy and beautiful Gina is. And such a lovely woman, too. Funny and kind. Maybe I was a little bit hasty.'

'A damn lot hasty.' Erin shook her head. 'But if Gina has got any sense she'll realise she's had a lucky escape and find someone who really loves her, and appreciates her.'

'I know I've hurt her. I shouldn't have been such a fool.'

'No, you shouldn't. But it's too late now. I doubt if she'd take you back even if you got down on your knees and begged.'

'Oh God, you're right—I can't face her.'

'Of course you can. Don't be such a wimp. Come on, shift yourself, we'll just manage to catch last orders if we hurry.'

'I'm way past hurrying.' Doug eased himself out of the rocking chair. 'But I could certainly do with a drink. And as long as you'll protect me if Gina lunges for my throat.'

'Not a chance,' Erin snorted. 'You brought that on yourself. Deal with it. Now come on before the pub closes.'

'Do I look OK?' Doug ran his fingers through his floppy hair.

Erin laughed. 'How vain are you? As far as I can see in this light—or lack of it—you look fine. Like a sort of shattered, scruffy, careworn, ancient surfer boy. And Gina, if she's got any sense, will be so over you that she won't give a toss what you look like. So, for pity's sake, come on!'

Doug locked the shop and, with arms linked, they walked across the green.

Shadowy figures were still hunched on the banks of the Nook and on the rustic benches and beneath the trees. Lazy, splintered conversations and the odd shout of laughter pierced the purple dusk. As they walked, Erin briefly filled Doug in on the events of the day.

'. . . and I don't want to talk about any of it again tonight,' she said as they reached the Merry Cobbler's crowded beer garden. 'OK?'

'Whatever you say, love,' Doug said with a shrug, as they walked through the propped-open door and into the furnace heat of the bar, 'but surely, this *mandap* thing—'

'Not another word,' Erin said fiercely. 'And I'm buying. Beer?'

Doug nodded, looking round the crowded pub. 'Please. And call me chicken, but I'm going to sit outside here in the garden. OK?'

Erin sighed, nodded, left him at an outside table and fought her way to the bar.

It was like a sauna.

'Yers?' Sam glowered at her. 'Time's getting on, nearly last orders. What can I get yer?'

'A pint of bitter, please, Sam. Draught. Uncle Doug's usual. And a pint of cider for me. Loads of ice. Thanks.'

'Damn silly new-fangled idea,' Sam muttered as he rattled glasses, 'putting ice in cider. Makes the drink go flat. Anyone knows that.'

'Makes it lovely and cold and refreshing though,' Erin said cheerfully, scanning the many faces in the pub. Most of the village seemed to be there— Part-time Pearl was busy serving Dora Wilberforce, and both the Blundells and Sid Duncan and the rest of the Yee-Hawers, as well as an awful lot of the

194

Nook Green yoof, but there was no sign of Nalisha. Thank goodness. 'And a long cold drink is exactly what I need after the day I've had.'

'You got problems with yer wedding?' Sam slid the drinks across the bar, took the money, dispensed the change. 'That don't surprise me. Too many people trying to interfere. It wouldn't have happened if your mum and dad were still here, or your nanna.'

Erin frowned. 'They wouldn't have made any difference, and anyway, no, we haven't got any problems with the wedding. Who said we had?'

'No one d'rectly. I just keeps me eyes and ears open in here, that's all. Seems to me this village is turning into *Mumbai Calling*—and all of 'em only want to do things their own way, as I sees it. And as it's your wedding, they should be told to sling their 'ooks.'

As this was far too close to home for comfort, Erin nodded but said nothing. Unfortunately, Gina had overheard.

'Sam! You stop that this minute! I've told you before about making racist remarks. There are laws, you know.'

'Ain't racist. Ain't breaking no laws. Simply telling the truth. I never said nothing bad about any of 'em. And I wouldn't. Young Jay and Kam and that there Nalisha is all smashing. And Jay's mum and dad, they're the salt of the earth. Polite and know what's what. Decent people. Could do with more like 'em round here. Ain't got nothing to do with race or colour or creed—got everything to do with interference. Sticking their noses in where it's not wanted. So there.'

And grumpily he staggered along the bar to serve

195

the next customer.

'He's not wrong.' Erin grinned at Gina. 'He's just the only one brave enough to say it.'

'You're right, but for God's sake don't let him know that. He'll be unbearable. Anyway, do you want to know what I've been doing tonight?'

'Pulling pints and warming lasagnes?'

'Much more exciting than that.'

Erin listened as Gina described the rehoming of the Indian gods and goddesses and the plans for Nalisha's first bhangra-cum-Bollywood dance class being held on Tuesday.

Erin thought that an ear-blasting influx of Bollywood via Dhanush, or Bhangra courtesy of Panjabi MC—see, she thought triumphantly, she *had* listened to Jay—in Nook Green village hall was going to be fantastic, even if it was all down to damn Nalisha, and wondered vaguely if they might like the *mandap* to go with the gods and goddesses.

'So, how did things go today? At the Swan? With all the last-minute wedding plans?'

Erin pulled a face. 'Don't ask. I was mad to think my wedding would be different to everyone else's and go without a hitch.'

'Oh really? I'm so sorry.'

'I'm sure it'll all work out OK in the end,' Erin said, actually pretty sure that it wouldn't, but too tired to care tonight. 'Now I ought to get this pint outside before Uncle Doug dies of dehydration.'

'Too scared to come in, is he?' Gina raised her eyebrows.

'Yes, actually.' Erin laughed. 'And serves him right. He behaved appallingly towards you. I'm so sorry.'

'It's not your fault. You warned me often enough

what he was like. I was silly to think it would end any other way.' Gina smiled. 'Made a bit of a fool of myself there, and not for the first time. But, you live and learn, don't you? I'm over it and I shall be more careful next time.'

'Next time?'

'Figure of speech,' Gina said quickly. 'Nothing more. But tell Doug he can come into the pub. I'm not going to deck him.'

'Shame.' Erin grinned. 'It might bring him to his senses. And, honestly, Gina, I think he's regretting it now.'

Gina held up her hands. Lots of bracelets rattled round her wrists and twinkled in the bar's overhead lights. 'Tough. Seriously. I was silly enough to fall in love with him. You know how much I loved him. And he didn't feel the same way. There's no going back. My only regret is that I won't be there to see you and Jay married.'

'What? Of course you will. Why wouldn't you be?'

'Because I was only going with Doug, wasn't I?'

'Rubbish. You're our friend. You just put on your slap and your best slinky dress and a knockout hat and make him realise what he's missing—with knobs on. Don't you dare think you won't be there.'

Gina beamed. 'Erin, that's made my day. Honestly. I was thinking earlier that I wouldn't be there and feeling really sorry for myself. And actually, there's something I really have to tell you—'

'Gina!' Sam barked. 'Stop all that jibber jabber, there's a good girl, and come and give us a 'and along here. Some of us do have homes to go to, and I'd like to see mine afore sunup. Pearl's gorn orf again. She's out the back crying. Thinks she's caught the Marburg virus from a dodgy pork pie.'

CHAPTER TWENTY-THREE

After a mainly sleepless night, where any dreams had been of the fretful naked-in-public or running-and-getting-nowhere variety, Erin eventually dozed off just as it was getting light.

It seemed only about five minutes later that Florence landed with a very ungentle whoomp on her stomach. Despite Erin pushing her away and explaining it was still the middle of the night, Florence kneaded and purred and demanded breakfast, so Erin, discovering that it was actually past nine o'clock, groaned, rolled out of bed and staggered groggily downstairs.

After grabbing her phone from her bag, she fed and watered Florence with one hand while checking her messages with the other.

Jay had texted her when he and Kam had returned from Picton's Farm in the early hours. Jay's text had been romantic and funny. Erin hugged the phone to herself as she made coffee and sashayed round Uncle Doug's cottage, giving the wedding shoes their Sunday morning workout.

The row was over. The falling out about the *mandap* was forgotten. Together they'd sort it all out. Sunday was a free day for both of them. They'd sneak off somewhere and have some time to be alone. Away from everyone and everything. Especially Nalisha.

So she texted back that she'd be ready in less

than an hour and would make a picnic. Nalisha, Erin decided, definitely wouldn't like picnics—not that she was being invited—but Erin loved them. So did Jay.

Pretty sure that even early on a Sunday morning Nalisha would look like she was prepared for a *Vogue* cover shoot, Erin quickly showered and dressed in the skimpy denim shorts that Jay always said made her bum look like Kylie Minogue's, and a turquoise vest because she knew it matched her eyes, and replaced the wedding shoes with glittery flip-flops. Then she used the straighteners on her freshly washed hair, left it swishing silkily round her shoulders, and applied full going-out make-up.

There! She surveyed herself in the mirror. It was OK. No, it was more than OK . . . It might not be smouldering Indian gorgeousness, but it was pretty damn good.

She shoved bread rolls and cheese and fruit and anything else that caught her fancy in the fridge and larder into a cool box.

Then she tiptoed back upstairs to check on Uncle Doug.

Doug was clearly having an uncharacteristic lie-in, or maybe, more truthfully, nursing a mammoth hangover. Doug's mates had managed to ply him with far too many pints of beer in far too short a time the previous night. Erin had helped him home in the darkness, staggering and stumbling across the green.

His earlier self-pity had turned to an alcohol-induced mawkishness and Erin had been glad to shove him into his bedroom and close the door, where he was, much to her relief, still snoring rhythmically.

Erin, now reassured that Doug was still alive, left him a note to say she'd probably be out all day with Jay and could he make sure Florence had plentiful supplies of biscuits and water, and then lugged the cool-box picnic across the Sunday-silent green towards Jay's cottage.

Please, please, please, don't let Nalisha be up and dressed and ready to make some catty remark.

The door to the cottage was standing open.

Erin grinned to herself. Jay was clearly as keen as she was to get away for the day and have some lovely, relaxing, romantic time together. Maybe, she thought, they could even escape before Nalisha woke up.

Yay!

Then her heart plummeted. Again.

Jay was in the doorway, not at all suitably dressed for al fresco frolics, and surrounded by veterinary paraphernalia.

'Erin.' He pulled her towards him. It was rather awkward because of Erin still holding the cool box, which bumped irritatingly against their legs and prevented them getting very close to one another. 'You look amazing.'

'Thanks. But I think it's going to be wasted, isn't it?'

'Sod it. Yes. I'm so sorry.'

'Oh no . . .' Erin dropped the cool box, stepped over it, and looked at him. 'Not a long call-out? Please tell me it's not a long call-out?'

'Sorry,' Jay said again, taking her face between his hands. 'Oh God, you have no idea how sorry I am. I got the call about five minutes ago. Gerry Banscroft. You remember him? Runs the new one-man-band practice out across the other side of

Bluebell Common? We met him at that barbecue last summer?'

'Yes, yes.' Erin nodded. 'Nice bloke. Pretty wife. Lots of kids. And?'

'He's got a really tricky emergency op. He's never carried out this type of surgery before. His locum's got tonsillitis, his nurse has a stomach bug and the Sunday agency replacement is scrub-only. He needs a hand.'

Erin sighed. 'Yes, OK, of course—but what about Kam? Couldn't he go?'

'He's already gone back to Picton's Farm with Renata. He has to make sure the procedures we carried out last night are working and he needs to blood test some of the other cattle and—'

'Sssh.' Erin smiled, then stood on tiptoe and kissed him. 'I get the picture, even if I don't like it.'

'And,' Jay added, kissing her neck, 'don't forget that Gerry Banscroft is standing in for me here on our wedding day, and his wife is doing all the animal-feeding, including Bella's menagerie and, more importantly, Florence—so I do owe him a massive favour.'

Erin sighed. Back of the net, Gerry Banscroft. No question.

'Go. Now. You've got to. The picnic will wait. And so will I.'

Jay kissed her again. 'Now I know why I love you so much. And why I don't want to go.'

'Go!' Erin, suddenly giddily swamped by a wave of love and lust, pulled reluctantly away from him. 'Please.'

So he went.

And she stayed and watched, waving and blowing kisses, as he collected his medical bags, unlocked the car and drove away. Then she turned and angrily kicked the cool box.

'Damn! Sod! Bugger!'

It hadn't made her feel much better. Was there, she wondered, as she wandered disconsolately back across the green lugging the cool box, anything worse than an empty Sunday stretching ahead when every person you knew was happily doing something else?

She glared with unnecessary ferocity at two small boys with fishing nets wading in the shallows of the Nook.

Sophie and Bella, she knew, had gone home to their respective parents for Sunday lunch and family pampering. Gina would be working in the pub. Doug was going to be massively hung over. Everyone in the entire world was doing something.

Apart from her and Nalisha . . .

Of course she could do boring stuff. Like opening up the shop and waiting for customers. The Old Curiosity Shop was a bit ambivalent about Sunday opening times and Sunday was always Erin's day off. Doug rarely missed Sunday altogether, though. Especially at this time of year when there were plenty of tourists in the Berkshire villages looking for something to spend their money on. Or there was always paperwork to catch up on, or tidying her knicker drawer.

None of it held any allure at all.

Oooh, sod it!

Then Erin brightened.

Hah! There was still the *mandap*! Yes, Jay had said he'd deal with it, but he had other more important things to concern him now, and she was at a loose end. It was clearly something she could tackle. And she would.

Much happier now she had something to concentrate on, Erin dumped the cool box back in Uncle Doug's kitchen, grabbed her mobile, and scuttled into the garden, finding a nice shady spot under the lilac tree.

With Florence on her lap, she kicked off her flip-flops and dialled Deena and Tavish's landline.

Deena answered. Erin sighed. She'd hoped it would be Tavish. Tavish would have been so much easier to deal with.

With only a brief mention of Nalisha and Kam, and after the initial polite enquiries about health and work, and Erin explaining that Jay was on an emergency call-out so wouldn't be sharing the phone call, Deena mentioned the wedding plans in general and how she and Tavish hoped that things were all going well.

This was exactly the cue Erin needed.

'The last-minute wedding plans—well, yes they're going perfectly, thanks. Jay and I went to the Swan yesterday to finalise the seating plans and—'

Deena giggled. 'And did you get a lovely little surprise, darling?'

'Well, we certainly got a surprise. Oh, it was really kind of you, but the *mandap* must have cost a fortune and—'

'Oh, a mere trifle, darling. If this was going to be proper Hindu wedding we'd have had to pay much, much more than we have. We were simply delighted to be able to contribute something at last.'

'Yes, and it's really, really kind of you, but you know we didn't need you to contribute anything.

And of course the *mandap*'s gorgeous, and under different circumstances it might have been exactly what we wanted, but—'

'As I said in the note, Tavish and I realise you and Jaimal can't actually get married in the *mandap*, not with the secular strictures of your ceremony, but maybe for the reception . . .'

'No, I'm sorry. I don't want to sound ungrateful, and I do appreciate how much this means to you, but we've already got our reception planned and organised. The *mandap* can't fit into the dining room at the Swan and—'

'Nonsense. I've been there. There's plenty of room. And I must say, our side of the family would be absolutely thrilled to see a wedding *mandap* erected. You and Jaimal can sit on the thrones after your ceremony, brief and rather dull as it clearly has to be, and be showered with all the lovely presents and—'

'Oh, please listen . . . I'm sorry, but we really can't use it. We're not going to be sitting on thrones, and we had already said we didn't want wedding presents from anyone because we've got everything we could possibly want and—'

'Well, of course, darling, we all understand there are to be no boxed gifts—no one these days wants several toasters or bath towels in the wrong colour, that's all so old hat, but it's traditional at Hindu weddings to give gifts of money and sweets and jewellery, and our side of the family will all still expect to do this, even though your wedding is, um, fusion.'

'Oh, I know about the sweets and things—that's a lovely tradition and of course, we'll adore having loads of sweets—but not in the *mandap*, and we want nothing else. Nothing at all. Not money or presents or anything. Oh, I know it must sound so churlish to you, but it's *our* wedding.'

'Yes, you've made that perfectly clear on several occasions. Quite frankly, I'd like to talk to Jaimal about this.'

'I'll get him to call you later. When he's back. But he'll only say the same thing. I know he will. He certainly doesn't want to offend or hurt you, and neither do I, and I know you were being kind and generous, but you really shouldn't have sent the *mandap* without asking us first.'

'And if we'd done that, you'd have said no, wouldn't you?'

'Well, yes, but—'

'Well, there you are then. That's why we didn't tell you. Anyway, darling, how long before Jaimal gets home?'

'I've honestly no idea. He's only just left. But—'

'No, let's not say any more. We don't want to fall out, darling, do we? Not so close to the wedding. Look, the *mandap* is yours to do with as you will. It's our gift to you. If you feel you really can't use it for your reception, I'll have a little word with Jaimal and we'll have to come to some other arrangement.'

'But, seriously, we know how expensive it was. If we arranged to have it sent back to you, surely you could claim a refund?'

'No. That's simply not possible. And I must say that I find your absolute refusal of a well-meant gift extremely insulting.'

Ouch. True. Erin winced. Back-pedal. Back-pedal—now.

The silence lengthened. Florence stood up on Erin's lap, stretched and jumped down to

205

find a more comfortable and cooler spot in the herbaceous border.

'Er . . .' Erin mumbled, 'yes, OK, I'm sorry. I apologise. That was very rude of me. It was just a shock, seeing this huge tent thing, er, the *mandap*, when we weren't expecting it. And honestly, I didn't want to insult you, but we simply can't fit it into our plans.'

'Apology accepted, darling.' Deena sounded as if she might be smiling. 'And as it's yours now, and you're a very resourceful girl, I'm sure you'll be able to find a home for it somewhere, won't you?'

'What? No—I mean . . . Oh, er, yes, probably, possibly, maybe.'

'Lovely! Now, tell Jay to ring me when he gets back, darling. And Tavish sends his love and we'll see you very, very soon. Byeeeee, darling.'

Erin snapped the phone off. And sighed. Heavily.

Oh, bugger.

That hadn't gone the way she'd planned it all, had it? How on earth had she capitulated so easily? Now, somehow, she'd agreed to keep the *mandap*.

Great.

And what the hell was she actually going to do with something that looked like a bad-taste circus tent?

Oooh, sod it.

'Erin?' A voice called over the garden gate, interrupting the gloomy train of thought.

Erin peered through the luxurious foliage but couldn't see anyone. 'I'm here—in the garden.' She scrambled to her feet. 'Hang on.'

'OK—I'm just so glad I've found you,' the voice continued. 'I've been ringing your cottage doorbell but no one answered.'

Clearly Doug was still sleeping off his hangover.

'Just hang on a tick. I'll unlatch the gate. It sticks a bit.'

Erin, having padded barefoot across the lawn towards the gate, squinting against the blinding white reflected light of the overhead sun, reached the gate and fiddled with the catch.

'Ah—hi.'

Nightmare.

Nalisha, looking even more stunning than ever, if that was at all possible, in ridiculously high sandals, skinny pink trousers and a fabulous floaty, strappy top, was smiling at her.

'Good morning.' Nalisha raised her enormous designer sunglasses slightly. 'Oh, Erin, you look absolutely gorgeous. Like a proper girl for once. Are you going somewhere nice?'

'I was.' Erin ignored the slight. 'But not now.'

'Oh, good. I'm not interrupting then. And is Jay here? There was no sign of him when I got up.'

'Sorry. He's been called out.'

'*Again?*' Nalisha frowned. 'On a Sunday?'

'Animals, like humans, can't actually plan their illnesses and accidents to fit into a five-day week.'

'No.' Nalisha shrugged. 'I suppose they can't. Honestly, I had no idea Jay was so busy. When do you two ever see one another?'

'We manage,' Erin said quickly. 'We're used to it now. It's part of our life.'

They stood in silence for a few seconds. The sun beat down relentlessly. Erin realised that Nalisha was going nowhere. She opened the gate.

'Come in, please. Grab a seat—there's a table and chairs under the trees. Can I get you a drink?

Or something to eat?'

'No food, thank you, but a drink would be lovely. Oh, what a perfect garden.' Nalisha sank on to a chair, looking like some glorious exotic flower blooming incongruously in an English meadow.

Florence, being a complete traitor, immediately emerged from the herbaceous border, entwined herself round Nalisha's legs, then jumped onto her lap.

'Oh, sorry—that's Florence,' Erin said quickly, remembering that whatever Nalisha had said to Bella, she really didn't like animals. 'Just shove her off.'

'She's OK at the moment.' Nalisha was tentatively tickling Florence under her chin and being rewarded by a lot of headbutting and purring.

Sighing at the treachery of women and cats, Erin headed irritably for the kitchen.

CHAPTER TWENTY-FOUR

An hour later, they were still there, sitting round the table under the shade of the lilac trees, drenched in the garden's heavy drowsy scent, halfway down their second jug of iced orange juice.

They'd discussed the purchase and rehoming of the Indian statues, and Nalisha had talked endlessly about her plans for Bollywood dance sessions. Erin, wishing Nalisha would spontaneously combust, had somehow mentioned the *mandap*, and Nalisha had sympathised but agreed that very few people ever bested Deena, and that she was sure they'd find a use for the *mandap* somewhere, and then they'd discussed Erin's small and scattered family, and Kam.

And then they moved on to Jay.

The previous revelations had clearly merely skimmed the surface.

Erin now knew everything there ever was to know about Jay's childhood, his teenage years and his subsequent growing up. All the gaps had been neatly filled in by Nalisha. Erin had learned about girlfriends he'd never mentioned; about holidays he'd taken with Nalisha—and other friends, too, but it was only the fact that Nalisha had been there that stuck; about his madly extended family—'we all become honorary cousins or aunts or uncles, it makes it so much fun when we all get together at parties'; and about how totally, totally wonderful Deena and Tavish were. Again.

It all simply served to reinforce Erin's ever-growing anxieties and insecurities. Nalisha knew more about Jay than she did. Far, far more . . .

Erin also now knew more about Nalisha being a corporate lawyer than she'd ever thought possible. And about living in California. And about dozens of other marvellous and amazing things Nalisha seemed to have managed to cram into her life.

None of it helped lift Erin's plummeting self-esteem one little bit.

In fact, by now completely demoralised—well, there honestly wasn't much mileage in her three average A levels, several very average office jobs before the Old Curiosity Shop, several very average youthful love affairs, and a very average life in the village until Jay arrived in it, was there?—Erin sighed heavily and wished yet again that Nalisha

209

had never, ever set foot in Nook Green.

'But you're the lucky one.' Nalisha stretched lazily. 'You live in this fabulous place, you have a great life, no one has ever pressurised you to do something you don't want to do, you've stayed true to yourself, you're only three weeks away from your fabulous wedding, and, most importantly, you and Jay are marrying because you love one another. You have a wonderful future to look forward to. Together.'

'Yes, well, put like that, it does sound pretty good. And I've always been happy with my life. But what about you? Don't you have a boyfriend? A partner? I mean, you must. I mean, look at you . . .'

'There have been one or two,' Nalisha laughed. 'But no one who ever made me want to give up my singledom. Some of them were even of my own choosing.'

Erin frowned. 'You mean your parents suggested suitable men for you? Set up introductions? Blimey, I thought that all went out ages ago.'

'You'd be surprised. Indian parents can be very persuasive. And, of course, as soon as we were old enough, my parents always wanted me to marry Jay.'

Ouch!

Erin felt the whole happy foundation of her world start to slide away. She sucked in some warm, sticky air. 'Really? Um, I thought you were just good friends.'

'We were. Are. But to my parents—and to Jay's—that's the perfect basis for a marriage. Even now. I know it sounds archaic, but if families can marry off their children to the children of their friends, they're generally ecstatic.'

Oh. My. God.

'And you?' Erin had to know. 'Did you feel that he was—or could be—more than a friend? Did you want to marry him?'

Nalisha swirled melting ice cubes in her orange juice. 'If he'd asked me I'd have said yes.'

Erin swallowed. There was a roaring in her ears. This really wasn't supposed to be happening.

'Because you loved him?'

'Yes.'

Feeling sick, Erin exhaled. Get a grip, she told herself. Jay is marrying *you*. You! Jay could have asked Nalisha to marry him at any time, couldn't he?

And if he had . . .

Oh . . . Erin sighed. How happy everyone would have been with that, wouldn't they?

Jay and Nalisha: the perfect beautiful Indian couple.

And they'd have been married in a temple, and embraced all the millions of poojas and weeks of parties, and they'd have definitely had the biggest damn *mandap* in the entire world, wouldn't they?

And probably white horses and painted elephants and a million Bollywood dancing girls and strutting peacocks and all the other Indian trimmings.

Jay and Nalisha would have had the perfect full-on Hindu marriage.

And there'd have been no mention of *fusion* at all.

And everyone in Jay's family would have been sublimely happy.

So, did that mean that Nalisha was still in love with Jay? And had Jay ever loved Nalisha?

And, oh blimey . . . had they ever been *lovers*?

Erin closed her eyes. What on earth was happening to her lovely, happy, secure life? Suddenly everything was being turned upside down. It was only three weeks to her wedding. The wedding that only a short time ago was so organised and planned and perfect.

Now the poojas and Deena's interference and even the *mandap* seemed pretty unimportant.

Erin stood up quickly. She simply couldn't sit there with Nalisha and imagine her and Jay *together*. She just couldn't.

'Um, excuse me . . . I need the loo, and I'm just going to grab my phone. Er, Jay might have finished the op early and left a message, and, um . . .'

Once back in the cool of the kitchen, Erin leaned her hands on the work surface and counted to ten.

It was OK. It *was* OK. Even if Nalisha loved Jay, it didn't mean Jay loved Nalisha, did it? Or ever had. Did it?

Erin grabbed her phone. Her fingers shook as she texted: 'Hope all going ok. I'm at home. Need you. Love you. Always. E xxx'.

Then she pressed send.

'You OK?' Doug drifted into the kitchen and peered at her. 'I must've overslept.'

She nodded. 'Mmm. I'm fine. Just texting Jay. Forget the note, we didn't go—he had a call-out.'

'Right. And you don't look OK. You look very pretty and done-up, but you look sort of . . . worried.' Doug sloshed water in the kettle and winced at the noise. 'Ooh, that hurts.'

'Not surprised. And I need to tell you something.'

'Oh, God, did I do something disgusting last

212

night? It didn't involve Gina, did it?'

'No and no. I've got to talk to some before I go mad. Listen . . .'

And she told him all about Nalisha. Everything. It had taken some time as Uncle Doug kept interrupting and asking questions.

'So.' he sipped his coffee and frowned. 'After all that, she's still here now, in the garden?'

'Exactly.'

'OK, but honestly, Erin, love, you haven't got any need to worry. Even if she is one of his exes, he's marrying you. He adores you. And she isn't here to split you up, is she?'

'No, of course not. Well, I don't think so, but she's so bloody devious, I'm not sure about anything any more.'

'Then have a bit more self-confidence, love. We all have pasts to deal with. Jay's bound to have had lovers before he met you, isn't he? But they're not the ones he's marrying, are they?'

'No, but she's so gorgeous. How can he prefer me to her?'

'Because he does. And you're gorgeous too. Oh, Erin, love, don't let doubts creep in and spoil the last few weeks before your wedding. This should be the best time of your life. You've got enough going on with Deena, without getting screwed up over Nalisha—who I've always thought was lovely, by the way.'

'I know. Everyone thinks she's lovely, but she's a cow. Trust me. I know. And now I just think it's karma. I was so bloody sure that our wedding was going to go smoothly, no hitches, no problems . . .'

'And it will.'

'Will it?'

'Of course it will. Jay didn't even ask Nalisha to marry him, did he? He asked you. Because he loves you. You. Not her.'

Erin hugged him. 'I know, but I just feel so, well, jealous when she talks about all the stuff they've shared.'

'Shared. Past tense. She's his past. You're Jay's present and future.'

Erin blinked. 'Wow, you're actually quite perceptive, aren't you? Even with a hangover. Thank you.'

'You're welcome. Oooh . . . Actually, I still feel pretty crap. Have you opened up yet?'

'No. It's Sunday. That's your job. And you do look totally awful.'

'Ta. Well, I'm going to go and say good morning to Nalisha and nurse my hangover in the garden and hope the black coffee works quickly. Then I'll open up the shop. While you—' he looked sternly at Erin '—stop looking like the sky's just fallen in and remember that neither Nalisha, nor Deena, nor anyone else can spoil your happiness, unless you let them. OK?'

'OK. Ooh, there's my phone. Please let it be Jay.' Quickly, Erin grabbed it and checked her messages. 'Oh shit. The operation is still on-going, and he doesn't know when he'll be home.'

Doug shrugged. 'Sorry, love. Look, you let me deal with Nalisha. I'll take her on a guided tour of the shop or something. Maybe suggest a spot of lunch somewhere? I'm sure you can find millions of things to do, can't you?'

'Oh yeah,' Erin sighed. 'Millions.'

And, feeling about as awful as it was possible to get, she slowly trudged upstairs to start tidying her knicker drawer.

CHAPTER TWENTY-FIVE

On Monday morning, Erin ran her hands over the writing desk. It was silky smooth and the intricate inlay shone from years of loving attention with beeswax. It would look wonderful in the Old Curiosity Shop, and would also be an ideal piece to photograph and display on their website.

It would, she was sure, be snapped up very quickly.

'Are you happy with the price?' She smiled at the elderly owner of the desk. 'And you're absolutely sure you want to sell it?'

Sod it. She groaned inwardly. Why had she said that? Why did she always say that? Uncle Doug was right, she was probably far too soft-hearted to be a serious negotiator.

'Too right I do, my dear. I'm off to sheltered housing. Lovely little flatlet I'm going to have, with a nice pocket-sized garden and a communal social room and a warden on tap. Can't wait. I've given my children first dibs of the furniture I didn't want to take, but none of them could find a home for this old desk. Too big and old-fashioned for them. So, yes, the price is just right.'

'Lovely,' Erin said, relieved. 'And I hope you'll be very happy in your new home. Now if we could just do the paperwork, and I'll arrange for Mr Boswell to come and collect the desk with his van when it's convenient for you. Shall I ask him to ring you to fix a time?'

'Yes, that would be grand. Any time in the next couple of days, my dear. I'm not moving out 'til Thursday.'

'And it's Monday today, so that gives us plenty of time. That's fine then. So, if you'd just like to sign here, and I'll sort out the money, and we're all happy, aren't we?'

Deal done, Erin stepped outside into yet another scorching cloudless blue and gold morning. The little semicircle of honey-coloured houses in the pretty village of Daisy Bank shimmered. Erin hoped that the desk's owner would have an equally lovely vista in his new home.

She thought, as she eased herself into the small oven that was her hatchback, that this morning's deal had been a particularly pleasant one. No tears, no sob stories and, most importantly, no spiders. If only all deals could go so smoothly, with such a happy conclusion.

Yay!

Then again, she thought, as she eased the car along Daisy Bank's narrow lanes and headed towards the Nook Green road, she deserved something pleasant after the weekend from hell, didn't she?

If she'd thought *mandap* Saturday had been bad, then Sunday had been truly awful. OK, Doug had mercifully kept Nalisha out of the way, but he really needn't have bothered. Jay hadn't returned until nearly midnight and had just sent a 'Sorry. Love You. Goodnight. xxx' text.

And she had the tidiest knicker drawer in Berkshire.

Anyway, she thought now, as she parked outside the Old Curiosity Shop and scrambled from the car, things—as Tony Blair had once rather foolishly said—could only get better. Surely?

'Erin!'

She turned. And laughed.

Jay was standing in the shadowy gap between the shop and the cottage.

'Are you hiding?' She grinned delightedly at him.

'Sort of. Waiting for you, actually, without anyone deciding they need to involve me in something. Please, please tell me you've finished work for this morning.'

'OK. I've-finished-work-for-this-morning. Just got some paperwork to file and—'

'Leave it.' Jay reached out and pulled her against him, running his fingers up her bare arms. 'I'm so sorry about yesterday. Did you have a nice day?'

Brilliant, she thought. Finding out all about you and Nalisha through the ages. Finding out that Nalisha loves you. Finding out that she would marry you.

Best day ever.

'It was OK.'

'Good. Look we haven't had any time alone together . . . well, it seems for ever.'

'Don't I know it.' Erin shivered with delight as Jay's fingers gently stroked her neck.

He moved away slightly. 'Sorry if I stink. I've just chucked off my scrubs and I'm still a bit scruffy and possibly still slightly smelly.'

Erin looked at him and thought he'd possibly never looked sexier, with his black hair awry and falling into his eyes, and in his jeans and T-shirt.

She pulled him back against her and held his face between her hands. 'You look fabulous and you smell of warm lemons.'

'The delightful aroma of post-op antibacterial hand-wash.' He laughed, then kissed her thoroughly. 'And I really should go away more often if I'm going to get this sort of reception. I know I haven't seen you for twenty-four hours— imagine what it would be like after *months.*'

'Don't even think about it. Sorry if the text sounded desperate yesterday—I was just a bit peed off. Did it go OK?' Erin murmured into his shoulder. 'The operation? Really?'

'Perfect. Gerry was delighted. We made a good team. He's a great surgeon.'

'So are you.' Erin kissed him again.

He laughed. 'You might be a bit biased.'

'Only slightly. Oh, I've got something to tell you.'

Jay frowned. 'That sounds bad.'

'It's not *that* bad . . . well, it's good really, I think.'

'Intriguing.' Jay laughed and held her at arm's length. 'Have you been practising a burlesque routine for our wedding night and you want to run it past me?'

'No.'

'You've bought several new bikinis for the honeymoon and want to give me a fashion show?'

'Nope.'

He sighed. 'Bugger. OK—so go on, tell me.'

'I've spoken to your mum and we're keeping the *mandap.*'

Jay grinned. 'Your decision or hers?'

'Well, it sort of sounded like mine, but I don't think it was really.'

'That sounds about right. I'm just glad it's sorted out. We'll worry about what to do with it later.'

'I thought you'd be pleased. It was stupid to fall out over it.'

'It was and you're fabulous,' he whispered. 'And I love you. Shall we just make a break for it now?'

'Sorry?'

'That's why I'm here. I've got no more patients until two-thirty. Bella's gone to the post office in Newbury. Kam is somewhere on a farm call and Sophie and Renata have gone home for lunch.'

'And Nalisha?'

'Has driven off in her BMW, roof down, on a sight-seeing tour of quaint Berkshire villages.'

'She didn't want you to go with her as tour guide?'

'She did. I said I was far too busy, and that I had other plans.'

Erin smiled up at him, insecurities and jealousies momentarily forgotten, and suddenly dizzy with delicious wantonness. 'Ah, right. Which means?'

'We have at least an hour, and my cottage is empty . . .'

CHAPTER TWENTY-SIX

'So, how are things going with the Jay and Nalisha reunion?' Gina asked Erin on Monday evening in the Merry Cobbler. She was working at one end of the busy bar while Sam and Part-time Pearl dealt with the other. 'Are you really OK with it?'

'What else can I be?' Erin swirled her cider. 'She's here for the duration. Jay's happy to have her here.'

'And you're not?'

'Truthfully?' Erin sighed. 'No. I wish she'd never set foot in Nook Green. Come on, Gina. How would you feel? She's beautiful and she's part of his past, and she's far better suited to him than I'll ever be.'

'Don't be so daft.' Gina slammed a glass down on the bar counter. 'You and Jay were made for each other. And I know you have your doubts about Nalisha, but I've always found her to be friendly and . . .'

'That's the trouble.' Erin drained her glass. 'She fools everyone. Oh, I'm not going to go over all this again. You like her, I don't.'

'Well, oh hang on.' Gina served two men in khaki shorts and vests with pints of IPA at the speed of light. 'OK—where were we? Oh, yes—yes, I do like her. She's always been very pleasant to me. Are you sure you're not just imagining things?'

'Because I'm jealous?' Erin shook her head. 'No, believe me, I have every reason to loathe the sight of the woman. Now, can we talk about something else? I just wanted to check with you that you're OK for my hen night? You will be able to get away, won't you?'

'Definitely.' Gina rapidly polished glasses and bent down to stack them beneath the bar. 'I have absolutely no intention of missing it.'

'Good.' Erin grinned. 'Because it's only thinking about the positives that's keeping me going.'

Gina smiled. 'Maybe I shouldn't say this, but it's a bit old-fashioned having the hen night only a week before the wedding, isn't it? Most girls seem to arrange it at least a month before to get over the hangovers.'

'I know. But I wanted to include my mum, and she won't be here until ten days before the wedding.'

'Ah, of course.'

Erin sighed happily. 'Oh, I can't wait to see her. And I'm so looking forward to my hen night—all elegant, nothing drunken or rowdy. A fabulous meal out in Newbury, insane cocktails, everyone in their best dresses.'

'Sounds perfect.' Gina mixed three vodka tonics. 'And what about Jay?'

'Jay and his stags are going to the casino in Reading. I have a feeling Nalisha would prefer to be with them.'

'Is she coming to yours?'

'God, I suppose she'll have to.'

'Look, Erin, can I just say something to you? About Nalisha—oh, I know you don't want to talk about her, but honestly, I think men and women *can* be just good friends. My best friend when I was growing up was the boy next door. We never thought of one another as anything but friends, and no, he wasn't the stereotypical gay either. He had girlfriends and I had boyfriends, but when we didn't we went out together—for meals, to the cinema . . . That's why I know that Jay and Nalisha's relationship is purely platonic. I've been there.'

'You're lovely, and I hope you're right.' Erin glanced at her watch. 'Oh God, I'd better fly. We're having supper at Jay's cottage tonight—Nalisha's cooking an Indian banquet.'

'Sounds lovely.' Gina poured Guinness. 'If a little ménage à trois.'

'She's invited Doug to even things up. And no, she's not even slightly interested in him before you ask. He's besotted of course, but I can tell she's just playing. Oh, sorry, maybe I shouldn't have said anything.'

221

Gina took the money for the Guinness and laughed. 'No, it doesn't matter to me at all, love. Not any more. I'm completely over it.'

'Good—and I hope he makes a total prat of himself over Nalisha and finds out what it feels like.' Erin grinned. 'Now I really must fly. See you!'

'See you, love. Have a great evening.'

Gina watched as Erin hurried out of the door and laughed to herself. There was no pain whatsoever when she talked about Doug. Result!

Gina was still smiling as Kam walked through the door.

'That's a great smile.' Kam, still managing to look devastating in his crumpled scrubs, pushed his way through the crowded bar. 'And just what I need tonight. I'm a man in need of cheering up.'

'You look like a man in need of a drink,' Gina said, her heart thumpety-thumping as she reached for a glass. 'Bad day?'

'Long, hot, messy, complicated.'

Gina slid the pint across the counter. 'No, put your money away. It's on the house. Staff perks.'

'Are you sure? Thank you.' Kam drank half his beer in one go. 'Oh, wow, that's better. You're a star. It's been like working in a sauna all day. I do wish this heatwave would break.'

'So do I. But not yet. Not until after the wedding.'

Kam grinned. 'Everything revolves around this wedding, doesn't it? Every conversation has something to do with the wedding. I've no idea how Jay and Erin are staying sane.'

'I'm not sure they are.' Gina took an order for food from a family who looked like they were about to melt. 'And Erin's just been in here talking about the hen and stag nights. I'm hoping they'll go without a hitch at least.'

Kam laughed. 'So do I. I'm sure it will be great—once they get over the shock. You didn't say anything? And your side of things is all organised?'

Gina raised her eyebrows. 'No, I didn't, and yes it is. Yours?'

'All sorted. We make great co-conspirators.'

'We do.' Gina looked away quickly. 'But I hope it doesn't all go pear-shaped. Poor Erin is stressed enough as it is. I mean, all the wedding plans were going really smoothly until—'

'Until our side of the family got involved?' Kam asked. 'Tell me about it. I've seen so many of my cousins practically on their knees by the time their wedding comes round because of all the family fall-outs and disagreements over the arrangements, and so many celebrations to be organised, and all the resulting arguments and stress—that's why I'm going to elope.'

Gina's heart plummeted. She hoped that her expression remained interested and neutral. She hadn't seen Kam with anyone, but that didn't mean he hadn't got a girlfriend. In fact, because he was so darn heartbreakingly beautiful, he surely *must* be seeing someone.

'Are you? Any time soon? With anyone I know?'

'God, no. I just mean, when—if—I find the right person and want to get married, I'd run a mile from all this exhausting, non-stop organised mayhem.'

Phew.

'Mmm, you did mention something about it before.' Gina hated herself for feeling so relieved. It was madness. Complete and utter madness. 'Right, now before my customers starve to death,

I'm just going to pop into the kitchen and nuke two veggie platters, a sausage and mash and a cottage pie. If you need a refill, just help yourself. Oh, and what about food? Shall I do you something? Or are you on call? Or going out?'

'Jay's on call tonight.'

'Is he? Nalisha's cooking him and Erin—oh, and Doug—an Indian banquet. I hope he gets time to eat it.'

'So do I. Can't believe I haven't been invited.'

'You could always invite yourself. You and Nalisha would make a lovely couple.'

Kam laughed. 'Nalisha's gorgeous, but she doesn't do it for me. She's far too high-maintenance. Can't be doing with someone who'd spend longer in the bathroom than I do. And that's a joke by the way.'

'Is it? Really?'

'Yeah, well, almost.'

Gina looked away. 'So, shall I do you some food? Or are you going out?'

'I'm so knackered I'm just going to have a shower and collapse on the bed with the windows open and the fan going full blast and watch whatever rubbish is on telly.' Kam grinned. 'But please don't tell anyone. It'll ruin my playboy reputation. If anyone asks, I'm out clubbing with a horde of A-list supermodels. So, yes, food would be great—but you don't have to.'

'I know I don't. But as I'm going to be in the kitchen anyway, one more meal won't make much difference. Tell you what, shall I concoct you a ploughman's platter?'

'Ploughman's would be out of this world.' Kam smiled. 'You do the best ploughman's I've ever tasted. Thanks, Gina. I don't know what I'd do without you.'

Gina drifted into the kitchen and tried really hard not to smile. It didn't work. Her mouth curved upwards at the corners and she danced towards the microwave.

*   *   *

Half an hour later, after swiftly redoing the worst ravages of her make-up, squirting on a quick spritz of Chanel No 19, removing her apron and making sure her shorts and top weren't beer-stained, and running her fingers through her curls, Gina carried the tray upstairs.

The very quick makeover, she told herself, had everything to do with maintaining proper landlady standards and not appearing to look like a wreck in front of her late-night punters, and absolutely nothing to do with Kam.

Nothing at all.

Hah!

She'd added another couple of bottles of beer and a fresh glass to the vast ploughman's platter. Kam would be starving, she was sure. He'd had a very long day and probably not stopped to eat. Jay, she knew, always maintained that he only kept his lean taut shape because there was simply never enough time to have a meal during the day. It was bound to be the same for Kam.

And Gina had always liked feeding people. It was one of the pleasures in her life. Oh, not just zapping pub grub through the microwave, but devising and cooking spectacular meals—particularly for Doug. Doug always loved her cooking.

How very strange . . . Gina paused for a second on the twisting staircase. She honestly could think of Doug now without any twinge of regret at all. She exhaled. She only hoped the cure wouldn't hurt more than the affliction.

Because, stupid as it was, Kam had been her cure.

But as long as he never, ever knew, then it would be OK, wouldn't it?

God, it was still so hot. From the landing window, the village seemed to be simmering in the rapidly falling darkness. Nearly closing time, thank goodness. The weather was fantastic for trade, but lousy for her state of exhaustion.

Gina laughed to herself. Thinking mundane thoughts about the weather and the pub was her way of blocking out the one thing that kept trying to sneak in. And frequently succeeded.

She tapped lightly on Kam's door. No reply. But she could hear the low murmur of the television. He was probably still in the shower.

Pushing away the very pleasant, and distinctly arousing, thought of Kam, soapy and naked beneath a torrent of water, Gina knocked again.

Still no answer.

OK, she thought, she'd just leave the tray. His double bedroom also had a tiny sitting area with a table, two chairs and a small sofa. The best room the Merry Cobbler had to offer. Of course.

Gina pushed the door open slightly and called softly. 'Kam?'

The room was in darkness apart from the oddly strobing effect of the television. The windows, looking across the green, were flung wide open, and murmurs of laughter floated upwards from the beer

226

garden on the stifling air.

Gina click-clacked in her high-heeled sandals across the polished floorboards, carefully avoiding the ones she knew from her housekeeping experience squeaked in protest when anything heavier than a feather escaping from the goose-down duvet landed on them.

Placing the tray on the table she turned round to leave.

Oh!

Kam was stretched out on the bed. Asleep. And naked. Well, she assumed he was naked. The white Egyptian cotton sheet pulled up to his waist contrasted with his smooth, butterscotch skin.

Gina just stared. Dear Lord, he was so beautiful.

His black hair, still damp from the shower, was spiky against the pillow. The long eyelashes threw dark crescents across the killer cheekbones.

Gina drank in the total physical perfection of him.

He was, without doubt, the most stunning man she'd ever seen in her life.

His chest rose and fell in deep sleep. His lips were curved slightly in a smile. Before she could stop herself, Gina moved silently closer to the bed. She could smell the glorious faint clean scent of his lemon shower gel and shampoo.

She leaned down and gently kissed his cheek.

'What the f—?' Kam shot up in bed, blinking.

'Oh God, er, sorry.' Gina stepped quickly backwards. 'I'm so sorry. I didn't mean to wake you.'

Kam shook his head sleepily. 'Gina? What . . .?'

'I, um, brought your food.' Gina wanted to die on the spot. 'It's on the table. Sorry for disturbing you.'

'Did you just kiss me?' Kam rubbed his eyes.

'What? Er . . . Good Lord, no. I was just, um, making sure that . . . er . . . you were OK, you know,' Gina floundered.

'Maybe I was dreaming?'

'Maybe you were.' She grabbed the lifeline. 'Or, um, more probably it was the breeze from the open window.'

Kam stared drowsily at the window where the curtains hung motionless in the stultifying night air, pulled the sheet up to rib level and exhaled. 'Yeah, maybe. OK, thanks a million for the food. Really kind of you. I hope I'll stay awake long enough to eat it now you've gone to all that trouble. Goodnight, Gina.'

'Um, yes . . . Goodnight.'

Gina hurried from the bedroom and shut the door behind her. Then she leaned against it and closed her eyes.

Oh. My. God.

He knew. She knew that he knew.

Oooh. She groaned in total embarrassment. What a bloody, bloody stupid thing to have done.

He knew, and she'd never be able to face him again.

CHAPTER TWENTY-SEVEN

Nalisha, dressed in a white and silver sari, all drifty and twinkling, like some ethereal Indian spirit, clapped her hands and beamed round the crowd gathered in the village hall.

'Thank you all so much for being here. So, are

we all ready for this?'

Everyone stopped chattering, stared at Nalisha, shuffled a bit and nodded in embarrassed anticipation.

'Eugh—look at her,' Bella hissed. 'Look at her! I mean, she's a nice woman, but now I feel like some huge bloated flump!'

Sophie giggled.

A collection of fans whirred their way through the stifling air, dust motes danced in shafts of evening sunlight splintering through the tiny windows, and the gods and goddesses still stared at their rather run-down new home with haughty disdain.

There were, Erin had to admit, far more people than she'd expected. The village hall hummed with a mixed assortment of Nook Greeners, including all the Yee-Hawers, and also quite a few strangers who must have seen the adverts plastered on every available surface throughout the village and surrounding areas.

Erin returned waved hellos from Dora Wilberforce and Gina and Renata and Julia and several other village friends and tried hard to summon some enthusiasm. Yes, when Nalisha had first mentioned the Bollywood dance classes, she'd been enthusiastic—but that was before she'd found out that Nalisha loved Jay. That Nalisha would have married Jay.

Nalisha and Jay—it was a mantra that insisted on pounding out its rhythm in her brain. Night and day.

So, when Sophie and Bella had suggested they should all have a girls' night out, Erin had leaped at the idea.

'This is *so* not what I'd imagined when you suggested a girlie night out to cheer me up,' Erin, standing between Bella and Sophie at the back of the village hall, leaned across and whispered. 'I really needed a completely trashy night—in every meaning of the word—to forget about everything. I did *not* want to be prancing around in the village hall in a heatwave to the sort of background music you get in every Indian restaurant and looking stupid to boot.'

'You didn't have to come,' Bella pointed out reasonably. 'Nobody forced you. You knew what was going to happen here. We told you where we were going. You could have stayed at home and sulked.'

Erin sighed. She could have done—maybe should have done—but, she admitted to herself, she was curious. And OK, she'd love it if Nalisha made a complete dog's breakfast of the whole thing.

'And now you're here you might as well enjoy it.' Sophie nodded. 'Please don't be grouchy tonight, Erin. What happened to the radiant, happy-as-a-lark, uber irritatingly cheerful bride-to-be?'

'Oh, she's been completely swamped by beautiful Indian ex-girlfriends and barking Indian rellies-to-be.'

Bella laughed. 'OK, I'll give you the mad family bit. And Nalisha is a bit too fab for my liking, but she's such a sweetheart, and she's not Jay's ex, is she?'

Erin sighed. 'I honestly don't know. He says they were just friends.'

'So believe him.'

'But she's gorgeous, and every time I mention she might have been something more, he just laughs.'

'In a scary embarrassed "ohmigod she's found out" way?'

'No, like it was the daftest idea in the world. He says he's always been close to her, but never thought of her as anything but a friend . . . a sister . . .'

'Well, there you are then.'

'But she's shared so much of his life. She knows so much about him. And Deena and Tavish adore her.'

'And he's marrying *you*, you crazy bat,' Sophie chuckled. 'So get a grip.'

'I'm trying,' Erin sighed, 'believe me I'm trying.'

Bella shook her head. 'Anyway, I thought your Uncle Doug was spending a lot of time with the fragrant Nalisha now?'

'Oh, he is. Every spare minute. He's doing his usual ancient hippie laid-back charm offensive, which seems to amuse Nalisha.'

'Auntie Nalisha,' Sophie laughed. 'It's got a nice ring to it.'

Erin groaned. 'Yeah, in his dreams. And my worst nightmare. '

Bella hugged her. 'See? You *can* joke. So, what else is bugging you?'

'Well, despite Jay saying he agrees with me about our wedding, now Nalisha's reminded him about all the zillions of Indian marriage ceremonies they've been to, together, I've got a sneaking feeling that my husband-to-be might just swap sides at any minute.'

'Oh, don't be so silly.' Bella sighed. 'Jay's one billion per cent with you on the wedding. Why on earth do you think he'd give in and go along with his mad family?'

'Because he's dutiful and gentle and hates upsetting anyone. Because I know he thinks, deep down in his heart, even if he doesn't say it, that maybe, just maybe, his parents are right and we should be having a more Indian-type ceremony.'

'Pffft,' Sophie sniffed. 'Rubbish. Wedding nerves. You're just getting stressed over nothing. You and Jay have planned your wedding exactly as you want it. End of. Forget the Indian rellies—and the Nalisha thing tonight—and have some fun.'

'Yeah, right. So, how do you suggest that I do that? Being here?' Erin sighed and threw her arms out dramatically, encompassing the gods and goddesses and Nalisha, looking every inch like the winner of the Miss India Pageant. 'It really isn't helping.'

'It might,' Sophie said placatingly, 'if you try to forget the Indian connection for a while.'

Bella frowned. 'That might be a bit tricky, don't you think, Soph? Given that Nalisha's Indian, we're at an Indian dance class, and the whole hall is surrounded by Indian idols. All we need is for someone to rush in with vindaloos all round and we'd have a full-house.'

Sophie tutted in irritation. 'That's not being very helpful, is it?'

'Bloody funny though,' Bella chuckled. 'Sorry, Erin.'

Erin shook her head.

Sophie tried again. 'No, but seriously. Exercise is good for the serotonin levels and serotonin is the feel-good hormone or brain chemical or whatever, so after all this shimmying and serotonin overload, Erin'll be back to being a sunny bunny again.'

'Don't think so,' Erin sighed mutinously. 'It'll take much, much more than serotonin. Several dozen cocktails and some mind-numbing music in a club *might* just have worked. This definitely won't.'

Sophie and Bella sighed heavily.

The rest of the villagers, clearly assuming that Nalisha no longer needed their attention, all started talking to each other again.

Nalisha, still looking supremely confident, shook her head and clapped her hands more loudly this time to attract their attention. Erin felt there'd probably be a lot of clapping needed tonight. The Nook Greeners, when they got together on social occasions, always forgot that they'd seen each other merely hours before and nattered and chattered about anything and everything.

Nalisha's bangles, earrings and multiple jewels glittered and jingled prettily. Again.

She raised her voice. 'I said, are we all ready to start our first lesson?'

The chattering stopped, and the affirmative answer was ragged but fairly convincing.

'OK, now we're all here—' Nalisha beamed a bit more '—I thought we'd just start with the basics. I've chosen some lovely lively music for you, and look what I have here . . .'

Erin frowned. 'Oh Lordy—what's she doing now? What's she dragging out? Is that a dressing-up box? Nooo—they're the biggest suitcases she brought with her when she first came to stay. Oh God.'

'Oooh!' Bella clapped her hands together in delight. 'We've got saris!'

'Oh, goody,' Erin muttered. 'Just what I need.'

'They're not all saris,' Nalisha said, overhearing

233

and adopting a bit of a supermodel pose and exposing her perfectly toned midriff. 'Now, I'm wearing a ceremonial sari. But we also have *lehenga cholis*. You get the petticoat—which you'd call the skirt; the blouse—which you probably think is more of a crop top; and the dupatta—which is the long trailing scarf.'

Everyone cooed enthusiastically.

Nalisha smiled encouragingly at her audience. 'You get dupattas with saris and Salwars too. Everyone wears a dupatta with everything. So useful and so glam and wonderful for dancing. And these—' she held up a handful of glorious, shimmering sequinned and jewelled rainbow fabrics from her suitcase '—are the Salwar suits, with lovely baggy trousers. And look, we even have some of Kam and Jay's long-forgotten kurtas for the boys.'

The boys—the majority of them over sixty—stared at the brightly coloured and lavishly embroidered tunics with mass typical rustic mistrust for anything sartorial that wasn't ginger cords and a nice checked shirt.

'Please don't be shy,' Nalisha called cheerfully. 'Dive in and find something lovely and loose and floaty. You can just pop something on over or drape it round what you're already wearing. There's no need to undress. Oh, and shoes and socks off too, please. We must all be barefooted for this. And once we're all ready, we can start dancing.'

'Barefooted, duck? We'll get splinters.'

The complaint came from several directions.

'No you won't,' Nalisha assured them. 'I've had the floor swept and washed and Mr Prior ran his sander over it and then washed it again. There are

234

no splinters. It'll be like dancing on glass.'

'I bloody hope not,' Ted Blundell muttered.

After everyone had tried sliding their feet tentatively across the floor to test out Nalisha's claims—just like children at infant school, Erin thought—shoes and sandals and socks were removed with varying degrees of ease and varying volumes of groans and sighs depending on the age of the wearer and the condition of their feet.

Bella, heading for the suitcase, frowned at Nalisha. 'Just one question—are all the clothes in a minus size eight? Like you?'

'Not at all. Sizing isn't a problem with most of these outfits.' Nalisha smiled. 'Indian clothes are amazingly comfortable to wear. You can drape and pleat and gather most of the saris, and the scarves are just well, scarves, and the petticoats and trousers have massive drawstring waists— like clown's pantaloons—so everyone should find something to fit them.'

Within seconds, the rural reticence had disappeared, and the would-be Bollywooders were all shrieking with delight as they pulled out vivid silks and taffetas and satins and held them up against themselves and each other.

All colours of the rainbow—and several more never seen in nature—wafted and billowed round the dusty village hall. There were oohs and aaahs of approval as everyone managed to find something suitable to wear.

Erin sighed and reluctantly followed as Sophie joined Bella and the rest of the chattering crowd round the open suitcases.

She was never usually so churlish, but dressing up in a sari—*honestly.*

'I think this pink and gold sari would look lovely on you, Erin.' Nalisha held out a fluttering armful of silk. 'Just wrap it round over your shorts and vest, and tuck it in at the waist—well, you know how it goes, don't you?'

'Yes. Thank you.'

'I'm so glad you came tonight.' Nalisha smiled kindly. 'It's great exercise and you look as though you could do with losing a few pounds before the wedding. Now! Come along everyone!'

Erin wanted to strangle her with the nearest dupatta.

'This is brilliant.' Sophie pranced round, waving her dark green and gold multi-beaded dupatta. 'Soooo pretty.'

Bella, in sparkly orange, lime and purple, sashayed with her. 'Yay! Look at us! Next time we go clubbing we'll have to wear this stuff. It's soooo cool.'

Nalisha smiled at them. 'You both look absolutely gorgeous.'

Bella and Sophie grinned like children. Erin shook her head.

Nalisha started to walk to the front of the hall, then stopped and looked at Erin. 'Oh, I knew there was something else.'

Something other than making her feel like a lard barrel? Oh, goody.

'Really?' Erin tried to sound disinterested.

'Mmm, I don't know if Jay's told you but Deena's coming down to Nook Green sometime in the next few days.'

'*What*? What the hell for? And no, Jay hasn't mentioned anything to me at all.'

She'd strangle Jay with the dupatta now, too—

236

once she'd finished with Nalisha.

'Jay probably forgot in all the excitement.' Nalisha gave the last word a frisson of rampant sexuality. 'But he's delighted. Oh, I know it's hard for you to understand because you're used to making all your decisions yourself with your parents being so far away, but I know Jay misses his mother. And I think she feels a bit left out.'

'Left out?'

'Of the wedding. You know how *Indian* she is about it all? I just thought it would be nice for her to be here, and be involved a bit more with the final arrangements.'

'*You* thought? You?' Erin said angrily. 'Did you invite her?'

'It might have sounded like an invitation.' Nalisha was all wide-eyed innocence. 'Anyway, I thought you'd like to know. Now, is everyone dressed? Good—let's get started . . .'

Oh, God, Erin thought, staring after Nalisha with total hatred, I really, really can't cope with this.

'I'm going home.' Erin tugged at her pink and gold splendour.

'Get a grip.' Bella frowned. 'Of course you're not.'

'You really don't know what a bitch Nalisha is, do you?'

Sophie shook her head. 'Whoa. Calm down, Erin. What on earth did she say to you?'

'She's invited Deena down to stay *before* the wedding. My wedding! And Jay's happy because he apparently misses his mum and—'

'Maybe he does,' Bella said reasonably. 'Maybe Nalisha was being kind. Maybe Jay would like his mum to be here to join in the last-minute stuff. It's his wedding as well, isn't it?'

'And,' Sophie said, 'your mum will be here too. It'll be lovely to have them both together, won't it? They can get to know each other before the big day. I don't see what you're getting so freaked about, honestly.'

'No, I don't suppose you can.' Erin sighed, hating herself for sounding so selfish and childish. 'And maybe Jay would like his mum here, too—what do I know? Oh, you're probably right.'

'Of course we are,' Bella said gently. 'And you're strung out with pre-wedding nerves so everything is being blown up out of proportion. Now, take a deep breath, forget about Deena for tonight, and enjoy yourself. Just look at all this. Isn't it wonderful?'

Erin was still simmering, but she looked anyway. The village hall was transformed. Even really old people like Dora Wilberforce had made some sort of effort to look like Bollywood divas. The men, at first reluctant to pull on the kurtas, now admired one another and admitted the long tunics were very comfortable and hid a multitude of sins.

The gods and goddesses, watching the gentle revolution taking place, seemed to be smiling at last.

If only the same could be said of her . . .

CHAPTER TWENTY-EIGHT

Nalisha, looking smug, returned to the front of the hall and clapped her hands again. 'You all look fabulous! If you can dance as well as you look, we'll have Sriram Raghavan and Dinesh Vijan wanting to sign you all up!'

'Who're they?' Sid Duncan frowned. 'More relatives of yours and young Jay and Kam moving into the village, are they?'

'Oh, I wish,' Nalisha laughed. 'One is a really famous Bollywood film director and the other a really famous Bollywood producer.'

'Ah.' Dora Wilberforce, wrapped in a crimson and shocking pink sari, nodded sagely. 'I could have told you that.'

Everyone stared at her. Dora stared back, daring anyone to contradict her. No one did.

'OK.' Nalisha paced up and down. 'If you get lost, follow me. Let's just go through the basic moves before I put the music on. Ready? Good. Now, first, put your palms together and bow your head . . . Lovely . . . Now, try lifting your arms to eye level and moving your hands up and down . . . Oh, that's really good.'

Nalisha's body simply flowed, and Erin, once she'd stopped feeling murderously angry and extremely silly in equal measures, found the gentle silky-smooth movements almost therapeutic.

'One foot in front of the other, raise your arms above your head and cross both hands over your head.' Nalisha's voice was soothing. 'Fabulous. Now step backwards and forwards, twisting your hands like you're unscrewing a light bulb at the same time. Oh, you're all naturals. That's really great.'

Ten minutes later, with walk-throughs and several more complex moves completed, including hip swaying and twisting, toe pointing and circling hands, shoulder shrugging and even a little bit of Indian head waggling, Nalisha decided they were good to go with music.

'Shall I just give you a little demo?'

There was a rousing cheer and a lot of nodding, but before Nalisha reached the village hall's ancient stereo system, the door flew open.

'Soz.' A multicoloured braided head peered round the hall, stopping briefly to gawp at the Indian gods and goddesses. 'Ooh, cool statues. Er, are we too late for the class?'

'I know him from somewhere.' Erin frowned at Rainbow Dreads and his shorter companion. Ah, yes! Of course. She leaned towards Sophie and Bella. 'It's, er, what's-his-name—oh, yes, David. He said he liked dancing. Oh, and the boy who stood up to Abbie. Aiden!'

'Uh?' Bella and Sophie frowned at her.

'David and Aiden. They both work at the Swan.'

'R-e-a-l-l-y?' Bella grinned. 'They're cute.'

'Too right.' Sophie shimmied her green and gold hips. 'I fancy the one with the dreads.'

'Good,' Bella chuckled. 'Because the little adorable one with the buzz cut is all mine. How good can it get? New dance class. New men. This village is starting to liven up nicely.'

Erin looked at them both doubtfully. 'Are you sure? About, er, them—the lads from the Swan?'

'Oh yes.' Bella nodded, wriggling her cleavage to its best advantage. 'Absolutely.'

'Men who can dance—' Sophie smiled '—are as rare as rubies round here. And I do like a man who's in touch with his feminine side.'

'But I thought you were both in love with Kam?'

Bella wrinkled her nose. 'We were. He's totally gorgeously divine, of course. But way too far out of our league. And we couldn't both have him, and we'd never fight over a man. So we've decided to back off. We've discussed it, haven't we, Soph?'

'We have.' Sophie nodded. 'And we think he's already got a woman anyway.'

Erin frowned. 'Kam? Really?'

'Yeah,' Bella said. 'He's got all the symptoms.'

Erin sighed. 'Go on then—share. Jay doesn't know, or if he does, he hasn't said anything to me.'

Bella shrugged. 'Doubt if Kam's even told Jay. It looks very much like a secret love affair to us. We reckon it might be one of the Pony Club mums or something. He's certainly been a bit distracted at work. He's got all the signs.'

'Well, I suppose it had to happen.' Erin continued to frown. 'But I wonder who? We'll have to ask him.'

'We will,' Sophie agreed. 'And threaten him with something nasty if he won't talk.'

They looked at one another and laughed.

Bella grinned. 'Anyway, Soph and I have decided Kam's a bit like Richard Armitage. Strictly fantasy only. You know, we can lust over him from a distance, but not get too close and risk having our dreams crushed.'

Sophie nodded. 'And so we're looking for real relationships with real men.'

'Yes, well, but those boys from the Swan are—well—boys,' Erin said.

'Mid-twenties, I'd say.' Bella gave them an expertly considered glance across the hall. 'A year or so younger than us maybe. And pretty fit. Perfect.'

'Totally,' Sophie agreed happily. 'So, as long as they're not attached, not gay and fancy us in return, that's us sorted nicely.'

Sometimes, Erin thought, looking at Sophie and

241

Bella, even though we've all been best friends for ever, I'll never, ever understand you.

By now Nalisha had efficiently welcomed the newcomers, run through the basic dance moves with them and had managed to find them kurtas.

David and Aiden, looking slightly embarrassed, slipped into place just in front of Erin, Sophie and Bella.

'Hi.' David turned round and grinned at Erin. 'Lovely to see you again. This is dead cool. I love the Indian gods; they'd go dead well with your tent thing.'

Erin flinched slightly.

David appeared not to notice. 'We've only just finished work. So glad we're not too late.' He looked across at Sophie and his eyes widened. 'Hello. I'm David and this is my mate, Aiden.'

'I'm Sophie. And this is Bella. Nice to meet you.'

There was a lot of mutual appraisal and grinning.

Erin shook her head and laughed to herself. They seemed to have passed all Sophie's criteria with flying colours. Poor David and Aiden—lambs to the slaughter.

'Right!' Nalisha did the hand-clapping thing again. 'Now we're all organised, I'll just pop the bhangra music on and show you a simple routine.'

The hall was instantly flooded with loud, vibrant, insistent, exciting music. The drumbeats echoed inside Erin's head as Nalisha swirled and twirled and shimmied round the floor, her hands telling a story, her body moving sensuously in perfect time.

'Wow,' Bella breathed. 'She's amazing.'

Erin nodded reluctantly. She certainly was. Bugger.

'And seriously seductive,' Sophie added.

'Mind you,' Bella said, 'don't forget the Indian heritage and roots are deeply entrenched in the culture that gave us the *Kama Sutra*. Maybe we shouldn't be surprised that Indians are naturally sexy?'

'And it's another reason to be deeply envious of Erin marrying Jay,' Sophie sniggered.

'It's an old joke,' Erin hissed, giggling. 'Heard it all before. Shut up. Please.'

As Nalisha finished her demonstration everyone clapped and cheered and stamped their bare feet on the dusty floor. Erin didn't. She simply couldn't be that shallow.

'Thank you.' Nalisha curtseyed. 'Now, it's your turn. Just follow me.'

Watching Nalisha intently, everyone attempted to put their recently learned moves to the beat. The results were varied, but the Yee-Hawers, clearly used to being choreographed, and despite their advanced age, were amazingly good.

And David and Aiden, moving sinuously and synchronised in front of Erin, were revelations. Sophie and Bella, clearly impressed by men-with-moves, certainly seemed to think so if the nudges and raised eyebrows and lascivious grins were anything to go by.

There was an awful lot of laughter echoing round the hall. Erin was quite surprised to find herself laughing at one point as she shimmied and swayed and twisted her hands seductively above her head and hip-bumped with Dora Wilberforce.

She was actually almost enjoying herself. How very strange.

Maybe Sophie had been right about the serotonin.

243

Rainbow fabrics swirled and sequins danced in the dusty sunlight.

Bollywood, Erin thought dizzily as, in company with the rest of Nook Green, she watched Nalisha and pranced and swivelled and twirled and finger clicked to the loud, exciting music, had definitely come to Berkshire.

CHAPTER TWENTY-NINE

As the music ended, Gina puffed to a halt and blew strands of her hair away from her face. Everyone in the village hall was laughing. Everything was twinkling and sparkling. The colours were dazzling. And yes, she had to admit, she'd thoroughly enjoyed losing herself in the Bollywood dancing.

Because she really needed to lose herself tonight.

She adjusted the turquoise and lilac dupatta, throwing it over her shoulder like she had with her old college scarf, and glanced at her watch. Nearly nine o'clock already.

As always when she was away from the Merry Cobbler, she felt a pang of anxiety. Would Sam and Part-time Pearl be able to cope without her? Should she even have come here tonight?

Yes, she thought, she should. And hopefully the pub would be quiet anyway as most of the regulars were in here. Yes—the business side of her life was OK.

If only the same could be said of the emotional side.

Kam wasn't here to watch as he'd said he would be. She'd known he wouldn't be, of course. She'd made a complete and utter fool of herself—again.

'Fabulous!' Nalisha smiled at them all. 'Totally fabulous! Now, while you just get your breath back, I'll walk through some more moves from some different dances, and explain to you the meaning of each of the movements and the stories they're telling.'

Gina wasn't really listening.

On the other side of the village hall, Erin, Sophie and Bella, looking young, fresh and gorgeous, were chatting happily and laughing with two boys she'd never seen before.

Boys . . . Gina sighed. Of course they weren't really boys. Young men, then. They *were* boys to her though. Far too young . . . As Kam was—clearly.

Oh Lordy—she'd made an idiot of herself with Doug, who was more than ten years her senior, and now with Kam who was her junior. OK, only by a couple of years, but her junior, nonetheless.

Maybe it was time to leave Nook Green and start again. But wasn't that why she'd come here in the first place? Could she really spend her life running away from her mistakes?

To give him his due, Kam hadn't mentioned anything to her about the kiss. But then he hadn't mentioned anything at all. Because she hadn't seen him. At all. All day. He'd simply left before breakfast, before she was even up, and not returned.

His supper plate and glasses had been washed up and put away in the kitchen. And he hadn't come back to the Merry Cobbler by the time she'd left for the village hall.

He was avoiding her—as she'd known he would.

'OK.' Nalisha clapped her hands again. 'You've all been brilliant. And if you've got those new moves fixed in your head, I'll put the music on again, and we'll just have one more dance. Ready?'

Everyone nodded.

Gina just went through the motions.

On either side of her, Dora Wilberforce and the Blundells and most of the Yee-Hawers were really moving well, twirling and crossing their hands, and pointing their toes and shaking their hips in a multicoloured swirl of silks.

Gina tried really hard to copy them but her heart simply wasn't in it.

The gods and goddesses on her side of the hall, particularly Durga and Shakti, seemed to be frowning down at her.

'Don't look at me like, that,' Gina muttered. 'I feel bad enough without you being all po-faced.'

'Talking to yourself, Gina?' Dora Wilberforce puffed. 'First sign, that is. And this is great, isn't it? Much better than Zumba.'

'What? Oh, yes, lovely.'

'Shame young Jay and Kam aren't here tonight. We could do with some nice young Indian men to show us how it's done, eh?'

'Er, yes.'

She wished her heart didn't lurch when someone mentioned his name. How juvenile was that?

'All this Eastern stuff is so exciting.' Dora twinkled. 'I simply can't wait for the wedding, can you?'

'No.'

'It's just what the village needs, isn't it?' Dora continued, flexing her hands in and out above her head as well as her rheumatism would allow. 'New

246

ideas and lovely young people.'

Gina stared after her as Dora shimmied away in sync with Mary Blundell, bending and sweeping and toe pointing to the music.

Young people, Gina thought, completely losing her choreographic thread and just shuffling on the spot. That's what everyone thought of Kam. A *young* person. Which of course he was. Not to mention exceptionally beautiful and clever, and too damn sexy for his own good.

Daft cow.

Gina watched Erin and Bella and Sophie across the room, dancing amazingly with those *boys* and shook her head.

'Not yer head, Gina love—' Sam Duncan shimmied past her '—you got to shake yer booty like Beyoncé.'

Gina shook.

And then mercifully it was all over.

'OK.' Nalisha switched off the music. 'That's it for tonight. You've all been absolutely amazing. I hope you've all enjoyed it.'

The roar of approval confirmed this and there was a huge Nook Green round of applause.

'And you'll be happy to make it a regular thing?'

More whoops of agreement.

'Good. But of course I'll be leaving the village soon.'

Catcalls and boos.

Nalisha laughed. 'I know—but London won't wait for ever—so I'll be looking for someone to take over. If anyone's interested, then come and have a word with me and I can pass on all the CDs and the saris and give you some DVDs as well.'

There was a universal shaking of heads and

reluctant groans of refusal.

As the rest of the Nook Greeners shed their polychromatic garments and found their discarded shoes and socks and chattered happily and noisily, Gina noticed the two boys who had been dancing with Erin and Sophie and Bella, approaching Nalisha.

They'd certainly been brilliant dancers, Gina thought, returning her swathe of turquoise and lilac silk to the suitcase. They'd be great replacement teachers.

And so young. Of course.

Pffft. She sighed crossly.

'We're all going back to the pub, Gina,' Dora Wilberforce announced. 'Well, you must be as well, We always had a last couple of drinks after we'd Yee-Hawed, didn't we? And we certainly all need one tonight. Who's working in there?'

'Just Sam and Pearl,' Gina said. 'And maybe, er, Kam. I hope they'll be able to cope with the rush, but I'll be back in a minute.'

'Pub, everyone!' Sam Duncan yelled. Then he looked at Gina. 'You're being a bit of a slowcoach tonight, duck, and I'm gagging for a pint. Can I give you the keys to lock up here?'

'Yes, of course.' Gina took the village hall keys. 'I'll give them back to you when I get to the pub.'

'Ta, duck.'

The Nook Greeners left the hall in a tidal wave.

Gina looked across at Nalisha. 'You can go, too. I've got the keys to lock up here. I'll see to everything. You were brilliant. It was really great.'

'Thanks.' Nalisha beamed. 'I'm so glad you enjoyed it, and it all went so well. Shame Kam didn't make it after all. He'd have had such a laugh.

248

And thanks for locking up here.'

'No problem.' Gina smiled, wondering if Nalisha was rushing off to see Doug and finding that she didn't give a stuff. 'See you later.'

Youth, again, Gina thought wearily, as Nalisha rushed out of the hall. Oh, to be that young again.

She started to check that no one had left anything behind prior to switching off the lights and locking the door.

OK, no lost property, most of the lights were off, the plugs were all unplugged, the windows all closed.

'Have I missed it?'

Gina jumped at the voice echoing from the shadows.

Kam uncurled himself from the wall just inside the door.

Her heart, thundering anyway, went into overdrive. 'Yes. As you well know. You must have watched everyone leaving?'

'I did, yes.'

Gina didn't look at him. She was grateful to him for coming here, waiting until they were alone, to have the conversation.

Kam walked into the hall. He glanced up at the statues. 'They really are impressive, aren't they?'

'They are, yes.'

Gina pretended to be packing up some non-existent last minute items. She really didn't want to look at him, tall and lean and spectacularly sexy in his jeans and T-shirt, or even to listen to that soft, caressing voice.

'Did you enjoy it tonight?'

'I did, yes,' she muttered again, knowing that she sounded irritable and hating herself for it. 'It was a huge success.'

'Good. And no one mentioned anything about our little conspiracy?'

'They didn't, no.'

'That's OK then.'

God, this was ridiculous. Gina sighed. Why didn't they just get it over? He could say that he knew, and she could apologise for being stupid and promise it would never happen again, and then they'd go their separate ways.

Kam would probably move out of the pub, of course, and she'd berate herself for ever.

But, hey, the story of her life.

'Do you know the stories of the gods? Their qualities? What they do?' Kam had stopped in front of Ganesh. He didn't wait for her to reply. 'Ganesh, the elephant god, the master of intellect and wisdom.'

Ganesh hadn't been on her side then.

'Saraswati, the goddess of creativity and music. Very suitable for tonight. And next to her, Shakti. She restores balance and gives energy. She probably came in handy for the dancing, too. And Durga— my favourite—he destroys poverty and suffering and injustice and cruelty.'

'Durga sounds like my sort of man,' Gina murmured. 'Don't you have a god or—more likely—a goddess, for silly, delusional women who seem determined to make a complete mess of their lives?'

Kam laughed. 'Not one that I've heard of. Why? Who needs one?'

Gina didn't dignify the question with an answer.

'Gina, look at me.'

She looked.

Kam smiled. 'That's better. Are you avoiding me?'

'Me? Hardly. You were gone before I opened up this morning. I haven't seen you all day. Even Nalisha noticed you didn't turn up here tonight. You *know* where to find me—so, no I think it's the other way round, don't you?'

'I've been working. Mrs Alexander, over at Daisy Bank, who runs the horse rescue place, had taken in a new consignment. Poor things. They were in a terrible state—but at least they'll all be happy now in their new home. It took all day to check them over, register them, prescribe medication and carry out whatever immediate treatment was needed. I've only just finished.'

'Oh, sorry.'

'Stop bloody saying sorry.'

'Sorry—oh, sorry.' Gina laughed despite herself.

Kam laughed too. 'So, did it all go well? Really? The Bollywood dancing? You weren't just being polite?'

'Yes, it did and no I wasn't.' Gina nodded, relieved at the change of subject, although she knew it was merely delaying the matter that had to be raised sooner or later. 'Even better than I'd thought.'

'Good. Gina—'

'Everyone enjoyed it tonight. It's going to become a regular fixture. Even when Nalisha's left the village. She's got a couple of willing apprentices lined up.'

'Good. I'll come and watch next time.'

Next time.

Gina groaned to herself. How silly she was to feel a little leap of excitement at those two words.

251

Silly, sad, delusional woman, indeed.

'And did *you* enjoy it?' Kam asked. 'And dress up?'

'Yes.' She nodded. 'I did. Both. Why?'

'Because—' Kam walked across the hall towards her and caught the ends of the lilac and turquoise dupatta '—you're still wearing this.'

'Oh.'

Kam was close. Too close. Gina moved away and he let the dupatta fall.

'Kam.' She looked at him. 'I know you don't want me to say sorry again. But I have to, because I am. I behaved stupidly. I've behaved stupidly all my life it seems to me.'

'Hardly.' He frowned. 'You're funny, clever and work harder than anyone I've ever known. You're independent, intelligent, incredibly sexy and very, very beautiful.'

'And you—' she smiled sadly at him '—have all the words that you think women like me want to hear. You're a flatterer, and a practised seducer.'

Kam chuckled. 'And you're reading from the PR sheet put about by my family.'

'Deny it then.'

'God . . . no, well . . . OK then, I've spent most of my life—well, for as long as I was aware that girls, then women, found me attractive—playing around, because I could. I studied hard, worked hard and played even harder.'

Gina nodded. 'Exactly. And I've spent my adult life loving the wrong men.'

'Tell me. About the wrong men.'

Was he mad?

'No. It's all pretty boring and you'll have heard it all before.'

'Not from you. Go on—please, tell me.'

'OK. There was one wrong man, actually. For a very, very long time. I felt very ashamed of what I did. I hated myself. When I came here, to Nook Green, I was determined to never do it again. But then of course I fell for Doug, who thought I was fun for a while, but not a keeper. History repeating itself.'

'Go on,' Kam said gently. 'I'm listening.'

'Like I said, it's a sad old story. Too, too familiar. Too, too boring.'

'I want to know why you're on your own. I can't understand why.'

'Because I'm crap at relationships. I'm rubbish at them. OK?'

'Tell me,' Kam said again.

'You really don't want to know.'

'Yes, I do. Please tell me.'

'OK, I was at college. Only an FE college, mind you—not uni—I was doing business studies. He was my one of my lecturers. I was completely besotted. He was married, of course. I didn't know that to start with, but by the time I did, it was too late for me. I was head over heels in love.'

'Did he tell you he was married or did you find out?'

'I found out. Eventually. He never kept me a secret, our love affair was very public, so I really didn't think he had a wife and three children tucked away in the next town.'

Kam shook his head. 'Is that when it ended?'

'I wish.' Gina frowned. 'No, he assured me he was only staying with his wife until the children grew up and left home and so on, that they led separate lives—the usual story, you know the kind

253

of thing. Everyone told me I was mad and that he'd never leave her, but I didn't listen.'

'No, you wouldn't.' Kam nodded. 'Nothing more potent than first love. Nothing more painful than first heartbreak.'

Gina laughed bitterly. 'And there speaks an expert? No doubt you've played that role many times. Anyway, as our affair was common knowledge, I reckon his wife knew all the time and didn't care much. He'd probably done it all before. But I hung on and it went on for years. Long, long after I'd left college.'

'Really? You believed him and trusted him that much?'

'Yes, sadly, I'm a very trusting person. And a fool. And of course he was part of my life. A huge part of my life. I really thought we'd one day play happy-ever-after. But, of course, I was simply his mistress—his bit on the side—and that's all I ever would be. By the time I realised it, I'd wasted half my adult life on him. So I moved away and came here and swore it would never, ever happen again.'

'And then there was Doug? But he wasn't married, was he?'

'No. And never likely to be. Another waste of time. Another opportunity for me to get it very, very wrong, to make a compete fool of myself, and end up being hurt.'

'And me?'

'You?' Gina laughed. 'Oh, you're more than both of them put together.'

'Meaning?'

'You don't need me to interpret.'

'Did you kiss me?'

'Yes.'

'And then you walked away?'

'Yes.' Gina knew her face was burning. She was so glad that the village hall was only dimly lit. 'It was a mistake.'

'The kiss or the walking away?'

'The kiss, of course. Kam, I'm so sorry. It won't happen again.'

'Bugger.'

'What?'

'Bugger. I was just so knackered. Half asleep. Thought I was dreaming. By the time I was awake, you'd gone. I can't believe I've missed not only my opportunity to tell you how I really feel about you, but also to kiss you.'

Gina said nothing.

Kam moved closer again. 'You're driving me insane.'

'*What?*'

'I think about you all the time. Right now, you're driving me completely crazy. I want you more than I've ever wanted anyone.'

Gina thought she must have misheard him. 'You can't.'

'Why not?'

'Because you don't really know me.'

'I know enough. I just want to see you, to touch you, and listen to you talking and laughing.'

Gina blinked at him. 'But, well, you're . . . well . . . you. You could have anyone you wanted. And I'm older than you, and I've got history, and I'm all jaded and faded really. You want someone young and beautiful and—'

'I want you.'

Gina laughed.

Kam frowned. 'It's not funny. I mean it.'

'Look,' Gina sighed, 'if you just want to spend the night with me . . .'

'This isn't about sex.'

'Really?'

'Oh—' Kam frowned again '—if we never had sex, I'd still want you. Want to be with you.'

'You can't.' Gina worked some saliva into her mouth. 'I mean you just can't.'

'Why not?'

'Because I'm not the sort of woman you want.'

'And what sort of woman would that be if it isn't you? I've never felt like this before. This is a first for me.'

'It can't be.'

'Oh, you're impossible. Come here.' And, grabbing the ends of the dupatta again, he pulled her against him. And kissed her. Properly.

Eventually, ages later, Gina, breathless and trembling, lifted her head and gazed at him. He meant it. He really, really meant it.

Oh, what the hell. You only live once . . .

She kissed him back.

'Wow!' A long time later she gazed at him dizzily. 'Oh, wow . . . So what happens next?'

'Um—' Kam smiled at her '—I don't suppose by any chance there's a back way up to my room?'

Gina nodded. 'A fire escape, yes. A very rickety outside iron staircase. And it means climbing in through your window.'

'Like eloping in reverse. I like the sound of that. OK, tonight we'll elope backwards.'

'You're crazy. Why?'

'Because I don't want to be seen dragging you through the pub.'

'Are you ashamed of me?'

'Are you kidding?' Kam grinned. 'I just don't want to get caught up in a million pub conversations when I can't wait to tumble you into my bed.'

'*My* bed, if we're being pedantic.'

'My bed, your bed, anybody's bloody bed. Just, please, Gina, can we go to bed? Together? Now?'

OMG, as Sophie and Bella would say.

Gina tried to smile. It came out all wobbly. 'Yes, er, yes, please. And actually, it might be a good idea if we kept this . . . well, this to ourselves for a while, anyway. You know what the village gossips are like.'

'Are you ashamed of me?'

'Yeah right.' Gina laughed and kissed him. 'Actually, I just like the idea of having a secret lover.'

'Which means we now have two secrets. That's pretty exciting. And I'll do whatever you want. Although I'd be more than happy to tell the entire world right now. But it's your call. Now, can we go?' He brushed her hair gently away from her face. 'Don't make me wait any longer, please. Now?'

'Oh God, yes, but . . .'

'But what?' Kam looked suddenly anxious.

'But I'm all sweaty and disgusting after dancing.'

'And I'm all sweaty and disgusting after working with the horses all day. We might have to have a shower.'

'Oooh, yes, we might. What a good idea.'

Remembering at the last minute to lock the door behind them, Gina grabbed Kam's hand, and together they ran, laughing like children, across the green in the sultry, steamy darkness.

CHAPTER THIRTY

'Uncle Doug? What do you want me to do with these?' Erin held up the largest of a collection of lavishly decorated ceramic jugs. 'They're really pretty. Do you want them displayed on the shelves once they're priced or would you rather have them put away in the storeroom so you can use them in the window when you next do the display?'

Doug, who was kneeling in the window of the Old Curiosity Shop making the final adjustments to his Indian Wedding Display, turned and squinted over his shoulder.

'Once they're priced, put them out on the shelves, please, love. Above the Poole pottery where it'll all look nice and bright together. Thanks. I won't be changing the window for a while, will I? OK, so what do you think of it?'

Erin cocked her head to one side and considered Uncle Doug's handiwork.

She smiled delightedly. 'Oh, it's lovely. It looks really, really good from in here. I'll have a look outside later when I've finished pricing up these jugs. But you've worked wonders with the Indian things you've got in there, and all that silk makes a lovely backdrop. And I love the random sparkly stuff too. Thank you so much.'

'I'm glad you think it's OK, because I want it to be perfect for you, well, and Jay too, of course. It's like putting out bunting for the Royal Wedding. I've nipped in and out to check the symmetry as I've been doing it,' Doug said happily, kneeling further into the window and making a few tweaks.

'It looked fine to me, too. You don't think it's too much, do you? And what about this "Happy Wedding Day Erin and Jay" banner? Not lopsided, is it?'

Erin laughed and shook her head. 'Not from in here, no. It's all fabulous. And seriously, the display is brilliant. I love all the colour and the scattered jewels and sequins, and all those little Indian gods and goddesses loaned from Jay's cottage look fabulous in amongst the sari silks. And goodness knows where you found all the incense burners and candlesticks and lanterns, or that entire herd of brass elephants.'

'They took a bit of digging out,' Doug admitted, pushing his hair out of his eyes as he moved the elephants slightly forwards. 'I knew I already had most of it in here somewhere, but Nalisha went to the temple in Wembley and bought me the rest. Wasn't that generous of her?'

Erin nodded and reached for another jug.

Nalisha seemed to have settled into being Doug's new best friend. Doug, it went without saying, was absolutely lapping it up.

In fact, Erin reckoned, anything that kept Nalisha away from Jay and the non-stop 'do you remembers' was a good thing.

And then there was the wedding . . .

Only ten days away, Erin thought giddily.

Well, OK there were still a few issues to sort out—like what the heck they were going to do with the *mandap*—but mostly everything was going absolutely perfectly. She'd been crazy to think Jay would want to rekindle any sort of romance with Nalisha. She'd been mad to think he'd side with his parents. She'd been so silly over so many things.

And tonight, she and Jay were picking up her mum and dad from Heathrow.

Erin did a little skippety-skip of excitement. Her parents were already in the air. On their way from Sydney. Oh, she so longed to see them again. They'd have so much to talk about. And a girl really needed her mum on her wedding day, didn't she? Skype had helped a lot, but there was nothing like the real thing, was there?

Of course, there was one rather irritating drawback.

Deena was arriving in Nook Green today, too. Well, in Maizey St Michael. And staying. In the Keskar's allotted suite at the Swan. And Tavish wouldn't be too far behind.

Jay had sworn he'd known nothing about Nalisha's phone call to his mother, but had admitted, yes, it might be a good idea for her and Rose Boswell to meet before the wedding, and no, he honestly *wasn't* missing his mum, but wasn't it sweet of Nalisha to think he might be?

Oh, yeah, really sweet.

Of course Deena had said yes, she'd love to come down and meet Erin's parents and it would be absolutely super to see Nalisha again—but there seemed little point in a flying visit, so why didn't she spend a few days making sure her beauty salon was able to run without her and, as soon as Tavish could find a stand-in pharmacist, they'd be able to come down sooner than they'd planned.

It would be so exciting, Deena had said, to be in on the very final stages of the wedding.

And, Erin thought now, as she blew dust away from the largest jug, it would be very small-minded of her not to welcome Jay's parents for the final

260

dizzily thrilling few days, especially as her own mum and dad would be here to share it.

And she and Sophie and Bella had been to Elle-Cee Bridalwear, and Linda and Carol had fitted them all for the last time, and the dresses had been pressed and swathed in their white cotton cocoons and zipped into their plastic covers, all ready for delivery on the day before the wedding.

And Deena's two Top Girls were coming down on Saturday afternoon to do a trial run of everyone's hair and make-up. Which would, Erin thought, be absolutely perfect as Saturday was her hen night.

And no one—absolutely no one—had made any mention at all of the mehendi or the *sagai* or the tilak, or any of it.

It was going to be a perfectly English fusion wedding.

Just as she and Jay had planned it all along.

Bliss.

'Oh, holy shit!' Erin hurled the jug away from her and leaped to her feet.

The jug shattered to smithereens against a bookcase. Dozens of porcelain pieces clattered to the floor like a brightly coloured mosaic jigsaw puzzle.

'Jesus!' Doug jumped, practically fell out of the window and landed heavily on the doormat. It rang. A lot.

'Get-off-the-bell!' Erin's teeth chattered.

Doug stepped off the doormat. 'What the hell's going on?'

'Spider,' Erin croaked, cowering against the rocking chair. 'Huge, huge spider . . . in that jug . . . Nooo, don't go near it. Well, yes, go near it. Get it.

261

Now.'

'That's probably about forty quid's worth of jug you've just demolished.' Doug frowned. 'And the spider's probably gone with it. For heaven's sake, Erin.'

'Sod the jug,' she said through clenched teeth. 'I saw the spider run and I'm not moving until it's out of here.'

'OK, love, stay there. Where did it go?'

'It landed by the bookcase. It ran underneath it, I think.'

'Great. One spider, one shop crammed with junk, er, collectibles. Needle/haystack come to mind?'

'Just-find-the-spider.'

'OK. God—now what are you doing?'

'Keeping out of the way.' Erin clambered onto the rocking chair. She had one foot on the teddy bear and the other on the kaleidoscope. The box of marbles rattled ominously as the chair pitched forwards. Erin held her arms out to either side to balance herself. 'Please hurry.'

'Whatever,' Doug groaned softly as he dropped to his knees by the bookcase, crunching bits of jug under him. 'I'll probably be cut to ribbons and I can't see a bloody thing under here. It's too dark. Can you fetch me the torch?'

'No. Sorry. I'm not moving.'

'Great.' Doug resumed his search.

The doormat chirruped cheerfully.

'Hello!' A country-casuals couple stood in the doorway. 'What a lovely little shop.'

'Thank you,' Erin muttered, teetering backwards and forwards on the chair, flapping her arms like a tightrope walker. 'Were you looking for anything in

262

particular or just browsing?'

'Just browsing,' the man said in plummy tones, frowning slightly. 'Er, are you all right up there?'

'Fine,' Erin said shortly. 'Thanks. Just feel free to look round. Please.'

'Oh, this is rather sweet, isn't it?' The woman, casting slightly bemused looks at Erin on her perch, and who also had a cut-glass accent, picked up a silver bonbon dish. 'It would look absolutely fabulous on our escritoire, wouldn't it, Henry?'

Henry nodded. 'Perfect, darling. How much is it?'

'No idea.' The woman squinted up at Erin. 'It doesn't have a price on it.'

'Oh, I think you'll find—oops.' The teddy bear slid sideways. Erin wobbled frantically.

'Ah, got the little fucker.' Doug backed out from beneath the bookcase and banged his head on a table. 'Bollocks!'

Henry and his wife stared.

'Um, Uncle Doug,' Erin hissed, 'we've got customers.'

'Ah, right—sorry.' Doug, his hands cupped round the spider, struggled to his feet and smiled. 'Pardon my language, I didn't see you there. I'll be with you in just a tick.'

Erin leaned forwards. The chair trembled under the shift. So did Erin. 'Uncle Doug, show me. No, not all of it—just show me. I don't want you to pretend that you've caught it.'

Doug uncupped his hands slightly. Long brown hinged legs waved angrily.

'OK, now I feel very sick. That's fine. Now take it away. And tell it to stay away. OK?'

Henry and his wife continued to stare as Doug

jumped over the doormat, hurried out of the shop and ran into the middle of the green, throwing his hands open wide.

'Run away and play and don't come back today or any other day.'

'Is he talking to us?' Henry's wife asked as Erin scrambled from her perch, spilling the kaleidoscope and the teddy bear and the box of marbles to the floor as she did so. 'Is everyone in this village insane?'

'Not everyone,' Erin said cheerfully, her heart rate returning to normal now the spider threat had gone. 'Now about the bonbon dish . . .'

'We don't want the bonbon dish,' Henry said quickly. 'Come along, Penelope. We're leaving.'

'Oh.' Doug frowned at them as they passed in the doorway. 'Are you going? The bonbon dish is Queen Anne, you know, and I can give you a really good price. No? OK then . . . sorry. Have a nice day.'

Erin chuckled. 'Sorry about that. But thanks.'

Doug shook his head. 'Forty quid for the jug and goodness knows how much we could have bagged for the dish. You owe me, Erin. I'll have to dock your wages.'

'Yeah, right.' Erin started picking up the scattered marbles. 'I'll get the dustpan and brush and sweep up the mess.'

'Leave it, love. Take the rest of the day off. I'll be fine here. I know how much you're looking forward to seeing Rose and Pete tonight. Go and get yourself ready.'

'Are you sure?'

'Absolutely. I've got a couple of dealers coming in this afternoon. One is interested in that writing desk you got from Daisy Bank, and the other one is looking for a job lot of china. That'll keep me out of mischief. And we might even get some ad hoc customers too if we're lucky.'

'As long as Henry and Penelope don't plaster the fact that we're madder than mad all over Facebook via their mobiles, yes, we might.' Erin hugged Doug. 'Thank you.'

'And, er, Nalisha said she'd be popping in later.'

Ah, now it made sense.

Erin laughed. 'You're old enough and daft enough to make your own mistakes in that area. I'm saying nothing. But I think you'll end up getting hurt.'

'Not me, love. Nalisha's a stunning woman. I'm so proud to be seen with her. She turns heads wherever we go. She's incredibly intelligent and excellent company. But I always know when to bow out of a relationship. Not,' he added quickly, 'that we're having a relationship in that way, of course.'

Euuuueeeeew.

'Good Lord, no—I wasn't ever going to ask that. Oh, yuk—no way.' Erin flapped her hands. 'But please, don't think Nalisha will stay here in the village after our wedding. Because she won't. Not even for you. You've been warned. Bye.'

She stepped carefully over the doormat and into Nook Green's solid, searing afternoon heat. From outside, the Indian window display, in its oriental golds and reds, looked wonderful. Erin stared delightedly at the wedding banner and gave a little jig of pure happiness.

Her wedding . . . Her marriage to Jay. Only days away . . .

Nothing or no one could spoil it now.

A minibus swerved off the little one-track road round the green and scrunched to a halt on the gravel outside the shop.

'Oi, love,' the driver said cheerily, leaning out of the window. 'Is this the Old Curiosity Shop?'

'That's what it says.' Erin smiled, indicating the sign over the door.

'Great, ta, love.' The driver turned his head. 'Right ladies and gents. Here we have a lovely little rural antique shop. Typical English. All ye olde worlde stuff you could ever want. Out you get. You've got an hour or so . . . enjoy.'

The doors of the minibus opened and at least a dozen rather elderly and very obviously American tourists poured out. And poured into the shop.

Erin laughed out loud. 'Good luck with that lot, Uncle Doug.'

And she ran across the green towards Jay's cottage, making sure that she avoided the place where Uncle Doug had released the spider.

Just in case . . .

CHAPTER THIRTY-ONE

'But I still can't believe you left him to deal with a whole bus-load of tourists on his own,' Jay murmured, stroking Erin's hair on the pillow. 'That was very cruel. Especially as he'd just given you the rest of the day off, and also rescued you from the Biggest Spider in the Whole World.'

'Don't mock—you didn't see it,' Erin sighed, drowsy and ecstatically happy. She turned her head and kissed Jay's naked shoulder. She loved the

266

feel and scent of his skin. Loved every inch of him. 'And he was just wishing for impromptu customers. And he adores Americans. They buy loads of things. He'll be dead happy. He might even meet a Betty-Lou from Kansas or somewhere to replace Nalisha when she leaves for London.'

Jay laughed and kissed her.

Erin squinted at him. 'Can I ask you something?'

'Yes. Anything you like. Except logarithms. Despite doing maths A level, I never did quite get the hang of them.'

Erin giggled. 'Ah, well, there I have the edge on you. I understand logarithms totally.'

'Not logarithms, then,' Jay sighed, 'thank goodness. Go on then, ask.'

'It's just that now we've mentioned Nalisha . . .'

'You've mentioned Nalisha.'

'Yes, OK. Well, she told me something and it's been bothering me, and I wasn't going to ask you, but . . .'

Jay propped himself up on one elbow. 'Why do I think I really don't want to hear this?'

Erin rolled away from him, lying on her back, staring at the ceiling. 'She said she would have married you if you'd asked her.'

Silence.

Oh God . . . Erin swallowed. 'And she said she'd loved you.'

Still silence.

'Jay?' Erin turned her head.

Jay just stared at her. 'And?'

Erin shrugged. It was a difficult thing to do lying down. 'I just wondered if . . . well, if . . .?'

Jay still stared. 'And you want an honest answer?'

'Yes. Of course.'

Or, maybe not . . .

'OK. Once upon a time—as all the best stories go—my parents and Nalisha's parents thought we'd be the ideal match. I'm sure she's told you that, too. And I asked Nalisha how she felt about it and she said she'd marry me if I asked her.'

Erin realised she'd been holding her breath. It escaped in a long sigh. So, it *was* true.

'And,' Jay continued, 'she told me then that she loved me.'

Oh God—it was *all* true.

Erin closed her eyes. 'And what did you say?'

'Erin, look at me.'

'No—just tell me.'

'Not until you look at me.'

She opened her eyes and turned her head. Oh God, he was gorgeous and she loved him so much, and even if he'd loved Nalisha once, he wasn't marrying Nalisha, was he?

It didn't help.

Jay smiled gently. 'I told her I loved her too.'

Oh God . . . Erin sighed.

'And that I'd marry her if she gave me all her samosas.'

'*What?*'

Jay laughed. 'We were at my Aunt Ganika's birthday party. We were eight years old.'

'*What?*'

Jay laughed again. 'True. And she said she wanted all the samosas to herself and broke my heart. And we've never, ever mentioned marriage or love again. Because I love her like a sister, and like her as a friend. We know each other far too well to ever want to move into a different sort of

268

relationship.'

Erin blinked at him. 'Is that honestly true?'

'Cross my heart.'

'So why didn't she tell me that you were just *kids*?'

'I have no idea. She probably thought it was funny. I can see, from your point of view, that it wasn't.' He pulled her towards him. 'You'll have to ask her yourself.'

'Oh, I will,' Erin said happily, wanting to laugh and scream and kiss the sky. 'Just as soon as I get up and get dressed and find her. But not yet—' she rolled even closer to him on the rumpled sheets, running her fingers over his gorgeous body '—as this is going to be the last time . . .'

'What?' Jay jerked his head away and stared at her. 'You mean? Us? In bed?'

'Yep. Until after we're married.'

'Phew,' Jay exhaled. 'I thought you were going to tell me something I really didn't want to hear. But why?'

'Because, darling, after today we'll both be heavily parented, won't we? There's no way I'll be able to escape my mum and dad—or yours—and sneak away like this.'

'No, I suppose not. Sod it. How the hell are we going to manage until our wedding night?'

'If you remember, we weren't going to be doing this at all for the six weeks before the wedding, were we?'

'No. But that was just silly. We both knew that wouldn't last.'

'Mmmm. But now we really will have to exercise massive restraint for the next ten days.' Erin giggled. 'Or longer, because everyone I know says they never managed to have sex on their wedding night because they were too exhausted. And the next night we'll still be on the plane on the way to our honeymoon. Blimey—that's ages of celibacy, isn't it?'

'Easy then.' Jay grinned at her. 'We'll just have to join the mile-high club, won't we?'

'Oooh, yes, or maybe no . . .'

'Which means—' Jay ran his fingers across her ribcage '—we ought to make the most of what little time we have left.'

* * *

'Jay!' The voice rang up the stairs. 'Jaimal! Are you in, darling?'

'Ohmigod.' Erin sat up, blinking the sleep from her eyes. 'Jay . . . Jay, wake up! We must've dozed off. It's your mum! She's here!'

'What? She can't be. Where?' Jay shook his head and peered drowsily at her through his devastatingly long eyelashes.

'She is. And here,' Erin hissed, scrambling for her clothes and not finding them. 'In the cottage. Downstairs.'

'Shit!' Jay rolled off the bed, staggering into the bedside cabinet. 'Ouch. Where the hell are my clothes?'

'With mine,' Erin muttered, remembering. 'On the stairs.'

Oh bugger.

'Jaimal?' Deena's voice was closer now. 'Why is all your laundry on the staircase, darling? You were never this messy when you lived at home. Are you decent?'

270

She knocked lightly on the bedroom door.

'No . . . yes . . . not really . . . Don't come in!' Jay muttered, stumbling as he wrapped himself in his hastily grabbed bathrobe.

'Don't be silly. I've seen it all before, darling. Have you been in the shower?'

About the only place they hadn't been, Erin thought, trying to hide beneath a corner of the sheet.

'I can't say I blame you on a scorching day like this.' Deena pushed the door open. 'I've just seen darling Nalisha in the village—what a lovely surprise that was!—and she said she thought you were here and—oh.'

'Hello,' Erin said brightly.

Deena just gaped.

'And this is another lovely surprise.' Jay's smile was a rictus. 'We weren't expecting you until this evening.'

'I don't think you were expecting me at all.' Deena sniffed. 'I'll go and wait downstairs, shall I?'

'What a good idea,' Erin said, trying not to giggle. 'And I'll make us all some tea.'

Tea. The cure-all. Even for being walked in on by your future mother-in-law.

'Once you're dressed, Erin, that would be lovely. Thank you. I'll see you both downstairs.'

She shut the door.

'Oh shit, shit, shit.' Erin giggled, threw off the sheet and padded to the door. 'I'd better go on a clothes hunt.'

Jay shook his head. 'If we'd had a little longer we might have managed to find something in the wardrobe. Oh God, I'm never going to be able to look at her again without laughing.'

271

'I'm never going to be able to look at her again full stop,' Erin muttered. 'How embarrassing was that?'

'One good thing,' Jay said, looking at the bedside clock, 'we won't have long enough to sit in uncomfortable silence over the polite cup of tea. We've got to be leaving for Heathrow in about half an hour.'

'Really? Wow. Just as well she woke us up then.'

'Yes,' Jay said, nodding, 'although I'd have much preferred the alarm clock. And, Erin, please get some clothes on before I drag you back to bed.'

CHAPTER THIRTY-TWO

Heathrow was very crowded and exciting. Erin and Jay mingled with all the other hordes of people at the arrivals gate, and Erin secretly wished they had a placard to hold up like all those rather intense men pressed up against the barriers.

'At least we'll be greeting your parents fully dressed,' Jay whispered. 'So there's a bonus.'

Erin, still on a complete high, laughed and curled her arms round his waist.

It had been excruciatingly awkward, kicking their heels in Jay's tiny living room, while Deena sipped her hastily made cup of tea, exchanging very brief polite pleasantries with someone who'd not only just seen you stark naked but who also *knew what you'd been doing*.

It had been a massive relief to escape.

'Oh goodness, why don't they hurry up?' Erin jigged up and down impatiently. 'Their plane

272

landed ages and ages ago.'

'They've got to get their luggage unloaded and then from the carousel and go through passport control and there must be hundreds of passengers on the plane,' Jay said reasonably. 'They won't be long. See, there are some people coming through now.'

The first trickle of passengers from the Sydney plane had started to filter through, appearing from the passageway, pushing loaded trollies or hauling wheeled suitcases. Several people ran forwards from the waiting crowd with cries of delight.

'Oooh, come on!' Erin muttered. 'Come on!'

Jay kissed her.

Children ran shrieking happily into fathers' arms; friends screamed greetings of recognition; parted lovers were romantically reunited; business colleagues greeted one another enthusiastically.

Then . . .

'There they are!' Erin shrieked, shoving her way through the crowd. 'I can see them! That's my mum in the beige . . . oh, and yellow and that sort of washed-out mustard colour, and look how much luggage she's got—oh and she's carrying a massive hatbox!'

Jay, who'd met her parents once before, laughed. 'And there's your dad with another high-piled trolley, still looking nothing at all like Doug. You'd never think they were brothers, would you?'

Erin shook with impatience as people insisted on getting in her way, but eventually she managed to force her way through and hurled herself into her mum's arms.

Then they both burst into tears.

Then Erin hugged and hugged her dad and cried

some more.

After several minutes of totally incoherent babbling and hugging and kissing all round, and Jay kissing her mum and shaking hands with her dad, and more kissing, and no one actually wanting to let go of anyone else, they staggered towards the exit.

'I've managed to park reasonably close,' Jay said. 'Just across the road here. Let me help you with some of this stuff.'

'If you could lose the damn hatbox before we get to the car,' Pete Boswell chuckled, 'it'll do us all a favour.'

Rose and Erin talked all the time. At the same time. And kept looking at one another as if they simply couldn't believe it.

'Oh, this is so exciting!' Rose beamed up at Jay. 'Your wedding at last. It's just so wonderful to be here. I can't wait to see Nook Green. Has it changed?'

'Not at all,' Erin said. 'Well, there are a few of Jay's relatives there already for the wedding, and they're all dying to meet you, especially Jay's mum. His dad will be down in a few days' time too, but otherwise, no. Everything's just as you left it. Oh, Mum, I've missed you so much.'

They hugged again as they reached the car, and Jay and Pete started on the tricky job of loading all the luggage into every available space.

'And is my reprobate brother still playing the field?' Pete asked.

'Yes. Sadly. The state of play's exactly as it was last time we Skyped.' Erin pulled a face. 'He's still got the hots for the lovely Nalisha, who as I've said, is going to leave him high and dry. And he'd be so much happier with Gina. Maybe you could talk

274

some sense into him, Dad?'

'Me? No way. I gave up doing that when he was fifteen,' Pete Boswell chuckled. 'And he didn't listen to me then, so forty-odd years on I don't think he's going to start now.'

Jay laughed.

'And *he's* even more lovely and handsome than I remember.' Rose smiled, watching Jay hauling cases from their trolley. 'You're a very lucky girl, Erin.'

'I know.' Erin giggled. 'But he's lucky too. Or so he keeps telling me.'

Rose sighed happily. 'Oh, you honestly do make a fabulous couple. I'm so happy for you both. And everything's gone to plan, has it? No hitches with the wedding? I know you've told us things on Skype, but you may have been holding something back.'

'Me?' Erin said. 'As if I'd ever be able to keep anything back from you. You've always been able to tell when I'm lying or trying to fudge an issue, even when I was really tiny. No, honestly, it's all gone wonderfully. Well, OK, there were a few glitches earlier—not worth bothering you with at the time— but they're mostly all sorted now. No, Mum, I can promise you, there is nothing on earth that'll stop us having the perfect wedding day we've always planned.'

CHAPTER THIRTY-THREE

'And are your parents still asleep this morning, darling?' Deena asked in Jay's cottage, the day after

275

the Boswells arrival. 'Are they totally exhausted?'

Erin nodded. 'Completely. Day's night to them at the moment. But Mum and Dad are really looking forward to meeting you—and Mum particularly is looking forward to discussing all the joint Mother-of-the-Happy-Couple stuff with you.'

'As I am.' Deena nodded. 'Will tomorrow be acceptable, do you think?'

'Perfect.'

'Good. And as for that little incident, yesterday . . . I think the least said about that, the better, don't you?'

Erin blushed a bit and wanted to giggle. 'Well, I'd prefer it if you didn't feel the need to share it with my parents, yes. But I'm not ashamed of sleeping with Jay. Far from it. Why should I be? We love each other madly. We're days away from our wedding. We adore one another. We—'

'I know, darling.' Deena patted her arm. 'And I was young once, too. I do remember what it was like. And it might have been a teensy bit my fault by just bursting in on you.'

Erin smiled to herself. She knew that was as far as Deena would go in admitting her culpability in the barging-in-unannounced situation. It was more than she'd expected to be honest.

'Anyway—' Deena smoothed down her vivid daffodil-yellow frock and, this time, Erin noticed, the jewels were citrines to match '—least said, soonest mended. So we'll say no more about it.'

'Good. Thank you. So, shall we go to the pub now? We're meeting Jay and Nalisha for lunch.'

'Yes, of course, darling. That all sounds lovely. I can't wait to see Nalisha again.'

Neither can I, Erin thought, laughing now at the

prospect.

Having locked the cottage door behind them, Erin indicated to Deena that they needed to cross the green. It was still scorching. Everything was dusty and drooping and baking in the sun. The banks of the Nook were crammed with children paddling and fishing and just sitting, too exhausted to move, dangling their feet in the crystal-clear shallows.

'Oh, that looks divine,' Deena said, teetering across the green's rock-hard and uneven surface. 'I was very tempted to do the same when I had my breakfast by the river this morning.'

Erin chuckled at the mental image.

'And,' Deena continued, 'I had a little word with Abigail, your wedding planner, this morning, too.'

Oh God. Nooo. Just when everything seemed to be going so well.

'Really?' Erin said. 'Lovely, isn't she?'

'She's very efficient, certainly. And I'm so pleased the problem with the *mandap* has been resolved. I knew you'd be able to use it, darling. I knew you'd love it. Didn't I say so on the phone?'

Erin gaped. She hadn't mentioned the *mandap* to Abbie again. As far as she knew, it was still packed up in the storage shed behind the Swan's swimming pool.

'Er, yes, you did.'

'Abigail said you were all a little dumbfounded when it arrived,' Deena laughed. 'But again, it's all been sorted out now, and I can't wait to see it in all its glory. Oh, your wedding day is going to be so wonderful, darling. I'm so glad that we've managed to meet each other halfway.'

'Um, yes, me too.'

277

Erin's head swam. Either she was suffering from pre-wedding amnesia and she'd completely forgotten some vital *mandap* conversation with Abbie, or Abbie was an even better peacemaker than Kofi Annan.

Whatever, it was something else to worry about later. Right now, there were absolutely no clouds on the immediate horizon.

'Here we are,' Erin said, leading the way through the brightly umbrella'd beer garden outside the Merry Cobbler.

'I've always thought this was an absolutely gorgeous little country public house, and the landlady—Gina?—is fabulous, isn't she?'

'She is.'

Erin led the way into the pub's cool, dark interior and threaded her way through the ever-present crowd.

Gina, looking young and amazingly sexily pretty in a very short rose-sprigged spaghetti-strapped frock and with her curls caught back with little rosebud hair-clips, beamed at them both.

'Good morning, Erin. Bet you're over the moon to have your mum and dad here at last, aren't you? Can't wait to see them and catch up. And hello again, Deena. Lovely to see you, and what a fabulous dress. Oh, I do wish I was as slim as you.'

Deena preened.

'And you're all booked in for lunch? Table outside suit you?'

'Perfect, thanks.' Erin nodded. 'Er, you look particularly amazing this morning. You look radiantly happy for the first time in ages. I'm so pleased.'

'Thanks,' Gina giggled. 'I feel pretty great too.'

278

'Morning, young Erin,' Sam called from across the bar where he was happily pouring beer slops into the waste bucket. 'And Mrs K.! Nice to see you again. Sight for sore eyes, you are, my love. Right little Reita Faria, you are, duck.'

Erin raised her eyebrows and held her breath.

Deena beamed. 'Well, thank you so much. That's a wonderful compliment.'

'Who's Reita Faria?' Erin asked.

'A former Miss India—she won Miss World in the nineteen sixties.' Deena preened even more. 'She was a doctor, too. An exceptionally beautiful and wonderfully talented woman.'

Well done, Sam, Erin thought.

'Ah.' Sam nodded happily over his slops. The smell was pretty rancid. 'Gorgeous, she were. And clever. Just like Mrs K., here.'

Deena almost purred with pleasure.

'Shall we sit here and have a drink?' Erin indicated a quiet corner table. 'Or would you prefer to be outside?'

'No, here's lovely.' Deena sat down gracefully. 'Oh, I do love this pub.'

'What would you like to drink? I'm having cider.'

'That sounds very refreshing, thank you, darling.'

Erin hurried to the bar and smiled at Gina. 'Two ciders on ice, please, and who is he?'

'Who?' Gina poured the drinks.

'The man who's put the oomph back into you.'

Gina laughed. 'Oh, I wish. There's no man, Erin. I'm just starting afresh, you know? I made a mess of things with Doug and it's over and I've moved on at last. It's like being reborn. I'm a whole new woman.'

'Well, if you ever want to share the secret—' Erin

grinned '—feel free. You look fabulous.'

'Thanks—Oh, hi, Kam.' Gina looked up and grinned. 'Er, surgery finished early?'

'Mine has.' Kam leaned on the bar. 'Jay's still working.'

Erin laughed. 'Blimey, I think you could do with whatever Gina's on. You look like you haven't slept all night.'

Kam looked at Gina and laughed. 'I know. I find it almost impossible to sleep on these hot nights.'

Gina giggled.

'Oh—' Kam squinted into the pub '—and is that your redoubtable ma-in-law-to-be I can see down there, Erin?'

'Yes, please come and say hello,' Erin said quickly. 'I'm going to run out of conversation in about five minutes.'

'Will do. I'll just get myself a drink—non-alcoholic, sadly. I've got a big op this afternoon.' He lifted the flap and wandered behind the bar. 'I'll be with you in just a moment.'

Erin paid for the drinks and took them back to the table.

'Thank you, darling.' Deena smiled. 'Is that Kam behind the bar talking to Gina?'

'Yes. He'll be over in a minute. He's just getting himself a drink. He works here sometimes.'

'As a barman?'

'Mmmm. Well, he has a room here until he finds his own place, and Gina's often really busy, so he just helps out.'

'Really?' Deena sipped her cider. 'How very odd. I wonder if he's told his parents?'

Erin tried hard not to laugh, wondering again if any Indian parents ever thought their children were

280

adults and deciding probably not.

Kam, clutching a St Clements, joined them, kissed Deena and uttered the expected compliments before he sat down.

'Erin's just told me you work here as a barman,' Deena said. 'I was very surprised.'

'Only on a very as-and-when basis,' Kam laughed. 'I'm not intending to give up being a vet anytime soon.'

'I should hope not.' Deena looked horrified. 'Not after all the sacrifices your parents made.'

Erin giggled quietly.

'Oh, they think it's pretty cool, actually. And I did work in a burger bar all through uni, if you remember.'

Deena remained silent for a moment. Then she sighed. 'Well, yes, of course you did. I'd forgotten. And Jaimal worked in that pet shop, didn't he? And Tavish said that Mr and Mrs Gupta's son worked in McDonald's all through his Oxford divinity course. And not just in the vacs, either. Sometimes he did evenings and weekends. Fitted his shifts in round his studies and he still got a First.'

'Good for him.' Kam nodded. 'But I don't think he's the greatest example to quote, do you?'

Erin frowned. *Why on earth not?*

Deena laughed. 'Well, they were obviously proud of the fact that he managed to support himself throughout his course, and of his final degree, but no, there were issues.'

Erin couldn't bear it. 'Why?'

'Because,' Kam laughed, 'Gupta junior went over to the dark side.'

'Uh?'

Deena pursed her lips. 'He abandoned his

281

Hinduism and became a Church of England vicar.'

'Jesus!'

Kam and Deena stared at her.

'Well, no sorry,' Erin muttered, 'but you know what I mean.'

Kam was still chuckling into his drink.

'At least this is a very nice class of public house,' Deena said, 'not rough or rowdy. And Gina seems like an extremely pleasant woman. Do you have bed and breakfast?'

Kam continued to splutter into his drink.

'Gina's great.' Erin stared at Kam, then looked across at Deena. 'Kam's very lucky to be here. I'm going to pop back to the surgery and see if Jay's ready to join us for lunch when he's finished, OK?'

'Lovely, darling,' Deena said with a nod. 'And Nalisha?'

'Oh, yes, and Nalisha. I think she's over at the shop with Uncle Doug at the moment.'

Deena raised her eyebrows. 'Really? Goodness me, that's not a relationship that will please her parents.'

'I don't think it's anything more than a temporary friendship.' Erin smiled 'Nothing at all to worry her parents.'

'Let's hope not,' Deena said. 'I know they have very high hopes for her making a suitable match, and pleasant as Doug is, he certainly wouldn't be their first choice. Or even their thirty-first. Now, Kam, come along. Tell me everything that's been going on here.'

Kam was still laughing as Erin left the pub. Men, she thought, grinning to herself, did they ever grow up?

282

CHAPTER THIRTY-FOUR

Erin was still chuckling when she walked into the vet's surgery.

Sophie was on the phone and made flapping movements with her hand.

'Yeah, me too, David . . . Yeah, it was brilliant . . . Oh, yes—tonight? Great. Can't wait. With Bella and Aiden—yeah should be a laugh. About eight o'clock, yes—oh, hang on a sec, Erin's here.' She put her hand over the phone. 'Hiya. Do you want Jay? He's in surgery with a booster jab and check-up puppy, and then he's got a patient waiting. Just the one. He should be fine for lunch. Just go in and wait.'

'OK, I'm just going to nip across to the shop and tell Nalisha that we're ready for lunch. Back in a minute.' Erin nodded at the phone. 'And give my love to David.'

But Sophie was already cooing again and didn't hear her.

*   *   *

Stepping carefully over the doormat, Erin peered into the cavernous gloom of the Old Curiosity Shop. There were a few people wandering about amongst the larger pieces of furniture at the far end and someone leafing through the collection of books. Dust motes danced round them in the shafts of sunlight like a summer miasma.

'Uncle Doug!'

'I'm over here. In the maritime section.'

Erin giggled. When Doug had a customer he was trying to impress he always tended to make the shop sound like an offshoot of the Ashmoleum. The maritime section had a couple of telescopes, two ships-in-bottles, a few flags and a battered model of the *Mary Rose*.

'Actually—' Erin swerved her way through a narrow gap '—I was looking for Nalisha. We're supposed to be going for lunch with Deena.'

Doug emerged from the maritime section clutching one of the ships-in-a-bottle, followed by a man who looked like Captain Birdseye.

'She's waiting for you in the garden. She's been helping me with some cataloguing.'

Hoping this wasn't a euphemism, Erin smiled her thanks, beamed at Captain Birdseye and headed outside again.

Nalisha, in a floaty pale green sari, was sitting reading at the table under the lilac trees with Florence sprawled on her lap.

Honestly, Erin thought, that cat has no sense of solidarity at all.

'Hi.' Nalisha looked up from her book. 'Scorching, isn't it? I thought I'd be used to the heat after California, but I forgot how stifling English summer days can be. Are we all ready for lunch?'

'Almost.' Erin flopped on to the opposite chair. 'Deena's in the pub with Kam, and Jay has a couple of patients still to see. Actually, I wanted to catch you on your own.'

Nalisha put the book down, cover upwards. Erin was disappointed to see that it wasn't a bonk-buster or a grisly police procedural, but a law book on historical torts.

Nice light reading . . .

'Go on then.' Nalisha smiled. 'I'm all yours—although if you're going to warn me off your uncle, I can spare you the trouble. He's been a charming escort while I've been here, I find the, um, antiques fascinating, and we get on very well, but I shan't be joining your family.'

Erin raised her eyebrows. 'No, I didn't think for one moment that you would. Actually I just wanted to talk to you about Jay.'

'More stories from his youth? Oh, are you going to make a bride's speech at the wedding and you want some ammunition?'

Erin shook her head. 'I'm leaving all that to Kam as best man. I'm sure he'll manage to be suitably rude and embarrassing. No, actually I just wanted to say that I think you were way out of line when you told me that you would have married Jay if he asked you, and that you loved him. That's all.'

Nalisha gazed at her across the table. 'Why?'

'Because Jay and I are together now, we're millimetres away from our wedding day, and it really wasn't what I wanted to hear.'

'But it was true.'

'Yes.' Erin stared at the gold tooling on the law book. It sparkled in the dappled sunlight. 'I know. I asked Jay. He said it happened when you were eight years old. You conveniently forgot to mention that bit.'

Nalisha laughed softly and tickled Florence's ears. 'Yes, sorry. I must have forgotten that part of the story.'

'No you didn't.' Erin was determined to stay calm. 'You did it on purpose. I have no idea why, but I just want you to know that I know now and that you can't do or say anything at all to make me doubt Jay, if that's what you were trying to do.'

Nalisha stroked Florence's head. 'I know, Erin. And I apologise. I was being a bit of a bitch. I am a bit of a bitch, you see. No, actually, I'm a lot of a bitch. That's why I've been such a complete cow. That's why I came to Nook Green. I wanted to hurt you. I'm very, very jealous of you.'

'Jealous of *me*? Bloody hell—why? You're supermodel stunning, you've got a ball-breaking career, you've got a car to die for, and designer clothes and—'

'I'd give up all those things to be in your shoes, even if they're about as far from Louboutins as it's possible to get.' Nalisha looked across the table. 'Because you've got Jay. And Jay loves you insanely. Jay can't wait to marry you. Jay can't wait to spend the rest of his life with you.'

Erin frowned. 'But you said . . .'

'The incident I told you about was at a party when we were kids, yes. But it's how I've always felt. Always. I'd have married Jay like a shot at any time. I've loved him all my life. But he does think of me as a sister, as a friend. He's never been interested in me in any other way.'

Erin stared. The birds seemed to have stopped singing. Florence had stopped purring. Nook Green was very, very quiet.

'You mean . . .'

'That you're the luckiest lady on the planet and that I really wanted to hate you, but I don't. I wanted to hurt you, and I tried but I can't because you're lovely—although I'll envy you for ever.'

Erin exhaled. 'But Jay has no idea how you feel, does he?'

'No. But even if he did, it would make no

286

difference. He'd never love me. He'd never want to marry me. I came here to see if I could make him change his mind.'

Dear God. Erin blinked. 'And?'

'And I realised that it was absolutely pointless. As soon as I met you, as soon as I saw you and Jay together, I knew it was a complete waste of time. Jay's totally, absolutely head over heels in love with you, as you are with him. But as well as that, you're close friends and partners. You understand and like each other. You're perfect together.'

Erin nodded. They were.

'And,' Nalisha said quietly, 'because he's the only man I want then I'll probably never marry. Anyone else would be second best.'

They stared at one another.

Nalisha smiled. 'And I'd rather you didn't tell him, OK? I'd like to retain some dignity and let him carry on thinking that the little jokey childish declaration at the party all those years ago was all there is to it.'

'Er, yes . . . OK. Of course. Whatever you want.'

Nalisha put Florence gently on the grass and stood up. 'Erin—thank you. And we've never had this conversation, have we?'

'What conversation?' Erin pushed her chair back. 'I don't remember talking to you at all.'

'You're lovely. I don't deserve you to forgive me. Jay's so lucky. And I'll see you for lunch in a little while? If you still want me to be there, of course.'

'I'll see you for lunch.'

Erin stroked Florence, smiled again at Nalisha and hurried out of the garden.

Then she scampered across the green and grinned and giggled and did a little happy dance.

The children playing in the shallows of the Nook all looked at her doubtfully.

She laughed at them. Because Jay, the most fabulous man in the world, loved her. And was marrying her. Very, very soon. Her—not the gorgeous, massively qualified, designer-clad, corporately employed Nalisha. Erin Boswell, in her Topshop shorts and T-shirts, in her scruffy jeans and vests. Erin Boswell with her three so-so A levels and her junk-shop job.

Erin Boswell, she thought gleefully, as she danced and skipped towards the veterinary surgery, was the luckiest girl in the whole wide world.

CHAPTER THIRTY-FIVE

Still grinning from ear to ear, Erin waved at Sophie and went through into the tiny waiting room, determined to keep as far away from the hunched figure with the cat-carrying-box as possible.

Her euphoria melted instantly away, the ear-to-ear grin faded, replaced by a wave of sympathy. She knew it was wimpy, but she couldn't bear it if the cat and the owner were about to be parted for ever. When the time came for it to happen to Florence she knew she'd never, ever recover.

Then she saw that the hunched figure was Callum, the Old Curiosity Shop's Saturday boy. And that he was crying.

Oh God.

'Callum?' Erin walked across the waiting room and spoke softly. 'Callum, are you OK?'

He looked up at her with swollen, bloodshot eyes.

Erin sat beside him. 'Can I help at all?'

'No. Thanks, though.' Callum swallowed and nodded towards the cat-carrier on his lap. 'It's Tootsie.'

Erin peered at the box. She could just see bits of ginger fur peeping through the slats. 'Oh, Callum, that's awful. I'm really sorry.' She slid her arm round his skinny shoulders, feeling him shaking. 'What's wrong with her?'

Callum dashed away the tears. 'I think she's broken her leg. I dunno if Jay can fix it. What if he can't?' He turned huge eyes to Erin. 'What if he . . .?'

Erin clenched her lips tightly together. It would be useless if she burst into tears now too. What sort of vet's wife would she be if she howled broken-heartedly with all the patients?

'I'm sure Jay will be able to fix it if it's only a broken leg.'

'What if it isn't? What if he can't?'

'Jay's a brilliant vet—you know that. He can work miracles.' She patted Callum's shoulder. She could feel the bones through his T-shirt. 'That's how we first met—me and Jay—when I thought my cat Florence was going to die.'

'And he sorted her out?' Callum looked hopeful.

'Completely. And she's still going strong. And will be around for years yet. I'm sure poor Tootsie will be fine as well. Don't worry.'

'I really love her,' Callum mumbled. 'I can say that to you, 'cause you understand. Some people would laugh, but I really, really love her. She's like my friend—she understands me when other people don't. And she's always there. I just can't face it if she . . . well, you know . . .'

'Oh, you don't need to tell me. I'm just the same with Florence.' Erin's heart went out to him as she sniffed back her tears and leaned forwards. 'I don't want to hurt her, but can I stroke her? Just gently? Sometimes it helps animals to be comforted and reassured when they're scared and in pain.'

'Yeah, course.' Callum brushed the tears away leaving a grubby streak across his cheek. 'Just don't touch her bad leg, OK?'

'No, I won't. You just open the box a bit . . . She's very quiet. That's a good sign—she can't be in too much pain. She'd be crying if she was in pain.'

Callum frowned but obediently opened the top of the box.

Erin gently peered inside.

Oh shit. Holy shit.

Every inch of her froze.

Tootsie was a tarantula.

A ten-inch wide tarantula.

A massive ginger and brown furred tarantula with seven equally massive ginger-striped, furred, hinged legs—and one that dragged behind her.

Erin whimpered.

'What?' Callum looked at her anxiously. 'Is it really bad? Do you think she's gonna die?'

No, but I might at any minute, Erin thought, feeling very sick and fighting the urge to stand up and run screaming out of the surgery and across the green and never, ever stop.

She averted her eyes from the carrier. 'No, er, I'm sure Jay will be able to, er, well, whatever.'

'Touch her, then,' Callum urged, fresh tears welling in his eyes. 'If you think it'll help her. I

290

stroke her a lot. She likes it. But I don't want to hurt her. You, being like getting married to Jay, you'll know how to do it properly.'

Oh, pulease, nooo.

Erin exhaled and tried to control the mounting panic attack.

Callum was watching her with large fearful eyes. One, two, three, Erin counted her breaths. Deep breathing helped, didn't it?

No, it didn't.

She held herself rigid and inched closer to the carrier box. Somehow, she willed herself to put one hand forwards and extend one finger. OK. Then she inched the finger closer to the opening in the carrier.

Tootsie waved one of her healthy legs. Erin whimpered.

Callum jumped. 'You know she's gonna die, don't you?'

'No, no, of course not,' Erin assured him. 'I'm just being, er, careful so that I don't hurt her.'

Oh, she'd just have to tell him that his beloved Tootsie scared her to death. That she was the biggest arachnophobe in the world. That she couldn't touch his beloved Tootsie without passing out on the spot. That just looking at Tootsie made her skin crawl, her heartbeat rise to danger levels and her entire body shiver with total terror.

Then she looked at Callum's face. He was absolutely relying on her to reassure him. And she remembered how she'd felt that morning when she'd first rushed in here with Florence.

And how she'd have felt if someone had offered her words of support and then immediately withdrawn them.

And Tootsie wasn't going to dash at her, or run up her arm, or disappear into her hair, was she?

And she was sort of furry . . .

'Er, it feels quite warm in there.'

'I've got a hot water bottle under the blanket. She's sub-tropical. Has to be kept warm at all times. And she's been out of her tank for about half an hour and I don't want her to die of cold, do I?'

Oh, no, of course not, silly me.

Erin knew, in the face of this all-encompassing love and impending heartbreak, she really couldn't do anything else.

Working some saliva into her mouth, trying to stop herself from shaking, and not looking, she pushed her finger into the carrier.

And touched Tootsie. Very, very tentatively.

Ohmigod.

The instinctive urge to scream, to be violently sick, to pull her hand out of the carrier and run away gibbering was extremely strong.

But Callum had stopped crying and Tootsie had stopped waving. And after all, Tootsie *wasn't* like a spider really, was she? Not-a-spider. Not scary.

Think of her as a little furry creature that needs comfort, Erin told herself. *Not* a spider . . .

Callum smiled. 'Oh, she likes you.'

How the hell can you tell? Erin couldn't quite manage a smile in return but at least she hadn't been sick on either of them. Bonus.

She moved her finger further into the carrier. And touched Tootsie again.

She felt such a rush of triumph that she actually itched to rush round the vet's waiting room with her T-shirt over her head and punching the air.

Yesssssssss!

The surgery door opened, and a large man with a very small bouncy puppy came out.

Bella beamed, more at the puppy than the man. 'Sophie will make your next appointment and sort out the payment, Mr Ball. Oh hi, Erin, catch you in a bit, we're nearly done, and, Callum, Jay will see you and Tootsie now.'

Erin whipped her finger out of the carrier at the speed of light.

Phew.

Callum fastened the carrier and looked terrified.

'It's OK,' Erin assured him, shaking now. 'She'll be fine.'

'Come in with me?' Callum stood up, looking as if his legs were about to collapse. 'Just don't tell no one I couldn't do it on my own. Come in with me—please.'

Avoiding meeting Bella's eyes, Erin smiled confidently and nodded and followed Callum into the surgery.

If Jay had to euthanise Tootsie, Erin knew she'd be a complete emotional heap.

Bella stood back as they passed in the doorway. 'Are-you-mad?'

'I-think-I-might-be. And so are you if you think Aiden the Dance King is your Mr Heathcliff.'

'Mr Darcy, actually. And Aiden is simply amazing. But, you do know that Tootsie is a—'

'Yes. Shush. I have a vet to see.'

When he saw her, Jay's eyes widened in total amazement. 'Er, hi—this is a lovely surprise. I certainly wasn't expecting to see you. Just Callum, and Tootsie.'

'Mmm, you know me. Always like the element of surprise in a relationship.'

293

Erin, still swamped by so many recent mixed emotions after the talk with Nalisha, found that actually all she wanted to do was to fling herself into Jay's arms and kiss him to death.

'Not that it's not lovely to see you, but I, er, actually don't think you'll want to be in here for this consultation, Erin.' Jay motioned his head towards the carrier, which Callum had placed lovingly on the examination table. 'Maybe you'd be better outside?'

'I asked her to come with me,' Callum muttered. 'I need her.'

'So do I,' Jay laughed. 'But she might have a bit of a problem.'

Erin shook her head. 'No. I'm OK. I know. About Tootsie.'

Bella, who was standing back in case she was needed, shook her head.

Jay exhaled. 'OK. You never fail to amaze me, and long may it continue, but—'

'Callum and I got talking in the waiting room. He told me all about Tootsie,' Erin said, willing neither Jay nor Bella to mention her spider phobia. 'Tootsie and I have already become acquainted.'

'No way.' Jay shook his head as he opened the carrier and carefully lifted the tarantula out. 'Honestly? And are you sure you want me to do this? Now?'

'Yes,' Erin said firmly, willing herself not to feel even slightly queasy.

'OK, but we'll keep the door open. Feel free to run at any time. Now, Callum, what's the problem with Tootsie?'

As Callum explained again about Tootsie's broken leg, Erin stood back from the table beside

294

Bella, while Jay examined the spider.

It's a spider, Erin told herself. A humongous spider. And you're not scared. Not at all. Not even a little bit.

Well, OK, not *that* scared.

'Please,' Callum whispered, 'please don't kill her.'

'I'm not going to kill her, Callum,' Jay said gently when he'd checked her over. 'Tootsie will be absolutely fine. Look, here—do you see where the hinge of her knee joint is on her damaged leg?'

Callum nodded.

'Well, inside there, on all her legs, there's a little valve, and it will eventually close off, so there's no more blood flow into the broken leg. OK so far?'

Erin had moved forwards and was now shoulder to shoulder with Callum. Tootsie was sitting quite calmly on the table. Wow, Erin thought, I'm sharing my breathing space with a tarantula and I'm still alive!

Wow.

Callum nodded again. 'And she isn't in pain, like, hurting, is she?'

'No. She's in no pain at all. And,' Jay said, his voice still wonderfully soothing, 'eventually the closed valve will make sure the damaged part of her leg will drop off. Like shedding unwanted skin. Or she might even bite it off herself when it's dead.'

'And that's OK, is it? It won't hurt her? And will it grow again?'

'Perfectly OK. And no, it won't hurt her at all. The leg won't grow again either, but she'll be absolutely fine with seven and a half legs, and she'll live happily to a ripe old age.'

'Really?' Callum looked wide-eyed at Jay. 'She's

going to be OK? You're not lying?'

'I never lie. Tootsie is very well looked after. I know you care for her properly, and if you carrying on caring for her as you have been, she'll live until she's at least fifteen years old.'

Erin brushed away a happy tear.

Callum beamed as he carefully scooped up Tootsie and placed her lovingly back into her box. 'Oh, wicked. Thank you. Thank you so much.'

'I didn't actually do anything much.' Jay smiled. 'But at least you don't have to worry about her now, do you? Go home and get her back into her tank.'

'I will.' Callum nodded. 'You're so cool, you two. Thanks, Erin. And you won't tell anyone about, well, out there?'

'Our secret.' Erin beamed. 'And Callum, thank you, too.'

'What for? I didn't do nothing.'

'Oh, you did, believe me.' Erin grinned. 'I think you and Tootsie might just have changed my life. Now, do as Jay says and get her home.'

'Yeah, cool. Thanks again. Both of you.'

Bella, trying not to laugh, left the surgery with Callum and Tootsie.

'OK—now explain to me what exactly happened there?' Jay pulled her into his arms. 'Have I just witnessed some sort of miracle?'

'Guess so,' Erin whispered, pressing herself against him. 'I just know I'll not be needing that arachnophobia therapy thingy any time soon. I think I could do with some other therapy though.'

'So could I,' Jay said softly into her hair. 'But aren't we supposed to be joining my mum for lunch in the Merry Cobbler? Wasn't that the arrangement?'

'Mmm, it was, and it still is. But we didn't actually fix a time, did we? And she's with Kam and I'm sure they've got loads to talk about. And, ooh, yes—' Erin grinned '—she said she'd spoken to Abbie at the Swan this morning, and apparently we've been in touch with her and made arrangements for the *mandap*. Have we?'

Jay shook his head. 'Hell, no. Well, I certainly haven't, and I'm guessing you haven't either, because I sort of think you might have mentioned it to me. How very odd. Maybe Abbie was just being diplomatic.'

'Yes, that's what I thought. Anyway, we'll talk to Abbie later. Let's not mention it again to your mum because she's currently *mandap*-happy.'

'Fine. I'll ring Abbie and find out what's going on.'

'Good idea. Just not now. OK?'

'Why—have you got other plans?'

'Mmm, I might have.'

'And are you going to share them?' Jay nodded, kissing her. 'Are they anything to do with how we can pass the next half an hour or so?'

Erin, now sky-high ecstatic because of Tootsie and Nalisha, curled her arms round his neck and giggled. 'Well, you know that other therapy session we just mentioned . . .?'

CHAPTER THIRTY-SIX

'Oh, no!' Deena gazed at Rose Boswell with ill-concealed horror. 'Oh, no, darling. Definitely no.'

Rose giggled. 'What's wrong with it? Does it really look that bad? I thought it looked rather nice, actually.'

It was two days since her mum and dad had arrived in Nook Green, and Erin, perched on the edge of her parents' double bed in Uncle Doug's spare bedroom and watching, with Deena, her mum try on her wedding outfit, held her breath.

'It looks, Rose, darling—' Deena steepled her beautifully manicured fingers together '—frankly appalling.'

OK . . . Erin exhaled. Enough. Time to intervene. 'I think appalling is a bit harsh, don't you?'

'Not at all, darling.' Deena beamed. 'Dear Rose is only going to be mother of the bride once in her life. It'd be a tragedy if she spent it looking frightful. Someone had to be kind enough to tell her.'

'Yes, but as long as Mum likes it . . .'

Deena held up her hands in mock horror. 'No, Erin, listen to me. Please. Rose, darling, that frock and that hat are, well, awful. And those colours . . . they simply don't go together, do they? They're so wishy-washy on your skin. Everything is so faded and dull. So terribly unflattering.'

Rose Boswell laughed, and turned to look at herself in the full-length wardrobe mirror again. Erin sighed. Deena did have a point. The peach cotton dress and jacket were cheaply finished and hung badly. The washed-out blue-grey ostrich feather hat was slightly too big and smelled a bit strange.

But if her mum liked it, then she, Erin, wasn't going to hurt her feelings. Never. Ever.

'Mmmm, maybe you're right.' Rose considered

298

her reflection. 'Maybe it does look a little bit dreary. I thought the peach outfit would look nice and summery, but of course it's not new and—'

'Not *new*?' Deena's voice raised several octaves. 'You mean . . . You mean, it's *an old outfit*? You're wearing *an old outfit* to your daughter's wedding?'

'Well, not exactly.' Rose smiled sweetly. 'It's new to me.'

'You mean . . .' Deena looked as if she was going to faint. 'You mean, it's *second-hand*?'

'Yes,' Rose said brightly. 'Most of my clothes are second-hand. I'm not really interested in clothes, as I'm sure Erin must have told you.'

Erin grinned and nodded.

'But surely, for your *only* daughter's *only* wedding . . .?' Deena trailed away, clearly too shocked at this lack of maternal pride to continue. She looked at Erin. 'Erin, darling, say something to your mother.'

'Nothing to say. If Mum's happy with that outfit, then so am I. I'm just ecstatic that she's here for our wedding. I don't care what she wears as long as she's here and comfortable . . . and happy.'

And not interfering, she thought, but didn't say so.

'Thanks, sweetheart.' Rose smiled some more. 'You know me so well. Honestly, Deena, I know you have my best interests at heart, but for me, an outfit like this is practically *haute couture*. I spent ages choosing it. And I've had it cleaned and pressed properly. And, truthfully, who's going to be looking at me? Or you, for that matter? All eyes will be on Erin—as they should be—and she'll be so stunning that no one will take any notice of the rest of us.'

Erin held her breath.

'I think they might.' Deena's voice was ever so slightly frosty. 'Indeed, I hope they will, because I have no intention of fading into the background. My wedding outfit is my statement of pride. My wedding outfit has been chosen to show my delight in my son's marriage to the woman of his dreams.'

Rose smiled benignly. 'Oh, that's lovely. Quite poetic. I can't quite say the same for mine, of course, but as I say, the outfit is new to me, and quite pretty. And I'll probably get some wear out of it again. Not the hat, of course. I'll probably leave that here when I go back to Sydney.'

Deena flapped her hands in despair. 'But have you no idea how terrible those colours look? Both together and on you? You're so pale-skinned and with that red-gold hair you need something to bring you to life, darling. Have you never taken advice from a colour consultant?'

Erin and Rose howled with laughter.

Deena looked affronted. 'OK, I can see that drastic measures are called for. I'm going to have to take you shopping.'

'Oh, please don't. I mean, do we have to?' Rose said quickly. 'I hate shopping.'

Deena looked shocked and horrified at this heresy.

Erin slid from the bed and hugged her mum. The ostrich feathers tickled her face. The hat really did smell very odd.

'Maybe if we all went together to look for something, Mum? Three heads would be better than one. We could all go. You, me and, um . . .'

Erin paused. There was always this dilemma of what she should call her future mother-in-law to her face. She couldn't call her mum—that would be too ridiculous for words—and saying 'Jay's mum' sounded stilted, and Mrs Keskar was far too formal.

She tried again. 'So, yes, why don't we all go shopping for a new outfit together? You, me and, um, Deena?'

Deena—there, she'd said it.

Whoa, she thought, Jay is going to be soooo proud of me.

Deena beamed. 'What a wonderful idea, Erin, darling.'

Brownie points all round, Erin thought smugly.

'Well, maybe,' Rose said reluctantly. 'But we've only got a little over a week now before the wedding. Aren't you going to be frantically busy with all the last minute things, Erin? And what about your work? Will Doug be able to spare you? I mean, is there going to be time to go shopping?'

'Oh, there's always time for shopping, darling.' Deena clearly sensed victory. 'And I know very well that Erin and Jay have got everything for the wedding organised perfectly. I think some retail therapy would do us all good. A nice bit of relaxation before the Big Day.'

Shopping with Deena would, Erin thought, be anything but relaxing. However, for the sake of peace and harmony and, more importantly, to stop Deena ever repeating to anyone that she'd seen Erin naked and in Jay's bed, she'd agree to anything.

'Well, Dad's happy as a lark working in the shop with Uncle Doug, so I won't be needed there, and I haven't got anything desperate to do for the wedding today, so I'm up for a shopping trip. But are you OK with that, Mum?'

'Yes, actually—' Rose still looked slightly

doubtful '—I think I am. It's been ages since I've been to Reading. Well, obviously—I've been out of the country for two years. Everyone says it's changed out of all recognition. I always loved shopping in Reading.'

'Oh, me too!' Erin laughed in delight. 'It'll be like when I was little, and we'd go in on the bus and have lunch at Lewis's and—'

'Reading? We're not going to Reading.' Deena's eyes flashed. 'We're off to London. In the morning.'

CHAPTER THIRTY-SEVEN

Erin gazed up and down Southall Broadway in open-mouthed amazement. Surely this couldn't be London? Well, almost-London, anyway? She'd been to London many times. With and without Jay. She'd never been to Southall Broadway.

How could this colour and crowd and noise and bustle and exotically scented Eastern-ness have been kept a secret for so long? Why had she never been here before?

Standing between Deena and Rose, she jigged with excitement.

Rose laughed at her. 'It's just like taking you shopping when you were a little girl, Erin. Only not in Reading. Oh, it's so lively and different. I love it.'

'Good.' Deena had suddenly turned into a tour guide. 'Now, we don't want to waste any time, do we? So let's just visit the shops I know will have exactly what we're looking for.'

'And what exactly are we looking for?' Erin ventured, as they were bumped and jostled by the loud and colourful three-abreast crowd who all looked like they'd just stepped out of a Mumbai travelogue. 'Do you have something in mind, Mum? *Mum*?'

'What? Oh, I have absolutely no idea.' Rose was still gazing in wonder at the multiple shops, their windows all crammed with haughty Asian mannequins in vividly hued saris and sari silks draped in multicoloured swathes, and the street-vendors, cooking and selling sweet and savoury snacks, and the market traders, with their wares tumbling out on to the pavement from their stalls, and the jewellers, with simply gazillions of bangles and necklaces and earrings all glinting in the sun like a hidden treasure mountain. 'I'm leaving it to Deena.'

Deena shook her head. 'But you must have some idea of what might suit you?'

'None at all,' Rose said cheerfully. 'Never have had. You have a blank canvas to work with, Deena. I'm in your hands. Only I suppose we shouldn't match or clash—so you'll be able to work out the colours . . . Oh, and something nice and comfy, of course. A nice elasticated waist—nothing that shows any bumps and bulges or needs me to keep sucking my tummy in.'

'But you'll be wearing a body-shaper, surely?' Deena raised both her voice and her eyebrows as they scooted diagonally across the road, narrowly avoiding the non-stop traffic in one direction and the wave of shoppers in the other.

'What's a body-shaper?' Rose shouted back as they leaped on to the relatively safety of the opposite pavement.

Erin could have sworn that Deena uttered a

303

profanity.

As Rose and Deena stood side by side, Erin smiled at the contrast. Deena, looking as always groomed and elegant in her smoky-grey body-con dress—which on anyone else on a day when the temperature was in the eighties would be totally unsuitable—and matching silver-grey heels, and Rose in baggy off-white linen trousers, a droopy orange T-shirt liberally splattered with faded butterflies, and ancient ballet flats.

And despite the heat, Deena's make-up was still perfect, while Rose's, like Erin's, had started to run and crease. And of course Deena's jet-black hair was still perfectly in place and gleaming, whereas Erin's, like her mum's was looking pretty limp and bedraggled.

Some things, Erin thought, were simply not fair. But at least Nalisha had declined Deena's invitation to join them on the grounds that this had to be an outing for the bride and the mums only. Erin had blessed her for that.

'Right, no time to lose,' Deena said briskly. 'Come along.'

They dived headlong into the fray.

'Oooh, excuse me.' Erin's stomach suddenly rumbled as she caught wave after fragrant wave of hot syrup and frying samosas, and tantalising wafts of every spice imaginable drifting from practically every doorway.

Neither her mum nor Deena appeared to have heard. Thank goodness. As she'd skipped breakfast, she really hoped that Deena had factored food into the shopping trip, but felt it was possibly best not to ask.

They came to an abrupt halt, due to the crowds,

304

and Rose turned and looked expectantly at Deena. 'Oh, there are so many lovely shops to choose from. As we've stopped, shall we try this one first, and then work our way along the row?'

'No, I don't think so.' Deena frowned at the window display. 'We'll leave these at this end until later. I know exactly where we need to be first. And if they can't suit, then we'll have to try again, so we can come back to this one. Just push your way through.'

Erin, now getting quite adept at sidestepping knots of Asian ladies in full-throttle, trotted alongside Rose as they tried to keep up with Deena. You had to admire the way she weaved neatly through the throng, Erin thought. Especially in those spiky heels. Conversation was impossible thanks to the noise of the traffic, the shouts of the vendors and the non-stop chatter of the shoppers, so Erin and Rose simply exchanged encouraging and slightly bemused grins.

It was all very exciting. And exotic. And very, very hot.

'Right, this is where we start and hopefully finish, Rose, darling.' Deena came to a halt in front of a double-fronted shop that looked much the same as all the others they'd passed. 'This shop is pretty special, and Rajesh is a miracle-worker, believe me.'

'Lovely.' Rose beamed. 'He'll need to be if I'm going to look as spectacular as you do. Is this where you buy all your clothes from?'

'No, not really.' Deena laughed. 'Only on very special occasions. Or when I don't buy direct from India. Or, of course, I can go to Leicester or Wembley for my Asian outfits, and I do—the shops there are equally as good.'

Rose shook her head in amazement. 'Fancy travelling all the way from Birmingham to London or Leicester just to shop for clothes.'

Erin closed her eyes and held her breath.

'Solihull,' Deena said sharply. 'It's Solihull. Tavish and I live in Solihull. *Not* Birmingham.'

'Isn't it the same place, though? Like a suburb?' Rose frowned. 'Or am I thinking of Edgbaston?'

'I sincerely hope not.' Deena looked a bit frosty. 'And as Erin will tell you, I personally find off-the-peg outfits from Per Una or Phase Eight suit me perfectly for my day-wear. And those, of course, I can buy anywhere. But, for an outfit for an occasion as exceptional as my only son's wedding, I couldn't possibly shop in a *chain store*.'

The words 'or a Sydney second-hand shop' hung unsaid on the hot, spice-filled air.

Unperturbed, Rose continued to smile happily. 'So, is this the shop where you bought your frock for the wedding?'

'No, Rose, darling. One, I'm not wearing a frock at the wedding. I'm wearing a ceremonial sari. And two, no, I didn't buy it from here. I had several designed and made specially in Delhi and flown over so that I could choose one at my leisure.'

'Bloody hell!' Rose looked at Deena in awe. 'I'm never going to compete with that, am I?'

'It's not a competition, Mum,' Erin said quickly, hugging her. 'You'll look gorgeous in whatever you wear.'

Rose laughed. Deena looked highly sceptical.

Erin ploughed on. 'You *will* look fabulous, trust me. You'll both look absolutely gorgeous. Anyway, shall we go in and get started?'

306

And then, she thought, there might be time to get something to eat. Was it very wrong to be craving a curry so early in the morning?

Deena pushed open the door.

'Oh.'

'Blimey.'

Rose and Erin stared round in complete astonishment.

The shop was vast, brightly lit with glittering chandeliers, and was floor-to-ceiling and wall-to-wall crammed with colour. There were racks and rails of ready-made saris and salwars, and bolts of every jewel-encrusted fabric under the sun, glimmering and shimmering and stretching into the far distance.

And customers. There were millions of customers. All talking at the tops of their voices without listening to the answers, hauling outfits from the rails, pulling pieces of fabric towards them, trying things on in the aisles.

It was completely manic.

'It's never like this in BHS,' Rose whispered to Erin.

Erin giggled. BHS was the only shop she'd ever known her mum buy new clothes in. Ever.

Deena, with Rose and Erin in tow, strode forwards through the mêlée, apparently not noticing the mayhem.

'Rajesh!' She held out both hands to a tall, middle-aged man at the back of the emporium. 'Lovely to see you!'

'And you, Deena. Looking as wonderful as ever.'

There was a lot of mwah-mwah air-kissing and ritual hugging.

'Raj.' Deena extricated herself. 'I want you to

work your usual miracles on my dear friend, Rose here. Rose is the mother of this lovely girl who will, next weekend, become my darling daughter-in-law. Rose, therefore, needs a spectacular outfit for the occasion.'

Raj looked Rose up and down with the sort of eye usually reserved for bloodstock specialists purchasing a new brood mare.

'Hmmm . . . That colouring . . . She's a typical English Rose.' He laughed at his own joke. 'And you, Deena, my dear, won't want to clash, I assume? The battle of the mothers is to be avoided at all costs?'

'Oh, absolutely.' Deena nodded. 'I'm wearing traditional red and gold.'

'But not purchased from here?' Raj looked a little hurt. 'I may be growing old, but I'm sure I'd have remembered fitting you in a wedding outfit. I didn't, did I?'

'No.' Deena tapped his arm playfully. 'Not this time. I bought direct from Delhi. Don't sulk, Raj, darling. Now, what do you suggest to make Rose look amazing?'

Rose leaned closer to Erin. 'Do you think all the mother-of-the-bride dress and jacket outfits are in another part of the shop? I can only see . . . well . . . Indian things so far.'

Erin frowned. 'I've no idea. We'll just have to leave it to Deena, but you don't have to be forced into anything you don't want, Mum. I know she can be very persuasive, but stand up for yourself. OK?'

Rose nodded.

Raj smiled at them. 'Rose, my dear, you have such beautiful porcelain pale skin, and that lovely hair the colour of sunlit cornfields. And your

308

eyes . . . such an unusual and captivating shade of blue.'

Rose preened.

'The very essence of Englishness. So, you must,' Raj continued, 'make the very most of the gifts you have been blessed with. You must harmonise and accentuate your natural beauty.'

Rose blushed.

Erin shook her head.

'So,' Raj carried on, smiling wolfishly, 'I think we have the very thing. Come along, ladies. Follow me.'

They followed, pushing their way through entire families wrapping themselves in various saris and posing in front of long mirrors, and grandmothers holding squawking children as younger women pulled on salwars, and gorgeous giggling young girls with smooth toasted-honey bodies sliding themselves into skintight silks.

'I knew the suits and what-have-you would be at the back,' Rose said happily to Erin. 'And Raj seems like a very nice man, doesn't he?'

Erin just smiled and nodded. Since she and Jay had been a couple she'd met many an entrepreneur like Raj. Charming, sweetly complimentary, they never let you leave empty-handed if they could help it.

'Here we are.' Raj eased his way through an archway so crammed with piles of material that it looked as though it would collapse at any minute. 'Here you can chose the perfect wedding *lehenga*.'

Deena clapped her hands.

Erin whimpered. Not a *lehenga*! Nooo. She'd seen Nalisha in a *lehenga*. On young and svelte Nalisha the *lehenga* had looked sensationally, sexily gorgeous.

But on Rose? Her middle-aged mum?

'Deena.' Erin touched her arm anxiously. 'Surely, a *lehenga* won't be suitable for my mum? All that exposed midriff and stuff? And I don't think, honestly, she was expecting to wear an Indian outfit. I think . . .'

'And I think, darling,' Deena said, patting Erin's hand, 'that we must leave it to Raj and Rose.'

Raj was rattling through rails, causing cascades of silks and satins and taffetas to billow around Rose like a falling rainbow.

'Ah, I knew I had one just for you.' He eventually pulled out a hanger from a rack of thousands. 'Rose, this will be absolutely perfect.'

Floaty acres of turquoise, lilac and silver drifted from the hanger. Multitudes of deeper blue and purple jewels and sequins glittered amongst the folds.

Rose clasped her hands together and grinned delightedly.

Oh dear God, Erin thought.

CHAPTER THIRTY-EIGHT

'Oh, it's so beautiful.' Rose stroked the fabric lovingly. 'Absolutely gorgeous. But, is it a frock? With a little bolero? Or a suit? I can't quite make it out.'

'It's a wedding *lehenga*,' Raj said smoothly. 'I'm assuming that as it's a Hindu wedding ceremony, and as mother of the bride, you'll be wanting to be not only traditional but also show-stoppingly fabulous?'

'We're having a fusion wedding,' Erin said quickly. '*Fusion*. A meeting of both cultures. And I think my mum was expecting to wear an English mother-of-the-bride dress and jacket or something.'

Rose flapped her hands. 'Well, yes, I was, but now I've seen this, um, *lehenga*? Is that right? Yes? Good. Well, I might just have to change my mind.'

Deena looked extremely smug. 'And honestly, Erin, darling, did you expect Rose to find a nice little suit in a shop like this? Why, darling, do you think we came to Southall Broadway?'

Probably so you could further hijack my wedding to your son, Erin thought, but seeing the absolute delight on her mum's face she didn't say it.

She shrugged. 'I don't know. It certainly never occurred to me that you were going to persuade Mum to wear an Indian outfit.'

'I've done no persuading at all.' Deena laughed. 'I'm just showing Rose that there are other options.'

'And,' Rose interrupted, still stroking the *lehenga*, 'I'm absolutely delighted that you did, Deena. This is simply beautiful. Can I try it on, please?'

'Of course.' Raj gave a little bow. 'Over here, madam . . . Would you like Deena and, um, your daughter to help you?'

'Ooooh, no thanks.' Rose chuckled. 'If I look truly dreadful I'd rather no one knew. If I need any help I'll shout.'

As Rose disappeared into the small fitting room and Raj drew the curtains behind her, Erin tried not to speak. Anything she said to Deena now would come out all wrong. And after the *mandap* fiasco and so close to the big day they really couldn't afford another fall-out. But, honestly . . . Her mum? In a *lehenga*? Oh, heavens, what on earth was happening to her previously perfectly planned wedding?

Deena and Raj immediately whooshed into a conversation about mutual friends, and clothes, and Jay and Erin's wedding.

Still determined not to join in in case she said the wrong thing, Erin stared instead at the other customers, all swarming and chattering and trying things on. Maybe Rose would decide the *lehenga* wasn't right for her, and they'd find a nice little silk suit somewhere . . . Please, please, please . . .

Then the fitting room curtains rattled back and Rose stepped out into the shop.

'Wow!' Erin blinked in delight. 'I really wasn't expecting that.'

Unlike Nalisha's, Rose's *lehenga* didn't have a midriff-displaying cut-off top, but one that fitted beautifully to the waist, with elbow-length sleeves to hide even the slightest hint of a middle-aged bingo wing.

The multiple layers of the skirt skimmed elegantly down to the floor like a jewelled waterfall. The colours made Rose's skin glow, her eyes shine and her hair gleam with fire.

It was, Erin had to admit, a gorgeous, totally fabulous, mother-of-the-bride outfit.

Even if it wasn't a nice frock and jacket from BHS.

'Mum!' Erin swallowed the huge emotional lump in her throat. 'You look amazing!'

'Oh, that's absolutely wonderful, darling,' Deena gushed. 'Perfection. Told you Raj could work

312

miracles, didn't I?'

Rose, stunned into silence, twirled in front of the mirror admiring the transformation, as with a superior smirk, Raj twirled his tape measure and tweaked and fiddled with various bits of the *lehenga*.

'As I knew they would be, the colours are exactly right for you, English Rose. However, I think I may need to make some slight adjustments. The petticoat needs shortening, even if you're wearing heels to the wedding.'

'I am. I've got a nice pair of two-inch courts,' Rose said, looking across at Deena. 'And they're brand new.'

'But highly unsuitable,' Deena said. 'You can't wear court shoes with a *lehenga*—you need lovely sparkly sandals. We'll sort those out later.'

Raj nodded and continued his tweaking. 'So, we'll need to shorten the petticoat to just sweep the floor so that your pretty shoes show in tantalising little peeps when you walk. And, see here, Rose, the blouse needs a bit of taking in on the waist as you're so lovely and slim and we need to show off your nice slender figure, but otherwise . . .'

'Oh no.' Rose stopped smiling and twirling. 'Alterations? We haven't got time for alterations. The wedding is just over a week away. I love it so much I'll take it as it is and use safety pins.'

'You will do no such thing!' Deena shrieked. 'Raj will make the alterations while we have lunch, Rose, darling. He's a wizard. We'll have something lovely to eat and come back and it'll be as if the *lehenga* was tailor-made for you.'

'Really?'

'Really.'

Raj nodded. 'Exactly as Deena says. And, just a little advice from me, when you wear this at the wedding, you just need to adjust the dupatta slightly to suit yourself. You see, you can either wear it like this . . .' He threw the long panel of floaty turquoise and lilac silk lightly round Rose's neck and dangled the ends rakishly over her shoulders. 'Or like this . . .' He draped it round her like a stole. 'Or again like this . . .' He deftly folded it and hung it loosely over one shoulder. 'So many ways to look so beautiful.'

And she did, Erin thought, sniffing back a happy tear. Totally transformed. The horrid peach suit and the dreadful ostrich feather hat could be donated to the charity shop and Rose would be as beautiful as—no, Erin corrected herself—even more beautiful than Deena at the wedding.

Hah!

'Right, now if Rose just pops back into her own clothes, we'll leave Raj to make the necessary alterations,' Deena said briskly. 'And we'll hurry along the Broadway and take care of Rose's footwear, and the jewellery of course, and find something to eat. And be back in what? A couple of hours?'

As Rose shimmied back into the fitting room, Raj nodded, looking up from scribbling down measurements on a pad. 'Perfect. Now I'll just need a deposit.'

'Oh, that's fine.' Erin stepped forwards and lifted the price tag. 'I'm paying for all of it. Mum doesn't know so let's get it all done before she comes out of the changing room. This is going to be my treat—eeeek!'

'Quality and individuality doesn't ever come

cheap,' Deena said smugly. 'Is it a problem?'

'No,' Erin lied.

Deena raised her eyebrows. 'Of course, you could always haggle.'

Erin shook her head. She couldn't. She knew Jay always haggled, so did Deena and Tavish. And she'd admired them for the skill. But she'd never been able to do it. She found it Britishly embarrassing.

Raj watched the exchange silently, clearly willing her to dare to *try*.

'No,' Erin gulped bravely, sliding her card into the machine. 'The price is fine, thank you. But—' she looked at Raj '—please get rid of this price tag before my mum sees it. She's never paid more than twenty pounds for anything to wear for as long as I can remember. She'd have a fit. Literarily. And refuse to have it. And if she asks, *do not tell her the price*, OK?'

'Of course.' Raj smiled, handing Erin the receipt. 'It's our secret. And I've already added the cost of the alterations on to the bill so there's nothing left to pay.'

Thank the Lord for that, Erin thought faintly, tucking the telltale slip deep into her bag.

She took a deep breath. 'Deena, thank you and I apologise. I was wrong on this one. Mum looks gorgeous. Obviously, a *lehenga* wasn't what either of us had planned on her wearing, but it's worked wonderfully well. It was very kind of you to bring us here and suggest this.'

There. She'd said it. Racking up the Brownie points today.

Deena beamed. 'Thank you, too, darling. But there's absolutely no need to apologise. I appreciate that you're a strong, independent woman with your own views. Jaimal wouldn't be marrying you otherwise. And as someone who has always fought her own corner I couldn't ask for more in my future daughter-in-law.'

Raj, who'd been listening avidly, beamed even more broadly. 'How lovely. Now you beautiful ladies go and enjoy the rest of your retail therapy and I'll see you shortly. Ah, and here's Rose back again—so, off you all go, then.'

And off they went.

Outside, it was even hotter, even nosier and far more crowded.

'Oh—' Rose linked her arm through Erin's '—I'm so happy. Deena, thank you so much. I never thought I would look like that in anything—ever. I simply can't imagine what Pete will say when he sees me.'

Neither can I, Erin thought with amusement. Her dad was as traditional as it was possible to get.

'You're very welcome.' Deena preened. 'And when my girls have done their stuff on the wedding day, you'll be absolutely stunning.'

'Your girls?'

'A couple of Deena's employees are coming down to do all our hair and make-up,' Erin explained. 'None of us feel we can do our own, and it's part of Deena's wedding present to me, and one that I'm truly grateful for.'

Unlike the bloody *mandap*.

'Oooh,' Rose practically danced. 'How fabulous. I've never had a professional makeover. This just gets better and better. And I never thought I'd wear an Indian outfit to your wedding, sweetheart. Never in a million years. But it's the most glorious thing

I've ever seen.'

Erin and Deena smiled at each other.

'And you look wonderful in it,' Erin said truthfully. 'And Dad will love it too.'

'I don't think he'll like the price, though,' Rose giggled. 'Do you know, I didn't even look at the price of it. I never usually do that. Oh, I do hope I can afford it. I reckon it might cost fifty pounds . . . think of it! Fifty pounds on a one-off outfit! How reckless would that be?'

If only, Erin thought. Fifty pounds would possibly have bought the dupatta. Maybe.

'It's all paid for, Mum. It's mine and Jay's present to you.'

'Nooo!' Rose squealed. 'You can't do that. It's far too much money!'

'It's all done.' Erin smiled. 'And if you lived here instead of an entire world away I'd have been able to treat you to loads of things all the time, so just think of it as an accumulation of all the little presents I couldn't give you.'

'Thank you so much, but I can't let you do it—' Rose shook her head '—it's still fifty pounds, sweetheart. *Fifty pounds*.'

Erin and Deena exchanged amused glances over Rose's head.

'And you're worth a million times that.' Erin hugged her mum. 'Now, I don't want to hear any more about it. So, are we going to do shoes and jewellery first—or food?'

'Shoes and jewels first,' Deena said, as they barged their way through the even more crowded pavements. 'Then we can relax and enjoy our lunch.'

'And I'm paying for everything else,' Rose said

firmly. 'Erin, love, you simply can't afford it. I know you can't earn much working with Doug, and it's so close to your wedding day and your dad and I haven't paid a penny towards it and—'

'Neither have Tavish and I,' Deena put in quickly. 'They wouldn't let us, either. So don't worry yourself about it, Rose. The children are having their wedding exactly the way they wanted it, and are paying for all of it, so us old fogies don't have a say. Tavish and I have given in gracefully and are just going to enjoy the day.'

'And Jay and I have been saving for ages,' Erin said, for once grateful to Deena. 'And we just want you all to come along and celebrate with us and have the best day of your lives. Now, about these shoes . . .'

An hour later, with Rose the proud owner of a pair of very pretty lilac and silver sparkly sandals, a pair of turquoise dangly earrings, a dozen purple and blue bangles and an amazing tiny clutch bag in all shades of blue and mauve and studded with diamanté, they headed back along the Broadway.

'I could eat an entire Indian banquet,' Erin muttered, greedily inhaling the hot air as they once more trekked through the ever-growing crowds. 'All these spices are driving me mad. I wanted a curry hours ago—now I'll just demolish anything that's put in front of me.'

'I'll just be glad of a sit down,' Rose admitted. 'My head's all of a whirl.'

Deena, still looking immaculate, smiled indulgently. 'Well, I do know a particularly nice little restaurant just round the corner. I'm sure we could have a bite there while Raj finishes his alterations. They do a lovely self-service buffet and—'

'Whoo.' Erin suddenly stopped outside a shop with crowds spilling out on to the pavement and stared at the men deftly cooking over griddles in the open air. 'What on earth is this place?'

The heat shimmered in an optical illusion over the burners and hot, sweet, mouth-watering aromas wafted along the jam-packed street, adding to the scorching, exotic atmosphere.

Erin jigged up and down. 'Oooh, Deena, look at that! They're making jalebis! This is amazing.'

'Ah, yes. This is Jalebi Junction.' Deena nodded. 'It's very famous.'

'Of course it is. Jay's mentioned it. Oh, and I love jalebis,' Erin groaned. 'Mum, you've never tasted anything like them. Jay and I have bought them before, but never from here, obviously. And I've never seen them being made. Look, they fry spirals of dough, and then dunk them in syrup and then when they're all golden and gorgeous and like little gooey cartwheels, they put them on the cooling racks to harden and . . .'

'They do look and smell scrummy.' Rose peered over Erin's shoulder, watching the hot, sticky sweets being snapped up as quickly as they could be shovelled into brown paper bags.

'Oh, they are,' Erin said excitedly. 'And look— it says they do *gulab jamuns* inside, too. I'll have to buy some of both to take home for Jay. They're his favourite things of all time. Hang on a second, Deena, while I pop in and buy something.'

'Wouldn't it be better to wait?' Deena frowned. 'We'll have lunch first, collect Rose's outfit, and then buy the little treats on the way home. Otherwise you'll spoil your appetites and—'

But Erin, followed by Rose, wasn't listening and had already elbowed her way into the Jalebi Junction crowd.

'Oh, really!' Deena shook her head as Rose and Erin eventually emerged from the hordes again sometime later. 'You've been ages—oh, and I see you've bought lots of things to eat.'

'Some are for Jay, of course, and I got some for Dad and Tavish as well,' Erin nodded, tucking the packages into her bag. 'And these—' she held a large bag of hot and sticky jalebis aloft '—are for us to share and eat now.'

'Us?' Deena squinted against the sun, looking horrified. 'Erin, darling, you surely don't expect me to eat in the street?'

'Of course. You have to eat them while they're hot. Jay taught me that.'

'I'm sorry—' Deena shook her head '—but if that's so, then Jay must have ignored all he's ever been told. I'll save mine for later, thank you. I've never eaten anything in the street in my life. Least of all jalebis.'

'Then you simply don't know what you're missing.' Erin lifted a wodge of steaming, gooey jalebi from the bag and managed to get most of it into her mouth. 'Whumph-grooomp-arrrmm.'

'Oooh.' Rose took a smaller bite from hers. Golden spirals dripped onto her T-shirt. She fanned her mouth. 'Goodness, they're delicious, but very, very hot.'

Deena looked at them both in dismay. 'And now you've got syrup on your chins and all over your hands and your clothes. And you probably won't be able to eat any lunch.'

Rose chuckled stickily. 'I know, Deena. Sorry.

But isn't this all the most amazing fun?'

Deena smoothed the unruffled body-con dress, inspected her own squeakily clean hands, looked at Erin and Rose, and then smiled.

'Yes, Rose, darling, actually, it is.'

CHAPTER THIRTY-NINE

'I do hope,' Gina said on the Saturday lunchtime a week before the wedding, 'that Erin and Jay will be OK about tonight.'

The Merry Cobbler was packed as usual. Gina, working with Sam and Part-time Pearl, was serving two people at once.

'Ah,' Sam said, juggling three pint glasses, 'they'll be fine. Shift yerself away from the IPA pump, there's a good gel. Ta. I'm looking forward to it.'

'So am I.' Gina poured shandies. 'But hen and stag nights can often go horribly wrong.'

'You worry too much about other people, duck. It'll all be grand, you'll see,'

'And we're closing the pub for the first time in living memory.'

'Ah, and that'll be all right, an' all,' Sam assured her. 'You've worked like a Trojan ever since you got here. We all deserves a nice night orf. Pub won't go broke for one night.'

'And next week for the wedding . . .'

'Two nights then. Don't you worry yourself about it, duck. Let yer hair down and have some fun.'

Gina, taking money for the shandies, grinned to herself.

She was actually having the best fun she'd ever

had in her life. And the best sex.

She laughed aloud.

'Can I do anything to help?' Nalisha, in a very pretty frock, appeared on the other side of the bar.

'No, love, I'm fine.' Gina chewed her lips together. She was sure everyone *knew*. 'What have you got planned for today?'

'Nothing much. I was going to have a little chat to Doug, though. He's asked me out for lunch.'

'Lovely.' Gina poured long, tall vodka and tonics. 'Anywhere nice?'

'Probably. All the villages round here are so beautiful and Doug seems to know some fabulous restaurants.'

He did, Gina thought, he'd even taken her to some of them.

'Oh well, have a wonderful time. But don't forget to be back early enough to get glammed up for tonight.'

Nalisha laughed. 'I won't.'

'I just hope Jay and Erin will enjoy themselves.'

Nalisha stopped smiling for a moment. 'They will. I know they will. They're so lucky. Loving one another the way they do. Anyway, I'll be back in plenty of time. In fact, I think I'll probably be back sooner rather than later.'

'Oh yes?' Gina raised her eyebrows.

'Mmm.' Nalisha nodded. 'I think Doug may have got the wrong idea about our . . . friendship. I need to put him straight.'

Gina gave a little mental whoop. About time someone did.

'Oh dear.' Gina hoped she looked sympathetic. 'Poor Doug.'

'I'm leaving the village as soon as Jay and Erin's

wedding is over and taking up my post in London,' Nalisha said. 'I always was. Doug seems to think that I'll stay if he asks me to.'

Gina chuckled. 'Sounds like Doug. Try to let him down gently then.'

Or not.

'I will.' Nalisha smiled. 'He's a really nice man and he's been very kind to me, but honestly, he's old enough to be my father!'

Gina was still laughing long after Nalisha had wafted sensuously out of the pub's door.

*   *   *

It was halfway through the afternoon when Kam returned.

Gina's heart did its usual double flip when she saw him. 'All done?'

'Yeah.' He grinned. 'We've worked miracles, haven't we? We make a good team.'

Gina pushed her curls behind her ears and started to pull a pint. 'We do.'

Because they did. In more ways than one.

Kam smiled at her. 'And is that for me?'

'Yes—why?'

'Because—' Kam slid behind the bar '—desperate as I am for a pint, I need something else more.'

Gina tingled. 'Not here . . . Not now . . .'

'Yes.'

Oh God . . . 'This is supposed to be a secret.'

'It is a secret,' he said, very close to her, his breath peppermint warm against her skin. 'And it's a very sexy secret. Although how we'll keep it any sort of secret for much longer, I have no idea.'

323

'Nor have I.' Gina's hand trembled on the glass. 'Still, it'll be fun finding out.'

Kam took the half-filled glass from her hand. 'I want to shout it from the rooftops. Tonight would be a good time.'

'Tonight belongs to Jay and Erin. As does next Saturday.' Gina looked at him and smiled. 'We'll have to try to be discreet. After that, I think we might go public—if you want to, that is.'

'God, I want to. You have no idea how difficult it is not to talk about you all the time. It's like being a teenager.'

Gina moved away from him and called along the bar, 'Sam! The lager's gone off this end! I'm just going down to the cellar to change the barrel! Can you keep an eye on things up here? Ta.'

She grinned at Kam. 'Oh dear. I'm such a feeble little thing . . . You know, I might need a nice big strong man to help me change that barrel.'

'I think you might,' Kam laughed, almost reaching the cellar door before her. 'Oh, be careful on the steps in those heels, shall I help you . . .'

After kicking the door shut behind him, silencing the happy roar from the pub, Kam swept Gina off her feet and carried her giggling down the steep stone steps and into the cool, dark cellar.

She laughed into his neck. 'Not the most romantic place in the world. All these utilitarian pipes and gauges and barrels and crates. However, there is a little storeroom just past the mixers where we keep a pile of emergency blankets for lagging when the frost gets really bad.'

'How convenient.' Kam kissed her, carrying her across the cellar and into the storeroom. 'Oh God, Gina, I'm sorry but I've got to say this.'

324

No! She screamed silently. No, please don't. Not now. Finish with me later, but not today. Not now. Not ever . . .

'I love you.'

Love . . .? She blinked at him in the half-light as she sank down into the pile of blankets. Love? No one had ever loved her before. No one.

'Sorry.' Kam stretched out beside her. 'Is that too soon? I had to tell you, Gina. This is a first for me. Being in love. Madly, insanely in love. I don't care if you don't feel the same way, maybe one day you will, but . . .'

'You are crazy.' She took his beautiful face between her hands. 'Of course I love you. I love, love, love you.'

He smiled at her, kissed her lips very gently then trailed his finger down her face and her throat.

'Thank God for that. And how long does it take to change a barrel?'

'Me? Oh, about three minutes.' Gina pulled him against her, loving everything about this sensational man: his beauty, the feel of his hard body, the scent of him and the way he needed her. 'Or in this case, at least half an hour.'

CHAPTER FORTY

Now it was Saturday night. Only a week to go before the wedding. Seven short days to go . . .

Erin jigged up and down.

It was her hen night. Although things weren't going exactly as she hoped.

'Where are we going?' Erin asked for the

millionth time. 'Why am I blindfolded? This is insanity. We're supposed to be going to Newbury for dinner and cocktails.'

'There's been a slight change of plan.' Bella giggled on one side of her.

'Just trust us,' Sophie whispered on the other.

'I want to go to Newbury and I don't trust either of you.' Erin was totally disorientated behind the satin eye mask. 'Tell me what's happening?'

'Just hold our hands,' Bella said, 'and do exactly what we tell you to do. You'll love it, Erin, I promise.'

Stumbling, unable to walk very well because of the combination of her heels and the special hen-night, slim-fitting LBD, and now madly irritated by her just-mascaraed-by-Deena's-Top-Girl-eyelashes catching on the inside of the blindfold, Erin sighed.

'OK. I know we're still in the village. We've only just stepped outside Uncle Doug's cottage. If you haven't got a helicopter waiting on the green to whisk me off to Monte Carlo or somewhere exotic after all this, I'm going to have a major tantrum.'

Bella laughed. 'No helicopter.'

Damn.

'OK then, there's a stretch limo waiting to take us to the hot spots of London's clubland to party with Premiership footballers, isn't there?'

'Nope,' Sophie said as they made unsteady progress across the green under the still-hot evening sun. 'Not even close.'

'Other girls have hen nights in Prague or Dublin or Barcelona. Hen weekends even. Sometimes even hen *weeks* . . .'

Bella chuckled. 'And you said you didn't want

anything like that. Keep it local you said. Keep it simple.'

'Exactly. Oops.' Erin stumbled and swayed. 'A nice elegant meal out with all my girlfriends and my mum and Deena. A few cocktails. Lovely chat, a lot of laughs. In Newbury.'

'As I said,' Bella laughed. 'A slight change of plan. It's OK. We cancelled everything. Everyone knows.'

'And,' Sophie added, 'at least we all look spectacularly glam.'

Erin, in her satin darkness, nodded. They did. They'd all bought new snazzy little dresses for tonight anyway, and after the wedding-hair and make-up run-through by Deena's Top Girls, they certainly looked fit to hit the town.

Only, obviously, they weren't going to be hitting any town tonight now.

Damn it.

Bella tightened her grip. 'Right, now be careful here, we're going to be going downwards a bit.'

Erin slipped and slithered and did a less than cute Bambi-on-ice on the heels.

'We're on the road now, aren't we?' she muttered as her feet stopped sliding. 'And you two can stop laughing. You can see. I can't. And I don't like it. And if we're still in the village, why is it so quiet? And the minute you let go of my hands I'm going to rip this bloody blindfold off.'

'Stop grizzling,' Sophie laughed. 'And it's an elegant black masquerade mask, not a blindfold. We're not going to execute you.'

'It feels very much like it. You know I hate surprises.'

'Mmm, that was a bit of an issue. But we know

you're going to absolutely love this one.' Bella squeezed her hand reassuringly. 'Seriously, Erin, we've been friends for ever. You don't think we'd do something you hated, do you?'

'No, not really, but . . .'

'But?'

'But I'm a bit scared and I'm really hungry—I haven't eaten anything all day to be ready for tonight—and I was so looking forward to a nice dinner and . . .'

'Oh, there'll be food,' Sophie said cheerfully. 'You won't starve. OK, here we are. Now step very carefully.'

Erin stepped.

She was aware of the change in air temperature. So they were inside now. The sun was no longer warming her skin. It was also very quiet. Absolutely silent. Eerily so.

'I don't like it.' She shook her head. 'I seriously don't like it.'

'It's OK. I think we're ready now,' Bella said. 'Just a couple more seconds.'

Oddly, Erin thought, because she couldn't see, her other senses were heightened. She knew that wherever they were, they weren't alone. She was aware of other people—two, maybe?—breathing, and the scents were intensified. She could smell warm skin and lemons and hints of musk and notes of ylang-ylang and sandalwood, and, surely, hot, stomach-rumbling spices . . .

Sophie and Bella were whispering, and there was another whispered answer. A man's voice. She wasn't sure whose.

'OK,' Bella said. 'We're ready now. Erin, Sophie's just going to undo your mask.'

She felt fingers in her hair, was aware of the sound of Velcro ripping, not hers . . .

Then the blindfold was off and she blinked rapidly, unused to the light.

Was she dreaming? Had she gone mad?

'Jay?'

'Erin?'

They peered blearily at one another in complete stupefaction.

Sophie, Bella, Gina—Gina, looking wonderful and radiant in a short strappy purple frock that showed off her endless legs—and Kam all stood back looking like proud parents and smirking.

'You're supposed to be in Newbury on your hen night . . .' Jay muttered.

'And you're supposed to be at the casino with your stags . . .'

'And—' Jay rubbed his eyes '—we appear to be in the foyer of the village hall.'

Erin looked at Gina, Sophie, Bella and Kam. 'What the hell is going on?'

They just laughed and looked smug.

'You look amazing.' Jay rubbed his eyes again. 'Totally gorgeous.'

'Thanks.' Erin tried to un-gum her eyelashes. 'You look pretty dead hot, too.'

Jay looked at Kam. 'Can you please tell us what's going on? Because this is our hen and stag night. The one night that traditionally we're *not* supposed to spend together. And I may have to kill you.'

Kam grinned. 'Ah, yes, but Gina told me how much you've both argued against tradition—and that you hate being apart—and I knew you didn't want to go down the multiple-party Indian route either, so we thought this would be a great idea and

329

that you'd love it.'

Erin, still completely bemused, sighed. 'So, what's happening? Are we all just going out together or what?'

'Oh, definitely "or what",' Sophie chuckled. 'As you're just about to find out . . . Hold hands.'

Erin gripped Jay's hand tightly. He squeezed her fingers. She was pretty sure this was going to be the worst evening of her life.

Oh, why the hell did people always have to *interfere*?

Gina and Kam threw open the doors to the village hall.

Ohmigod!

Erin blinked at the blaze of light and colour. At the rainbow of pleated silks swathing the ceiling in a canopy and dropping to the floor, at the thousands of sparkling dancing fairy lights, the tall flickering candles, the flowers, the gods and goddesses bedecked with garlands of roses and lilies, the golden cloths on the little side tables all scattered with multicoloured sequins, which glittered like a manic solar system, the long trestles with their dozens of gold and silver dishes piled high with sweet and savoury treats.

And then at everyone they knew: the whole village, their families, their friends, waiting silently, expectantly, smiling, crowded beneath the exotic canopy.

Jay squeezed her hand even tighter. 'Holy shit.'

'Couldn't have put it better,' Erin whispered. 'And is this the *mandap*?'

'No, that's still at the Swan. Abbie said so yesterday. This one's handmade.'

'Blimey, then it's spectacular. They've gone to an

awful lot of trouble. I'm probably going to cry now.'

'Ladies and gentlemen!' Kam clapped his hands and raised his voice. 'I give you our hen and stag! Erin and Jay!'

Then the crowd erupted in cheers and whoops and massive applause, and threw deluges of rose petals like a pale-pink snowstorm as they all rushed forwards to embrace the almost-happy couple.

Most of the women, Erin noticed rather dizzily, picking rose petals from her lip gloss, were wearing glittering jewelled dupattas over their Best Clothes, and some of them had brightly coloured silk stoles, and some of the men were in kurtas, and, wow, there was her mum looking gorgeous in a pale-green sari, and Deena, stunning in a regal blue one, and Nalisha, pretty in pink.

East meets West. And then some.

Everyone hugged everyone else. Everyone kissed. Everyone shook hands. Everyone talked at the same time. Then someone put some madly catchy bhangra music on the stereo, and the village hall was transformed.

'I can't believe they kept this secret from us,' Erin muttered. 'No one has ever kept a secret in this village in its entire history.'

'I know—' Jay pulled her closer to him '—I never even got a hint either. It must have been Kam's idea.'

'And Gina's.'

'We'll definitely kill them later.'

Deena and Tavish came forwards and kissed them on both cheeks; Pete and Rose did the same. Then everyone in the hall simply lined up and followed suit, Uncle Doug and Nalisha—but not together—and Bella and Sophie with Aiden and David, and Renata and Julia, and Dora Wilberforce and all the Yee-Hawers, and even Sam and Part-time Pearl. And the rest of the villagers. And then their friends from school and college and beyond.

Erin's face ached from smiling and her arm ached from shaking, and her cheek was covered in a hundred different lipstick traces, but it was just wonderful to know that everyone, simply everyone, had turned out tonight for this. For her and Jay.

Even if it wasn't anything like the hen night she'd been expecting.

Gina waved and headed towards the little stage. The music stopped and Gina held up her hands. 'We'll have more music in a minute, I promise.'

Nook Green cheered.

'First, I'd like to thank everyone not only for coming here tonight, but also for managing to keep the whole thing a secret. You were amazing. I don't think Jay and Erin had a clue, did you?'

They both shook their heads and made not-quite-jokey 'we'll get you for this later' gestures.

Gina beamed happily. 'Jay and Erin had planned to have a traditional English stag and hen night. They've also planned a lovely fusion wedding, which we'll all be celebrating with them this time next week . . .'

More whoops and foot-stamping and, sadly, one or two ribald comments.

'So, it meant that some of the Indian pre- and post-wedding ceremonies wouldn't get a look-in. And this seemed a shame as Kam explained to me that Indians, even those who have never actually been there, do love a good party . . .'

A huge roar of approval.

'So,' Gina continued, 'to keep everyone happy—' she looked quickly at Deena '—Kam and I decided we'd put on a little fusion night of our own. Only our fusion is a hen and stag night mixture of all the Gujurato Hindu pre- and post-wedding rituals. As Kam and Jay and Nalisha—and probably Erin— know, these are not being held in the right order or on the right days, but we know you're all going to love them.'

'Clever,' Erin said admiringly. 'Very clever. Everything your mum wanted and we refused to have added to our plans, all in one place at one time, and heavily disguised as a party.'

Jay nodded. 'And very diplomatically done, too. No one can be offended, and honour is satisfied. Nice one.'

'There will of course,' Gina said with a laugh, 'be plenty to eat as you can see, and also to drink, as I've set up a little free bar in the kitchen.'

A massive roar of rural approval.

'And lots of dancing too, of course. Bhangra and Western. But the ceremonies which Kam has chosen for tonight, and which will also incorporate the *sagai* and *sanji* festivities which Jay and Erin can't have on their secular wedding day, are the mehendi, which is henna tattooing—completely optional but a lot of fun—and the tilak, which means Jay's stags get to do whatever they like to him—and a couple of poojas.'

There were a few snuffling giggles.

Gina smiled down at Erin. 'Apparently, you're going to have the Ganesh pooja, which brings good luck and prosperity to the families, and the Griha Shanti, a pooja which is the blessing for a happy and peaceful married life.'

'Thank you,' Erin whispered, now completely overcome, 'that sounds wonderful.'

'Mmm.' Gina looked across the hall at Tavish. 'Kam says we should have a pandit for that one, but as this is strictly fusion, Tavish is going to do it. And as a finale, we're having a Garba Raas.'

Nook Green looked blank. Kam laughed. Jay groaned.

'What,' Erin whispered, 'is a Garba Raas?'

'You'll never know,' Jay hissed, 'because we won't be here for it.'

Erin giggled. 'It can't be that bad, surely?'

'Worse. It's like mad Indian Morris dancing. Everyone gets into pairs and skip-dances with *dandiya* sticks. It's the most embarrassing thing ever.'

'Can't wait,' Erin chuckled. 'And let's face it, the Yee-Hawers will love it. They were mostly all members of the Maizey St Michael Morris before it disbanded. Anyway, hopefully by then we'll all be too drunk to care.'

'I will never, ever—' Jay leaned down and kissed her '—be drunk enough for Garba Raas.'

'Right!' Gina clapped her hands again. 'That's more than enough from me. And can I just say a massive thank you again to you all for managing to keep your mouths shut! Let the festivities commence . . .'

The bhangra music flooded the hall again, and Nook Green prepared to party.

CHAPTER FORTY-ONE

It was, Erin thought some time later, simply the best night of her life.

She had a very small henna tattoo on her thigh, applied carefully, if a bit shakily, by Rose, as was the custom. Deena and Nalisha had supervised and explained that Jay's name had to be incorporated in the design and it was traditional that he had to discover it on their wedding night.

Rose had blushed and Erin had giggled.

Then nearly all the women mehendi'd each other. It had all become a bit messy, but the results were impressive.

Bella and Sophie were extremely proud of having David and Aiden's names hidden from view amongst peacock feathers and exotic blooms. Erin reckoned there was no chance they'd stay a secret for a week, or even until the end of the night.

Dora Wilberforce, Nalisha and Gina had some spectacular designs on their hands, and Deena and Rose had matching spirals and seashells on their arms.

While the mehendi was taking place in one part of the hall, Jay's stags had thrown themselves into the tilak with howls of merriment. Erin was delighted that her dad and Tavish, who had instantly become firm friends, both had tears of laughter pouring down their cheeks.

And the poojas had been really moving and meaningful and Erin had cried, but her newly done mascara had miraculously stayed put so she didn't look like a panda. Result!

And she and Jay had slow-danced to even the most raucous bhangra music, and everyone had eaten and drunk and hurled themselves into the fusion night with gusto.

'You're going to have to be going some to beat this at your wedding reception,' Gina grinned, as she and the elderly Sam foxtrotted past Erin and Jay to some wild Punjabi folk tune.

'Oh, I think we'll manage it,' Erin grinned. 'Thank you for organising it. It's amazing.'

'You're more than welcome. I'm just so glad you're not cross.'

'Cross? How could I be cross? It's simply sensational.'

Gina grinned, and then was whisked away into the crowd by Sam.

'You know—' Jay smiled down at her '—there is one thing that's been bothering me all night.'

'I know. It's the Garba Raas.'

'No, not just that. I can, and will, avoid that. It's Kam.'

'Why?' Erin stopped dancing. 'He's still here, isn't he? Is he OK?'

'He's on his own. He didn't bring anyone. And he hasn't even glanced at your old school friends or anything, has he?'

'No, he hasn't, and they all look pretty sexy and they've been drooling over him and giving him the come-on all night.' Erin shook her head. 'Funny that. Sophie and Bella said that they thought he had someone, you know. That he was acting like he was madly in love.'

'And they'd know.' Jay laughed. 'But, yes, now you come to mention it, he has been a bit distracted lately. Perhaps the miracle has happened and

336

Kam's really fallen in love.'

'Then why isn't she here with him? Why isn't he writing her name all over his pencil case, or whatever equivalent vets have?'

'She's probably married.' Jay shrugged. 'A lot of them have been. He could hardly turn up here with someone else's wife, could he?'

'S'pose not. Maybe he'll bring her to the wedding—we've left a space for his plus one, haven't we? As long as there are no interruptions from furious cheated husbands. Ooh, and look, it's so nice to see Uncle Doug being mostly ignored by Nalisha—she must have told him he has no hope there.'

'Poor Doug.'

'Not at all,' Erin said. 'It serves him right. He's dished it out enough times—he needs to know what it feels like. He'll find someone else by next week anyway. He always does. And clearly Gina doesn't give a toss. I've never seen her look happier or more beautiful. She's well over Doug, thank goodness. I just wish she could find the love of her life, too.'

'Like you have?'

'Like I have.'

They gazed at one another.

'Shall we go now?' Jay whispered. 'No one will miss us and . . .'

The music stopped.

Deena, looking slightly embarrassed, clapped her hands. 'OK, everyone—now please put down your food and drink, and take your partners and get into your pairs for the Garba Raas. I'll talk you through it while Kam's handing out the *dandiya* sticks, but it really doesn't matter if you get a bit lost. All you

337

have to do is just follow everyone else and skip and enjoy it.'

'Oh, bugger,' Jay sighed. 'Just a fraction too late.'

'And you're not going to dash off and hide in the loo, either.' Erin giggled. 'You're going to do exactly as your mum says—you're going to skip and enjoy it.'

'Sometimes,' Jay muttered, 'I really don't know why I'm marrying you.'

'Yes, you do.'

'Oh, yeah, maybe I do.'

'Here we go, lovebirds,' Kam said cheerfully, handing them a pair of thin, glittering and madly embellished sticks. 'Have fun, children.'

'Kam—' Jay nodded '—thanks a million for organising all this. Oh, not the bloody Garba Raas—we both know how gruesome that is—but the whole evening. It's been brilliant. And you must have worked really hard.'

'We aim to please.' Kam grinned. 'Gina and I have been like undercover agents ever since I suggested the idea. I'd been told I had to get you to toe the party line and Gina, being Erin's friend, knew you didn't want to, but neither did you, or we, want to upset the oldies, so this seemed like the perfect compromise.'

'It is.' Erin kissed his cheek. 'It's been totally wonderful. More than I could have ever dreamed of. And so, where's your partner tonight then? You can't dance this mad Garba thingy on your own, and we won't allow you to sit it out.'

'Oh,' Kam said, 'you know me. Why settle for one chocolate bar when you can have the whole sweet shop? But tonight I'm going to dance with Nalisha.'

Jay and Erin watched him go, handing out sticks, laughing and joking.

Jay frowned. 'Do you think . . . Kam and Nalisha?'

'No, actually I don't. But he's got someone,' Erin said quickly, knowing that whoever it was, it certainly wasn't Nalisha. 'He's on such a high. He's definitely in love.'

'In love . . . Kam? Blimey.' Jay considered his cousin thoughtfully. 'Kam has a secret lover?'

'And I think we owe it to ourselves to find out who it is, don't you?' Erin grinned.

'Absolutely. It would be rude not to.'

They laughed together.

And then, following Deena's instructions, and accompanied by some really loud music—like an Irish jig crossed with Bollywood—they threw themselves into the Garba Raas along with everyone else.

It was total mayhem as people ran amok and clashed sticks and hit each other and themselves and got completely lost and then found their way again.

'I don't know why you don't like this,' Erin panted as they crossed couples with Deena and Pete, 'it's total fun.' She laughed as Rose and Tavish went in totally the wrong direction, still skipping wildly.

'It's not as bad as I remembered,' Jay admitted, puffing slightly then wincing as Dora Wilberforce's *dandiya* stick caught him a blow on his shoulder, 'and there is one saving grace.'

'Is there?'

'Oh, yes.' He sucked in some air and ducked as Kam and Nalisha galloped past. 'After all this

339

tonight, there can be no hidden Hindu surprises thrown up at our wedding, can there?'

'No, I don't suppose there can be—ouch!' Erin nodded, wincing as Renata and Julia, both waving their sticks like they were bullying off in a hockey match, hit her shins. 'Which means . . .'

'We'll have the fusion wedding we planned all along.'

'And nothing and no one can change it. Oh, what a relief. Nothing to worry about at all any more. It's just going to be fabulous. And I can't wait.'

CHAPTER FORTY-TWO

It's my wedding day . . .

The words ran merrily through Erin's head.

Then she spoke them aloud for the first time. 'It's my wedding day . . . It's really and truly my wedding day.'

At long last.

Oh, wow!

Florence, on the end of the bed, looked up at her with disinterest and then buried her head beneath her paws.

'Thanks for your support, Flo,' Erin chuckled, dropping a kiss on the silky grey head. 'You're going to be well looked after. And I'll miss you so much while we're on honeymoon, but you probably won't even notice I'm gone, will you?'

Florence purred and snuggled in even more.

'Breakfast for the bride-to-be.' Rose, in her dressing gown, popped her head round the door. 'How are you, sweetheart? Nervous?'

'Not at all, I'm fine, Mum. Honestly. Oooh, lovely—a tray. Thank you so much. Toast and honey and coffee . . . and is that a Buck's Fizz?'

'A very weak one.' Rose nodded. 'I know you probably won't want to eat anything, but just try a little bit.'

'Actually, I'm starving.' Erin looked sheepish, taking the tray and curling back on the bed. 'Is that wrong?'

'Not at all.' Rose sat beside her. 'And anyway I'm nervous enough for both of us. And as for your dad—well, he's all fingers and thumbs. And practising his speech for the umpteenth time.'

Erin bit into the toast and mumbled round the crumbs. 'Tell him not to worry. He hasn't got to do anything he doesn't want to do. This is going to be a very relaxed wedding.'

'Really?' Rose broke off a corner of toast and nibbled it. 'It's all seemed a bit of a mad whirlwind to me. I think Deena and Tavish are lovely, but they have some very fixed ideas and—'

'Mmm, they did have. Jay and I have more or less worked round them all. Everything's perfect now, especially as Nanna and Colin are safely here and ensconced in their room at the Swan. Do you know what she's wearing?'

Rose laughed. 'No, but whatever it is she'll look like the Queen Mum, you know she will. And Erin, honestly, you're OK with me wearing the *lehenga*, aren't you?'

'Absolutely.' Erin gave her mum a sticky honey hug. 'You look totally fabulous in it. I don't care what anyone wears, Indian or not, just as long as they're there today.'

'And your dress—' Rose looked longingly at the

341

fabulous Ian Stuart creation, hanging on the back of the door '—is the most astonishingly gorgeous thing I've ever seen. I still can't quite believe how intricately beautiful it is. No wonder you've kept it a secret. You'll look like a princess. And I'll cry.'

'So will I,' Erin said. 'But we'll be fine because Deena's Top Girls are doing our make-up later and that mascara will withstand a tidal wave.'

'Thank goodness for that—' Rose kissed her '—because it'll need to. Oh, I'm soooo excited . . . Now, do you want to use the bathroom first, or shall I nip in while you're finishing your breakfast?'

'What about Dad and Uncle Doug?'

'Oh, they've both been in and out. They're getting dressed.'

'You go first then. I'll just enjoy my breakfast in a leisurely bride-to-be fashion.'

Rose laughed. 'You're far too cool for your own good. I was a bag of nerves on my wedding day. Spilt everything, dropped everything, cried . . .'

Erin sighed. 'Oh, we've been through all that. There were plenty of times in the last few weeks when I thought today—the day Jay and I had planned so carefully—would never happen. But now, with him, I can face anything. Anything at all.'

'I'm so happy for both of you, sweetheart. He's wonderful.'

'I know, Mum. And this is going to be the best day ever.'

'Oh, don't . . . Now I'm going to jump in the shower before I cry.' And Rose, sniffing happily, left the bedroom.

Erin sipped the Buck's Fizz, finished the toast and coffee and slid out of bed and padded to the window.

Glorious. The sun shone from a cloudless flax-flower sky, and there was no breeze at all. Nook Green, preparing for the Big Day, shimmered in the early morning heat. It was lovely, Erin thought, leaning her hands on the sill, to think that in nearly all those cottages and houses people were getting ready for her wedding.

Her marriage to Jay.

She gazed at Jay's pretty cottage across the green and longed to hear his voice. But they'd agreed not to ring or text one another this morning. It was all going to be done the old-fashioned way.

Was he awake now and feeling as unruffled and serene and ecstatically happy as she was? She thought he probably was. He'd have Kam to calm him down, if not.

He'd insisted that Kam and only Kam was necessary for his wedding preparations. Deena and Tavish were advised, gently, that they'd be staying put in their suite at the Swan until the wedding party arrived. And Nalisha had moved out and joined her own parents at the Swan too.

And after today, after their honeymoon, Erin thought, that beautiful cottage would be her home. Her home with Jay . . .

Could life ever get any better?

*   *   *

'Well, wow then!' Bella said, looking at them all crammed into Uncle Doug's living room. 'How stunning are we?'

'Pretty damn stunning,' Sophie agreed. 'Not quite as stunning as Erin, of course, but pretty hot nonetheless.'

Erin, feeling every inch a fairy-tale princess, walked tentatively on the wedding shoes, loving the feeling of the petticoats, layers and layers of net and lace, swishing against her legs.

'Very elegant.' Bella smiled at Erin. 'You're so very beautiful.'

'We all are,' Erin said, her voice wobbling slightly. 'And Deena's Top Girls have done a great job.'

They had. Everyone—including Rose—now had glorious glossy wedding hair and supermodel make-up.

'I look like I've been airbrushed,' Bella giggled. 'Aiden won't be able to keep his hands off me.'

'Oh, wow, Mrs B.!' Sophie gasped as Rose, in the wedding *lehenga* and bangles and little sparkly sandals, drifted in. 'You look a million dollars.'

'Thank you, sweetheart. So do you. Those bridesmaids' frocks are incredible. How funny this is—you've talked about this day since you were all little girls together, and now it's here.'

Bella, Sophie and Erin looked at one another. A dream come true.

Rose kissed Erin. 'I've got to go now, darling. You look sensational. So very, very beautiful. Oh Lord, don't let me cry . . . and our car's outside. Are we all ready, girls?'

There was a last-minute flurry of grabbing overnight cases, as everyone was staying at the Swan, and fluffing at hair, and adjusting hems and topping up lip gloss, and then Erin made sure that they all had their bouquets and, with squeals of good wishes and everyone kissing everyone else, and general giddy giggling, Rose and the bridesmaids trooped out of the cottage.

344

It was suddenly very quiet.

'So—' Pete Boswell looked at her '—it's just you and me now, love. I'm so proud of you.'

Erin hugged her dad as much as the voluminous skirts would allow. 'You look great, Dad. Really smart. And Mum looks beautiful. And you walking me down the aisle is going to be another dream come true for me.'

'And for me, love. I'll be the proudest man on the planet. Oh, what on earth is that?'

A raucous blast of bhangra music echoed across the green.

Erin, slightly hampered by her dress and the furniture, eventually made it to the window, and laughed out loud.

'It's Kam and Jay leaving! Oh, don't let him see me—it's bad luck—but, Dad, look at them!'

Kam's car, with Jay in the passenger seat, snaking slowly away from the cottage and around the green, was completely covered in Indian trappings. Flags and drapes and tapestries, all in very over-sequinned gold and red, hung and fluttered from every surface. Massive exotically hued paper flowers nodded and danced. Red and gold balloons waved from both bumpers, entwined with matching sparkling ribbons. And from the stereo, through the car's open windows, bhangra pulsed at top volume.

'It looks like something out of a Bollywood film,' Erin laughed. 'Mad—but somehow perfect.'

'It'll make our departure and arrival seem very staid by comparison.' Pete grinned. 'But it's a great touch. Wonderful. Happy and colourful—just the wedding day you deserve, darling.'

'Don't make me cry.' Erin hugged her dad. 'I've

345

done so well so far. Oooh, here's our limousine just appearing round the green. Oh, look at the traditional white ribbons, and the red and white roses. Not quite so much Bollywood glamour for me.'

'A nice contrast.' Pete nodded. 'And perfect for a fusion wedding.'

Erin swallowed as the car pulled up outside the cottage. 'Oops, now I do feel a little bit shaky.'

'You'll be fine, I promise you.' Pete reached for her hand. 'Remember when you were a little girl and used to wake up from a bad dream and I'd tuck you back in and smooth your hair and tell you you'd be fine?'

Erin, swallowing the lump in her throat, nodded.

'And you were, weren't you?'

Erin nodded again.

'And you will be again now. You're the most beautiful girl in the world. And I love you.'

'I love you, too.' Erin hugged her dad tightly. 'Thanks, Dad. OK—you're right. I'll be fine. Just let me find my bouquet and say goodbye to Florence, oh, and remember to lock the cottage door and then we'll be off.'

CHAPTER FORTY-THREE

The Swan looked magnificent in the sun. The river glinted, the tiny streams criss-crossing the sloping lawns glittered. The rose arches were a mass of blooms and the air was sweet-scented.

'Like a film set,' Pete exhaled, as the limousine purred majestically to a halt on the gravel. 'OK

346

now, love?'

Erin nodded. 'Yes, thank you. I'm fine again—as you knew I would be. I just can't wait now.'

'Well—' Pete slid out of the car and smiled slightly awkwardly at the uniformed chauffeur who was holding the door open and touching his cap '—you'll just have to wait there a little bit longer, and I'll make sure everyone is in the marriage room and in place. OK?'

Erin sank back into the warm leather. The fabulous dress billowed round her and the perfume rising from her flowers was richly tropical. She felt like a queen.

The car park was crammed with cars. Including Kam's with its amazing Bollywood bling. Jay was here . . .

And in just a very few minutes, she'd be gliding—hopefully if all the wedding-shoe practice sessions had worked—down the aisle in the beautiful cream and oak-panelled marriage room and Jay would be waiting for her.

At last.

Pete came back and leaned into the car. 'OK. They're all ready for you, love. Do you want more time?'

'No, absolutely not. I'm really calm and happy now. Let's go, Dad.'

With a lot of help from the grinning chauffeur, Erin managed to get out of the car with her frock intact. And then, on Pete's arm, she walked into the Swan.

Sophie and Bella were waiting outside the marriage room door.

'Wow, wow, wow!' Bella grinned.

'Fabulously perfectly stunning!' Sophie nodded.

'Thanks, you too.' Erin smiled shakily. 'And thank you both for this today, and for everything.'

'Shut up!' Bella groaned. 'I haven't cried—yet.'

Through the open doorway, Pete nodded to the registrar standing at the head of the marriage room, and the beautiful strains of Handel's 'Arrival of the Queen of Sheba' gently filled the air.

Then, with her hand resting on her dad's arm, Erin stepped slowly into the sun-dappled, flower-filled room, followed by Sophie and Bella.

As she passed each row and the guests saw her in her wedding dress for the first time, there were gasps of delight and a mass intake of breath. Erin smiled, still only vaguely aware of her surroundings.

She knew everyone was there: Jay's right-hand side of the room was like a dazzling, glittering sea of colour with so many women of all ages in their saris and *lehengas*, and the men in their kurtas. And on her side, she briefly glimpsed everyone she knew and loved, the whole village, all dressed up to the nines, some in Indian clothes, too. Gina was looking so very beautiful in a fabulous pink and lilac sari. Oh, and there was Colin and her lovely nanna—yes, looking exactly like the Queen Mum in a duck-egg blue duster coat and a massive matching hat riotous with feathers—and Doug looking very 1970s in his rumpled cream linen suit and his thin tie. On Jay's side, Deena looked completely stunning in her richly embroidered red and gold ceremonial sari, jewels in her hair, round her throat and wrists, and a lovely ruby bhindi trailing down her forehead.

Nalisha, sitting on an aisle-side chair, with her parents, glanced up at Erin as she passed and smiled. Erin, praying that Nalisha wasn't going to leap up at the last moment and belt out Yvonne

348

Fair's 'It Should Have Been Me', smiled back at her.

'I'm so happy for you,' Nalisha whispered.

Erin swallowed. 'Thank you.'

And then—there was Jay.

Jay, standing beside Kam, waiting for her, looking incredibly handsome and divinely sexy in his cream Nehru suit.

As they reached the end of the aisle, she looked down at her mum and smiled. Rose dabbed her eyes and smiled tremulously back.

Jay just looked at her.

'Oh . . . wow!'

She smiled at him, and sniffed back a tear as her dad slid into his seat beside Rose, leaving them together.

'You look totally incredible,' Jay whispered. 'I never dreamed . . . Erin, I love you so much.'

'I love you too.'

The registrar beamed at them both, then at the gathered audience.

'Ladies and gentlemen, let me welcome you to the wedding room of the Swan, where we're all gathered together for this very happy occasion, to share in the marriage of Jaimal Keskar and Erin Boswell . . .'

After that it all passed in a dream.

Erin made her promises in a steady voice, as Jay did, never once taking their eyes from each other. Cameras flashed and someone—one of Jay's uncles, Erin thought vaguely—was standing to one side with a camcorder.

Then Kam stepped forwards with the rings and, as they slid them on to their respective fingers, they repeated the words they'd practised, giggling, so many times. Only today they didn't laugh. Today it was real. Today they meant every single word.

And then they were married.

The registrar smiled kindly. 'And I now pronounce you man and wife. Jay, you may kiss your bride . . .'

He did. And Erin kissed him back and clung to him, happier than she'd ever been in her life.

Married! She and Jay were actually married!

And then they were kissing one another again and laughing and crying and everyone was clapping.

'Just the register to sign now,' the registrar reminded them gently. 'This way—with your witnesses, please.'

And followed by Kam and Rose—because Erin had known she couldn't ask either one of Bella or Sophie and not the other to be her witness—they stepped up to the little desk, which was smothered with lilies and roses. And as Prokofiev's *Romeo and Juliet* overture played softly, they made their togetherness legal.

And then somehow, with all their guests nosily and happily clapping and stamping their feet—as she and Jay had known they would—to Strauss's rousing 'Radetzky March', they drifted out of the marriage room with everyone laughing and smiling as they passed.

'Outside now for the photos,' their photographer said bossily. 'Glorious weather, fabulous grounds— I'll do you two together and then do the set pieces. I'll just get everyone organised.'

The photographs, it seemed to Erin, went on for ever and ever. But she didn't mind. She and Jay just clung together, and chatted to everyone in between shots, and kept looking at one another in total wonderment.

The sun shone on and on, and they posed on the little bridges and in front of the Swan and down by the river and practically everywhere else possible.

Their guests swarmed across the Swan's grounds, clutching glasses of champagne, chatting, the smokers snatching the opportunity for a sneaky cigarette.

'You look so beautiful,' Jay said for the millionth time. 'That dress . . . I was just blown away when I saw you walking towards me. I'm so bloody lucky.'

Erin leaned towards him and kissed him. 'You look wonderful, too. And I'm definitely luckier than you and we've done it. Do you realise we've actually done it?'

'We have. And everyone was here, and nothing went wrong . . . and this is without doubt the most incredible day of my life.'

'And mine.'

'Darlings.' Deena sashayed towards them once the family groups had been photographed. 'Darlings, congratulations, again . . . You look fabulous, Erin, darling. That's the most amazing dress I've ever seen on any bride—ever. The ceremony itself was a little brief and functional, but that's very British, I suppose, and as may be. This is all going wonderfully, darlings, and I couldn't be happier.'

They stared after Deena as she linked arms with Rose and they were swallowed up in another crowd of laughing, glittering women from both sides.

'Blimey.' Erin giggled. 'Was that an acceptance?'

'I think so. Nothing short of a miracle. Oh, Erin—I love you.'

'I love you, too. And isn't this just fabulous?'

351

'Mmm, and it's not over yet . . .'

*   *   *

At last the photographs were over, and the maître d' called them to form the greeting line-up outside the dining room because the wedding breakfast was ready to be served.

And again, after another age of kissing and congratulations and handshaking and hugging, the guests filed towards the Swan's dining room. There was a mass intake of breath as they walked on scattered rose petals, beneath a swathed archway of red and gold silks, passing a massive, garlanded golden Ganesh.

The dining room was now a glorious sea of even more red and gold silks. On the tables, tiny red tea lights danced and towering floral decorations of ornate golden filigreed lanterns and red lilies complemented the tablecloths and cutlery, and every inch of every surface was scattered with a glitter of red and gold and silver sequins and tiny sparkling jewels. There were also tiny crystal Ganeshes as gifts for everyone.

'Oh!' Deena clasped her hands together. 'Darlings! How wonderful! An Indian banquet!'

Yessss! Erin squeezed Jay's hand really tightly as they all found their places.

Rose and Pete, beside Erin on the top table, looked round in total amazement. So did everyone else.

'Fusion is clearly the way to go,' Jay leaned towards her and whispered delightedly. 'They all absolutely love it.'

'So they should,' Erin giggled, as the Swan's

352

waiters and waitresses glided round the room with the first course of pakoras and samosas and naan breads and dishes of dhal. 'We *knew* it was going to be perfect, didn't we?'

The banquet roared on, course after delicious Indian course, with the wine waiters replacing champagne bottles in the ice buckets the minute they became empty, and was clearly a huge success. Everyone chatted and ate and drank and ate some more, and laughed and ate and drank. On and on.

It was all absolutely wonderful.

And then it was the speeches, and Jay and Pete managed to get through theirs without hesitating, and Kam's best-man speech, of course, was hilarious and quite rude, and everyone screamed with laughter and pretended to be shocked.

And the cake-cutting went without a hitch and even Deena couldn't fault the perfect layers of chocolate confection from one of India's top delicatessens.

The fusion wedding, exactly as they'd planned it, swept blissfully on.

And then Jay stood up and called for silence.

'The bar will be open and free until it's been drunk dry.'

Screams and shouts of approval.

'And in a moment, the ballroom, through the far archway will be up and running for those of you who want to demonstrate the moves that Nalisha's taught you. We have a rock band, a bhangra band and a disco—so something in there for everyone.'

More shrieks and applause.

'Later, there will be a fish and chip supper, with veggie options, of course—oh, and bacon rolls because Doug said we had to include them—for the

353

evening reception.'

Doug looked a little shamefaced as there were loud declarations that no one would be able to eat anything again—ever.

'And through here—' Jay nodded towards two Swan-uniformed men who were standing in front of a black curtained-off area, '—just in case you get bored, we have . . .'

The dining room was filled with a sudden blast of Elvis growling 'Viva Las Vegas!'

'. . . a casino!'

Screams of delight and ear-splitting applause broke out as the Swan's men drew back the curtains to display blackjack tables, roulette wheels and several fruit machines, all beneath another golden glittering canopy.

Erin and Jay looked at one another in absolute triumph. It had worked. All their plans had worked.

'We're so clever,' Jay whispered, kissing her and pouring more champagne.

'We are. Everyone is smiling. Even your mum.'

'Erin—' Uncle Doug had left his table '—who is that stunning lady over there? The one in the dark-blue uniform?'

Erin peered. 'Oh, that's Abbie, our wedding planner. Why?'

'Because I may have to ask her for a dance.' Doug grinned. 'She's exactly my type of woman.'

Erin nudged Jay, and they watched as Doug smiled at Abbie, doing the pushing-his-hair-back-and-letting-it-flop-down-again thing, and she dimpled and went all girly, and laughed. Then they walked away together.

'Blimey.' Erin shook her head. 'That didn't take him long. Another one bites the dust.'

And then, even later, when Jay and Erin had had their first dance to Lonestar, locked in one another's arms, aware only of each other, Kam appeared beside them.

'It's been bloody fantastic.' Kam beamed. 'Amazing. I never dreamed it would be anything like this, and now, I have another little surprise for you.'

'Come on,' Gina said as she joined them. 'Follow us. Just you two for now. Kam's sorting everyone else out.'

'Any ideas?' Erin whispered to Jay.

'None at all. But as we're well and truly married now I don't think we have too much to worry about.'

Erin, clutching Jay's hand, sincerely hoped not.

CHAPTER FORTY-FOUR

Frowning, slightly doubtful, Jay and Erin left the dance floor and followed Gina out of the ballroom and along the cool stone corridors to the rear of the Swan.

Gina opened a pair of heavy doors, and the evening darkness flooded in across a stone terrace and down an ancient twisting wide stone staircase.

'Oh—wow!'

'Ooh—it's unbelievable!'

Erin and Jay laughed out loud.

Down across the sweeping laws at the rear of the Swan, the golden *mandap* glowed, illuminated by thousands of little pinprick lights in the swathed silk ceiling and hidden in the folds of the silken walls, and the thrones and pillars and cushioned sofas, all gilded, gleamed and glinted in the flickering light from hundreds of tall golden candles.

And in front of the spectacular *mandap*, forming a guard of honour with nine on each side, were the Indian gods and goddesses.

Erin clapped her hands. 'It's the most gorgeous thing I've ever seen.'

'Took us bloody ages to arrange and set up,' Kam muttered, appearing behind them. 'Ages.'

'It must have done. I simply can't believe it.'

Erin turned her head. Everyone was lined up behind Kam. Everyone completely in the dark as they had been, but now seeing the *mandap* for the first time, all laughing and pointing.

'Darlings!' Deena screamed with delight. 'I knew you'd use it! Oh, this just makes this totally wonderful occasion absolutely perfect. And look at the statues! I've never seen anything like them outside the temple. Oh my word.'

'You—' Jay grinned at Kam '—are one devious sod. But you're bloody brilliant.'

'And that goes for you, too.' Erin grinned at Gina. 'I've no idea how you managed to organise it, but I'm so delighted that you did.'

'It was fun, actually.' Gina giggled. 'In fact, I've never had so much fun in my life.'

'All you have to do,' Kam said to Jay, 'is lead your bride in processional splendour down the steps, across the grass, through the guard of honour, and take up your places on the thrones.'

Laughing, Jay and Erin tried really hard to manoeuvre her dress in some sort of dignified manner along the terrace and down the steps. It took ages, and together they eventually bunched up a side each, and staggered down the stone staircase.

'Whoo, that's better,' Erin said, rearranging the layers of tulle and net and steadying herself on her heels. 'OK, I think I'm ready. I can't believe this, can you?'

'No.' Jay shook his head and hugged her. 'I told you Kam was crafty, didn't I? And he's clearly been a very bad influence on Gina, getting her involved . . . but wow—though—it's just amazing, isn't it?'

'Absolutely fantastic—oops,' Erin agreed, stumbling and clinging on to Jay as her heels sank into the grass. 'Oh, look at it. It's sensational.'

They approached the statues, towering in their inscrutable imperious splendour, and walked slowly between them, towards the *mandap*'s fabulously exotic golden-lit interior.

They stepped up on to the glittering tiered floor.

'Madam.' Jay laughed, bowed, and held out his hand.

'Sir.' Erin giggled, managing a clumsy curtsey, and took his hand, as he led her towards the thrones.

'Blimey, they're high. You'll probably have to lift me up,' Erin chuckled. 'This dress makes even the basics tricky—you do not want to know how I managed in the loo—ooh!'

Jay grabbed her round the waist, and swung her up and onto the throne, laughing as she temporarily vanished in a wave of taffeta and net.

'Ooh, thank you.' Erin struggled into an upright position. 'Ah, that's better. It's just like being an Indian Posh and Becks, isn't it?' She giggled, gazing round at the high-backed, heavily jewelled thrones, at the unimaginable glittering splendour of it all. 'Oh, this is just like a dream . . . our own little golden palace. Here's Kam, now—and everyone else—oh, and he's giving them all little bags of something.'

First Deena and Tavish, and then Rose and Pete, gazing round them like children who've stumbled into a fantasy fairyland, handed them tiny delicate organza bags of sweets, and then everyone crowded into the *mandap*, squeezing on to the seats and the sofas and between the pillars, all of them with gifts of sweets and cakes and rose petals.

And then Nalisha and her parents, followed by the more senior members of Jay's family, all the chattering, smiling sari-clad aunts, and the dignified, grey-haired uncles, handed them red and gold envelopes.

'Money,' Jay hissed at her. 'Don't open them now. Just say thank you.'

'OK . . . of course.'

Erin smiled and said thank you. Thank you. Thank you. Over and over again.

'Wow.' Erin gazed at the pile of envelopes growing on the steps of the raised dais. 'Well, just—wow.'

And there was more laughter and kissing, and Erin, sitting beside Jay, on her golden throne, thought again that the *mandap* was the most fabulous thing she'd ever seen.

'Deena.' She leaned towards Jay's parents. 'Thank you both for this. You were right and I was wrong. It's wonderful. I absolutely love it.'

'Of course you do, darling. I told you you would, didn't I? I'm never wrong.'

'OK.' Kam clapped his hands. 'We'll leave the happy couple to enjoy the privacy of their very own wedding *mandap* for—oh—all of fifteen minutes.

358

We'll go back and carry on the dancing—and the gambling.'

Everyone cheered.

'And—' Kam looked sternly at Jay and Erin '—you do seriously only have fifteen minutes. There's still an awful lot of dancing and eating and drinking to do. Any longer, and I'll come and get you.'

Everyone laughed and clapped again and started to make their way back to the Swan.

And then, eventually, they were alone. Even if it was for a very short time.

Erin, practically swamped by sweets and flowers, giggled. 'I still think I'm dreaming. This . . . this *mandap* was my biggest nightmare, and now it's just the most wonderful thing ever, isn't it?'

Jay leaned over from his throne and pulled her towards him and kissed her.

'It is. It's the perfect finale to our very clever enormously English Monsoon Wedding.'

'Which—' Erin glanced towards the Swan, with lights spilling from every window, and the splintered sounds of laughter and loud music floating on the warm night air, 'looks like it might be carrying on until breakfast time.'

'Mmmm, it does. I suppose we ought to go and join them again before Kam appears and turns into a nagging Best Man. Anyway, your nanna says I've got to dance with her.'

'Then, much as I don't want to leave the *mandap*, we'll have to go.' Erin giggled, gathering up the dress to make the return journey. 'No one dares to cross my nanna.'

Jay, having collected up all the lovely red and gold envelopes, helped her to her feet. 'This really is just the best wedding day anyone's ever had in the entire history of wedding days, isn't it?'

'It is.' Erin nodded happily. 'And we've still got the rest of our lives to look forward to yet.'

CHAPTER FORTY-FIVE

Two hours later, Erin and Jay stood alone on the Swan's beautiful back terrace in the darkness. The trapped heat from the ancient veranda's sun-warmed stones rose upwards, pleasant now, as the night set in with a slight early-September chill.

Somewhere in the distance, the River Maizey lapped lazily against its banks, and from inside the solid walls, the shrieks and yells and laughter and music of the still-ongoing wedding reception echoed.

Jay's arm was tightly round her waist and her head rested on his shoulder. Erin felt blissfully happy and completely exhausted.

'It's been such a totally perfect day, the most wonderful day of my life, and this time tomorrow we'll be up there. Miles up there.' She stared up into the velvet black sky studded with diamonds. 'On our way. Does anyone else know where we're going, yet?'

'No.' Jay's voice was low and slightly husky from the non-stop laughing and talking. 'No one at all. Just you and me, Mrs Keskar.'

'Mrs Keskar.' Erin savoured the words. 'I really do like that.'

Jay laughed and kissed the top of her head. 'That's just as well. Oh, it's great to be out here, just us, together, for a little while, isn't it?'

Erin nodded. 'Although no doubt we'll be missed soon, and someone will be sent to drag us back in to do "The Birdy Song" or "Agadoo".'

'I think we can count on it. Despite having jitterbugged me off my feet, your nanna's now got me earmarked as her partner for "YMCA". She says Colin gets the moves wrong.'

'Well, I hope you won't. Nanna's a stickler for getting all the party dances spot on.'

'I know. I've noticed.' Jay laughed. 'It couldn't have been more perfect today, could it? All the things we planned just fell into place, and all the problems we thought we'd have simply didn't materialise. And, against all odds, the *mandap* was just the cherry on the top of it all. And everyone's had the best time ever. A perfect day.'

'Even the weather was beautiful.' Erin turned her head and kissed his cheek. 'Honestly, it's been the best day of my life. Thank you. I'm the happiest girl in the whole wide world.'

'And I'm the happiest man,' Jay said. 'And does that make us sound slightly smug?'

Erin laughed. 'A bit. But who cares. No one's listening. See?' She cast her arms wide over the shadowy darkness. 'There's nothing but silence out there. No one but us and the night and the moon and the stars.'

They leaned together, not needing to speak.

'Actually—' Jay leaned forward slightly '—I don't think we're entirely alone. I think there's someone in the *mandap*.'

'What? Who? No, surely not.'

Erin squinted down the sweep of age-foot-dinted steps and over the grassy slopes, all night-black now, and across the Swan's lawns to where the *mandap* stood, deserted, in all its golden, flickering, fairy-lit glory.

The sequins on the distant thrones and the pillars danced in the moonlight, and the glorious silken drapery moved very softly in the lightest of breezes. The vast embellished interior was empty.

'No, there's no one there. You're imagining it.'

'I'm not. I'm sure I'm not. I saw something move,' Jay said. 'Just a shadow, but definitely a movement.'

'It's probably just a fox clearing up all the sweets and goodies that were dropped.' Erin smiled in the darkness. 'Good luck to him. I hope he enjoys his wedding night supper and—' She stopped and stared. 'No—did you see that? It can't be a fox— well, not unless it's a circus fox and its walking on its hind legs. You were right, there's someone in there.'

'Told you,' Jay laughed. 'I'm right. You're wrong. Now you have to pay a forfeit.'

Erin giggled. 'Oh God, not out here—and not when my nanna's still waiting to dance with you. Hey—' she leaned forward over the stone balustrade '—there it is again. A shadow. Did you see it?'

'Yeah. Two shadows,' Jay said. 'Someone's using our *mandap* for a clandestine lovers' tryst.'

'Blimey, that's poetic. I'm impressed. Are you going to quote romantic poetry to me on our honeymoon?'

'No.'

'Shame. Ooh, I wonder who it is though? It must be either someone who works for the Swan, or one of our guests, as we have exclusivity. Oooh, I wonder if it's Uncle Doug and Abbie? I do hope not. Eeeuwww.'

'Mmm, not a pleasant thought. But why would they be in the *mandap*? Doug's got a room here tonight and Abbie probably lives-in anyway. They wouldn't need the *mandap*, would they? Oh, well, good luck to them whoever they are.'

Erin looked at him in surprise. 'Aren't you even slightly curious to know who they are? Won't it keep you awake all night, wondering?'

'I'm hoping—' Jay smiled slowly '—to be kept awake all night by something else entirely.'

Erin chuckled.

'But actually, yes. I suppose it would be fun to know,' he admitted. 'Especially if it's some wildly unsuitable couple. Like Nalisha and Dreadlock David.'

'Or Dora Wilberforce and your posh Uncle Samir.'

Jay pulled a face. 'Please don't—that could give me nightmares. Come on then Little Miss Inquisitive, we can just be taking a romantic wedding-night stroll in the moonlight, can't we?'

'We can.' Erin gathered up the masses of her glorious dress and multiple net petticoats. 'And I'll never breathe a word that you're simply as nosy as I am. Oh . . . I'm going to need a hand down these steps again.'

'You could always take your dress off.'

'No way,' she laughed. 'It'd take far too long. It'd be sunrise before I was down to my vest and knickers.'

'Bloody hell, that doesn't bode well for my intentions later.'

'Later,' Erin giggled, 'I promise you I shall just ask you to unzip, unlace, and unhook me and I'll leap out of it from a standing start.'

'Really? I'm impressed. And you can't do that now?'

'Nope. But if you hold my hands I'm going to kick off these shoes. I can't walk across the grass in them and my feet have been numb for about the last five hours. Aaah—bliss.'

Erin's height dropped dramatically as the insanely high—and even more insanely expensive—cream-satin and silver-net-delicately-studded-with-tiny-organza-rosebuds wedding shoes now lay discarded on the terrace.

'Just the dress to deal with now. Look, I'll grab this side if you grab the other. Ta.'

'Yes, m'lady.'

Giggling, they carefully negotiated the layers of dress on the downward curve of wide stone steps again, and walked silently hand in hand across the damp grass. The hem of the dress, dragging on the lawns, would probably be ruined, but Erin absolutely adored the cool dew on her bare feet and between her burning toes.

Total, total heaven.

It was, Erin thought, simply fabulous to be outside, in the cooling night air. To be able to feel her feet again. To be with Jay. Just with Jay. Yes, of course, she was a bit curious about the inhabitants of the *mandap*, but more than that it was just lovely to be alone with Jay.

Her husband!

'OK,' Jay whispered, as they walked between the gods and goddesses forming their silent towering guard of honour again, and reached the *mandap*'s opening. 'Now we just peep in, and whoever it is, we don't say anything. Not a word. We just look and walk away. OK?'

'OK. And can we laugh when we're out of earshot?'

'Yes, or maybe not, depending on who it is.'

'Oooh, yes—and we don't want anyone to think we're peeping Toms, do we?'

Trying not to giggle, Erin bunched up the layers of her dress and they tiptoed towards the entrance and peered in.

The candles had been extinguished, but the zillions of pinprick fairy lights in the pleated silken ceiling gave a gentle golden glow.

Oh . . .

Kam and Gina, oblivious to anything or anyone but each other, were entwined on one of the deep-cushioned sofas.

Erin swallowed. The way Kam was looking at Gina needed no interpretation.

She tightened her grip on Jay's hand and tugged him away. 'Come on,' she hissed. 'We really shouldn't be here.'

'No—' he shook his head '—we shouldn't. But . . .'

'Sssh. Quick. Before they see us.'

'Right now they wouldn't notice if we had an earthquake and a hurricane combined. But yes, let's go.'

Hand in hand, keeping to the grass so that their footsteps were muffled, they ran as fast as Erin's dress would allow back to the terrace.

'Gosh,' Erin said breathlessly once they were back leaning against the stone balustrade. 'Kam and Gina. I'd never have guessed that in a million years, would you? But how absolutely fantastic.'

Jay nodded. 'Wonderful. And clearly they want

to keep it a secret, so we'll never ever let them know that we know.'

'Kam and Gina,' Erin murmured again, beaming. 'Gina and Kam. Perfect. Oh, I'm so happy for her—she deserves a lovely man. And no wonder she's been looking like she's discovered the elixir of eternal youth.'

'And Kam has been looking like the cat that got the cream for ages,' Jay chuckled. 'And he must be very serious about her because he hasn't breathed a word—usually he's bragging about his conquests from the rooftops. And I've never seen him look at another woman the way he was gazing at her. He's head over heels.'

'Oooh.' Erin leaned back against Jay. 'Isn't that just lovely? I'm so happy for them both. What a wonderful ending to a wonderful day.'

'It's not quite over yet.'

'Oooh, no—you've still got to party-dance with Nanna.'

'I was thinking more about our wedding night— and our honeymoon.'

'Mmmm, me too. Are we going to tell our parents when we get there? Mum and Dad are bound to worry if I don't.'

'Of course. I thought we'd let everyone know we've arrived safely when we land at Keshod.'

'Oh, yes.' Erin grinned up at him. 'You're very wicked. And I love you insanely.'

'Good. I think it's in the rules. And as soon as we mention Keshod, Mum and Dad will know straight away that we're in Gujarat, won't they?'

'Going back to your—and their—roots for our honeymoon.' Erin laughed softly. 'They couldn't ask for more, could they? They'll be amazed when they find out where we are.'

'They will. And it's something we planned all on our own, without any family interference at all. Come here.' Jay pulled her against him and sighed. 'Damn—this dress is fabulous, but I can't get close enough to you.'

'You'll just have to wait until the leap from the standing start.'

'You're a hard woman.'

They laughed together.

Erin sighed happily in his arms. 'Can you picture your parents' faces when we tell them that we're staying at Mandvi Beach? In a honeymoon *mandap*. A glorious all mod cons silken tent on the sands. With a huge carved queen-sized bed, and having traditional Guajarati barbecues beside the ocean.'

Jay nodded. 'Oh yes. But I think we'll keep all the details to ourselves until we get back. I know everything worked out wonderfully in the end, but they could have caused so much trouble with their interfering and trying to force us into a Monsoon Wedding. If they hadn't been quite so pushy and obvious, maybe we'd have told them about our plans, but as it is . . .'

Jay kissed her. Very, very slowly.

Then he lifted his head from hers and smiled. 'I think we can manage our Monsoon Honeymoon very nicely on our own, don't you, Mrs Keskar?'

'Oh yes,' Erin sighed blissfully, curling against him. 'I *know* we can . . .'